THE BOTTLE COLLECTOR

THE BOTTLE COLLECTOR

BY

TOM MANAGHAN

ScrivenerPress

Library and Archives Canada Cataloguing in Publication

Managhan, Tom, 1951-
    The bottle collector / Tom Managhan.

ISBN 978-1-896350-45-5

    I. Title.

PS8626.A488B68 2011   C813'.6   C2011-905492-2

Book design: Laurence Steven
Cover design: Chris Evans
Photo of author: Tina Managhan

Published by Scrivener Press
465 Loach's Road,
Sudbury, Ontario, Canada, P3E 2R2
info@yourscrivenerpress.com
www.scrivenerpress.com

We acknowledge the financial support of the Canada Council for the Arts, the Ontario Arts Council, and the Government of Canada through the Canada Book Fund for our publishing activities.

 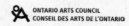

With love, for Carol

Acknowledgements

I would like to thank my writing mentor, Joan Barfoot, for her valuable input on an earlier draft of this novel and especially for teaching me the value of what's necessary and essential, and for making the case regarding character vulnerability. As well, I would like to thank Laurence Steven, of Scrivener Press, in general for his commitment to the entire project, and in particular for the insights and astuteness that resulted in considerable improvements to the book's cohesion. The cold beer and fine chats on his patio certainly enhanced the enjoyment.

Finally, I would like to acknowledge those who have inspired me—my mom, and my dad who died much too early. I would like to have spent more time with him in my wiser years. Then, there are my children, Tina and Brien, who are always greatly encouraging, who provided thoughtful commentary on earlier drafts, and who were good for the spirit during the subsequent process of seeking publication. Above all, I wish to thank my wife, Carol, for her unfailing support and her loving involvement with all aspects of my writing—and especially for helping me look forward to the completion of each chapter with her calls for a grand reading, complete with wine and wonderful critique.

1

Heading South

THE FINALE BUILDS TO ITS CRESCENDO, rattling windows, straining speakers, threatening to blow apart the truck before coming to an end, the final notes echoing, subsiding, and then slipping through my mind to find their comrades who have gathered to welcome them home. They embrace, celebrating both their accomplishment and their sense of belonging, each satisfied with its contribution, feeling especially lucky to have their home in Beethoven's Ninth Symphony, their "Ode To Joy."

Notes to be envied.

Silence follows, the noises from my truck and the giant transports blowing by me on Highway 401 diminished by the sounds that came before. I look around to get my bearings, realizing that London has passed without notice and that my destination is now less than two hours away. The drive from Sault Ste. Marie to Windsor is a long one and though I could have taken the shorter Michigan route, I opted to drive around the lakes so I could say goodbye to this part of Ontario, just in case things don't turn out for me. Last night during a stopover I said goodbye to Toronto, made some purchases at my favourite book and music stores including the TSO's version of the Ninth Symphony, the one I just finished listening to.

The terrain flattens between here and Windsor making it possible to see great distances across the increasingly prominent farmland. Before long I'll be able to spot the Detroit skyline poking through the horizon, the anticipation reminding me that Detroit is where I heard Beethoven's Symphony for the first time. Maybe it wasn't such a good thing to have heard it first as a teenager; perhaps my teenaged brain didn't know how to handle all that inspiration and all that hope that over the past thirty years has wilted and fallen flat as the highway that ends just ahead with nowhere else to go.

2

THE GREAT TEMPLE

I'VE OFTEN RETURNED TO THAT TIME, believing that if there's a key to be found it must lie in the wonder of that evening, hiding like a single note in a symphony. Yes, something, perhaps a passageway for my future was supposed to have been discovered that evening.

If only I'd been able to step through the door.

The invitation had come as a fluke, but once underway the events had taken little time to engulf me, stirring sensations bordering on hallucinogenic. And now, closer to the motor cities than I've been for a long time, the memories resurface clearer than ever and take me back once again.

It was a Friday evening in May when we came, dampened by drizzle, to the entrance of a great structure. Cars swished past on the busy street, pounding to the sounds of Motown, oblivious to curbside puddles lying in ambush for my best pair of slacks. The year was 1969, I was finishing high school, Marvin Gaye was at the top of the charts, and astronauts were packing for the moon.

Inside, crescent-shaped steps led upwards. Marble walls ascended to a heaven where pot-bellied cherubs sat on pedestals, smiling sinister smiles. Directly overhead, oil-painted ancestors, some scantily clad, others draped in tunics, mingled with angels and floated among castles sitting weightless upon clouds. Heaven radiated with an amber glow, compliments of the chandeliers hanging below. At floor level, statues watched from arched recesses, as though waiting to be called upon for the wine and hors d'oeuvres. Undeterred by their nakedness, they whispered to me, or so I imagined, speaking words of reverence such as *hallowed, divine, power,* and *glory.* However, when I moved closer, hoping to hear more, the whispering stopped.

People, mostly middle-aged and old, filled the lobby. The men arrived cloaked in navy and beige trench coats, the women packaged in furs and ornaments. Unlike the cherubs, their expressions were sober. Carefully, they peeled off their outerwear and released their fragrances like flower girls casting rose petals. Most smelled like florists, some like soap. Still others had a prickly chemical quality. I wondered if breathing this stuff would affect my sinuses and leave me talking like them, nasally inserting *ee* sounds that didn't belong: "My son learns f*ee*ast, my daughter enjoys music pr*ee*actice."

My friend Malcolm was feeling as misplaced as I. "If it weren't for Cathy," he murmured, "I could be down the street at the Joe Louis Arena right now."

"The Red Wings would be gl*ee*ad to see ya."

"If they knew I was here, they'd be very m*ee*ad at me."

I looked around, still taking it all in. "It would be nice to see a hockey game," I agreed, "but there *is* something intriguing about this."

"Oh yeah? What exactly?"

"Hard to explain but I think I'm feeling a little déjà vu."

"You're not telling me you've been here before."

"Not here, but maybe somewhere like it." I knew, of course, I'd been to no such place.

I asked him if he was sure about the Wings playing at home. "Yep, Boston's in town." Malcolm would know.

I checked my watch. "They're probably on the ice right now, warming up."

He frowned and tapped his stomach. "Yeah, and I'd be at the concession stand downing one of those fat, juicy, frankfurters."

"Good luck finding a hot dog stand in here." I craned my neck, pretending to search the premises.

Playing along, Malcolm did the same. "Hell, can you picture anyone in this crowd chomping on a hot dog?" I couldn't, everyone was so sedate, so formal. If they spoke at all, they conversed in undertones, like visitors to a funeral parlour.

"Oh well, I'm sure Cathy will have a special treat for me later this evening. I'll just have to wait."

"Wishful thinking."

He smirked. "It *is* my eighteenth birthday, and we *have* been going together for a while. Wouldn't you think I'm due for…you know, an adult type of gift?"

"Doesn't matter what I think. We are talking about Cathy, cross bearer for the staunchest Catholic family in Maidstone—so like I said, sounds like wishful thinking to me."

"Yeah, but you know what they say: once those Catholic girls cut loose—anyway, I'll be sure to let you know." Then, spotting what he was looking for, he drew my attention to an alcove on the opposite side of the lobby where people were checking their outerwear. "Let's get rid of these coats."

As the attendant gave us our tags, an older woman wearing too much makeup stepped up to hand over her furs. Not helpful to her appearance was the sour expression she wore under the orange rouge that matched her hair. At first, I thought she was worried about entrusting her coat to the young attendant, but that wasn't the problem.

The problem was me. She was giving me the once-over and clearly disapproved of what she saw. Her gaze shifted quickly from me to Malcolm and back again, obviously to make a point. She looked at my sweater, her chin dipped, her lips pursed in rebuke. Malcolm was wearing the proper attire, a sports jacket, a white shirt, a tie, and I wasn't.

Damn right I wasn't. I hated ties, all the way back to when I was eight years old and complained to my parents about having to wear a neckerchief with my Boy Scout uniform, explaining how it choked me and left burn marks on my neck. Of course, my dad took a fit like he always did when I had a complaint. "What's your problem?" he roared. The correct answer, the one that could have put an end to his rage was a chastened, "Nothing's the problem," but I had a defiant streak, and so I answered his question directly. "The tie, I have a problem with the tie." Growling his favourite name for me, "Mr. Smart Guy", he charged, fist shaking, red-hair blazing, blood vessels straining, his whole head appearing to swell to the size of a buffalo's, yelling that if I didn't know enough to shut my face, then he'd do it for me, and then he tried to do just that, delivering what he referred to as a biff alongside the ear—a biff that knocked me to the ground. Losing control, he raised his other hand, but my mother intervened as she usually did, leaving me to wonder if he would have killed me had she not been there. I tried my hardest not to cry, hating myself for the few tears that escaped. Later, my mother told me I shouldn't goad him like that, pointing out that my dad wore a tie every day for his job as a customs officer, asking how I could put him down like that, especially when he had sacrificed so much for me. As I got older, my aversion to ties only grew stronger as I felt society in general taking over the role of keeping me in check, suggesting in particular, it seemed to me, that my gender had an instinct to rape, plunder, and pillage, and, thus, had a responsibility to wear ties, like dog leashes, that could be grabbed and yanked on when needed.

And so I resented this woman's rebuke. Moreover, just as it hadn't been my intention to goad my dad, it hadn't been my intention to dress down for the concert. In fact, I'd taken care to purchase a nice sweater, hard-earned from waking up early winter mornings to shovel snow from neighbours' driveways. As the stare from the woman with the orange makeup lingered, I stared right back, noting the options that *she* had exercised—the satin dress, the fancy earrings, the strings of pearls draped loosely around her neck. Had my dad been there to witness this impertinence I would most certainly have received a biff, and maybe a double whammy, one for each ear, but he wasn't there, and the woman turned away, looking appalled, clutching her pearls protectively.

When the doors opened to the main part of the auditorium and people began to file through, I was struck by our blind conformity, lining up, shuffling politely in whatever direction the ushers indicated. No one stopped to check the surroundings before entering. No one turned an ear to listen for sounds that didn't belong. Approaching a doorway, I looked up and saw the cherubs with their smiles, wondering what knowledge they had that we didn't. An usher wearing the same kind of smile handed me a program. I noticed the doors were made of thick steel that once closed and bolted would be impossible to break down. What if the ushers were aliens rounding us up as specimens for zoos and medical experiments? We'd be in the air headed for outer space before anyone noticed.

Once inside, I heard the sounds of scratching and scraping coming from behind the stage, sounds that animals might make trying to claw their way out of captivity. Everyone seemed oblivious until an extra loud shriek turned some heads, but even then for only a moment. Seconds later, another shriek pierced the air, this time followed by grunting and whining, and I imagined some form of ancient being awakening and giving birth at the same time. And then, it wasn't one being that was stirring but many, one sound waking another, and these two waking others, until the noise swelled to a cacophony of yawning, squealing, and groaning, threatening to burst through the walls. The pressure mounted on my eardrums—crickets, beetles, and mosquitoes the size of dinosaurs, agitated from being trapped inside walls over the course of generations. My mind knew that these sounds had been heard in prior lifetimes, but for me that evening, in the temple known as the Detroit Cadillac Auditorium, the beginning of the symphony was the birth of sound, itself.

Previously, I would have shared Malcolm's preference for a hockey game, no contest, but at that moment things changed. Something inside me began to scratch and claw to get out, and it was at that moment, when the musicians stopped their warm-up exercises, the moment when their sounds became music, that I was won over.

The idea of attending a symphony would have never occurred to me. I knew nothing about classical music and neither did Malcolm. As a birthday present, he'd been given a pair of tickets by his girlfriend, Cathy, who figured he'd be more receptive to the idea if he could take me along. Cathy was also at the Cadillac Auditorium that night, but not with us. She was there to sing in the Border Cities Teenage Choir, and the choir was there to accompany the Detroit Symphony Orchestra for a performance of Beethoven's Symphony No. 9.

Soon after taking our seats in the balcony, and after the screeching and shrieking stopped, the lights dimmed, the whispering died, and silence filled the hall. Seconds later, like the early shudders of a cataclysm, a high pitched quiver stirred the air. And then, as tension turned to exaltation, as darkness gave way to dawn, the goddess of sound gave birth. So began the first movement of the Ninth Symphony.

Waves slammed against rocky cliffs, flinging spray high into the air. Again and again, the sea reared up and charged headlong against the shore. I closed my eyes and felt the power of it, felt the undertow tugging at me, offering to take me along. Abruptly, the first movement ended, quelling the thunder and the fury, and the music turned its focus to an outcrop of rocks where rivulets of water were trickling back to the sea and where nature was revealing another side of itself. The rocks were covered with fiddler crabs scuttling this way and that as fast as they could, lurching forwards, backwards, and sideways, all in a panic to find their mates, jealous over whose claws might find them first—nature demonstrating a sense of humour. I could discern that one instrument was leading the way but would not have been able to identify who was playing it had it not been for the motion of the oboe player who carried the second movement, her head bobbing and swaying, unable to restrain the joy. And then the tempo slowed, the tone mellowed. In a wooded area, back from the shoreline, cedars flickered in a light breeze. From a grassy patch within, a fawn rose and stood on shaky legs while its mother took a drink from a nearby stream, and I could imagine a world where important things are not so complicated: the appreciation of music, the sound of a lover's heartbeat—where tears come from joy.

Oh for God's sake, Mark. Fiddler crabs? A new-born fawn rising on shaky legs? Cripes, sounds like Bambi and friends resurrected from old Disney movies. God only knows what I might have imagined had the symphony gone on longer. The tearful passing of Old Yeller? A lover's heartbeat that turns a toad into a prince? I wince from embarrassment, made worse by the realization that these images, as vivid as ever, remain with me as part of the music. Of course, I could try to replace my private juvenalia with society's mass-marketed tripe—milk commercials and Hollywood action heroes. I murmur an apology to Beethoven on behalf of all of us.

Between the third and final movement, the music paused to welcome the choir which positioned itself, quietly, behind the orchestra. For the next while the choir remained motionless as the orchestra resumed, at first thrashing notes around from the first three movements before finding its way, and until the lone baritone stepped forward and startled everyone with his call: "O Freunde, nicht diese Tone!" On perfect notes, he shouted the words and flung them from the stage. "Freude!" Joyfully, the rest of the choir joined in.

I was in a reverie, imagining myself as one of the soloists when I caught an elbow in the ribs from Malcolm. He was whispering, asking if I'd been able to locate Cathy in the choir. Having been told exactly where to look, he knew her position but wasn't going to leave me alone until I located her as well. And so I searched again hoping to appease him so I could go back to concentrating on the music. Finally, I found her in the second row, fourth from the right, singing her heart out, at one with all the other straining necks and perfectly formed mouths. Where Cathy was looking I couldn't tell. Unlike her ever-widening mouth, her eyes were indistinct. She could have been looking at the hairdo of the person in front of her, at the conductor (most likely) or she could have been searching, longingly, for Malcolm. From our location, I couldn't tell where anyone in the choir was looking, and, of course, would have no reason to care had it not been for the girl on Cathy's right. She startled me almost as much as the tenor had with his outburst of "Freude!" She was dark-haired and dark-featured, about the same height as Cathy. This girl's eyes I could see; I could see them as though she were standing six feet from me. Her eyes were dark like the rest of her features, and deep, and for some reason, overwhelmingly familiar. For the duration of the symphony, even though I remained immersed in the music, I could not keep from looking back to her, because every time I did, I could swear that her eyes were fixed on one place, and in that place was me.

It was as if the music was communicating with me, that I was its guest of honour, that it was maintaining connection and eye contact through a member of the choir—and what a connection. But why?

When the finale arrived I couldn't believe that almost an hour and a quarter had passed. The grand finale, the finale of all finales, emerged triumphantly from the depths of everything that came before it, and from the earthly stage it began to rise. With awesome force, the tempo quickened, then accelerated to a feverish pitch before reaching a breaking point. There, with unbearable tension, the music hovered, the same four notes pulsating over and over, before finally breaking free and dashing for heaven.

In Detroit's Cadillac Auditorium, on the evening of May 7, 1969, the final note resonated like an echo in the canyon of my soul, unleashing a spontaneity I'd never before expressed, at least not in public. Jumping to my feet, I pumped a fist in the air and shouted, "Bravo!" I was the first one standing. Malcolm must have thought I'd lost my mind. I didn't know if shouting bravo was still considered appropriate, my experience of it coming only from old movies, but I didn't care. "Bravo!" I shouted again.

Gradually, I noticed the others around me, Malcolm slouched in his seat looking down, playing with his tie, the woman on my left twisting away, trying to turn her back to me. A man a few seats over leaned out and gave me a look. With his crew cut and square jaw he looked prepared to restore order if need be. I chuckled and gave him a wave. If they didn't appreciate my enthusiasm then too bad for them.

The conductor nodded at the orchestra, acknowledging the triumph of each musician before turning to receive the thundering applause. No one in my immediate vicinity stood, refusing to be led by an impetuous and tieless teenager, but far away, on the main level, a few people did stand, and then a few more, and then in a wave, everyone. The ovation lasted for several minutes while the conductor took his bows, after which he motioned for the musicians to stand. Bravos erupted, and I clapped until my hands were sore.

Leaving the auditorium, I felt liberated, like breaking the bonds of my script and dashing away. I felt expansive, larger than the expectations that had been shaping my future. There could be little doubt that Beethoven's creativity had come from natural talent, but with the type of self-discovery that could only be achieved by defying customs and expectations along the way. Accordingly, I wanted to discover my uniqueness, pursue my own path.

By the time we got back to the car, I'd decided I was not going to accept the invitation to attend the University of Windsor the following September. Instead, I was going to work for a year, save up some money to buy a used sailboat and learn how to sail it as I sailed northward through the Great Lakes. For no particular reason I'd had recurring dreams about doing just this, dreams of slicing through sparkling waters by day, and lying on the deck by night, watching the aurora borealis dance in technicolour. I'd have to deal with my dad and his edicts, a major one being that I was to stay in school and get an education, this being, in his opinion, the only option for one who, obviously, had no natural abilities, a conclusion he arrived at because I didn't have the same aptitude or interest in woodworking that he did. The consequences for defiance would be dire. But so be it. I was going to go, and I felt exhilarated.

Malcolm had plans to stop off at The Ribs Restaurant on the Windsor side of the border to meet Cathy and some of her friends from the choir. He asked me along, attempting to entice me with visions of girls who'd be horny and eager to party, high from singing their joyful ode. Malcolm was a good friend but quite capable of leaving me stranded if he thought there was a chance to get laid. I wasn't in the mood for picking up chicks, as he put it, and so I asked him to take me home.

It wasn't until he dropped me off that I thought about the dark-eyed girl and the possibility of her showing up at The Ribs, though I figured the chances were slim. Malcolm had mentioned that the majority of the choir was American. Odds were that she was one of them, but even if she was Canadian and returned on the bus to Windsor, there'd be no guarantee she'd end up at the restaurant. Still, I did some second guessing. If she were there, I could ask her about the eye contact. Yeah, right. Wouldn't that sound like the worst pick-up line she'd ever heard? So no, I'd made a good decision. I had some planning to do and I wanted some time to start doing it. I was going to sail north. It had to be done, and absolutely nothing was going to stop me.

3

THE DEATH OF A DOG

BUT HERE I AM, HAVING NEVER DONE the Great Lakes trip, having never done much of anything. Aspirations tend not to work out, circumstances intervene, lives change, some lives end prematurely—my dad's did. Apparently fate had another plan for me, prescribing a path, confining me to it, turning on me whenever I deviated or even thought about it.

And now, finally on a path of my own choosing, I suspect that fate will interfere, but so be it, there isn't much to lose.

Have I passed Chatham? As the fields are indistinguishable and have little to say, the past seeps back to keep me company, challenging me to recall how, once again, I decided to take charge of my life. My first inclination is to start with how I met Zoe, but no, the actual moment came just before that.

Damn dog. It appeared on the knoll that bordered the parking lot, materializing as always like the Indian warrior who suddenly appears atop a ridge in Western movies to scout the wagon train. Prior to my vacation, the encounters with the dog had been occurring almost every morning as I left my apartment for work. Whether I was a few minutes late or a few minutes early, ever since I'd given him a piece of granola bar about a month before, he'd a knack for predicting my schedule. The act of charity had been uncharacteristic. I had no use for dogs, not even chocolate brown Labradors with pleading eyes. Unlike the Indian warriors, Rover did not swoop down the hill exuding glory. With tongue dangling, ears flopping, and legs flailing, he looked more like a bag of groceries falling from a moving truck.

And now, incredibly it was back. It was a Monday in early September, the sense of vacation freedom was waning, the scent of freshly packed lunch bags tainted the air, school bus lights were flashing. Everyone was returning to the production line and I was in no mood to be slobbered on. I was already ticked at the intrusion, the idea of something perched on the edge of my awareness wanting something from me. You'd think the world could wait for me to get to my office and resume my duties as a psychologist, a fraudulent one who let people believe I could fix their problems.

I didn't like infringements on my personal space, not of any kind, so when Rover poked me with his nose, cold and wet like the inside of a grape, I had to restrain myself from lashing out. Other than brushing him off, I did my best to ignore him. Maybe he was extra hungry that morning, tempted by the smells of baloney and ham sandwiches—who knows what prompted him to jump on me, but when I saw the streak of mud on my slacks, I lost it.

"You stupid animal," I screamed.

He cringed, caught off guard, and I let loose with a backhand that would have ripped an ear off had I been aiming. He rose from his haunches, but only enough to get his tail between his legs and scramble away. I wanted to scare him off so he'd run back to his home and never come back. And so I charged towards him clapping my hands like cymbals as he ran down the driveway towards the street, before he slowed sensing the danger. But he didn't sense it soon enough, because he was still in a trot when he entered the street. At the moment he looked back to check where I was, he was hit by a van.

I heard the sound of brakes, a thud, and a yelp. The driver stopped and got out of his vehicle. A woman on the sidewalk, walking a Scotty dog, gasped and stepped back from the horror. The fleeing Labrador had put considerable distance between us so that neither witness had seen me. The woman with the dog collected herself and approached the injured animal. The driver was already bending over and reaching towards it, but then refrained from making contact.

"The thing ran right out in front of me. I didn't have a chance." The driver looked up at the woman, seeking confirmation. I thought she was about to say something but the words seemed caught in her throat, and she looked away.

Slowly, I walked closer, close enough to see, but not close enough to get engaged. The impact had flung the Labrador against the curb. His flank was rising and falling, but his breathing was laboured. I couldn't see his injuries, maybe they were internal. Though he was skinny, his coat was thick and rich, a pure chocolate. His neck and head were stretched back as though he were still looking for me. And then, I was there in his dying vision, getting absolved of blame by the saddest, most forgiving eyes in the world. The eyes tried to reassure me that if I had it to do all over again, I'd give him a pat on the head and maybe even share another piece of granola bar. Then, slowly, his eyes closed.

I felt angry, wanting neither reassurance nor forgiveness. It wasn't my fault. I hadn't asked to be stalked. I hadn't asked to be jumped on. All I'd wanted was to be left alone.

A car came from the opposite direction and stopped. The driver, a guy wearing a suit, was getting out his cell phone, looking confident like he knew what to do. As the delivery driver and the woman with the dog watched him make his call, I took the opportunity to walk away.

The Algoma Mental Health Centre is a catch-all for people strug-
gling on the edge. It lurks on the outskirts of Sault Ste. Marie, buffered
from blue collar life by fifty acres of lawn. In contrast with the surrounding forest, the grounds are flat and rock-free, an open expanse
except for the odd flower garden and smattering of trees. So impec-
cably aloof are these trees and so rigid are their limbs, that one could
suspect they're here to be treated for catatonic schizophrenia. They
stand about the grounds, displaced from where they belong, looking
forlorn, helpless, perhaps dazed by drugs.

The main sidewalk leads from the parking lot to the buildings,
while a smaller sidewalk forks to the left towards a red-brick structure
that resembles a prison. This is the old psychiatric hospital. Patients
who follow this path tend to stay awhile. Farther along the main walk,
and to the right, lies the more modern short-term assessment and
treatment centre. It's made of cinder blocks and smoky windows and
looks like a mausoleum. Patients refer to it as The Ashtray. My office
is in this building. Located between the old and new sections, but farther back from the sidewalk, sit the maintenance and laundry buildings, the latter stinking like a freshly opened diaper pail. That day, the
clatter of laundry wagons leaving the back of the hospital tricked me
into looking in that direction, upwind, directly into the stench. The
urine odor of freshly mowed grass only added to the effect.

Good God, what was I doing here? Good God, how many times
had I asked myself this question? How had I always ended up working
in institutions when I hated them so? How had I chosen a profession
in psychology, always meeting and dealing with people when I really
preferred to be on my own? Fate kept finding ways to sabotage other
options, and seemed to take great delight in keeping me miserable,
adding little touches like sending me the dog and the laundry wagons
on my first day back from vacation. I had often considered quitting,

23

even without having another job lined up, thinking that desperation might be the catalyst needed to reinvent myself. But I also wondered at those times if fate was setting a trap that would leave me with nothing except for the depression that nothing would leave me with. I could imagine fate rubbing its hands gleefully at the irony of a psychologist getting swallowed by depression. Depression is like quicksand; once you've stepped in it you have only seconds to get out before it's too late. You feel the strength of its pull and the sense that it's bottomless, or at least that's how I remember my own close call, an experience I never wanted to feel again and that always convinced me to carry on with what I was doing until something else could be found.

Perhaps the encounters with the dog and the laundry carts helped me realize that my crappy existence was never going to change unless I did something to assert control. And even though drastic action could make matters worse, any sense of hope was dying by the day, regardless. So, right then and there, outside the mausoleum, I made myself a promise: that if one more thing went wrong that day, if someone made a wrong comment, if I got assigned to one more useless committee, if a black cat crossed my path, I'd quit and take my chances.

I felt better already.

Midway through the morning, a gaggle of professionals settled around an oval table. The dull yellowish walls of the conference room were bare except for a poster extolling the virtues of old age. Under the slogan was a picture of an elderly couple, well matched with beautiful white hair and smiling kindly like everyone's favourite grandparents, a picture of contentment. Yeah, yeah, everything so wonderful, life so glorious, except for the diapers I thought they might be wearing below those toothpaste smiles. Geezus, what a miserable cuss I could be. When had I become so mean-spirited? I looked again at the poster, the perfect hair, the perfect teeth, the tanned skin, imagined the couple's boat sitting in a nearby yacht club, and reassured myself that it wasn't the couple who had triggered my cynicism as much as the unrealistic portrayal of life. Okay, so I had a little bitterness about my own failings and found that projecting them harmlessly onto a stupid poster defended against excessive self-hatred. An understandable ploy, I guess, except that the awareness of it made me feel worse, more sad than angry, not a good thing, for anger, at least, gave me some fight.

"Welcome to the psychogeriatric unit, Dr. Weathers."

The greeting came from Dr. Hoshi, the unit's psychiatrist and chief of staff, leaning forward in his chair like a camp counselor checking that all the children were accounted for. Always with a polite grin stretched across his smooth-skinned face, Dr. Hoshi had a small, cushy body, and except for the three-piece suit, resembled a miniature Buddha. Conscious of our difference in height and my outfit of beige slacks and fisherman sweater, attire appropriate for hunting oysters, I took a seat across the table so we wouldn't look ridiculous sitting together. He brought the meeting to order.

"Dr. Weathers is giving us some of his valuable time to help out with Mr. Forster. Does everyone know Dr. Weathers? He's the chief psychologist in the developmental disabilities unit."

From across the table, the ever-bubbly social worker, Cheryl Cranston, tried for eye contact, wanting to let everyone know we were acquainted. I denied her the satisfaction.

"Maybe first, we should go around table to introduce ourselves." Dr. Hoshi's voice skipped musically, like the bouncing ball in old sing-alongs. He turned to his left.

"I'm Kathleen Plunkett, the discharge planning nurse." Her manner was 'ho hum' clearly unimpressed, conveying the resistance of one who couldn't believe that psychology had surpassed the enema as preferred practice. Having nearly gagged on the overly ripe fragrance that greeted me upon entry to the geriatric unit, I felt relieved she didn't provide a description of the discharge work she performed.

"Brad Simmons, primary worker." Such a low voice from one so skinny. Primary worker of what, he didn't say.

Around the table we went. How many hundreds of times had I endured this ritual? Monica, the physiotherapist was next. I was acquainted with her and knew she could be quite funny. I said a silent prayer, hoping she'd say or do something out of the ordinary, perhaps pull a baton from under her chair, plaster a smile across her face, lead us into the talent portion of the program, do some twirling, tell us how she'd like to make the world a better place.

"Monica Robitaille, physiotherapist." A smile. That was it.

I wanted to scream, but knew, of course, that screaming wouldn't change a thing. These conventions knew how to survive, year after year, decade after decade, if anything, they only grew stronger.

The conference room door cracked open and a woman I hadn't seen before edged through the opening, trying her best not to draw attention. She looked to be thirty-something, but wore the freshness of a college girl arriving late for her first class. Her morning shower hadn't rinsed the dreaminess from her eyes, and her hair, clove-coloured with highlights left from summer sun, was still damp from insufficient time with the blow-dryer. I could imagine her sitting in the stands of a college football game while I tried to muster the nerve to sit beside her. Carefully, she pressed the door shut behind her, looking pleasantly frazzled. I was discreet in my scrutiny, not wanting to get caught checking how her derriere squirmed inside her corduroy jumper like a child trying to hide under the covers.

Unless she had a voice like Daffy Duck, the meeting might be worth sitting through after all. And Zoe Kasparis, occupational therapist, did not speak like Daffy Duck. Far from it.

Nothing else went wrong that day. In fact, things took a significant turn for the better and over the next little while, for the first time, a sense of purpose gradually crept into my life.

4

Wayward Souls

ZOE WAS ASSIGNED TO ACCOMPANY ME for my consultation with the Forsters as she had already familiarized herself with the family, having made some initial recommendations to Mrs. Forster on how to deal with her husband and his progressing Alzheimer's. Only recently had I started to take on Alzheimer's patients, using the principles of applied behaviour analysis to minimize wayward behaviours. Following the team meeting I suggested that we go for a coffee to review the case and discuss strategy. So off we went to the hospital coffee shop, formerly a gift shop that had been taken over and converted to join the chain of Tim Horton's.

Lo and behold, separated by nearly two years and seven hundred miles, I spot a Tim Horton's at the interchange to Tilbury, a town that lies about an hour away from the Lake St. Clair Yacht Club. Having driven for hours without a break, fatigue is weighing on my eyelids, and now, in the flat and monotonous landscape of Essex County, is trying to tug them shut. I like my suv, it's comfortable and has a quality sound system, but I have no wish to be killed in it, and in particular I have no desire to put other lives at risk. Death, I've decided, should be purposeful, and at best, warrants an act of defiance. Preparing to sail the Great Lakes on Antonie, my twenty-five foot sailboat, without the requisite experience to do so—now, there's an act of defiance. But I'm getting ahead of myself, and must first make it safely to the marina. A stretch, a breath of fresh air, and a coffee should help.

I take my coffee to a picnic table on a patch of grass beside the parking lot. The table looks short and fat, like one half of a comedy team, the other half the tall, skinny, garbage barrel beside it. Spring is farther along here than it is in the Soo. The grass has obviously been mowed and the trees (the few that exist in this area of the province) are in full leaf. Across the fields, but widely scattered, lie tufts of greenery upon which farmhouses stand alongside barns, sheds, silos, and rusting machinery. Otherwise, the land is one huge tabletop of earth, ploughed and drying from winter, but still too wet for planting. The acreage extends for miles in all directions, unobstructed by wilderness, the farms separated from each other by fences and ditches, yet tied together by the perpetual rumble of transport trucks racing down Highway 401. I look up to see a caravan of auto carriers and I'm reminded that the fields end thirty miles down the road, where the auto factories and their feeder industries begin.

As I stare across the landscape, memories of corn and soy beans in endless rows lends the realization that their planting and harvesting is not unlike assembly lines in the auto plants. This is a county of mass production where people are known by what they make. The methods of production are well established and people are measured by how efficiently they can carry them out. Despite what the farmers see when crops begin to sprout, their justifiable pride notwithstanding, there is no nature here, for once something has been harnessed, controlled, and shaped in the service of something else, it is no longer natural. Here, nature has been annihilated by a tribe of producers, a tribe to which I don't belong. I'd like to meet the stork that wasn't paying attention when it delivered me—I have some questions.

Back on the highway for the final stretch, my thoughts return to Zoe, not a good thing, as these thoughts, even those associated with our first innocent meeting, can pull me down into bad places. Distraction and staying busy can provide a buffer, but eventually I tire or let my guard down and the memories spring loose, especially during mindless activity such as highway driving. At night, getting to sleep is difficult unless a good book can take me hunting for the Holy Grail, or take me fishing for marlin off the coast of Mexico. During the day, I create distractions and invent projects like this sail from Windsor to Thunder Bay. The sailing project, however, has taken over from all the rest, having been conceived and developed as a final reckoning. I plan a pace that will take me two to three months, fully appreciating that a freighter could come along on the first day and crunch us (Antonie and me) like popcorn, or that a storm on Lake Superior could sink us with much less effort than the thirty foot waves it mustered to swallow the Edmund Fitzgerald. So what? Come and get me I say.

When I'm driving, classical music helps. It induces imagery and the imagery never includes Zoe, perhaps because she was never a fan of classical music. I choose Beethoven's Concerto for Piano and Orchestra #5, otherwise known as "Emperor," and my mind drifts back to a live performance I once heard. It was at the Roy Thomson Hall in Toronto and the guest pianist was a seventy-year-old woman from Russia. Slowly and sedately she walked across the stage, her short body seeming to shrink along the way, yet remaining poised and purposeful as she approached the piano. The bench seemed too high for her, and the effort it took her to mount it seemed to extract a toll, as she never did assume a proper posture. Instead, she played with hunched shoulders and rounded back, giving the appearance of a precariously balanced, queen-sized lady bug, one that had long flowing arms, lithe fingers, and fluid wrists, one that could play an audacious and effervescent version of the Emperor. Apparently, genetics, having decided she would be a world-class pianist, had carefully designed her right-brain, her arms, wrists, and fingers, connected them well, and then called it a day, showing little regard for the non-essentials. I was envious. I hadn't been endowed with *any* spectacular gifts, except for the rather spectacular capacity to appreciate talent and beauty, combined with equal capacity to experience torment from my own lack of such.

Finally, I see the Detroit skyline, the towering glass silos of the Renaissance Centre. It seems strange that I can't remember them being constructed. They weren't there when I was a boy. They came along after the race riots (I can remember seeing the smoke drifting across the river) when the city wasn't known for much other than cars, boarded windows, and murders. Renaissance, revival, a new birth—that had been the plan. Unfortunately, except for the isolated pockets, where the Red Wings or Greek restaurants entertain, a mecca the city is not. I look further along the skyline and see skyscrapers I don't recognize—when did they spring up—and then look back to the RenCen towers. As grand as they are, I note that they're too small for the blue sky and patches of cloud reflected by their windows and now seemingly trapped within them, in the way that cages are too small for eagles.

I try to think positively, wondering if the word renaissance is applicable to my circumstances. I am back at the start, not where I ever belonged, but nevertheless where I was born and raised. And except for a boat and money, I'm back with nothing from the intervening years. It's a Monday in the middle of May and I'm neither at work nor on vacation. One has to have a work life to be on vacation and I no longer do. I'm like a mule unburdened from a lifetime of packs and rolls and saddlebags and mountainside treks. Never again will I attempt to undo the brain damage of people born with developmental disabilities, or to reverse dementia in the elderly—a relief, indeed. In over twenty years of practice, I've never cured a single case of mental retardation, autism, or dementia, not that I ever thought I could—but wasn't I supposed to do something profound and doctorish when people came to me with hope? So, relief now, certainly, but not a renaissance. At mid-life, I haven't achieved anything and have no prospects for doing so. My trip is all about an ending—about leaving, reflecting, trying to figure out if anything at all ever made sense, about ending my life if by the time we reach Superior's lakehead I haven't found meaning. That's the plan. But, committed to making the most of this final opportunity, I shan't dwell on what might be the most likely outcome. Nature should clear my mind and freshen my thoughts. Sailing should keep me from wallowing. Hopefully, I'll enjoy the freedom and appreciate the moments. The contrast with my past life should provide perspective. Should any insights come to me, I'll be where I want to be, should no insights come to me, I'll be where I want to be, should an awful storm hit me, I'll be where I want to be.

Absorbed by my musings, time passes quickly, and I find myself at a busy intersection inside the city, not far from the marina. I roll down my window, anticipating the smell of fish, of docks draped in seaweed. The woman driver alongside me is staring, alarm on her face from something she's witnessed. I tend to get animated during intense, internal monologues, so perhaps she noticed my gesticulations which might have seemed a bit vigorous considering I'm alone in the truck. In my liberated state I wave to her, and admittedly my wave is a little more exuberant than appropriate. I note the gasp, how she slinks back in her seat, clearly unaccustomed to crossing paths with an uninhibited madman. When the light changes she holds back, waiting for me to pull ahead. Well then, if that's how she wants to be. I gesture like a gentleman deferring to a lady at an entranceway: 'After you, ma'am'. And immediately after, I grin like a maniac. Oh dear. What does she do? A horn blares from behind. The woman steps on the gas but her motions are jerky and she overcompensates by stomping on the brake. Brakes squeal behind her and I grimace, waiting for the crunch which fortunately doesn't materialize. She doesn't end up like the dog.

I pull away from the intersection, from the feeling of lightness, from the consternation on my mother's face as if she's watching from her house only a few miles away. It's the closest I've been since the self-imposed exile following my father's funeral, his death from a damaged heart, the heart that failed for good during a heated exchange with the son who'd been shielded by his mother until he was old enough to fend for himself, until it became necessary for the mother to stand more firmly alongside her husband, the husband who had wanted to develop his woodworking hobby into a full time business, but who needed income for a few more years from his wife, a lawyer's clerk who worked for a lawyer my dad hated but who nevertheless went back to work following the birth of her first son, but who, for some reason, couldn't return to work after the birth of her second son, the son who was hated as much as the lawyer as though my dad saw in them an alliance against him. I could never quite figure it out.

Why does causing grief come so easily to me while no amount of effort results in anything good? Perhaps effort without talent is like sailing without wind. What if the poor woman in my rear view mirror had a bad heart? What if she had once been traumatized by a person who looks like me? What if this, what if that? God only knows how much damage I've done. But wasn't I minding my own business while she was the one peering into another person's vehicle, infringing on privacy, making judgments? To hell with it, I'll soon be boarding Antonie. Big water beckons—big water, where people are sparse.

5

Antonie Awaits

THE BOATS ARE RESTLESS, SHIFTING to and fro, looking anxious to get underway. Some appear to be shivering, especially those exposed to the blustery weather blowing in from the river. There's a lot of boat chatter going on, pinging and clanging—high-pitched voices attempting to be heard above the flumph-flumphing of flags and the crashing of waves against the breakwater. It takes me several minutes to spot Antonie. Her mast, rigging, and sails are in place as promised. She arrived the week before on the back of a flat-bed truck after I had paid small fortunes to both the transport company and St. Clair Yacht Club to ensure she'd be set, ready to go. Although looking smaller here than at home on Whisky Lake, she is no less distinguished in her cream-coloured gym outfit with the sharp, black lettering. As a racer/cruiser, her profile is more symmetrically pleasing than the larger, more expensive vessels in the berths next to her. She's a diver sandwiched between a weight lifter and a basketball player.

I, too, am anxious to get things underway. Most of the preparations were finished before I left Sault Ste. Marie, the grocery list completed long ago and the non-perishables stored securely on board before Antonie was lifted aboard the truck. All that's needed now is for me to pick up some fresh produce, wine and beer.

Ah yes, the food and drink. Fine dining aboard Antonie has always been a delight and will be a regular feature of the trip. For breakfasts, the menu will include misty morning coffee, freshly squeezed orange juice, french toast, and pancakes. My french toast is made with orange and cinnamon, my pancakes with whole wheat flower, oatmeal, and blueberries. Later in the trip I plan to pick my own blueberries, fresh from rocky shores. Lunch will be light, either grilled cheese sandwiches made from a blend of cheeses, or salmon sandwiches with dill, as long as I can find fresh dill. The stern-rail barbecue will take care of most suppers. With a beer in one hand and a brush for marinading in the other, I'll savour the sizzle of coriander burgers, or Cajun chicken strips, or if I'm lucky, the fresh catch of the day. If I'm really lucky, the gentle swaying from Antonie and the love-making sounds she makes with the water will entice dessert-bearing mermaids. Later on, when the sun is setting, I'll choose a wine, a complementary cheese or pate, and of course, classical music to fit the mood. A diet to nurture the soul.

The CD player is permanently mounted (I hope) in the main berth, connected to four speakers strategically placed to create a surround-sound effect in which the cello is clearly distinguishable from the bass, the oboe from the clarinet, and so on.

As I step aboard I feel Antonie shift slightly to welcome me home. My love for being on the water has made me wonder if I was supposed to be a fisherman, a lobster fisherman perhaps. That would fit. I unlock the hatch and descend into Antonie's cozy interior, as if I'm Gulliver entering a shrunken world. My head comes close to touching the ceiling and in the main part of the living quarters I can, without moving my feet, reach almost everything—the stove, the fridge, the sink, the table, the cupboards, the nautical lamps of amber on the wood-paneled walls. Fortunately, everything seems to be in order. The fridge, cabinet, and cupboard doors have all remained shut and there are no signs of spillage. The fuel containers are strapped in place, a hanging rack is still full of navigational charts. I open the narrow closet, half expecting to see clothes off their hangers, but every item's in place, looking relaxed and casual—jeans, shorts, t-shirts, and sweatshirts. One pair of dress pants and shirt are on board in the unlikely circumstance I come across an up-scale cultural event or gourmet restaurant.

Over the table, my novels stand as I left them in the crib-like shelf. I take a moment to review the titles. Several are new, a few are favourites I wish to re-read. I reach for one of the new ones and open it to read the synopsis. I like the weight of it in my hands, something that isn't chronic or burdensome that I can enjoy and then put away when I'm done. A Toronto musician crosses paths with a museum guide in Vienna, and of course, these two major characters were fated to meet. Freakish circumstances intervene and threaten to play havoc with the people closest to them. In mere seconds, I'm halfway to Austria and I'm reminded of the fact that there's no better place for reading fiction than on a boat. But the afternoon's moving along, so I'd better run my errands, buy my booze and groceries.

By the time evening arrives, except for having to review some charts which can wait till morning, I'm feeling prepared. I contemplate some of the Italian Chianti just purchased from the liquor store, but the blustery weather has turned cold and my special blend of Spanish coffee will better fit the occasion. The clanging of halyards and fluttering of flags have intensified to a feverish tempo as the pounding of waves against the breakwater fills the air with spray. I don't think it's rain, not yet, although overhead, mud-coloured clouds tumble across the sky. I love this. Yes, I'll make some Spanish coffee then throw on a jacket to drink it outside in the cockpit. I'll face the wind, rest the edge of my cup between my lips and blow into it so that the warmth comes back to bathe my face, so its vapour fills my head with the scent of alcohol—and it will occur to me that some people need prescription drugs to feel like this.

Afterwards, I'll curl up and read my novel until my mind is ensconced in another time and place. And then, I should be able to sleep—I hope. Other thoughts and memories will need to be dealt with, but my intent is to schedule these on my terms.

6

Fog

I WAKE EARLY, BUT FREE FROM the wailing of an alarm clock. Of course, I've had that privilege before, on weekends and holidays, but it's different this time. Now, it's permanent, for however long that means. Previously, time existed only as an instrument of working life, bedtime determined by whether I had to work the next day, leisure determined by the designated breaks, but things have changed since my alarm clock passed away a little while ago—after I took a hammer to it. And yet, old thoughts attempt to intrude, whispering about tasks to be performed, goals and objectives to be met, fantasies to be sacrificed. I can thwart these thoughts, but they are deep rooted and will require tenacity to eradicate. Time, I realize, so needy, so exploitive, has a personality characterized by narcissism, a characteristic I have little tolerance for and, thus, which I shall drop from my caseload. It may complain of not getting the entitlement it deserves, of not receiving the cooperation it needs from those unworthy of empathy, it may threaten desperate measures should I turn away, it may promise ethical rewards for my involvement, sermonizing that hard work makes a good man, but "tough titties," I say, for I shall not respond.

Yes, things are changing.

The air is raw, the wind blustery. Cables are clanging, docks are creaking. I snuggle under the Hudson's Bay blankets, and in the warmth and coziness remind myself to accept the comfort, that it's okay, I'm not doing anything wrong—and before long I'm back to where I was, where dreams swim about like jelly fish.

After awhile when daylight pries open my eyes, the first face I see is the face of freedom. It doesn't care if I wake or sleep. "Hallelujah," I whisper. Freedom.

Slowly, I pull my arms from under the blankets and rise from my berth to open the hatch that's directly above, stick my head out to see what's going on. A morning mist rinses away the remnants of sleep and leaves me light-headed. All I'd have to do is let go, and I'd float through the hatch and into the air, up, up, like a balloon. Looking down I would see people stuck to their designated pathways like flies to flypaper. But I don't let go. I fear getting blown away in directions I'll have no control over. I love the wind, but on water I'll be able to negotiate my pace and direction.

Traffic noises jack-hammer their way into my head from the street above, where the high-rise skyline peers down with smog-filled eyes, presiding over its kingdom, judging the offerings made by its subjects. I've got to get away from the city. Maybe now's the time to untie and slip away, under cloud cover and mist.

The mist is turning to rain. It swabs the deck, washing over my head as though it were just another navigational device. Lousy weather for sailing. I duck below and turn the radio on for a weather report. A robotic-sounding voice states that the wind is coming out of the southeast at twenty knots. The voice remains the same whether reporting dead calm or gale force winds. I understand—I, too, was taught to remain objective. The voice drones on, sticking to facts, telling me that the barometric pressure's been dropping.

I pull on a pair of jeans, a sweatshirt, and windbreaker, and take a walk down the pier that borders the marina. At the end, I look beyond the slimy seaweed and over the open waters of Lake St. Clair. Because the wind's blowing off shore, the water doesn't look as unruly as it should. Farther out, I see scattered whitecaps, but they lack menace and after rising a bit to bare their teeth, they roll quickly onto their backs. If I leave now, I won't have to worry about navigating around other sailboats. Too early in the season for regattas, there'll be no sailors charging alongside to steal my wind. Unfortunately, it's not too early for the freighters. The ice is out and that's all they need.

Visibility isn't great, but I think I'd see or hear something the size of a football stadium if it were floating down the river, and there appears to be nothing out there, not now, anyway. Maybe I've overestimated the flow of freighter traffic, I hope so. Nonetheless, a course that hugs the eastern shore will keep me away from the main shipping lanes, at least until we're forced to funnel into the St. Clair River, a situation I'll have to worry about that when we get there. But what the hell, what's the point of being free if I'm going to worry about everything. I've taken very few risks in a life that could end up being relatively short. And the safe, conventional life has revealed little in the way of meaning. Lousy weather be damned. I decide to go.

Antonie and I back out of the slip and motor down the channel alongside the breakwater. At the end, we turn to the lake and feel the first rocking from the waves, nothing significant, not unlike Whisky Lake on a breezy day. Still, I stay with the motor for longer than I need to, worried about conditions that may be waiting offshore. No, that's not right—I'm not worrying. What I'm doing is being cautious; responsible sailors practice caution. After all, Antonie and I have never sailed on a Great Lake. St. Clair might be the baby of the family but it's still bigger than anything else we've attempted. Moreover, we're sailing in a heavy mist under heavy skies towards a destination we can't see. Okay, so what if I have a little trepidation? What I'm afraid of is the unknown, the bogey man under the bed. I reassess my notions of freedom and anxiety and the question of whether one can truly be free if he can't choose a situation that frightens him. No, of course not. This is profound. Day One, not quite clear of the harbour, and already I'm becoming a philosopher. Hell, maybe I'll have the meaning of life figured out by morning's end and be back in time for lunch. Given all the preparation, however, it would be a shame not to get a little more sailing in first. Up goes the mainsail and I put a reef in it. Antonie approves, digging in her keel while leaning at a steep angle from the wind.

Out from shore, the water gets rougher and three foot waves slap against our sides. My legs get soaked from the spray and mist and I realize I've forgotten to put on the lower part of my rain gear. Visibility is poor. Mist, sky, and water, have turned from grey to darker shades of murk. As planned, we keep a safe distance east from the main shipping lane—or so I figure. The direction of the wind has us on a beam reach, one of the easiest, most straight-ahead ways to sail, and Antonie, happy to be underway at last, cuts loose into a frolicking romp.

A few hours go by and Antonie has helped me into a comfort zone, at one with wind and waves. At the helm, I'm wet and cold but I accept this as my chosen environment, relishing how quickly I've blended into the elements. Good for me, I'm where I belong. Should I catch a cold I'll wrap myself in warm blankets and whip up some more Spanish coffee, confident of transforming myself over time into a hearty, seafaring rogue, who develops immunity to such landlubber ailments. Already my confidence has strengthened. True, we've maintained the luxury of a beam reach but I'm ready to navigate these waves with tacks and gybes should the need arise. The waves may get bigger than I'm accustomed to but the required skills are the same as on Whisky Lake. After conquering this lake, I'll motor down the St.

Clair River and out to Lake Huron, an expanse that will open in front of us as large as the ocean. On Huron, I'll maintain a course where I can stay within sight of land, seeking shelter from storms and rough seas. As I gain experience, I may grow bolder and tackle conditions of greater challenge. The sailing part of things will be fine, likely not as difficult as I thought.

But fate, I soon discover, has been busy setting an ambush, tricking me, seducing me with false hope. Behind us, through the fog I see the outline of an island that isn't marked on my chart. How can this be, and how could I have sailed so close to a land mass and not notice? It doesn't make sense. I've kept a steady course with the wind, and the wind certainly hasn't changed direction. The fog is playing games, making things appear and disappear, distorting everything. "Settle down," I tell myself. The lake isn't that big. All I have to do is get closer to land, crawl along and watch for landmarks. After a minute, I look back, expecting the island to be gone, swallowed by the murk. But no, it seems even closer now. What's happening? The wind's been pushing us back? I've turned us around? How in hell…oh shit…the land mass is too high, much too high…a fucking freighter…we're in its path. The fucker isn't making a sound. How can something so big not make a fucking sound? Bastard! Only now do I hear the slosh of water against its hull as it emerges from the fog, huge anchors carved into its bow like the teeth of a jack-o'-lantern. I can smell the iron of its breath. There's no time. Dive overboard and swim like hell…yeah, right…die like an idiot. Now, a low guttural rumble…the tremors of an earthquake…Shit! Shit! Shit! There's no time, no option except… veer to starboard. I glance up and see streams of rust running down its side…see its name: 'Frontenac,' the last word I'll ever see? What a joke. I close my eyes.

Incredibly, like a near-sighted monster, the freighter rumbles past, but leaves its wake to chase us down—what fun it would be to roll us over. Again, we escape, unscathed, except from the fright that has my heart gasping for blood, my stomach ready to retch. Needing to get the hell off the lake, I take down the sails, start the motor, and peer through the fog, hoping to see shore. Suddenly, the keel scrapes bottom, nearly hanging us up, but momentum is just enough to get us through. First fog, then a freighter, and now sandbars—how naïve to think that this would ever be easy, how naïve to let my guard down so early when I knew fate would be waiting for such an opportunity. And here it is, having come to teach me a lesson: How dare I try to break free?

I veer to avoid something in our path, a small boat, or maybe a tree that, just for me, has sprung from the middle of the lake, but as we pass I see that it's a buoy, and I keep to the direction that promises a channel towards land. Before long, I see the outline of a dock, carved into berths. We slip into one and tie up, unable to see land at the base of the dock, so thick is the fog. God only knows where we are.

I can't stop shivering. Maybe if I make a hot drink, maybe a hot buttery rum, but I can't muster the energy. Maybe after I crawl under the covers and sleep, calm myself down. Yes, that's what I need to do—go below, warm up, get rested—and then court further disaster by lighting the stove. Why not have everything blow up in my face? What will be, will be, but I shall not be deterred. No way. Defiance, I find, brings a small measure of satisfaction, and as I crawl under the covers, I tell fate to go screw itself.

7

IVAN THE
BOTTLE COLLECTOR

DOPEY FROM A DEEP SLEEP, I crank open the hatch, wondering where we are and wondering how much time has passed. The fog is gone but whether it's late afternoon or early morning of a new day I can't tell. We appear to be alone in the small marina, so with no one to ask I scan the surroundings for clues.

At the base of the dock, a cement building stands crumbling in a patch of weeds. I'm guessing that the washrooms and showers are inside, closed for the off-season if not for good. To the right, a driveway curves up a wooded slope towards a blue-tinged sky. Behind us, a haze smeared red and yellow by a setting sun hangs over the horizon, informing me that I haven't slept through the night, and that I've yet to make it through the disastrous first day of the journey.

I try not to wallow, reminding myself that I don't need to be anywhere, that time is irrelevant, that I can sleep for days on end, that I can choose not to continue. But continue I shall, though obviously, I'll need to temper the defiance and impulsiveness that leads to stupid decisions, such as the one to set sail in terrible weather. For the duration of the trip, or until I decide there's no point, I'll use sound judgment and put health and safety first. For now, it's time to eat. Minutes later, equipped with the necessities, beer and spatula, I'm grilling a burger on the stern rail barbecue when a movement from shore catches my eye. A man carrying a sack and wearing boots the size of bread boxes is coming down the driveway, criss-crossing from side to side, moving with the ploppity-plop saunter of a shopping mall Easter Bunny. Any second now, he's going to look up and see me, and then he's going to forget all about the bottles or whatever he's looking for, and he's going to come over and make a pest of himself. Of this, I have no doubt. He's a king-sized rabbit and I'm Farmer McGregor's vegetable patch. Where other people manage to attract a little good fortune here and there, I attract intrusive characters, like beggars in need of spare change, or past acquaintances who look me up, brimming with flattery and pretense before pitching their pyramid scheme. And now it's a giant Easter Bunny wearing a hunting cap and rubber boots.

"Ahoy there."

Ahoy there? Good God. I pretend not to hear.

"Ahoy there!" He calls out twice as loud this time.

I don't look, but of course it won't occur to him that he's being ignored. No, he'll think I'm deaf, and he'll come over and wave in my face, and then he'll mouth the words so I'll be able to read his lips: "A-H-O-Y T-H-E-R-E." I'm holding myself perfectly still, like a child who believes that doing so will make him invisible. He's on the dock. Five, four, three, two, one…"How ya doing?"

Without turning, I wave, hoping to convey it's the best I can do at this crucial phase of the burger grilling. Seconds later, I feel Antonie dipping to one side. What? The guy's boarding my boat! No friggin way. I spring across the cockpit to block his entry. "What do you think you're doing?"

"Just dropping by to say hello. Not here to cause trouble—nope, not me, not no more." For several seconds he stands there, burlap sack at his side, shaking his head no just in case I didn't understand the part

44

about him not causing trouble. "I come around to keep an eye on the place for the owner." And then, as if he's just presented his passport, he looks for a way around me, glancing to my left. Un-friggin-believable. I shift to the left.

"Sorry. I'm getting ready to have my supper." I gesture towards the barbecue.

"Cooking a hamburger, eh?"

"Yep."

"Not having anything with it?"

"Oh yes. I'm having beans with it. Beans and a baked potato," I lie. "I'm cooking those down below in the cabin. I'd better go and check on them." He doesn't take the hint. "It's been a long day," I tell him. "I want to hurry up and eat so I can go to bed and get a good sleep." The sun chooses that very moment to break through the haze, setting aside the dusk.

"It's a little early for going to bed, don't you think?" For some reason he thinks this is funny. "Huh yuh, huh yuh, huh yuh."

"I'm very tired."

"It's pretty bright out now. You won't be able to sleep when it's this bright." He's gloating, thinking himself clever and, maybe, on the verge of an invitation.

"I can make the cabin very dark inside, and I am very tired. I'll be asleep before my head hits the pillow."

He stands there, stymied, but seemingly incapable of changing the channel. Then, he hears the hissing and spitting from the grill, the sound of my burger betraying me. "Sounds like your burger's burning."

Shit, he's right, I can smell it. Still, I'm not about to leave my post as the instant I do, he'll step aboard and attempt to settle in for the evening. Obviously, I need to be more direct.

"Well, it was nice meeting you, Harvey. Good-bye, now. Hope you have a nice evening." I raise a hand, half waving, half shooing him away.

His lips purse and his brows furrow. "My name's not Harvey. Why'd you call me Harvey? Are you joking? You're joking aren't you? Huh yuh, huh yuh, huh yuh. My name's Ivan, not Harvey."

Ivan, hmm. There's something familiar about him. "Sorry, I'm bad at guessing names." Now, with a hand on his arm, I'm steering him physically. "Bye now."

"Yeah, I better get going if I want to find some bottles before it gets dark."

Thank God. I tell him his plan's an excellent one.

"Don't worry, though. I'll come around first thing in the morning to see how you're making out."

"That would be great." I decide right then on an early departure.

As he steps away I offer an encouraging wave. He hesitates and looks back at the burning burger.

"Your hamburger's going to be black on that side and won't be any good."

"That's the way I like them. Well done on one side, rare on the other."

Instantly, I realize my mistake in extending the conversation. He starts walking back. "Raw hamburger isn't good for you. You'll get sick."

Geezus. "I'm joking," I tell him. "I'm going to cook it well on both sides." My hands are gesturing again, waving, shooing. "Good luck finding those bottles."

He breaks into a grin. "Well, I'm glad to hear you're not going to eat raw hamburger. You like to joke don't you? Huh yuh, huh yuh, huh yuh, huh yuh."

"See you in the morning."

Finally he walks away and keeps going. As for supper, I'll have to throw the blackened burger to the fish and start again. At the base of the dock, he turns and waves, a picture of contentment and obliviousness. He kicks around the weeds, sees something he likes and moves quickly to retrieve it. As he stashes the prize he looks up to see if I've witnessed his discovery. It's a simple pleasure that wouldn't kill me to acknowledge, yet I look away, pretending to be at work with my spatula until he heads up the driveway.

I try to regain my resolve, but soul-sucking thoughts energized by Ivan's visit come dancing from the recesses of my mind, ridiculing my search for meaning, laughing at my plan to sail the Great Lakes, scoffing at my inexperience and corresponding inability to distinguish smart decisions from stupid ones. Doing a jig, deriding my delusions, they mock my belief that I've taken control over anything. They ask to hear the part about my latest plan, smirking and snickering, reminding me that whether or not I leave first thing in the morning will depend on the weather. Marco, Marco, the fog could roll in, worse than today's, and who's to say an early-morning storm won't be dying to greet you with thunder and lightning? But one thing you can be sure of; not even a hurricane will deter another visit from Ivan. You'll hear the cloppity-clop of footsteps, you'll feel the weight on the boat, you'll hear the knocking on the door as you try to hide: "Ahoy there."

To distract myself, I take down the navigation charts and spread them on the table. Where are the marinas? Which one are we in? Perhaps Ivan could have told me and contributed something useful. I leave the charts to put the kettle on. Having slept earlier, I'm worried about getting to sleep tonight and hope to benefit from a hot toddy of rum, lemon, and honey. Ivan! Suddenly it comes to me. Ivan The Terrible. I do know him, from the institution he terrorized with his temper tantrums, and that, no doubt, terrorized him for most his life, from the institution where I accepted my first job as a psychologist. And here we are, years later, both having escaped, him seeming carefree, as happy as can be, and me being miserable and snubbing him, perhaps never having truly escaped.

Saying that I accepted that position is not an accurate way of expressing how I came to the job, having accepted it as much as a man accepts incarceration for a crime he didn't commit. Encouraged as a doctoral student who had already published research demonstrating the impact of physical environments on human behaviour, I had planned to become an environmental psychologist, intent on designing communities where people would feel safe, where they'd take collective ownership for their neighbourhoods, where they'd feel a sense of belonging. Yes, this would be my contribution. I'd situated myself at the leading edge of an exciting new field, thrilled about the possibility of helping create better communities. Unfortunately, a recession came along to thwart the aspirations of environmental psychology, at least as something that would have applied value, laying it to rest in journals and textbooks buried in university libraries. A university teaching position would have been fine, a job with the government doing some type of social research would have been acceptable, but the recession smothered these possibilities as well. Diligently, I studied the career sections of every major newspaper in the country looking for something even remotely related to my interests and background.

Then, lucky me, on the very day of my graduation, only three months after I'd defended my dissertation, my parents discovered something for me, something "lying right under my nose." They'd taken me out for dinner and had saved the surprise for dessert, my mother pulling an envelope from her purse and waving it at me from across the table as if it were the winning lottery ticket—mine if I were quick enough to grab it from her; except it wasn't a lottery ticket, was an ad cut from the local newspaper: "The Erie Regional Centre Is Seeking A Psychologist To Assess And Develop Training Programs For Individuals With Developmental Disabilities…" It would be a bit of a commute they said, but "boy oh boy, talk about having a horseshoe up your butt, to have an opportunity like this fall from the sky on the very day you receive your degree." Leaning forward, holding their breath, they awaited my reaction, eager for relief from the em-

barrassment of having a son who'd become a "professional student,"
forgetting how they'd always told me to "stay in school, get an education," while lamenting from the start my interest in psychology, "a
wishy-washy profession that has little to offer the real world." And so
I applied and was offered the job, and figured out soon enough why
the chief psychologist had waited for my acceptance before giving me
a tour of the place—a chamber of horrors, born of overcrowding, staff
shortages, and barren wards that left residents prone to aggression and
self-injurious behaviour. But I sucked it up and weathered the irony of
believing I could help design better communities only to end up in a
place from hell—a place that refused to open its gates even after the
recession, because by then no one was interested in a psychologist
who had only worked in an institution for the "mentally retarded."

And so, here I am, free from institutions, but docked in the middle of nowhere, not a soul around except for Ivan The Terrible, a soul
I don't wish to see, a soul I wouldn't have seen had I not got lost in
the fog. What are the odds? Again, I check the charts, but this time I
glance towards the south and east, grumbling to myself when I realize what I'm doing. Yes, I get it now. Crossing paths with Ivan is a
sign I need to turn back, head south, down the Detroit River, beyond
Windsor and into Lake Erie, so I can go visit my first place of full-time
employment. If the point of this trip is to seek meaning from my adult
life, then, of course, I need to start there, despite how the very thought
of it makes me cringe. You want me to face it, don't you Ivan?

And yes, I get that you're no longer living in an institution, that
you're free to visit places in your community, that you take an interest
in meeting other people, that you're free to develop your own pas-
times, that you find enjoyment in life's little pleasures, that somehow
you've overcome your past to find contentment, succeeding in these
things far more than I've been able to. You've made your point and
good for you. And I'm sorry Ivan, for being such a jerk, for turning

you away from my boat, for not seeing you and wanting instantly to celebrate your new life. And yes, I'm well aware of the advantages I've had with status, with money, with good health, and that I should be appreciative of these things. At times, I have made resolutions to be appreciative, but you know, Ivan, the acceptance of who I am and what I've done never amounts to more than a mental exercise—I've never felt a spirit or soul that says: "Yes, this is you, this is what you're meant to do, this is where you're meant to be." It just never seems true, what can I say? And I'm guessing that's the reason I resent you showing up like this, reflecting for me my insignificant life, while at the same time making me feel guilty for not being more thankful for what I do have. Sorry, I shouldn't take it out on you, but I need to achieve something that makes a real difference, that says I've been here and that it mattered. If that's impossible, then there's no point to living. Can you understand that Ivan?

I take a good gulp of my hot toddy and burn my tongue. His voice comes to me as clear as if he were standing next to me: "First your burger and now you're tongue—you need to stop burning things and pay better attention to what you're doing–Huh yuh huh yuh huh yuh."

Gee whiz, thanks Ivan, don't know what I'd do without you.

8

THE BAYSIDE TAVERN

I CHOOSE BEETHOVEN'S SYMPHONY #6 for this evening's pre-bedtime music, hoping that its peaceful melodies will help lull me to sleep. The selection also prompts me to resume reading Beethoven's biography, something I'd been planning to do for a long time. I go directly to the part where the biographer describes Ludwig's motivation for composing The Sixth, already knowing from information accompanying the CD that the symphony, subtitled, The Pastoral, was composed as a tribute to nature. How wonderful it would be to not only have a passion for something but the ability to do something creative with this passion. When a friend asked Beethoven prior to the symphony's first public performance if the composition could be compared to a painting, the composer replied: "More an expression of feeling than a painting." He promised his friend that if he were to listen to it, really listen to it, the music would come back to him whenever he'd take a moment to appreciate nature's beauty, warning him not to get preoccupied with other, less important matters. Ironic that Beethoven didn't take his own advice.

As I'm putting Beethoven away for the night, another book on the shelf, Great Lake Treasures, grabs my attention. I brought it along thinking it would be interesting to read about the various highlights as

I come across them on the trip. I open it to the section on Point Pelee National Park, the most southerly point on the mainland of Canada, my favourite place for family picnics when I was a kid, and later, when I was a teenager, my favourite place for year-end, class parties. I'll have to pass right by it as I travel back into Lake Erie.

Although I already knew that the park was famous for its marshlands I didn't know that it contained rare species of plants and animals that, in sheer numbers, exceeded any other region in Canada. I had no idea that this included 600 species of plants and flowers with names like wild blue phlox, pink herb Robert, and the pink-flowered swamp rose mallow, along with 70 species of trees such as the hackberry, shagbark hickory, and chestnut oak. I knew that it was a favourite place for bird-watchers, but I didn't know that over 370 species of birds have been sighted in the park and surrounding area, spurring their avid viewers, I'm sure, without the slightest hint of sheepishness, to call out the names: "tufted titmouse!" "Acadian flycatcher!" "yellow-breasted chat!" I knew that the park was the site of an annual gathering of Monarch butterflies preparing to migrate the 3000 km. to the mountains of central Mexico, but I didn't know about the 27 species of reptiles and 20 species of amphibians. Impressive, and a little distressing to think I'd been there so many times without learning more about it.

Heading east, on the far side of the Point Pelee peninsula, I find the marina at Roxton. The entry channel is located next to a two-storey pile of gravel waiting for action from the rusted-out crane that stands alongside. Accustomed to the pristine waters of Whisky Lake, Antonie can't believe I'm steering her into this sludge. Sorry, Antonie, if I don't want Ivan's voice with me for the rest of the trip I'd better drop by the Erie Centre and be done with it. I promise her the trip will get better. Eager to put this visit behind us, I decided to pass Point Pelee without stopping. Thinking about Beethoven's advice, I tell myself, "maybe on the way back".

Roxton is a resort village well past its prime, its cottages more dilapidated than when I left southern Ontario all those years ago. The Bayside Tavern is looking even more rickety, though work is underway to give it a face-lift. As I approach, workers are climbing down from the scaffolding, packing it in for the day. When the job's finished, the new shingle exterior will enhance its maritime theme, no doubt in the hope of attracting more boat traffic. Who knows, maybe sailors will be fooled into believing they've arrived at Kennebunkport.

Inside, the first thing I recognize is the oval bar in the middle of the floor, designed to look like a shipwreck. To its right I see the same two pool tables and the same shuffleboard, they haven't budged. Somehow, they've survived the beer spills, the cigarette ashes, the stale breath, the assaults from poor losers and drunkards, with no reward except for the view of female breasts dangling above. Against the wall on the left sits a cigarette machine. It lives for dirty dancing, either men or women will do. Next to it sits a jukebox. I walk over to see if she'll play one of my old favourites and am gratified to see she's devoted to the sixties: Nowhere Man, Let Me Be, Sitting On The Dock Of The Bay, Get Off Of My Cloud, MacArthur's Park. I slip her the cash and she begins to purr, her inner workings clicking. She still has it, for now. The whole place has it for now. My whole generation still has it, but the *it* is only what we've had—lost potential. I consider singing along, maybe it will help me figure out how the cake got left in the rain, or at least if I have any chance of re-finding the recipe.

The only other customers are two guys with matching hockey jackets sitting at the bar. Decorated with crests, the jackets boast of championships in old-timer tournaments and of men in their thirties and forties pretending they haven't given up. I walk farther into the fire trap, under the wooden beams that run across the ceiling, over the wooden floor worn smooth and shiny like wool pants pressed too often, take a seat among a group of tables surrounded by barn wood and cheap paneling, and pull out the menu that's propped between the sugar and napkins.

A couple minutes later, a waitress armed with an order pad approaches my table. Her skin is wrinkled like the shell of a walnut, her hair springs from her head like a wire brush. She's wearing a black t-shirt with white lettering that says Bayside Tavern. Thank goodness, now I won't forget where I am. Her black jeans are pulled up too high, well past her waist, drawing attention to sagging breasts. She reaches above her ear and flicks out a lead weapon, setting it to the order pad like a switchblade to someone's throat.

"Have you already decided, honey, or can I tell you about our specials?"

I was considering the clubhouse, simply because … well, how bad can a clubhouse get? But then there's the chicken, mayo, and food poisoning to consider.

"Specials? Sure, tell me about the specials." My voice comes out flat, the result of not talking all day. A good part of me is still riding the waves with a mind that's been wandering. I'm trying to recall if a waitress younger than fifty has ever called me honey.

A voice tells me I have a choice between a rack of lamb and chateaubriand, both served with brandy to be set ablaze at my table, the lamb accompanied by fresh vegetables, the steak accompanied by fries and coleslaw. "I'll have the clubhouse on whole wheat and … sorry, did I just hear you say … ?"

She grins and jiggles her eyebrows. "That got your attention, didn't it? Now, tell me honey, do you want to hear about the specials, or not."

"No, no, I heard. I'm thinking about the chateaubriand, especially because it comes with both fries and coleslaw. Quite the bonus! I usually get a stupid tomato, baked with an herb topping, or green beans done in onions and garlic, or a stuffed potato sometimes done with a hint of caraway."

"La-dee-da."

"Yes, exactly. Never fries and coleslaw. How's the béarnaise sauce?"

"Heavenly. Chef Pierre gets it perfect every time. Wish I could do that. Doesn't it just piss you off when it separates?"

"Royally." I look around her, towards the kitchen door. "Chef Pierre, is it?"

"Most of the time he goes by Pee Wee."

"Pee Wee?"

"Yeah. He only comes up to about my chin. Picked the name up when he was a kid and it kind of stuck. Anyway, I'm just realizing that the steak and lamb were last night's specials—sorry. Tonight, it's between chicken parmesan and liver with onions."

"Perfect. I'll have the clubhouse on whole wheat with a little mayo."

"You want a beer or something with that?"

"Blue Light."

"It's all yours, honey."

As she walks away I see her, fondly, in a captain's hat, as a weathered old salt who owns a fishing boat. Her name could be Sally. People would call her Sal. But where did she learn about chateaubriand and the hazards of overheating béarnaise sauce? What's her history? How did she end up here? I consider asking but decide against the risk of insulting her.

Oh no, the hockey jacket guys are leaving the bar and heading my way. Of course, with multitudes of tables to choose from, they have to choose a table right next to mine. To make matters worse, they pull together two other tables, obviously expecting others, and then, as if there aren't a hundred chairs to choose from, "Hey Mac, can we take a couple of your chairs? You're not using them, are ya?"

I gesture as if intending to introduce them to my chairs, "Go ahead."

"Thanks, Mac."

Over the next few minutes their teammates arrive, same jackets, fill the three tables. Some come close to backing into me, pushing out from their table to stretch their limbs. All I'd have to do is turn my chair around to become part of the group—like that's something I'm dying to do. The construction guys who were working on the building enter next. Fortunately, they stay clear.

"So much for a nice quiet dinner," Sal says, returning with my beer. She says it loudly so the others can hear.

"Hell, who goes to a bar to be alone?" one of them quips.

Another one calls out, "He's going to need a lot more beer than that," and he chuckles loudly at his own joke. They're glancing at me for a reaction.

"Oh well, at least they like hockey," I tell Sal, loud enough for everyone to hear. This brings various grunts of approval. Everything's cool.

"If they get out of hand, just give me the word and I'll have the lot of them thrown out," she promises. After she winks and turns to listen to their debate on how many pitchers of beer they'll need, I attempt to establish my separateness by fixating on an overhead television that's tuned to dirt-bike racing, an event as interesting to watch as popping popcorn.

"Eating alone tonight, Mac?"

Apparently not. The overture comes from one of those extroverted types who can't fathom how someone could be within hearing range and not want conversation. A social eager beaver, his eyes bulge from the effort he puts into not wanting to miss anything. Even his front teeth are prominent, ready to start stripping away my bark.

"Yeah, sometimes it's nice to get away." I smile but refrain from eye contact.

"I know exactly what you mean. That's what I'm doing tonight. The wife doesn't like it." He looks up to see what I'm watching. "She puts up with it but that's about it."

I allow a grin, nothing more.

He shifts his attention to the group but I sense it's only a matter of time. A couple minutes later he turns back. "You like watching that stuff?"

I guess from his question that he doesn't. "Yep." My eyes stay glued to the television. "I'm just starting to get into this sport."

"I know exactly what you mean, I haven't been able to get into it either. All they do is go round and round, jumping over the same bumps—how the hell are you supposed to know who's winning?" He leans closer, his head and eyes oriented upwards just like mine. We're now watching it together. Soon we'll have two straws and be drinking from the same glass. "So, do you have any idea who's winning?"

I tell him I don't.

"See what I mean, man? You and me both. Like I said, what's the point?"

We're on the verge of acknowledging the close bond developing between us when the pitchers of beer arrive and a teammate interrupts my buddy, 'Eddie', offering to fill his glass. A tall guy wearing aviator glasses stands to propose a toast for the occasion of their third annual hockey pool.

Not long afterwards, my sandwich arrives along with a second beer I didn't order. "You'll be needing it," Sal tells me. Moments later, Eddie and his teammates get their platters of wings, caps, and skins.

"Hey, I'll trade you two chicken wings for a quarter of your sandwich and four fries." The offer comes from a character named Bill, an adult version of a Campbell kid, from the soup family. Round-faced and freckled, he's grinning from ear-to-ear, pleased by his wit. I want to tell him that he's quite the wag. Instead, I laugh, snorting the air like it's so spontaneous I can't help myself.

The chicken bones get thrown into a shallow bowl brought out specifically for that purpose, and when the bowl is full enough to resemble a mass grave the NHL draft gets underway. Eddie and Bill, the two closest to me, have pulled out their notes. Bill, satisfied to be picking fourth, produces a sheet of statistics and nonchalantly reaches back to set it on the edge of my table for easy reference. His pick is coming up. He's torn between Sakic and Sundin. He asks Eddie, but Eddie's grumbling about drawing eleventh and tells him he's on his own. He looks towards me but sees that my mouth is full of sandwich. The third pick is a risky one—Lindros, a player who's had trouble with injuries. I feel a little mayo at the corner of my mouth and reach for a napkin. Amazingly, without forethought, a word jumps from my mouth: "Sundin."

Bill frowns, letting me know he was leaning towards Sakic. The moderator calls out, wanting to hear from the person who has the fourth pick. Bill takes a breath, on the verge of taking Sakic. His eyes dart from the moderator, to his stats, to me.

"Let's hear it Bill. We have a long ways to go."

Bill shakes his head no, trying to resist, but can't. "Sundin," he says.

I nod and give a thumbs-up. The next time around I tell him, quietly, with authority, to go with Selanne. I'm the mysterious stranger with the inside scoop. As Eddie's second round pick approaches, he too, seeks counsel. I have no idea why I'm doing this, but it's amusing to see the impression I'm making. For the remainder of the proceedings, Bill and Eddie look to me before finalizing their selections. A couple of the more competitive types don't like what they're seeing, scowling whenever we go into our huddle.

Towards the end, Eddie reaches for an untouched glass of water, pours the contents into an empty beer pitcher, fills the glass with beer and hands it to me. That makes three, my limit for such a brief time span. When Sal comes with two new pitchers of beer, she sees that I'm in the circle, sort of, and tells them they should have brought me a jacket.

At the end of the draft, Eddie and Bill thank me for my assistance. Eddie extends his hand. "Eddie Newton," he says.

"Mac Adams," I reply.

"Get out of here. Your name is really Mac? How did I know that?"

Another hand comes out. "Bill Turvall," says the voice that belongs to it.

We're one big happy family. It's absurd, yet half of me is entertained by the other half. The participatory half cooperates through the chit-chat, the game of let's get acquainted. Where do you live? Where do you work? Do you have family? How long has the team played together? You've been doing the annual draft for how many years? You're sailing where? How long will it take you? I have a cousin who lives in the Soo. Norman Newton, he works for the city and appears on television sometimes, as the city's spokesperson. Ever heard of him? (Normie Newton, now there's a guy I want to meet). I tell them I don't watch much television. Eddie says I'm not missing anything, that his cousin comes across as a snob, and then he gives me a friendly slap on the shoulder as if to congratulate us for not being snobs. I feel a pang of remorse, but for what exactly? My behaviour, while not terribly outgoing, has not conveyed snobbery. If I had exercised the more honest option, announced my need for solitude, moved to another table—now that would have been considered snotty. Should I need to feel guilty about wanting some time alone, and not frustrated when others refuse to see this and intrude upon my privacy to satisfy their own needs? Unfortunately for introverts, extroverts are more interested in making up the social rules that everyone gets judged by. So doesn't this make the extroverts the snotty ones? And doesn't this make my private, albeit snotty thoughts, a personal defense against the anticipation of being judged a social failure? Trouble is I shouldn't be blaming others, not when by my own standards I judge myself a failure. God, now I really feel shitty, like it would be easier to just give up and die. Damn this psychologizing, does nothing but open the door to the unbearable grief that will surely kill me if it gets the upper hand. If I hope to proceed with my trip, anger, not grief will help me survive.

"Hey, there's Stan," Eddie says, craning his neck to get a better look at the couple who have just walked in.

Bill looks and then leans over to inform me that it's Stan and his old lady. He's looking at me for a reaction and when I don't come up with one he looks towards the couple and then back to me, slowly, hoping that I'll track his gaze and comment on what I see. But, it's Eddie who makes the comment. "If only all ladies could look so old."

The couple has stalled a few feet inside the door, disoriented while their eyes adjust to the darkness. Stan is burly and bear-like, has hair that starts with a wave at the top of his forehead and then drops straight back. Later, I learn that he owns a fleet of trucks as well as some local cottages. A few of the players work for him, including Bill. Janis is lithe, wrapped in form-fitting leather that clings to her like plastic wrap on angel food cake. She has nearly-blonde hair that bounces around a slender face and down past her shoulders. Sculptured cheek bones. She could be a hairdresser or a beautician. At first, they're unable to see the players waving for their attention but as Janis scans a second time, I see the flicker of recognition. Quickly she looks away and tries to lead Stan to a table closer to the front. Stan's on the verge of sitting down when he spots the group, brightens, and points us out to his wife, who tries to perk with enthusiasm, but whose body moves languorously when they come to join us.

The players move about in a quick game of musical chairs. Without thinking, someone realigns my table as if I've been part of the group all along. The social loop is reconfigured and it takes me no time at all to see that Stan is being deferred to, that he assumes the role of kingpin. When Bill and Eddie orient themselves towards him and away from me I feel a tad ambivalent, and surprised at the possibility of having appreciated the camaraderie.

Within minutes I learn that Stan and Janis have come in from the city to work on their own cottage and that a twenty-year-old son is going to be responsible for renting and maintaining the others. Janis doesn't look that old. I deduce that the son belongs to Stan and that Janis may be the second wife, perhaps the younger model that hastened the demise of the first. Stan doesn't let her say much, but when she does, he qualifies her comments without looking at her. He's more aloof than nasty about it, the boss who allows his secretary to interrupt a meeting with coffee as long as she comes and goes quickly. Coyly, however, she steals attention from the boss without him knowing. Her eye contact is studious and tends to linger longer than necessary. When she does look away, she leaves behind a suggestive smile, a hint that the evening's just getting started. I'm guessing it's a tactic that keeps her from getting bored.

Truck-driving stories take over the conversation, skirmishes with customs officials a favourite theme. Truck drivers are the valiant distributors of essential goods, the economic lifelines of the country, while customs officials are pompous jerk-offs, generating useless paperwork to preserve their jobs. I'm surprised by sudden anger, that my dad isn't alive and here to defend himself. Is this the way he encountered the world? Was this the way that others treated and defined him? It never occurred to me in my image of him as big and scary, that he could ever have been on the receiving end. I feel relieved when the conversation moves on.

For awhile I sit silently, absorbing without participating. Just as I consider leaving, Ron McLean appears on television. It's Hockey Night In Canada and the Montreal Canadiens are preparing to meet the Pittsburgh Penguins. Something about the combination of recreational hockey players, truck driving stories, a blonde temptress, an old salt of a waitress, and a retired psychologist posing as a sailor, all cavorting in a ramshackle bar on Lake Erie, makes me decide to stay. Perhaps it's the casual sense of community that reminds me of the old general store where I used to hang out as a kid, listening to the cross-section of others who also hung out, especially the farmers with their eccentricities discussing their shared interests—the price of soy beans, bets about who's going to win the Stanley Cup. Besides, it occurs to me that this may be the last hockey game I ever see. It's spring, the hockey season's winding down, I'll be on the water most of the time, and...well, who knows how things will end? Besides, I think I've just finished my fourth beer and it's been a long time since I've had more than two or three at one sitting. Walking away like a competent, beer-drinking male might not be easy.

I'm lost in reverie when suddenly I hear my name mentioned. The voice belongs to Bill. "Mac came into the marina this afternoon by boat. He's planning to sail all the way to Thunder Bay."

"Wow, from here?" Janis's eyes fly open and even in the dim lighting I see how blue they are. Much of their expressiveness comes from her long, dark lashes—rarely do I notice eye lashes—but I notice hers. "That's an awful long way, isn't it?" For the first time since she and Stan arrived she seems truly interested.

I tell her the trip will take me most of the summer, stating it matter-of-factly, shooting for understatement.

Stan has made a decision about how the conversation should go. "So, what kind of job allows you to take that amount of time away?" His voice, louder than it has been, has taken on a sneer. He's a self-appointed guardian for the work ethic and he wants everyone to know it.

In an instant, my feeling about him jumps from mild to intense dislike. He's forgetting that not everyone in the world reports to him. Fool. I give him the stare of a boxer coming out to centre ring, and the challenge spreads disquiet over the group. They're hoping I'll back down so everyone can get back to feeling comfortable. A commercial has ended and there's a lull in anticipation of the opening face-off. Finally, it's Eddie who can't stand it any longer. "Mac works at some kind of a mental clinic in Sault Ste. Marie."

"Sault Ste. Marie? You're a long way from home." Janis says this, clearly impressed and wanting Stan to know it.

Hearing that I do have a job (which I don't), Stan doesn't know quite where to go with this. He's on the spot, however, and needs to do something. I decide to help him out. "No. I worked there until recently but don't any more." I haven't blinked.

"So where do you work now?"

I've given him new life and he's given one to my facetious streak. "My parents were the Duke and Duchess of a place near Sault Ste. Marie—Iron Bridge. Maybe you've heard of it. Unfortunately they were recently killed in a moose-hunting accident, but left me with a huge inheritance." I let this dangle for a moment, sensing wariness that a lunatic has infiltrated the group's hockey pool. I wonder if Bill and Eddie are still satisfied with their picks. "Nah, I'm pulling your leg, Stanley. I'm a consultant in private practice." Guessing that he doesn't like to be called Stanley, I watch the tips of his ears turn red and can easily imagine them laying back on his head like a mad dog's. "You'll be happy to know I've worked for twenty years without taking any time off at all." I pause to stroke my chin, trying to remember. "I may have taken the odd Christmas off. So, now I'm taking the summer off—kind of like a sabbatical."

Stan is working up a bit of a hate, but still doesn't know what to do with it.

"Why am I not surprised to hear that you've spent some time in a mental centre?" His sneer deepens, a couple of his buddies snicker.

I smile and shrug, letting him know I have no problem with the innuendo. This annoys him even more.

"We have a mental institution just down the road from here. Maybe you should check in, apply for a job. Maybe you could stay as a patient." He laughs. His buddies laugh. If I give him a smart-ass answer I wonder if he'll invite me to step outside. In a way I'd love to shut him up, right in front of his friends. At the moment, the group is split. Some are energized, eager to find out what's going to happen, others are uncomfortable, having come for the hockey pool and a pleasant night out.

Janis is the next to speak. "It's not really a mental institution. It's a place for retarded people." Slowly, Stan turns and glowers. It's the first time he's given her eye contact. Its message is clear—she's to shut her face.

"Good idea," I say. "I think I will drop in for a visit."

Stan relaxes a bit, satisfied that he has the upper hand. He pours himself another beer and motions to those around him, offering to fill their glasses as well. Everyone can tell he has more to say.

"I have a cousin who worked at the Erie Centre for a long time, worked his way into a supervisor job, probably didn't have the luxury of taking any sabbaticals along the way. Then one day some young professional type fresh out of school becomes his boss, just like that accuses him of having sex with a retarded woman. A blind retarded woman. Can you imagine?" No one can. They answer him with groans and grimaces. "As the story goes, the retard sits on this traumatic event for a couple of days and then decides to tell her tale to a couple of staff. The staff members—who knows what they did to plant the story in the first place—tells the professional and he believes it. His superiors listen to this because, of course, he's a goddamned professional." Again, the chorus acts as it's supposed to: Some shake their heads in dismay, others shrug. What can you expect is what they seem to be asking. "Fred had a nice wife at home—as if he had to have sex with a blind retard." Stan shakes his own head in disgust, picks up his beer, swirls it around and gulps it down.

"So what happened?" someone asks.

Stan wipes the froth from his mouth. "The professional tries to get my cousin fired. The investigation goes on for a while until Fred gets fed up with the whole thing and tells the assholes that run the place where they can shove it—ended up taking another job, losing all his years of seniority, poor bastard."

"Incredible," someone offers. "Why'd his boss have it in for him?"

"Probably just trying to make a name for himself. I think he was some sort of doctor. Maybe it was his dream to be champion for the retards."

A cheer explodes through the tavern. The Habs have scored. The players in red and blue are gleeful, engaged in a group hug. The tavern has filled, the beer is flying.

I wait for the commotion to die down.

"Dastardly," I say. I like the sound of the word and so I say it again. "A dastardly deed." Eddie looks at me in protest, thinking I must be a Pens fan. "No, not the goal," I assure him, "the blind woman. I wonder if anybody bothered to check out her story, weigh the evidence."

Stan pipes up. "You think someone can interview a blind retard about a two-day-old story and hear anything that makes sense?"

"Yes."

"Fucking professionals. I suppose you're one of them."

"It has nothing to do with being a professional."

"Oh yeah?"

"Yeah. It has more to do with my sister. She has a developmental disability—and she never lies." I glare at Stan. It's a lie I've made up on the spot.

Before Stan can recover and before anyone else can resurrect the banter, I stand up and leave.

Stan belches as I walk past.

9

What Did You Want to Be When You Grew Up?

LATER, A NOISE COMING FROM OUTSIDE the boat wakens me. I listen for a few seconds, at first wondering if I dreamt it, but then it comes again: Knock, knock, knock. Someone's on my boat. My mind races through the possibilities—the marina operator dropping by to collect dockage fees, thieves checking to see which boats are unattended—Ivan. I dismiss these as fast as I think of them, until Stan comes to mind, perhaps drunk, looking for excitement, accompanied by some of his boys. I reach under the berth, feeling for my rifle and the box of ammunition lying next to it. The knocking comes again, no talking, no shuffling, just dainty little raps that leave me second-guessing, doubting drunkards would be capable of such stealth. Quickly, I'm sitting, pulling on my sweats. "Who's there?"

No answer. I'm out of my berth, turning on a light. "Who is it?"

"Mac?" A woman's voice, little more than a whisper.

"Yeah. Who's there?"

"Janis."

I open the hatch and there she is, squatting forward in the cockpit, her arms wrapped around herself to keep warm. The air is fresh and a little fishy under a starlit sky that lacks the sparkle it has over

Whisky Lake. I stare, expecting her to say something. She stares back, says nothing. I have no idea why she's here, but guess it's not to borrow a cup of sugar. She's shivering. I ask if she wants to come inside.

Her shoulders droop as they would at the end of a sigh, perhaps dispirited by body language I hadn't intended. She glances into the darkness over the lake. "They're in the cottage playing cards. Eight of them." She looks back towards land and fixes her gaze as if she can see them through the walls, sitting around the table. "The cottage is full of booze, smoke, and loud-mouths. The walls are like paper so there's no way I could get to sleep. I don't sleep well at the best of times."

So what would she have done if I hadn't been here? I shrug and wave her in. She starts down the ladder and hesitates, twisting around to take a quick look, long enough to see that things look innocent in a galley that's cozy as candlelight. "I hope I didn't wake you. This isn't very thoughtful of me." She closes the door behind her, and instantly I smell the alcohol.

"No, hadn't fallen asleep yet, was just lying on my berth feeling queasy from drinking too much." This isn't true, but I'm hoping she takes the hint. "I'm not much of a drinker I'm afraid."

She steps off the ladder, reaches into a tote bag and produces a flask. "You know what they say about fighting fire with fire."

"What kind of fire you got?"

"Cognac."

"Go ahead," I tell her, "would only make things worse for me." Damn, I hope she's not drunk. If she is, I don't hear it in her speech. I tell her to take a seat at the table as I get her a glass. She thanks me, pours a little, and slides it across the table at me.

"Just take a sip to see how it tastes," she says. "It's good, will warm you up on a night like this."

It is as she promises but I settle for the sip.

She reaches inside her bag to dig out some cigarettes. "Do you mind?" Noting my hesitation, she glances around before slipping the pack back inside the bag. "Yeah, it's a little confined for smoking if you're not a smoker. You're not are you?" It's more a statement than question.

I thank her for her understanding. Immediately, as if to make up for the deprivation, she tops up her drink, takes a gulp and begins to talk, free to say whatever she wants because I'm the stranger on the train she'll never see again. She speaks in clips, perhaps from habit, afraid of getting cut off at any moment. She tells me the card game will last for hours—stop. She tells me that once Stan takes to boozing he forgets completely about her—stop. She tells me she started the habit of late night strolls a year ago after discovering he was having an affair—stop. "We're not married," she says, "but still, he pledged it would never happen again. Not surprising, though, he was married when he had an affair with me." So I was right about that. At first she considered forgiving him but has decided he's not worth it. She pauses to take another gulp, offers a toast: "Isn't it great to speak your mind and have nothing to lose?"

"Go nuts," I tell her.

She chuckles but her expression shows more resignation than pleasure. "So are you comfortable on your boat?"

"Yeah, when I'm not hung over."

"Is it alright if I take off my jacket?"

"Sure." What's wrong with me? All I have to do is ask her to leave.

She unzips her jacket and slips out from behind the table to pull it off. I get up to take it from her, a gentlemanly gesture that, unintentionally, brings us face-to-face in the cramped quarters. Along with the jacket comes a sweet bouquet of perfume—the fragrance fresh, given the hour. Automatically, she preens, sucking in a stomach that's already flat, slipping hands inside pants to tuck in her top, reaching behind for her shirt-tail, stretching, revealing braless breasts as they press against her blouse. I wonder how much of the posturing is intentional. It doesn't take long to find out. At the closet door, she's beside me, craning her neck, wanting to see what's on the other side. I offer to provide the grand tour from where we stand. Enthusiastically, she nods. "Okay," I begin, "as you can see, this is the clothes closet. It's well enough stocked to allow me a change of clothing at least once every other month." I say this, facetiously, but I guess with too much of a poker face because she doesn't react. I have to tell her I was only kidding. I pivot, back up a step, and point to the left. "This is the bathroom. In sailing terms it's called a head."

"Yes, I know. Sounds kind of crude, don't you think? Excuse me but could I use your head?" Slyly, she smiles, trying to hold my gaze.

"Don't ask me why they call it that. Head seems to be a favourite word in the sailing world. The top edge of a four-sided sail is called a head, the top of the mast is the masthead, altering your course to face the wind is called heading into the wind." My diversionary tactic backfires.

"I had an old boyfriend who took me sailing once." Her gaze is unwavering and it's hard to know where to look. "Seems to me he mentioned another term for heading into the wind…Hmm, I can't seem to remember." She plants her finger to her chin, pretending to concentrate. "You're a sailor…don't you know?" She knows, but wants a reaction.

"Hardening to the wind."

"Yes, that's it, 'hardening up' is how he put it. The term was stuck on the tip of my tongue."

I ignore this and open the door to reveal the sink, toilet, and a cubicle the size of a phone booth. "It even has a shower. You'd be out of luck if you weighed two hundred pounds, but you certainly wouldn't have to worry."

She asks if I'm hinting that she needs a shower. I assure her I'm not.

"For your information, I had one just before I came."

I step further towards the bow. "And this is the berth, my bedroom." I flatten myself against one side so she can see. She leans forward, placing a hand on my shoulder for balance.

"Hmm. There's more room inside this boat than one would think."

"Yep, and it's all I need."

"Is it?" She turns to face me and we're so close I can feel her heat—or is it my own heat I'm feeling? She leaves the hand on my shoulder.

I feel a stirring that's been absent for a long time. Bless her heart, but it's not something I want—a path that goes nowhere, leading from one soulless moment to the next. I try to picture this woman with Stan, figuring if anything can kill the arousal— She looks towards the berth and then back to me, tempting me to look with her. When I don't, she nudges closer, placing her other hand on my shoulder, her eyes glistening as they stare into mine. "I'm thinking that you might need more. I'm thinking that you need to alter your course a bit." She presses forward so I can feel the length of her. "I'm thinking you need to harden up as they say."

The image of Stan isn't coming and so I set my hands on her waist and hold her away. "I'd better sit down before I throw up." Hunching over and holding my stomach I try to make the ruse as convincing as possible, barely managing to get back to the table.

"Great. Just great. Why can't it be my jerk-face partner who gets sick when he drinks? He never gets sick, just more and more sickening." She follows me to the table. "I'll stay for a couple of minutes to make sure you're alright." Still standing, she reaches for her drink but changes her mind when she gets it to her lips. She swivels and pours it down the sink. "Hell. Obviously, I've had enough to drink, too." She asks if I'm okay

I nod.

"You're a decent guy." Her seductiveness falls like a mask at the end of Mardi Gras, uncovering a face scarred with regret. "You're probably thinking I'd be willing to sleep with anybody."

I shrug as if it's no big thing and then shake my head to deny any bad impressions of her.

"I don't, you know." She goes for her pack of cigarettes before remembering. "Shit, I don't know what to do with my hands."

"You can pull out a cigarette and fidget with it if you'd like."

"Very funny, you're so helpful." But she retrieves one and does exactly as I've suggested. "Feeling a little better?"

"A bit. The wave of nausea has passed. It's better when I sit."

"It was probably me and my come-on that was making you sick."

"No. Just too much drinking."

"I've had a few too many myself."

"Happens to the best of us."

"Still doesn't account for me being here, does it?"

"The noise, the loud-mouths—"

"Yeah, that too, but there's more to it—to be honest, I kind of liked the way you took on Stan." She pauses, but only briefly. "He thinks he owns everything. Besides the trucking business and some cabins which he does own, he thinks he owns his employees, he thinks he owns me, he thinks he owns the Bayside and most of Roxton." She straightens, tosses her head to flip some hair from her eyes. I note again how beautiful her hair is, the colour of honey in the amber lighting. "He's a bully who has money, so most people pander to him—I'm guessing you noticed."

"The audience was important to him, no question about that."

"No kidding. Not being able to intimidate you in front of the others really pissed him off. Anyway, I kind of liked that, that and the thrill of doing what you're doing, hopping on a sailboat and taking off, leaving everything behind."

"But you're still a couple?"

"Not really. We're in limbo I guess, biding our time, putting off the hassle of a separation agreement."

"Sorry it hasn't worked out."

"Don't be. I'll be better off." She chuckles, but with more bitterness than optimism. "So tell me what it's like to be a maverick. I'm curious, or envious is more like it."

Now it's my turn to chuckle. "Ha, you don't know what I'm about."

"Maybe not, but maybe I want to know, maybe part of why I came was to see if you were really different from Stan and all the others who would like to fuck me if I made myself available, just because I'm pretty—to see if such a thing is possible for a guy."

"Well, you still don't know, do you?"

She looks at me, puzzled.

"I was feeling sick. Not a true test."

"Tell me something." She cocks her head and squints a little, as though the truth is more easily seen this way. "Are you really feeling that sick?"

"You say you were testing me. What would you have done if I'd accepted?"

"Hmm, I guess I would have let you get lucky."

"Okay, lucky me, but how about you?"

She shrugs. "If you have any more sensitivity than a jack-hammer, it would be better than it's ever been Stan. Who knows? I've even heard it can be good."

"Not a jack-hammer, but believe me, you're wrong to think I'd never take advantage."

"So tell me about it," she says. Crossing her arms, she leans across the table, all ears and eagerness, more alive and less contrived than a minute ago when she was making a move on me.

"Won't take long." I explain that I was married once, got divorced, and then screwed around a lot with women who were pretty and available, with women I didn't love, some I didn't even care for. I tell her how I'd pick them up in places like the Bayside Tavern, going in to get something to eat and coming out with a strange woman. "Not that I was any great prize—but not caring made it come easy, somehow. Must be a law of physics or something."

"And now?"

"And now, unfortunately, I don't care for much of anything and don't seem to have the energy."

"You're impotent?"

"Impotent? A few minutes ago, when we were looking at my bed—I guess we weren't standing as close as I thought."

"Oh yeah." She smirks. "And, um, you're right, we were standing close, and I did notice. Silly question. So what are you, depressed or something?"

"No, I wouldn't say that. It's just that every time I picked up a strange woman, I felt another piece of me falling away, until one day I realized that there wasn't much left, that the remaining parts were losing faith and preparing to jump ship."

"There's been no one special since your wife?"

I shrug.

"So the pieces of you that jumped ship...you're sailing around now, trying to find them?"

I smile, appreciating her insight. "I haven't thought of it that way."

She puts the cigarettes away and leans back from the table. "You didn't tell us what you did at that mental health centre, or what kind of consultant you are."

"You haven't told me how you spend *your* time."

She frowns. "I work in the office at Clarkson Chevrolet in Chatham, not really an office, more like a miniature bar that sits in the middle of the showroom. I sit on a stool, take down personal information, fill out forms, and look at new cars all day."

"Hmm, so when male customers come in to take a look, they see you and start to imagine the possibilities—if only they owned one of those sexy cars."

"Yeah, that's pretty much my job—me and Shelley perched beside each other on our stools, day in, day out. Shelley's the phone receptionist, a twenty-five-year-old redhead with a nice voice." She pauses, candy-coats her voice, bats her lashes. "Hi there, how are you today? See anything you like?"

I wonder how many would notice the sneer behind the smile. "Anything about the job you like?"

"Oh, I don't know. Most of the time, I'm detached. I suppose at some level I like the attention—I don't give it much thought." She's shaking her head no. "Now, your turn. You worked at a mental health place. What kind of consulting do you do?"

"I'm a chaplain." It's the first thing that pops into my head. "I visit various places, mental health centres and other types of clinics, providing spiritual support to both patients and staff, helping them find the strength needed to cope with their challenges." I had no idea that anonymity would make it so easy to invent stories. Without trying, the cadence of my speech changes, becomes more paternal and reverent. Maybe this was the calling I missed.

"A chaplain? Holy jumpin."

"Holy, indeed."

"Christ, I mean crap, I see someone in the bar who strikes me as interesting and he turns out to be a god-dam ... a gall-darned chaplain. Sorry, that's not meant to be an insult. I'm sure there are many interesting chaplains, it's just that ... Wait a minute. You just got done saying you used to screw around a lot. What happened? You been born again or something?"

I'm feeling guilty, surprised I fooled her so easily. "Hell, I'm not a chaplain. Are you kidding?"

"You're not?"

"No way."

"Well, you're an asshole then. You just wanted me to feel like an idiot, is that it?"

"Sorry, I was only kidding. I wasn't expecting you were going to believe it."

"Oh yeah, it's my fault. I don't know you, you seem sincere, how am I supposed to know what to believe? Jerk."

"Sorry. I really am. I'm sorry."

She shakes her head, "You know what? I don't give a shit what you do for a living. Forget it. You're probably a shrink who enjoys messing with people's heads."

"Close," I tell her. "Look, I wish I could take it back, you deserve better." I reach across the table offering a handshake. "Hello, I'd like to introduce myself properly. My name is Mark, kind of like Mac, except with an r—but no more story-telling."

"Good." She takes my hand and shrugs. "Hello, and my name is still Janis."

The idea comes to me suddenly. "Do you have a car?"

She pulls her hand away and scrunches her face. "Do I have a car? Why do you ask?"

"Like I said, no more lies. A long time ago, I worked at the Erie Regional Centre, my first full-time job, so thought I'd come to visit the place as an appropriate start to my trip, before heading north. And you guessed it—I'm a psychologist, though I've never enjoyed messing with people's heads."

"You are?"

"Yep." I note the dubious look. "Honest. I'm not joking. My career has covered several places, up to Sudbury and all the way to Thunder

Bay. Sault Ste. Marie was the most recent. You might say I'm retracing my steps. But, I hadn't figured out how I was going to get to the Erie Centre from here, so, do you have a car? I'll gladly pay you for the gas and your time."

"I have the keys to *his* car."

"Great. And there's no way you can get to sleep, right? The card game is going to go on for a while?"

"You want me to take you now?" She can't believe what I'm asking.

"If I remember correctly, it's within fifteen minutes of here. Hell, we'll be back within the hour. You wanted to know what I did for a living? I'll tell you about my life as a psychologist. That'll take all of ten minutes, and I'll give you forty, fifty bucks for your trouble. Come on. Let's go." I get up and grab my jacket. She follows. "The place is very spooky at night. I won't ask you to get out of the car or anything."

"Why? Are you planning on getting out? You're not leaving me in the car by myself, no way. "

At night, from a distance, a glow can be seen over a rural area where everything should be dark, as if an alien space craft has landed in the middle of a farmer's field. And then it appears, sitting far back from the road, illuminated by row upon row of lights, a monolith with a thousand eyes. In an instant, the memories rush back and I can see everything as clearly as if it were daylight. I direct Janis to the administration parking lot close to the building's main entrance. She pulls into the spot reserved for the director of training, leaving us half in the shadows, half exposed by a street lamp. "This place is huge," she says. "I didn't realize. As close as it is to Chatham, I rarely come this way and I've never really paid attention."

It is huge, I'd forgotten how huge, about three times the size of the Algoma Centre—everything about it is bigger, the buildings, the parking lots, the grounds, and seeing it brings back the familiar churning in my stomach. "A hundred acres of abomination."

"What?"

"Sorry, I was just muttering to myself about the wretchedness of this place." I note an exercise area enclosed by a high fence, the water tower, the giant smoke stack, thinking that armed guard-posts with searchlights wouldn't look out of place. A single light from one of the windows blinks off and I sense something sinister, as though someone's standing in the darkened space watching us. I roll down my window to let in some night air. "We must be upwind." She lets me know that I'm muttering again. "We must be upwind, or we'd be able to smell all the urine-soaked laundry." Merely saying it stirs the stench from memory.

"Oh yuck."

"Those smells can make you vomit if the conditions are right." For a moment, we sit quietly, allowing me to remember. "The floors in these places are pretty much all terrazzo." I sit back and close my eyes. "You have to be aware of where you're walking because you never know when you might come across a trail of shit. It can sit undiscovered for a while, sometimes until a resident finds it during a tantrum and scoops it up for ammunition."

"Oooh, shit."

"Exactly. It's good policy to avoid leaning against the walls. Sometimes in the clean-up, spots get missed."

"Didn't I hear that this place is going to be closed?"

"Yeah, but it'll take a while. I've heard hundreds still live here. Used to be over a thousand."

"Are they all retarded?"

"Yes, but developmental disability is the term they use these days. Advocates change the term every five years or so."

"Your sister doesn't live in there, does she?"

"My sister? Oh no, I don't have a sister. I made that up for Stan's benefit."

"You seem good at that."

"I'm sorry for lying to you, but not to Stan."

"Do you think cousin Fred really had sex with the blind woman?"

"Yes." I open my eyes to look at her. "I was familiar with the case."

"It wasn't you who helped her was it?"

"Ha. Help? I'm afraid that trying to help was always a waste of time." I close my eyes again. "Roll down your window and listen."

"Why?"

"You'll hear things." She does as I ask. "Just wait." After several seconds we hear a scream. It's hideous, like nothing human. Seconds later we hear another. The screams pierce the windows, permeate the bricks. I look up and see a shadow move against a window, trapped behind the unbreakable glass.

"What the hell's that?"

I tell her the screams could be coming from David, a resident I once knew, thwarted from plucking out his remaining eye as he did the first one, because almost everything he saw terrorized him—or from Gregory, infuriated with the helmet he's forced to wear due to his insistence at running head first into permanent fixtures like sinks and toilets. I tell her that Gregory is quite ingenious at finding ways that will get staff to remove his helmet—like chewing off the end of his tongue. I tell her I could be wrong, that the screams could be coming from far back in the building, from Horizon House, the ward that houses the sixteen residents who have multiple handicaps, meaning they're blind, deaf, and profoundly mentally retarded. "I'd like to see Hollywood make a 'feel good' movie about that—about sixteen of these tormented souls wandering around, banging into walls, colliding with each other."

"This is too gross," she says. But she leaves the window down, as helpless as I am to help or to heal.

"Some were born with gross genetic defects or physical deformities, but others were just a little slow at learning. At one time they had a school right inside the building, slow learners would get sent here, they'd learn bizarre behaviours from the others and then they'd get left here because of it. Some who were legally deaf or blind and not retarded at all got sent here because their community schools didn't know what to do with them. Can you imagine?"

"How could their families allow such a thing?"

"Times were different, beliefs were different. As recently as thirty years ago, many physicians specialized in convincing families that this was the best option for their kids because of all the resources and specialists that were centralized here. And if you couldn't trust physicians, who could you trust?"

"What did you do as a psychologist?"

"My job was to try to make them behave," I tell her. "They scream, they rip their clothing off, they smear feces. They mutilate themselves, they scratch and tear at each other, and my job was to stop it all. After all, I had all that schooling …You've come to cure them, eh? So, let's see this magic of yours—make yourself useful, Doctor. So I practiced behaviour modification—that's what we called it—reward good behaviour, punish the bad. Too bad the environment didn't provide much opportunity for good behaviour. That's what I did here for six years, earned myself some promotions doing it. Ivan knew. That's why he sent me back here—to remember."

"Who's Ivan?"

"He's a bottle collector I ran into the other day at a small marina on Lake St. Clair."

"A bottle collector?"

"Yeah, he was trying to tell me something about appreciating life."

79

"Bottle collecting?"

I laugh. "No, not exactly. He wanted some little thing from me, that's all."

"A bottle, maybe?" Janis chuckles, realizing we're on different wavelengths.

"I didn't have an empty bottle to give him, didn't have anything to give him." I think back to how excited he seemed when he found a bottle in the grass. "I wonder if, when he was a boy, he spent time thinking about what he wanted to be when he grew up."

"Probably. Every kid thinks about that."

I turn to look at her. "Yeah, you're right. What did you want to be?"

We hear another scream, followed by a bang. Perhaps it came from a ward directly across from us, or perhaps it came from an entirely different wing, the wind carrying it from a half mile away.

"First, can we get away from here?" she asks. "I don't like this place."

"Sure." I take a quick look around. "Yeah, I'm done with it."

As we start down the driveway, she rolls up her window. I look back and allow myself to think about the lifetimes that were spent here, from childhood to death, the fact of such existences. No particular feeling comes to reveal the meaning, nothing fills the emptiness. I roll up my own window to help shut out the memories, knowing as I've always known that there's nothing I can do to help. We flee.

A short distance away, she tells me. "When I was a little girl, I loved the water. My mother used to tell me my body was made for swimming. I wanted to be a lifeguard." She doesn't elaborate, speaks nothing more of aspirations or disappointments. I look through the dim lighting of the instrument panel and can imagine the little-girl innocence, the pig-tails, the lithe body that was made for swimming—and suddenly, inexplicably, I want to reach out. The next few seconds come in a rush. I want to put my arm around her, but to do so now would be weird and would surely be taken the wrong way. I want to tell her that she's still young with all the time in the world to try other things, but that could insinuate she's a failure. I want to tell her I'm sorry about Stan and about the other males in the world like him, but that would change nothing. I want to apologize for trying to dismiss her so easily with that chaplain nonsense, but I already have. Surely, there must be something. She saw me, must have hoped for something worthwhile, and so she came to me. And now she's here, only a couple feet away, neither deformed nor locked away in an institution where there are so many others that one has no idea where to start. The desperation to reach out builds to panic. I muster all the energy I have and reach inside, deciding once again to risk failure, for surely I must have something to offer. Something. Anything.

Nothing. As quickly as they came, the seconds expire and I cross back to the shadows where I resume my existence as spectator from the other side of the glass.

10

THE RUIN OF HOCKEY

THREE DAYS AFTER SETTING SAIL, and after motoring all morning through the rain, we're right back to where we started, at the Lake St. Clair Yacht Club. As I tie Antonie to the dock, I hear the splish-splash of traffic on the streets above, dampness everywhere inducing thoughts of catching a cold—just what I need. Cool, thick, air, prickles my nose, smelling as if a stranger has sneezed in my face. I go below to put on coffee, thinking about what I should do for the afternoon. Though tired, I'll try to last the day, hoping the result will be a better sleep tonight.

My truck is in the parking lot where I left it so I decide to take it for a tour of my home county. It's been a while.

After a quick pass by the psychology building at the University of Windsor, I head for the hub of the county. Out on old Highway #3, I travel within a half mile of where I grew up and pass the home of my first girl friend, Mandy, who was also the first girl I ever kissed, the first girl I ever fell in love with, the girl who was sent out of county to attend an all-girl Catholic high school after her mother caught us necking in the barn. A few miles later, I spot my old high school and pull to the side of the road to look it over. I scan the classroom windows, all divided into little squares, not knowing why I'm looking for the site of my grade thirteen literature class. Locating it, I imagine Mr. Neilson looking out from inside, pretending to lose himself in reverie, away from his students and whatever novel they're studying—most likely something by Callaghan, Greene, or Updike. Perhaps imagining himself a character from the novel, he narrows his eyes, trying to focus on something in the distance, something transcendent, for this is his shtick. He focuses on the farmer who's working the field across the road and starts talking to himself, but loudly enough to be heard: "I wonder what needs to be done today?" A dramatic pause. "I guess it's up to him to decide." A smile spreads across his face, accompanied by a second dramatic pause. "Look at him there on his tractor. Up and down, up and down, over the endless field. I wonder what he's thinking about—the amount of sunlight left in the day, the crops that will grow and be harvested from the very seeds he's planting?" His dreaminess caused one of my classmates, Judy Bishop, to fall for him, to spend a weekend alone with him at his cottage. Judy's best friend turned out to be poor at keeping secrets, news of the liaison spread, and that was the end of Mr. Neilson's teaching career. The last I heard, he had moved to Barrie and was managing a hardware store, but who knows?

I carry on into the town of Essex, to the main intersection where I'm stopped by the traffic light. Surprisingly, Davidson's Apparel is still in business on one corner, but I wonder how much longer it can last. Its pin-headed mannequins with their badly outdated hairstyles look tired of posing in mid-conversation, trying too hard for too long to emulate the models from Sears' catalogues. On the opposite corner, the sight of Bloomingdale's Grocery, the sponsor of my first hockey team, stirs a twinge of nostalgia, bringing to mind the team picture, the red Bloomingdale sweater hanging down past my hockey pants and over my Toronto Maple Leaf socks, everyone wearing a different style of helmet. That was when hockey was simply fun and thrilling.

The arena, located on the far edge of town, sits at the end of a long, pot-holed driveway. A single car, probably belonging to the maintenance guy, is parked near the entrance. Finding the large metal door unlocked, I walk in, greeted by a large glass cabinet full of trophies. A few of them bear the name of championship teams I once played for. At the time, the trophies looked more expensive, the gold and silver more shiny, the figurines more noble. Now, the metal looks worn, like old silverware sitting in a bargain antique shop, and the figurines look like painted plastic. Inside another set of doors lies the ice surface, clean and white, glowing softly in the dim cavern. All's quiet as strands of mist snake across the ice like ghosts reluctant to leave a recently completed season.

Taking a seat in the stands, I wait for a visit from another ghost, one who soon appears in the form of a free-wheeling boy slaloming from one end to the other, performing tricks with stick and puck, deking around opponents, setting up teammates. But suddenly he's older and no longer playing. He's in the third period of the final game in something called the playoffs. The aura of innocence has left, the magic is gone.

Fans, many of them parents, are engrossed, yelling at players on the opposing team, players who are the teenaged sons of other parents: "Hey pizza face, good thing you have lots of pimples because you're not going to get any goals." "Nice try lard-ass, if you'd take off a few pounds you'd be able to skate." Of course, not all the cheering is reserved for the players. The referees get their share of encouragement. "Get some glasses, Harrison, you wouldn't know an off-side from your arse-hole." The boy has never grown accustomed to the ugliness—in fact with every game it sickens him more.

The boy scores his second goal, putting his team ahead by three with only a couple of minutes left in the game. His coach taps him on the shoulder and reminds him about the scout sent by the Red Wings to watch him. "I'm thinking he'll want to have a little chat with you later." But it's time for the losing team to forget hockey and to inflict whatever damage it can. The boy is quick and keeps his head up but the whistle has blown and he doesn't see the goon who keeps coming, who takes his stick and rams the end of it into the boy's right eyebrow, drawing blood. The goon gets sent to the penalty box. The boy goes to his bench, dazed, asking his line-mate what happened. The line-mate tells him, but encourages him to forget it, reminding him about his two goals, about how they're on the verge of winning.

Some opposing fans decide to get in on the fun. "Hey Weathers... what's the matter... can't take it?" "Got a little booboo over your eye? Better show mommy... get her to go out on the ice with you cause there's more where that came from."

The boy looks across the ice and sees the goon looking at him, drawing a line over his left eyebrow, taunting him, smirking. The boy feels neither anger nor fear, simply maintains his gaze for a moment before looking away, towards the penalty clock. He fixates on it with a single-minded focus that intensifies as he listens to his instincts. With less than a minute left in the game the penalty expires and the goon dashes for his bench, looking towards the end of the rink where his team is hemmed in. He's not paying attention to the action coming from his opponent's bench, where the boy has jumped over the boards, is charging towards him, picking up speed. Only one of them is prepared for the impact. The goon goes down, hits his head on the ice and stays down, motionless, for several tense moments, before teammates help pull him to his feet.

Afterwards, in the dressing room, the celebration is wild, everyone woo-hooing and slapping each other on the back, congratulations in order for just about everything: the goals, the assists, the penalty killing, and especially the blind-side hit on the goon. The coach sees the boy wiping his eye, winks at him, tells him to take care of his new battle scar. Later, the coach takes him aside and passes along the scouting report: that the boy is a fine hockey player and would surely be drafted if only he were bigger. The coach, of course, disagrees about him being too small for the physical play. The scout has asked the coach to pass along his congratulations on the two goals and championship. The scouting report is secretly welcomed, letting the boy off the hook when he has already decided to quit competitive hockey. It's getting ugly, the yahoos are taking over—another tribe he doesn't belong to.

I sit for another minute, thinking it would be nice to strap on the blades and go for a skate, swirl around for a while with the mist. The thought occurs to me that only a month passed from the time the boy left his team's dressing room to the time he was leaving the Cadillac Auditorium in Detroit, promising to head north, a promise more easily made than kept. So many dreams that wouldn't turn out.

11

ROBYN'S LIGHTHOUSE

FINALLY WE'RE GETTING SOMEWHERE, having made it through Lake St. Clair and the St.Clair River and well into Lake Huron as far north as the Bruce Peninsula. Sailing conditions have been mostly favourable, with westerly winds that stiffen to about fifteen knots by mid-morning and remain reasonably constant until evening, granting us a steady course on a beam reach. I had wanted to track the beaches of Grand Bend, Goderich, and Kincardine, but was unable to pick them out without their sand castles, sun umbrellas, and bikinis bouncing about in games of volleyball. By hugging the eastern coastline we haven't had to worry about freighters, and, in general, have seen few boats of any kind. Still, I remain cautious, even wary, frequently checking the charts and listening to my weather radio every chance I get.

Until yesterday afternoon, the forecasts had proven accurate, and the earlier part of the day brought the nicest weather yet, sunny with hints of summer warmth. During a mid-afternoon lull, I hove-to, content to drift a few minutes while I sat back with a cold beer, relaxed but not sleepy. Unconcerned about the storm that was predicted for the southern part of the lake, however, I drifted in more ways than one, and was shocked when I woke to a cold and angry sea. Ink-coloured clouds stained the sky, lightning licked the horizon, and waves were smacking us broadside. When did all this develop? I couldn't have slept that long. Fortunately, we weren't that far from Port Elgin and its marina, and I was able to start the motor and get us in. No doubt, fate had come to pay a visit, had come to mock me for my soul-searching, to remind me that any decision I make about living or dying will have no bearing on the outcome—that even should I decide to take my own life, fate will have the final word, and if nothing else will rob me of the timing.

In the evening, between downpours, I walked along the beach, dwarfed by waves taking runs at the breakwater, trying to hurdle over. The sand felt good, pressing cool and crumbly between my toes. Later, when the storm subsided, I took a cup of hot chocolate to the beach gazebo and watched the sunset, a curtain of black and crimson satin going up in flames.

And now, the day after, we're back to making good progress, reaching just north of Tobermory, rounding the tip of the peninsula in waters famous for their shipwrecks. Heading into Georgian Bay, a body of water that is more Great Lake than bay, the swells rise under winds that come from all directions. The swells, like giant hands, lift us by the stern as if by the seat of our pants, impatient to move us along. Time after time, Antonie wriggles away before shooting down the waves, racing free until the next wave catches up, the knot reader showing speeds we've never reached before. This is thrilling at first, before I start to worry about nosediving, racing down at such a steep angle that the bow goes under, and then, inevitably, the rest of the boat. Overhead, seagulls squawk in warning, haunting sounds like cellar doors on rusty hinges. A lighthouse appears from the mainland but it stands stone cold, unwelcoming, a middle finger raised from the back of a hand. I lose track of the wind and abruptly the mainsail slingshots from one side to the other, coming within inches of decapitating me. I try to restore our course but can't read the winds. Spooked, I start the motor and lower the sails: time to look for anchorage.

I see an island several miles ahead and aim for it, hoping to find a sheltered bay. Sure enough, on the lee side of the island is an inlet with a flagpole at its base overlooking three wooden berths. What luck. Better yet, the slips are empty and the island shows no signs of habitation. I slip into a berth straightaway, tie up, step onto the dock and listen. The place is so well sheltered I can barely hear the surf that's pounding on the windward shore. On this side, the wind is little more than a pleasant breeze. I look to higher ground and through the trees spot a lighthouse rising from an eight-sided structure, looking less imposing than most. Perhaps it's this modesty and the fact that it's painted like a candy-cane that makes it inviting, certainly more than the one we passed a while ago. During daylight hours there's no way of knowing if it's active or not, but even if it is it would likely be automated, having lost the need for a lighthouse keeper decades ago. Seeing a path that leads up the hill, I decide that a hike to the lighthouse is just the activity needed to stretch my muscles.

Nailed to a tree near the entrance of the path is a sign engraved, 'Welcome to Cedar Island.' The path is well worn, probably by boaters like me looking for a safe port from which they can hike, picnic, or enjoy an overnight stay. Smaller paths branch out from the main one, reinforcing the notion that the island is used for hiking and perhaps blueberry picking later in the summer. In places, the trees are sparse and the pattern of low lying shrubbery on rounded rock suggests a blueberry paradise. Part way up, I catch another view of the lighthouse, farther away and higher than I'd originally thought. The path meanders in a series of switchbacks to make the climb less steep. For a moment, the breeze dies, and instantly I'm attacked by blackflies, but quickly the lull passes and the little buggers are dispersed for duty elsewhere. Finally, I come to the barren plateau on which sits the lighthouse. The base structure, a combination of stone and wood, is well kept, with that appearance of being painted every year until the coating grows to a thick rubbery skin. It's quaint, cabin-like, with checkered curtains tied back from the windows, and I'm surprised that the windows aren't boarded up—surprised even more that they're intact. I'll be able to take a peek inside, but first, I go to the edge of a cliff which is much higher than it appeared from below. The view is breathtaking, an armada of islands appears to be approaching, moving in unison, a large one surrounded by smaller ones, arranged like an aircraft carrier and its entourage.

I turn back and look to the top of the tower, imagining what the view must be like from its catwalk. In addition to displaying the panorama where lake meets bay, it would provide a bird's eye view of the island itself.

Not surprisingly, however, the door's locked. I wonder if there might be a spare key—a series of rocks, also painted red and white, border the walkway leading to the door and I look under all of them, but there's nothing, too obvious. A few feet away, two Canada geese stand staring at each other under a window. Because they're wooden and can't fly far, it's possible they may have found employment as the key keepers. I frisk them both, head to foot. Nothing. I rise from my crouch to look around.

THWACK—a blow to the head nearly sends me to my knees, blackness threatening to envelop me. I've been hit by the mast—no, no, I'm on land…the lighthouse…I've set off a booby trap…oh, God, I hope like hell I haven't been shot. What if this is it? Is this what happens—one's granted a few seconds of semi-consciousness before death? I hear a voice. Damn, the association of pain with another person suggests I've either been shot or clubbed with a baseball bat.

"Excuse me. This is private property."

"Sorry, what's that?"

"I said: this is private property you're on. What do you think you're doing here?" The voice is female.

"Right now, my best guess is dying." I'm wobbling around like a boxer facing a referee with two heads and fifteen fingers. What the hell does she think I'm doing?

"You alright?"

Good question. I check for damage over my right ear and note that my hand comes away with a smear of blood. That I don't feel a hole in my head is a good sign, I hope. I tell her I don't know if I'm alright or not.

"You're on private property."

"Yes, I think we've established that. As soon as I regain conscious-ness, I'll be on my way. Just point me in the direction of the path as I'm not seeing so well." I try to move in the right direction, wherever that is, to let her know I'm not a threat. "You'll have to excuse me if I'm a little woozy."

"I didn't mean to hurt you. I saw you sneaking around and then I saw you ducking under my window. What are you, a peeping Tom or something?"

Slowly, I get my faculties back. I'm surprised to see that the voice is coming from *inside* the house with only an open window and a few feet separating us. So that's what happened—just as I was straighten-ing from frisking the geese she swung open the window to see who was snooping, and wham, the corner of the window caught me over the right ear.

"I'm on a sailing trip. I decided to call it a day and saw the emp-ty berths, had no idea that the place was inhabited—so, yes, I was snooping." I press my hand to the wound and check again for blood, finding just a taint. "It's an interesting piece of property, thought I'd do some exploring."

"Would you like a band-aid?"

"No thanks. I'm getting this weird feeling I'm on private property—think I'll be moving along before someone shoots me." I take a few steps and wave to bid farewell, though the visit's been anything but fare and well.

"Hold on a minute. I'll get you a band-aid. My husband will be home any minute now. He's a busy man and I don't think that dealing with a dead body is the first thing he wants to do when he gets home."

"Thanks, but if my injury's fatal I doubt a band-aid's going to make much of a difference."

When I turn back to the window, she's gone. Time to leave. Trouble is, I didn't mark the entrance to the path and the ground looks the same everywhere I look, nothing but rock. The door slams and out she comes, keeper of the lighthouse, bailiff of the island, striding towards me in an over-sized plaid shirt, chin held high, lips tucked tight, either a bandage or a warrant for my arrest pressed between her fingers. She's a small woman and about my age. A golden retriever follows close behind.

She thrusts the band-aid at me. "Here." It's the size of a waffle. "What's wrong?"

"Nothing."

"So why the look?"

"What look?"

Both she and her dog raise their eyebrows.

"It's a little big, that's all."

"After trying to break into my house, that's the thanks—"

"Wasn't breaking in, I was looking for a key."

"Yeah, what would you think if it happened to you, if it were your home?"

"Thought it was a lighthouse, not a home. Kind of looks like a lighthouse."

"Ever think of knocking?"

"I can't put this on. When I go to remove it, it'll rip out half—"

"Don't then." She squats to pat the dog, hugs it, allows it to lick her face.

"Thanks, though."

They carry on as if they haven't seen each other for years. It *is* a beautiful dog.

"What's its name?"

She cups its face, croons: "Oooh, Samuel, you're not an *it* are you? You're my big boy, my big fella, aren't you Sammy?"

Good grief. I glance around, hoping to spot the path. No luck. I'll have to ask her to point it out and to tell me where I can find the closest public dockage. Crouched beside her dog, she looks even smaller, in greater need of security. "You're right, I'd be unnerved seeing someone snooping that close to my house."

"Oooh, you look out for me don't you, fella. No one messes with us do they? No sireee."

"Sorry, I didn't mean to scare you."

"We weren't scared were we, Samuel—we take care of things don't we?"

"No kidding. Damn near knocked me out."

Suddenly, Samuel breaks free and jumps on me, a mass of fur and dog-breath trying to lick me.

"Well, look at that would you?"

I bob and weave trying to avoid contact with his tongue, but otherwise do my best to pat him. "Good Samuel, nice boy."

"He *never* takes to strangers."

"Yeah, well—"

"Consider yourself lucky. Previous intruders haven't fared so well."

"I can only imagine."

"See that cliff over there, how steep it is?"

"Yep, pretty steep."

Samuel bobs and weaves as well, looking for an opening.

"You're not looking."

"Saw it on my way."

"After knocking them out, we drag them to the edge and throw them over. The tide takes them out to sea." She turns, hiding her expression.

"Georgian Bay has a tide?"

"What? You're saying you know this bay better than I do?"

"Course not." Samuel drops to his feet but isn't finished with me. He circles, sniffs at my legs, my feet, pokes his nose into my crotch. Geezus, what is it with dogs?

"Aren't you afraid the tide will bring them back, wash them up on shore?"

On cue, Samuel trots to a bone lying a few feet away, lies down and starts gnawing on it.

"It's happened," she says, shaking her head as she watches him chew. "I *do* tell him to leave them be, show some respect," she shrugs, "but he is a dog after all, a retriever at that."

"Tell me you don't strip them of their jewelry." Her face scrunches as if she's stepped in dog poop. I've carried it too far.

Samuel looks at me, licking his chops.

"Well then I do apologize, and thanks again for your concern, but seems like I'm fine—so if you'd direct me to the path—"

Ignoring me, she slaps her thigh, "Here boy." He goes to her eager for a pat on the head.

I ask her about public dockage.

With raised chin and hands on hips, she asks, "Something wrong with my dock?"

"No, it's just that—"

"Did you want to see the property or not?"

"Uh, I don't know, I've seen the view from the cliff and it's spectacular, but why should you, and, you know, your husband ... and considering what you just told me, I should stay away from cliffs."

"If Sammy didn't like you, he would've had you for dinner by now."

"Nice Sammy, good boy."

"He's the best judge of character I know, and I don't know what he sees in you, but—"

"Nice Sammy, smart dog."

"Obviously, you wanted to see the house."

"I wouldn't want to intrude."

"Hell. Minutes ago you were like a teenager prowling around a girls' dressing room."

I look back at the house, shielding my eyes from the sun. "I've never seen the inside of a lighthouse." Sammy's at my feet again, sniffing. "Your husband won't mind?"

"No," she murmurs, "he won't mind."

"You live here year round?"

"Yep."

"A beautiful spot."

"A slice of heaven." She says this wistfully, making me wonder—a slice of heaven, *but?*

"I'd love to see your house."

She breaks into a big smile and extends her hand. "Robyn Galloway."

"Mark Weathers."

Relieved, we both look at Sammy, acknowledging his role.

The exterior rises, stark and bold to confront the elements. The interior embraces, warm and relaxed to soothe the soul. Wood abounds, on the floor, in the furniture, through the rafters, on the walls, and I tell her how much I love it.

"Me too." She makes a sweeping motion with her arms. "This is the grand room," she says. "My great grandfather built the entire place from materials that came from the island."

Many photographs hang on the walls, mementos sit on bureaus and end tables. She shows me the kitchen, which, as the base of the lighthouse is made of stone. Pots and pans hang from a metal rack, preserves, cans and canisters fill the cupboards. She sees that I've spotted the staircase and tells me she'll take me up in a minute, that there's more to the lower level.

She leads me back through the grand room and into a short hallway, gesturing to the wall on our right. "This is my son, Brent." The wall is covered with pictures, the same person at different ages, a visual history from infancy to early adulthood. She beams as she steps aside to let me look. "He works at an outfitter's near Killarney Provincial Park. The owner just promoted him to manager." The most recent photos portray a fit and friendly looking fellow with the round face and outdoor glow he shares with his mother. On a small table sits a canteen, a compass, and a pair of binoculars. On the opposite wall, another shrine awaits my perusal. "Beth." She says it like a museum curator drawing attention to a famous painting.

"Your daughter?" She obviously is, small like her mother, with the same smile.

"She's a professor of anthropology at the University of Waterloo."

Anthropology texts, and scary masks sprouting coarse black hair, are arranged on a shelf.

"Beautiful children."

"I'm lucky."

"You don't look old enough to have adult children."

"Hmm." She's studying a picture of baby Beth, tapping at it. "Time passes too quickly. Before long, my face will be long and drawn and I'll look as frightening as these masks."

I doubt it. "Even if that were true, there could be advantages."

"For instance?"

"You could scare the hell out of trespassers by just looking at them."

"Not funny and that's no way to impress your host."

"Sorry."

She shows me the master bedroom and yet more pictures, these of her entire family, her two children and a handsome man wearing a familiar looking plaid shirt who I assume to be her husband. I wait, expecting her to tell me his name, but she turns to leave without mentioning him.

"So, what does your husband say about you stealing his shirt?" I'm thinking she'll be impressed with my powers of observation.

She leads us from the room without answering and it's not until we get back to the staircase, a narrow passage that spirals through the stone, that she stops and turns. "At first, before Sammy gave his approval, I wanted you thinking I had a husband. "Tim, my husband—" her voice quivers and she bites her lip, "sorry, I'm being silly, I rarely get like this." As she makes a *stop* gesture with her hand, she takes a breath and then resumes. "Tim died six years ago."

"I'm very sorry."

"A brain aneurysm. He lived with it for many years, realizing it could let go any time." She pauses, a pensive smile on her face as she looks around the kitchen, no doubt remembering them there together. "But Tim was a man who knew how to live and he made the most of those years. Come on, I'll take you up the tower."

We climb round and round in a staircase walled by photos, all scenes of nature, each picture fascinating and unique, and I pause to examine one of a tree, its silhouette embedded on a harvest moon like a giant tattoo. I want to ask about the photographer, but Robyn's three steps ahead and higher than me so I'll have to wait.

We emerge through a trap door and into a small chamber. Robyn lowers the door behind us and points to an opening in the wall. "This way. Hope you're not afraid of heights."

I am. In fact, I'm terrified, walking into the sky like this, separated from death by a see-through catwalk and steel railing. The steel seems sturdy but I imagine it breaking away from mortar crumbling with old age. Gale force winds rip at my clothes, threatening to parachute me off the ledge. I hear a voice asking if I like the view. Pins and needles prickle my legs, try to hypnotize them "Jump, jump," they urge. I feel her take my arm. "Over here," the winds roaring and she has to shout to be heard, "I want to show you something." To avoid glancing down, I watch some seagulls overhead hovering in the wind, waiting for the right moment to swoop away like kites cut from strings. Slowly I level my gaze to the horizon where the water glistens like gold. The panic eases to simple fear. Robyn points to my boat, tells me she'd like to take a look at it. "Sure," I reply, not looking, and when she points out her boathouse, a glance is all I can manage. "But what I really want to show you is over here." She leads me farther along the railing and stops at a red stripe painted on the steel. "Way across there," she says, pointing, "beyond the peninsula, past places called Hanover and Drayton, Beth is in Kitchener packing their suitcases. She has a husband and my little granddaughter. "

"Where they going?"

"They're coming here for the long weekend, leaving tomorrow after work." Her gaze is fixed as though she's watching her daughter pack, and then suddenly she smiles as if relieved to see that Beth has remembered those extra sweaters. "Come, come," she says taking me by the sleeve. I can guess what's next.

On the north side we come to another red stripe. "Nothing but water," she says, "between here and Brent."

"Do you see him often?"

"What?" She leans closer. "Sorry, can't hear you over the wind."

"Do you get to see him often?" I shout.

"Yep. He and his wife are coming too. They got married last summer." Slowly, she nods *yes*. "They're all coming. It's a rite of spring. We'll have from Friday night right through till Monday." She leans against the railing, one foot propped on the bottom rung, her rear-end jutting south. I'm having trouble hearing her, especially with the wind blowing her hair between us. I move to her other side.

"Sounds wonderful."

"It's great to see them together."

"So tell me about your great-grandfather, how he got to be a lighthouse keeper."

"What?"

"Your grandfather, how'd he get to be a lighthouse keeper?"

She looks back and laughs. "Pippy was never a lighthouse keeper." She moves closer, shouting and pacing her words. "He ran a small sawmill on the Bruce, but he'd always loved lighthouses and had always wanted to live in one. When he was eighteen, he went to a dance in Wiarton and part way through the evening overheard a girl tell her friend that she wanted to live in a lighthouse. Pippy went over to her, introduced himself, and told her directly that he was going to marry her."

"Get out—what'd she say?"

"She was horrified, slapped his face." Robyn chuckles and shakes her head.

"And?"

"Didn't deter him at all. Told her he'd loved lighthouses from the day he was born, asked if she had any favourites, told her he was preparing to build one to live in."

"I'm sure it was the most original pick-up line she'd ever heard."

"Oh yes. She grabbed him by the collar, apologized for slapping him and asked if she could make amends by giving him the next dance."

"And he accepted, right?"

"Well, kind of. He told her that his jaw was very sore, maybe broken, that one dance wouldn't do it, that it might take the entire evening of dancing."

"And she accepted, right?"

"You know what she told him?" Robyn lowers her voice to a growl, *one dance at a time, mister.* And that was that. They danced every dance."

"What a story."

"And this is the lighthouse he built. He asked Mimmy to marry him the day he finished painting it."

"So they lived happily ever after as lighthouse keepers."

"Well, yes and no. They lived happily ever after, but they were never lighthouse keepers." She laughs at my expression. "Have you seen any lights? This isn't a real lighthouse. It's a good replica, but it's never been an operating lighthouse. Pippy was always a sawmill operator."

"Incredible. Made his dream come true."

"Sorry, what?"

I shake my head to indicate I'd said nothing important.

Silently, we gaze out over the water. I've mustered the nerve to hold the railing but can't bring myself to lean on it. "Tim loved this place almost as much as Pippy did." She says this quietly, right when there's a lull. Her eyes are watery, but maybe it's the wind, and that's all she says. I feel bad for her having lost her husband, for her children having lost their father. But I also feel the life ingrained in this place, in these people connected by generations, the fulfillment that digs deep into the earth, rises in the sky to overlook north, south, east and west, keeping watch over the next generations. The realization hits me more than ever before that I will have contributed nothing towards the future. It won't have mattered that I came and went. The seagulls continue to play. The sun dips in the west.

Back in the kitchen Robyn makes us tea. It's a soothing contrast to the blustery wind that roars yet in my ears. I ask about the pictures in the staircase and she admits to being the photographer—and yes, all scenes are from the island. She tells me that taking up photography was a life-saver when her husband died and that she gets to sell some of her pictures while she runs a part-time framing business, sharing space with a friend who has a small art gallery on the mainland in Tobermory.

"Ah, so you don't get too lonely, then."

"Not at all. I have several friends on the mainland. I visit them, they visit me. If only I got to see my children as often. Would you like a cinnamon roll?"

"No thanks."

Sammy comes trotting in from the other room, still working on the bone from outside. "Oh yeah, the mention of food and you're up like a jack-in-a-box. Too bad sweets don't agree with you. You've got your bone so go lie down."

He circles around and goes back to his rug.

"It must be nice to have such a sense of belonging."

"He loves it here, has the run of the place; what dog wouldn't?"

"That's nice but I was referring to you."

"Oh," she snickers. "A sense of belonging for sure." She tells me she and Tim raised their kids on the mainland where their schools and friends were more accessible, and that the lighthouse was their summer place. "Even at that," she says, "the Bruce Peninsula was fine when they were young but they weren't enthralled with it as teenagers. They wanted transportation to go and do things outside of Tobermory but we only had one car. It was tough. And, I think they resented their father at times, well, not resented him, but you know, they weren't free to get angry or frustrated with him for fear of setting off the aneurysm." She frowns and tells me I don't need to know all this, that it was just the usual stuff families go through. "Anyway, when he died, the kids were both away at school and I came to the island to grieve, and ended up staying." She gets up from the table. "So yes, I have a strong sense of belonging—my favourite memories are from here. Would you like a refill of tea?"

"Please."

"How about you?" she asks, as she pours. "Where do you be-long?"

"Belong? Nowhere really." Not intending my answer to come out like a declaration, I add quickly, "On my boat for now. I'm taking some time off, to explore the big lakes. I don't have any amazing tales to talk about yet but I'm enjoying the journey. Good tea by the way. What kind is it?"

"Thanks. It's a ginger tea. So where do you call home?"

"I was living in the Soo before the trip but I've traveled around, was raised in a rural area outside of Windsor."

"Is that where you call home?"

"Not really. You know, the more I think about that cinnamon roll—"

"No problem," she says agreeably, though frowning at the inter-ruption.

"You know, I'd love to have a place like this to call home."

"How about family? Do you have family?" She's like Sammy with his bone.

"Nobody immediate. I was married a long time ago, but not long enough to have kids. It only lasted for four years. Never got remarried."

"What happened?"

102

Women—always interested in this stuff. "My wife married a grump, gave up on him after four years, justifiably so."

"What was he grumpy about?"

"Life wasn't unfolding the way he wanted."

"What was he hoping for?"

"This is a great cinnamon roll. Home-made?"

"Come now, really."

"Okay, he was hoping to do something meaningful, accomplish something, you know, in a man-build-a-pyramid type of way." I shrug. "It didn't work out, but it doesn't work out for many people, so no big deal."

"Given that the pyramids were already built, what would he have liked to accomplish?"

"Oh, I don't know, maybe he wanted to become a scientist who discovers something, or an athlete who masters a particular event, or a composer who leaves behind beautiful music—a Beethoven, somebody like that. Silly eh?"

"I've seen pictures of Beethoven. He looks grumpy if you ask me."

"I'm reading his biography and you're right, he was grumpy."

"What was his problem?"

"Over time, he lost his hearing, was pretty much deaf by the age of thirty. He couldn't think of anything worse than for a composer to have his hearing taken from him. At this stage in the biography he's stomping around a lot, shaking his fist, cursing fate."

"That would be a blow wouldn't it, not being able to listen to his own music?"

"Not being able to listen to his music, or to the sounds of nature—and he loved nature."

"But nature is something you see, mostly."

"Not for Beethoven. For him it was something he listened to—it inspired his composing."

"How so?"

I tell her about the first four notes of the Fifth Symphony, the famous da da da dum, about how he'd been strolling through the woods when he heard two birds singing these same notes to each other over and over again, how he used them to establish foreboding in a tale of adversity versus perseverance, with the latter emerging triumphant in the end. I tell her how he tried every cure he could think of to halt the deafness. "The poor soul. It makes me wonder how much of his music he would have been willing to sacrifice to get his hearing back."

"Did he have family?"

"Not his own."

"Any idea why?"

"Apparently he favoured women from social classes above his own and even had affairs with some. In those days, the nobility hired composers as they did servants. They had their cooks, their gardeners, and they had their composers to impress and entertain at parties. So, you see, none of these women were willing to consider marriage, and this pissed him off, royally."

"Beethoven with the status of a servant—that hardly seems right."

"Lots of things pissed him off. Even his friends had to tip-toe around his moods, never knew what might trigger his next tirade."

"His music ended in triumph. Did he?"

"Haven't got that far. He's only in his early thirties. He lives to be fifty-seven so I have a lot more reading to do."

"How the hell did we get on to Beethoven, anyway?"

"Grumpiness."

"Oh yes. Isn't it ironic? You were grumpy cause you couldn't be like grumpy Beethoven. What do you do for a living?"

"I'm a grumpy psychologist."

"What? If anyone ever wanted to do something meaningful, have an impact on people's lives—"

"Trouble is, psychology is a very young science, and I hate to say it, but we don't know very much yet."

"You don't believe that psychologists can help people?"

"Oh, sure, anyone can help others, but only those most in need go to psychologists. Think about it. The clients might have chemical imbalances, they might have dysfunctional families, they might be carrying traumatic experiences 24/7, and I'm supposed to make a difference in an hour, every other week."

"You must have *some* success."

"Not nearly enough."

"Hmm. People go to you for help but you've come to believe it's futile so you jump on a boat and head for the middle of the lake where people can't find you. Is that about it?"

"I don't know. It's not that I don't like people. Am I acting like I don't like you?"

"But what happens after your trip? You planning to switch careers or something?"

"Unfortunately, to have an impact, one needs talent and I don't have much, not the true, raw, predisposition for an ability that some people come into the world with."

"Poor you?"

"Not at all. I'm fairly good at this and I'm fairly good at that, but all mediocre stuff that's not enough to make a difference. I was born with keen senses so I can appreciate many things, but I guess it frustrates me to appreciate without being able to create. Look at you, you have a creative way of seeing things, like an artist. I'm betting you didn't go to school for thirty years to learn how to see that way. You just do."

"Maybe you should forget about building pyramids and composing symphonies and do something you enjoy."

"Hey, the topic of me is getting boring. Look at this place, it's beautiful, a one of a kind. I should be savouring it."

"Okay, but after I ask one more question. Are you at least optimistic you'll find something?"

"Haven't got that far yet. I have a long way to sail."

I thank her for the snack and tell her that I should be getting back to my boat, that she has a big weekend to prepare for. She says she doesn't have much to do, that she has lasagna and meatloaf in the freezer and the kids are bringing stuff. "There's only a salad to make. I used to do a lot more but we all agreed I spent too much time preparing and not enough time visiting, so we've changed all that."

"Hey, I have a great idea."

"Yeah?"

"I've seen *your* home, why don't I show you mine? You said you'd like to see my boat."

She ponders for a moment, not quite sure, but then agrees.

"Tell you what. I'll get a head start, get some food ready and make you supper."

"You don't have to do that."

"I know I don't have to, but why not? I like cooking, it's one of those things I'm fairly good at and it will save you a little work. You have to eat, how about it?"

"You're trying to avoid people, remember?"

"Just promise me you won't have a panic attack when you see barbecued salmon accompanied by a nice white wine—I'd hate to have to switch into psychologist mode. How about an hour from now?"

Again I note the hesitation, until, "That would be wonderful. Thanks."

"And bring Sammy along, I'm sure his role of chaperone is important to him, and besides, you say he likes me. I don't know why, but—"

"It's probably your smell."

"Gee, thanks."

"What else does he have to go on?"

"How about my cheery disposition?" I get up from my seat. "In an hour, then?"

"Sure thing. Sammy will be delighted."

The temperature has dropped and they come prepared, she in a yellow wind-breaker carrying a lantern for the walk back, Sammy still in the coat he was wearing earlier. The baby potatoes are on the barbecue slathered in oil and rosemary, to be accompanied by zucchini. The salmon steaks from Kincardine are ready to go. I give her the tour and open some wine, asking her if she'd prefer drinking it inside or out. Her choice isn't surprising, coming from the outdoorsy, hardy soul that she is.

Conversation flows and the meal goes well. Part-way through, Sammy, disappointed with the salmon and lack of space, gets up and traipses off. When the conversation drifts back to her weekend she offers an interesting confession: "I'm a little concerned about how things will go this year."

"Oh?"

"I've invited a friend from Tobermory to join us for our Saturday dinner."

"Do your kids know her?"

"No. His name is Ralph and they don't know anything about him."

"Oh."

"Exactly."

"Surely they aren't thinking you should be put out to pasture at your age."

"I'm not so sure. What I do know is that they don't like family traditions being encroached on."

"You haven't warned them?"

"No, should I have?"

I give her the look.

"I know, I know. I've been meaning to, but keep chickening out."

"Well, well. Robyn, keeper of the lighthouse, bailiff of the island, afraid to tell her kids about her boyfriend. How serious is it?"

"Not as serious as he'd like it to be."

"Hmm, Ralph is it?" I can't resist the impulse. "Ralph and Robyn. Robyn and Ralph." It's pretty obvious that destiny's at play."

"Alright, alright, I'm not crazy about his name either, Dr. Smart Ass."

"Sorry, it's a problem I have."

"*A* problem? It seems like there's several."

"It seems like the boat has two smart asses on board."

She pauses for a sip of wine and comments on how dark it's getting. The temperature has cooled as well, but I refrain from asking if she'd like to go below, afraid she'll take the opportunity to call it an evening. "Given the risk with your kids, I'm assuming Ralph must be worth it."

"He's thoughtful," she says, rather weakly. "Oh hell, I don't know. He's a friend. What can I say?"

"A friend who's trying to court you." By now I'm feeling mischievous.

"Trying to *court* me? What century are you from? Next, you'll be calling him my suitor." A sour look crosses her face which she quickly wipes away.

"Have you thought about how Ralph and your kids are going to interpret his inclusion?"

"I know. He was fishing for the invitation and I offered it without much thought."

"You want to do anything about it?"

"It's too late to take back the invitation."

"Yeah, I'd agree with that, but how about the interpretation of things, starting with your kids?"

"What do you think I should tell them?"

"I have no idea, and it doesn't matter what I think. What do *you* think?"

"Probably the truth, that he's been a friend for a while, that I've invited him for supper, that maybe I shouldn't have, that he's a nice man, that we're not serious—well, that I'm not serious."

"When you going to tell them?"

"I don't know. Soon I guess. Does the exact time matter?"

"I don't know that either. You think you should wait until just before he arrives?"

"Well, no."

"How about a couple hours before?"

"I'll have to tell them before then."

"Tonight on the phone?"

"No, this is something we need to talk about in person, tomorrow night after they've arrived and settle in. But when should I talk with him—you know, so as not to mislead him?"

I raise my eyebrows.

"Yeah, yeah, I know." She ponders for a moment. "Some time next week. The sooner the better."

She leans back to look at the sky, where the first stars are appearing, pinpricks against the deepening blue. I see the strain in her neck and would bet anything she's fighting the sadness of remembering Tim. The sadness is pure and private, unfiltered by words that couldn't do it justice, and unexpectedly her sadness spreads and grips me by the gut. Like fumes near a fire, emotions threaten to ignite, but Robyn turns and smiles and her strength saves us both.

She thanks me for listening to her about Ralph, and to lighten the moment I suggest that my listening skills might have made me a good hairdresser. A little later, when she announces she'd better get back, I insist on walking with her. On the way, I ask permission to explore the island the next morning before setting sail, and she tells me to feel free, as long as I drop by for pancakes. At the top she thanks me again, tells me to take the lantern, offers advice about the hiking trails then says she'd better get inside because she'll need time to figure how to tell her children about a man named Ralph who's attempting to *court* their mother.

I rise early and find the path that winds in and out, up and down, along the shoreline. The water's calm and small fish approach the rocks seemingly curious about the two-legged creature. Where the path veers inland I spot the "Yoda trees" described by Robyn, ancient cedars gnarled and twisted, clinging to rock and moss, fighting for survival each and every day, deformities and all. In the lowlands within the woods, the trail is soggy from winter thaw and spring rain, and shades of yellow-green spread overhead and beneath, feasting on the skeletal remains of winter. At their tips, evergreens are showing new growth, becoming older and younger at the same time. Pollen infuses the air with a lemon scent, like the juice I sprinkled over last night's salmon. Birds sing and a few yards away, tucked under an enormous pine, a rabbit twitches. I freeze, hoping not to scare him off, while cautiously he turns its head to check me out. In our battle of nerves I observe his breathing and wonder if he can notice mine. His head pivots and I spot the clump of green in its mouth. As he nibbles, his nose twitches as if he has an itch that can't be reached while the clump of green shrinks and disappears. Uncomfortable, I shift a little, and that's all it takes. He bolts, zig-zagging into the woods until the cotton of his tail blends with the flicker of white birch. Farther along is a lookout where boulders, like marbles left at a picnic by the children of giants, lie scattered on a flat plateau. But as oddly situated as they seem, they do belong. Everything I see on this island belongs— the cliffs, the paths, the cedars, Samuel, and especially Robyn and her lighthouse—all of it enduring, evolving with the change of seasons. I realize that here, the old don't die, but thrive as the foundation for what comes next, the life that's sprouting everywhere. How this place must love the spring, its virility, its impulsiveness.

Imagining the smell of maple syrup I head back, looking forward to seeing the everlasting Robyn one more time.

12

THE NORTH CHANNEL

AS CEDAR ISLAND SLIPS FROM the horizon, the image of Robyn anticipating the arrival of her kids sticks in my mind. How satisfying it must be to have a family that perseveres, celebrates the seasons, and gives new life. Had I not planned on having my own family one day, once I felt solid enough about myself? Where has the time gone? Did I let opportunities slip by? Depression beckons, wanting me to confess once and for all my insignificance, but after witnessing the tenacity of life on that island, I'd feel ashamed to give in. Seeing first-hand how nature has no time for wallowing has taught me resolve if not optimism.

Favourable winds and a promising forecast have spurred me to aim for Parry Sound, straight across the widest part of the bay. For the first time, I unleash the spinnaker, which curls and luffs and then snaps open, its broad stripes billowing, taking to the wind like a hot air balloon. With wind and sails doing the work, I can relax a little, lean out over the water, let goose bumps tickle my skin, then sit back to let them warm in the sun. I close my eyes and listen to Antonie slapping away the waves, but I keep the moment brief, remembering what happened when I let my guard down the last time. As we approach the eastern shore I'll need to be on high alert to navigate the shoals that appear suddenly like whales surfacing for air.

For now, only the adjustment of sails needs attending to, an easy task involving the slackening or tightening of lines managed with the help of cleats and winches. My movements are fluid, my handiwork is deft—maybe I could be a rodeo cowboy who breaks records for hog-tying. Ah, what a line in my obituary that would be. Something Robyn said comes back to me, something about good things coming naturally from pursuing one's passion. Maybe she's right. I've read about people who, in mid-life, identify a passion, who leave their jobs to raise goats, or grow sunflowers, or build saunas. Apparently, live happily ever after. Of course, only the success stories get published. How many end up with nothing but a yard full of goat shit? The Robyn in my head smacks me with a window. It's hard to like a cynic. I don't like cynics and I've been intimate with one for a long time. I make a pact with her to try to be more positive, to keep an open mind about the possibilities. She smiles, Samuel licks my face.

Having managed the islands and shoals, I'm relieved to see the Canadian Coast Guard base appear as I round Three Mile Point. Behind it, lies Parry Sound, a town I've often driven past, but have never stopped to visit. I'll stay the night, spend Saturday, and leave Sunday morning. After checking my guidebook, I decide to hike the town's shoreline fitness trail and visit the Bobby Orr museum. Having interests has never been a problem—the problem is figuring out how to make a living at one of them.

On Saturday I come across a great little bookstore that besides the current best sellers and some classics carries a collection of books about the Great Lakes, the early explorers, the shipwrecks, the light-houses. The store also sells CDs, featuring classical musicians who have performed at the town's annual Festival Of The Sound, and it has an art section showcasing paintings from local artists along with prints from Canada's Group of Seven. What a great idea, a store that so perfectly matches its environment. I probably have the money to open a similar store in a town or city somewhere north of here. A woman with long grey hair and wearing a multi-coloured shawl asks if she can be of assistance. "Just browsing," I tell her. She tells me to take my time and to give her a shout if I have any questions. I ask if she's the owner, and she tells me she is.

"It's a wonderful store."

"Thanks. This is my tenth year at it."

"Good for you. You must get crazy busy in the summer."

"Don't know about crazy. Thanks to July, August, and December, I break even, a good year lets me buy an extra pair of shoes—"

"And maybe a Caribbean cruise in March to help shorten the winter?"

"Hasn't happened yet, but it's not really about the money." She picks up a CD and wipes away some fluff. "If it bothered me to live in a tiny apartment, I wouldn't be doing this. It's having this stuff around me and getting to meet new people—it's perfect for me."

"I can see how you'd love it." What I can't imagine is living cooped up in a tiny apartment.

She smiles, but just then the phone rings and she goes to answer it. A few minutes later, having abandoned the idea of opening a book store, I leave with my only purchase, *The Lighthouses of Lake Huron*.

Before leaving Parry Sound, I head for The Log Hut restaurant, advertised in the town's weekly newspaper as having the best Sunday brunch north of Toronto. I arrive early, hoping to reserve the better part of the day for sailing. The log building with its huge stone fireplace provides a warm ambiance, and although the buffet table is ready and waiting, I sit back with a welcoming cup of coffee, take a few minutes to absorb the atmosphere. Among the early arrivals is a fit-looking, middle-aged couple who sit a couple tables over. As the server pours their coffee, they pose questions about the restaurant—what date did it open, has it been busy, is Morrie around? When the server confirms that he is, the guy breaks into a big smile and asks her to convey the message that "Gus is here and demands to have a word with the new owner." Within minutes, a man wearing a chef's jacket appears from the kitchen and goes directly to the couple. Hugs and kisses follow, as do compliments regarding one another's health, and then congratulations on the restaurant, apparently a new venture for Morrie, one that has him beaming with pride.

Wouldn't this be perfect, running a restaurant on the waterfront, a wonderful setting with good food, at the same time greeting old friends and chatting with patrons to make sure everything's okay? Over brunch, I'll observe carefully, see if I can anticipate needs, imagine what I might do differently, gauge my readiness to be patient and flexible in ways similar to a psychologist, except with a greater chance of success, satisfying appetites no doubt a much more realistic goal than modifying even a single personality, given the brief hour or so to work with.

I notice a commotion a few tables over as a family of four prepares to leave, or, as it turns out, the mom, dad, and daughter are preparing to leave—the three or four-year-old son, an attractive little guy, is having no part of it. He's kneeling on his chair, very focused, arranging toothpicks into a special design on the table. When his parents get to their feet, tap him on the shoulder, tell him it's time to go, he flaps his hands, smacks his head, and lets out a shriek. EE-EEeeeee. Dad looks at mom who tells her son it's okay, he can take a couple minutes to finish, but after that he'll have to leave the toothpicks so they can go home. They've learned. A minute later, mom issues a reminder, "One more minute," but when the time expires and they try to move him, he reacts even stronger. The ear-piercing shriek draws glances from the other patrons, branding mom, dad, and the daughter, no doubt like they've been branded many times before. Dismayed, they've also learned that what works one time doesn't necessarily work the next time. Big sister takes a stab at it, crouches down, takes some toothpicks from the small glass container and, using the carrot and stick approach attempts to lead him away. EEEEeeee, FLAP, SMACK. Growing increasingly agitated with the interference, he begins to rock. Looking frustrated, dad runs a hand through his hair, wishing only to be able to take his family out for breakfast without all hell breaking loose. I've talked with enough families—I know. Mom sits down looking completely baffled, watches her son, wishing more than anything that he could talk so he could try to explain why his designs are such a life-and-death matter. She slumps, resigned to waiting till he's ready. Dad sits as well, but pushes his chair back, angling away from the others. Big sister stays standing, her arms crossed in front of her, chewing on her bottom lip.

Do I or don't I?

It's a family matter and who am I to intervene? Already, I've invaded their privacy by just paying attention to what's going on. From the parent's perspective, I'm an on-looker who doesn't understand but probably blames them for being bad parents. On the other hand, I feel their anguish and won't feel free of it for as long as the episode continues. I get up and go over, pondering the awkwardness of how to introduce myself. As I cross into their space, they stiffen, no doubt expecting something bad.

"Sorry, but couldn't help but notice your dilemma."

Their looks are hostile.

"I have an idea, something I've seen work before—can't promise."

Mom and daughter soften a tad, moving from hostile to wary, not so the dad.

"Sorry, maybe you're a kindergarten teacher or something but your sing-song problem-solving isn't going to work here, so if you don't mind—"

I understand his anger but don't appreciate his insulting sarcasm, even though he's talking to someone who can be just as much of an ass.

I look towards the mother. "Do you have keys to your car?"

She hesitates but then reaches into her purse and pulls them out.

"What's your little boy's name?"

"Joey."

"Try setting the keys next to Joey's design and ask him where they belong."

Suddenly eager, she follows the suggestion. At first, nothing.

"Say, Show me where the keys go, Joey."

Again, she does as suggested. Joey flaps a bit and then suddenly grabs the keys and bolts for the door. Dad almost falls out his chair but gives chase, big sister close behind. Mom hurries to put money out for the bill, snaps shut her purse, and looks at me, speechless.

"Transition item," I say with a shrug. I nod towards the door, her family heading for the car, and off she goes, stopping just before the exit to turn around. I see the pink, blotchy patches on her face as she mouths, "Thank you."

For the most part, parents were thankful for my efforts, even, as incredible as it seems, for the initial assessment and diagnosis that informed them their child had autism. I suppose it's because I took the time, did my best to answer their questions, offered recommendations, and maybe most of all, appreciated their child, got to know him or her just a little, and recognized the good. What they didn't know is how heartsick I felt once they left my office, the same way I feel now, knowing that if dad takes the scenic route home, interrupts the routine, turns right instead of left, all hell could break loose again, bringing the life span of my contribution to an end in five minutes or less. Of course, the family knows that disaster can strike at any time, but the fact that knowing this didn't take away from the small victory they felt as they left the restaurant makes me feel worse—that they, the ones who live with the condition can accept the small triumphs and I can't.

But how can I? Ten years of university, I have a doctorate, I'm Doctor Weathers, the psychologist families often called, their voices full of hope, asking if I was the autism guy, only to have me fail them, offering little more than a label with strategies that work for some but not for others, or that proved helpful until a new week brought a new problem to replace the old. I'm a fraud and it's killing me. I must be something else. I must be.

Back at my table, I watch as another family enters the restaurant, two couples, three children between them, and an elderly gentleman shuffling behind. As the family heads towards a table for eight, a boy, around six years of age, heads in the opposite direction.

"I wanna sit next to the window," he shouts.

One of the women, presumably his mother calls back, telling him that the tables by the window are too small.

"We can put them together." He tugs on a chair and tips it over, and then silverware falls to the floor when he pulls on the tablecloth.

Oh boy, here we go.

The havoc he creates is non-stop. I learn from his mother's yelling that his name's Jackson. Once seated at the family table the server brings the kids crayons and something to colour. Jackson tosses them, finding it more fun to agitate the others.

I head for the buffet wanting to get a head start on Jackson and company. The selection's good and I fill my plate with a cold course of herring, shrimp, smoked salmon, and potato salad, saving the hot food for a second course. Thank goodness I got there first. Minutes later, the fish section's getting sneezed on, Jackson spraying his germs all over the same herring, shrimp, and smoked salmon. I imagine I'm the chef-owner and one of the servers comes back to the kitchen to inform me of the predicament. What do I do? Give the stuff a good rinsing and put it back, the herring without its marinade, soggy smoked salmon? No, I'll have to throw it out, try to remain calm, remind myself that the pricing allows for this type of waste.

Now, the little girl I assume to be Jackson's sister is shaking her head no to everything on the buffet. At the end of the line, she's holding an empty plate with her mother squatting beside, trying to talk her into something. Just then, Morrie arrives with two more platters for the table, sees what's going on and asks if there's anything he can do.

"Jackie's asking for the cereal she has at home," Mom explains. Then, sheepishly, "You wouldn't have any cocoa puffs would you?"

"I don't have cocoa puffs, but I think I could find some rice krispies," he says with an encouraging smile."

Jackie resumes the head shaking. Mom gets another idea. "How about some toast? You like toast and jam."

Apparently, not today.

"Why not, you eat toast at home?" The girl points and mutters something. Mom looks up at Morrie. "The toast is cut on the diagonal, I always cut it straight across for her."

"Hey, no problem. Give me a second to set these things down and I'll go and cut some toast the right way—straight across, coming right up." Good for Morrie. He's patient, good-natured, and obviously devoted to customer service. "You can wait at your table," he tells them, "I'll bring it to you."

Shortly after, he's at their table presenting the toast. "Toast for Jackie, cut just the way she likes it," he's almost singing. Everyone's looking, waiting for her reaction. She folds her arms, shakes her head no. "What's the matter honey?" her mom asks.

"I don't feel good."

"Does your tummy hurt?"

Morrie's working hard to stick with it. "Would ginger ale or something like that help?"

Nope.

Mom looks up and says, "Thanks anyway." Morrie retreats, scratching his head, still trying to think of something. Meanwhile, Jackson's up and down from the table, running around, annoying the other patrons.

Later, the server comes with my bill, nods towards the family, tells me she'll give me a discount if I go over and do the car key trick with Jackson.

"I'm afraid the little bugger would jump in the car, start it up, and drive away. We'd all be sued, Morrie would lose his restaurant, you'd be out of a job."

I leave my money on the table and leave, truly hoping that Morrie does well with his new restaurant, knowing that he's a better man for it than I.

That day, I sail as far as Killarney, acting on another of Robyn's suggestions—to stop often and smell the coffee. I remember coming here with Zoe to spend a couple romantic nights at the Mountain Lodge Resort and to take her cross-country skiing in the adjoining provincial park, a jewel of geography that's every bit as beautiful in its winter whites as it is now in its feathery greens.

The snow was deep and except for the groomed trails sat unblemished, freshly prepared it seemed, just for us. The intermediate trail, the *Carlyle*, took us along the shores of interconnected lakes and over snow-covered ice where the wind was chasing ghosts and nipping at us with its icy teeth. The bland, office-dwelling psychologist, Dr. Weathers, was fading behind as I felt the change come over me, becoming more like the impassioned, snow-encrusted Dr. Zhivago, slipping away from captivity and into the forest to pursue his beloved mistress. Zoe told me she had never felt so exhilarated despite the head wind that was making her face "feel like the lid of an ice-cream carton." She preferred the wooded sections, finding shelter amongst the pines that stood ramrod straight, like sentinels in white tunics arching their arms, protectively, overhead. Occasionally, clumps of snow tumbled from branches and landed in muffled thuds, punctuating our huffs and puffs and shushing skis. Over a long stretch of herring-bone climbs we stopped on a narrow plateau and fed each other slices of cheese and squirted cabernet from a wine skin into each other's mouths. Once, when Zoe thought I was ready, she squirted some on my chin and it went down my neck, causing me to make a face that made her laugh hysterically until I scooped some snow and threatened to wash her face with it. Finally, at the summit we were rewarded with a panoramic view of wilderness, the rocks, lakes, and woods, all hibernating under a duvet of snow extending forever under the cloudless sky.

Restlessness and disappointment had taken a backseat to the love of a woman. Like magic, like Zhivago, I'd found meaning in life and this made up for everything else that had come before.

"What if you've got me pregnant?" Zoe asked.

I almost choked. "You're on the pill, right?"

She chuckled and told me to take it easy. "It's only a hypothetical question, promise."

However, she made it clear she wanted an honest answer and asked me to think about it before I responded. I told her I'd want her to have my baby and that together we'd be able to work things out, conquer whatever obstacles lay in our path. After that she leaned into me and we stood silent for a long moment, until I closed my eyes and told her I felt like an eagle on the edge of a cliff, that I could lean forward, open my wings and take flight.

"Fly like an eagle? All those times you let me get ahead of you on the trail—you were sneaking wine, weren't you?" She told me to take off a glove and to give her my bare hand and when I did she rubbed it till it was warm and then slid it up under her jacket and sweater and held it there asking if I could feel her heartbeat.

Yes, I was intoxicated—from the wine, from the surroundings, and especially from the feel of Zoe's skin.

Stop! I nearly shout it aloud. I had promised myself not to revisit this time period. More than a year has passed and I refuse to dwell on it any longer. I have a journey to complete. I look around to concentrate on what's before me, to erase the winter scene that snuck up the moment I let my guard down. I turn my attention to how the region provides a haven for summer activities—hiking, canoeing, kayaking, and cycling. Robyn's Brent must work somewhere close to here. An outfitter's business—yes, how could I go wrong? I'd sell tents and sleeping bags, camper stoves, skis, dried foods, survival equipment, outdoor wear. I'd rent out bicycles and canoes. During the brief off-seasons I'd explore, get to know the networks of inland waterways, become an expert in the business of outfitting. What a nice change that would be, giving happy and healthy people advice on how to enjoy life even more.

I rent a bike and cycle the road that winds through the wilderness to the major highway, stopping to visit three outfitters. Three within the first twenty miles—the market is saturated with them. So much for that idea.

Still, the area is so beautiful, harmony for Mark Weathers has to lie somewhere around here. Back at the village, docked in front of the Sportsman's Inn, is a tall ship with polished masts the colour of honey, draped with ropes, webbed together it seems by giant spiders. Mounted on the bow is a plaque: "The Great Lake Adventure Cruise." Ah, I could invest in a small yacht, something manageable, and start a cruising business in the North Channel. I could call it Paradise Tours. It's feasible, isn't it? My sailing skills are improving and I have the time to explore.

I leave Killarney first thing in the morning, planning to plot different routes to satisfy different interests. I'd adopt the role of both captain and chef. I list the menus of fish, the wild game, and the barbecue delights already in my repertoire, all manageable for groups of six to eight adults. The brochures and ads would make it clear that, "Regretably, Due To Safety Precautions, Paradise Tours Are Not Suitable For Children (at least those named Jackson)." I think of how I could hire students looking for summer jobs that offer adventure. I chart a beach package, envisioning how it would be advertised on my pamphlet, "White sandy shores and turquoise waters where sand ripples underfoot as you step out for a refreshing swim," hoping they'd be amused when the icy water turned them blue. I chart a history package that would point out the ruins of settlements and fishing factories that nature has long since reclaimed, that would include going ashore to visit small community museums. The first course charted, however, would be the scenic package, highlighting the La Cloche Mountain Range with its white, quartzite mountains speckled in green pines looming over the sky-blue water, followed by the Benjamin Islands in their garments of pink granite. I'm overwhelmed by the beauty, and there's so much of it. This is great, I'm on my way, discovering islands with nicely worn paths that lead to spectacular look-outs, exploring waterside villages with farmer's markets and other attractions, like the summer theatre in Gore Bay on Manitoulin Island.

On a sunny morning during my stopover in Gore Bay, I test my ideas with the marina employee who's filling my propane tank.

"Things seem pretty busy."

"Our busy time for sure."

"Some pretty good sailing around here."

"Reckon there's none better. Where you from?" Lanky, in baggy overalls, he moves easily, efficiently, giving the impression he could do it all blindfolded.

"Not far, the Soo, but it's my first time sailing in the Channel. I'm honing my navigation skills, trying to graduate from novice."

"You could sail for years and not see it all."

"I'm guessing there's businesses devoted to just giving tours."

He opens a valve on the supply tank, letting loose a rotten-egg fart. "Don't know of any. There's some who do tours, but mostly it's an aside to other things."

"Hard to believe that tours wouldn't be more popular."

"Sailing season's short and people from the big cities down south don't drive this far—the ones who do, come to visit their camps. Others come by water, they already have boats."

Shit. Shit. Alright, Mark, don't give up, not yet. I think of Robyn and Cedar Island and remind myself to persevere. Grudgingly, in the absence of natural talent, I've often laid claim to being tenacious. So prove it, be the pine that takes root on the side of the cliff and won't let go. And I've always been a hard worker, so maybe I'll diversify, do several things at once, protect myself from failure should any one thing not work out. Maybe I should look for a small resort on the north shore, where I can dock a sailboat and take people out on simple day tours, where snowmobilers could come in the winter, where I could use my investment in psychology to advertise getaway workshops and seminars on personal growth and life cycle changes, such as retirement planning. Yes, I'll try that.

I head for Bruce Mines, on the westerly edge of the channel. It's not far, and it's within striking distance of Sault Ste. Marie, not a large city but large enough, and situated at the locks that join Lakes Huron and Superior, it does draw some tourists. In the winter, the locals love their snowmobiling. And having lived and worked there, I know of no other psychologists who conduct workshops on life cycle adjustment.

13

RONNIE MCDOUGALL

FROM THE AERIAL PHOTO, the marina at Bruce Mines resembles a comb with missing teeth. Although it offers space for fifty boats, it's the height of boating season so I head in early. With the St. Mary's River, Sault Ste. Marie, and Lake Superior all lying a short distance to the west, Bruce Mines will serve as an excellent base for stocking up on supplies and for researching real estate on the North Shore. Moreover, the marina is right in the middle of town within short walking distance of the restaurants, the grocery store, the liquor store, and, hopefully, a real estate office. The approach is easy, right down the middle of Bruce Bay—perhaps too easy. Already thinking I've arrived, I blunder.

Of course, there has to be an audience, people sitting on a picnic table at the end of the pier, a few sailors milling around their boats, a woman walking with her little girl near the open berth, people who, having witnessed my sailing prowess can be crossed off my list as future customers. I have Antonie all lined up with just the right momentum when I cut the engine and scamper towards the bow to grab the dock. At exactly the worst possible moment, a freak gust attacks from the south, catching us broadside. The gust pauses, inhales, and blows again, stronger this time, blowing us beyond the targeted berth and into a collision course with a steel fishing boat that sits like a can opener waiting for something to open. I grab the oar and paddle frantically, like a ridiculous cartoon character, the coyote who's off the cliff and scrambles in mid-air to get back to land. Everyone on shore knows how it's going to end. With the crunching of fiberglass seconds away, I brace for impact, aiming the paddle at the other boat, leaning, preparing my arms as shock absorbers to soften the blow, suspecting it won't make a difference except for adding to the farce.

Right then, I see the woman and child running towards me, arms outstretched, calling for me to throw them a line. There's no time, if I drop the paddle… She's clapping her hands, yelling: "Now!" and I do it. She catches the line on my first throw and tugs, digging in with her heels, keeping her hips low, as if she's pulling on a rearing horse, the young girl joining in. The bow jerks to a halt but the stern continues to swing, and again I grab the paddle to push against the other boat, crouching and pushing, pushing, pushing, until we stop. The woman and girl have saved me. Applause comes from a few of the others and I wonder if I should bow. Thank you, thank you, Clutzy the Clown has arrived.

As I tie up at the stern I glance up to see the woman tying us at the bow. She finishes before I do, her movements clean as a seasoned sailor and looking the part in her cut-offs and blue-striped t-shirt. The girl I assume to be her daughter looks to be about six or seven years old. They wait for me at the base of the berth where I try to be gracious, but it's difficult, feeling as I do, like a doofus.

"Thank you. You just saved my boat."

"I'm glad we happened to be walking by."

"Not half as glad as I am, not half as glad as Antonie," I say nodding towards the boat. "She would have suffered significant injury, for sure."

"She's a very pretty boat." After an awkward pause she tells me to enjoy my stay and begins to move away, recognizing my need to escape the moment. "Come on, Shannon" she says, reaching with her hand. Shannon, the little darling, isn't so eager.

"Shouldn't he have kept his motor on, gone past the dock and then come back against the wind?"

"Sometimes, Shannon, a breeze comes up very unexpectedly"— again, she's trying to help me out—"and you don't have time to do anything about it."

"But isn't that why you should always keep your motor running?" Thanks, Shannon. Her mother offers a pained smile and pulls her along.

I go below to conduct inventory and make a list of what I need and, yes, to hide for a while, hoping the people on the picnic table will be gone by the time I come out. When I emerge an hour later with my backpack and bag for carrying groceries, there's no one around, only seagulls in a flap about something on the rocks at the shoreline. I smell it before I see it, a bloated fish being picked apart by the hooked, yellow beaks, competing for parts. How irreverent are these scavengers, feasting on death and stench, wearing their lily whites and their looks of indignation. One stops to stare at me, perhaps thinking that fish and sailors reckless enough to smash against the shore have no business questioning the value of those who clean up after them.

Looking towards the base of the pier I notice a cinder-block building. In addition to housing the washrooms I see a telephone booth mounted on the side. Good, where there's a public phone there's a phone book. If I don't see a realty office when I walk through the town I can look one up. Across a laneway, a stone's throw away sits the Bavarian Inn, advertising both Canadian and German food. I'll have to give it a try, either tonight or tomorrow night. Behind the washrooms is a footpath that arches over a wooden bridge and leads to a small park with picnic tables, a gazebo, and a quaint amphitheatre. The grass is brown and brittle as a bird's nest and the only trees are young saplings held upright by stakes attached by straps cut from garden hose.

In the soil that forms a circle around each, flowers wilt from need of watering. On my way to the grocer's, I note that the entire town is in need of watering.

It has its bright spots, the Bavarian being one of them with its window boxes jammed with freshly rinsed flowers. Other highlights include a mariner's style church made of stone, a log-cabin gift shop, and what looks to be a giant doll house, brightly painted and housing a combination pizza parlour and ice-cream shop. Abandoned businesses lie between, ramshackle buildings surrounded by weeds. A large sign announces the town as the first mining site in North America and asks travelers to check out its museum, a wood structure that sits atop a rock looking shunned, like a schoolhouse in July. One of the abandoned buildings wears a faded sign that says, Alice's Art Supplies—in a town of 600? A couple doors away sits another business, advertised by a sign that reads, Norm's Upholstery & Live Baits. Unlike Alice, Norm must have considered the village's population and diversified. Trouble is, I don't know how much I'd want my favourite lazy-boy reupholstered by the guy who packs earthworms and dirt into Styrofoam containers, but who knows, maybe there's a wall inside separating the two portions of the business. I wonder which side represents his true passion.

I find the liquor store and then the grocery store, both well stocked for a community this size. After selecting some thickly cut steaks for barbecuing I head for the produce section hoping to find fresh mushrooms. Find them, I do, loose in a bin, speckled with black dirt which I'm careful to flick away, wary of escapees from Norm's business.

Although I don't see a realty office, I do see a number of For Sale signs, all advertising the same realtor, so I write down the number with a plan to call her first thing tomorrow.

A large cabin cruiser, gleaming white with yellow trim, has pulled in next to Antonie. What a contrast, a sleek, ultra-modern cabin cruiser and an old, steel-grey fishing boat serving as bookends to a small, day-sailing cruiser. I'm in the cockpit slipping off my backpack when I hear a booming voice from behind, the kind that tumbles from the high reaches of a hockey arena, its insults timed perfectly so everyone can hear them.

"Hey buddy! I bet you didn't find hee-aff the supplies you were looking for." I turn to see a wide-shouldered man wearing aviator sunglasses and a Detroit Tigers baseball cap, waving with a motion a person might make to smear another with a cream pie. "Thee-at's what I find in these shit-ass little towns. They advertise hee-aving a marina but when you stop for a visit, they offer shit all. They sure as hell don't know how to deal with tourism."

"Actually, I didn't do too badly," I call back.

"Us? We bring a lot of our own stuff from down home." He hesitates and I know he wants me to ask him were he's from, but I don't. "It's a long way from Port Huron, but we hee-ave a lot of storage space. There's an ice-locker on this baby that's unbelievable." Just then he hears something that I don't. "The missus is calling me for supper. Better not keep her waiting."

I wave. "Nice talking to you."

"She's still pouting about me bringing her here. Everybody tells me I've got to see the North Channel. Hell, there's nothing here but rocks and trees. Shit, I can see rocks and trees anywhere." He takes off his cap, looks at it, and then as if to give it a good dusting, whacks it several times against the railing. "You gotta cook your own dinner?" This time I hear a woman's voice calling from inside the boat. "Yeah, yeah," he answers, "I'm coming."

"I'm going to the Bavarian Inn. The food's supposed to be good." I make my mind up on the spot.

He scrunches his face. "Don't blame you for wanting to get away from thee-at stinking fish boat you got next to you, all those fish guts and shit."

I don't smell anything but assume from the lack of activity that the owner's not around to hear the insults. "She's sitting pretty high so I doubt she's carrying any fish."

"You don't ever get fish-stench out of things, not even steel. Say, after you're done eating that kraut food, why don't you come over for a drink. *The Petroleum Princess* would be happy to have you." What a crappy name for a beautiful boat. "I'll give you the tour, got some see-atellite technology you'll want to check out." This time, when the voice from below rises in anger, he grimaces and starts to move. "So, give me a shout after."

I return his wave, already thinking of ways to avoid him.

The sign inside the restaurant says, Seat Yourself, and I'd be happy to do that except I can't find an empty table. I'm on the verge of leaving when a young couple notices me, and as they hurry to take a final sip of coffee, motion that I can have their table. Nice of them. It's not often I catch a break like this and it's even a window seat. The décor is true to its theme, from the plate rails lined with beer steins, to the giant cuckoo clock on the end wall. Only the waitresses depart from the theme, no braided hair, no blouses with puffy sleeves and fancy embroidery, just plain white blouses with black skirts, and the industrious smiles one associates with a women's auxiliary putting on a community dinner. The one who serves me, an older woman with grey hair and a tight smile, wears a name tag that says, Alice, and I hope she's not the same one, having to give up on her dream to do this. She tells me about the special of the day, the hunter's schnitzel, and asks if she can bring me something to drink. The German beer sounds good.

Outside, campers, cars pulling boats, but mainly transport trucks roll by, at times, a half dozen or so all in succession. Through a break in the traffic I notice an elderly couple trying to make it up the steps of the community hall across the road. She's leading the way, pulling herself hand over hand up the steel banister—he's holding on to her. They could be life-long mates who still love and depend on one another, or they could be long-embittered combatants heading for disaster when one of them snaps and does bodily harm to the other. I'll know when they reach the top, depending on whether she pauses and turns to check on him or forges ahead without a glance. I'm hoping she pauses. Otherwise, what would be the point of having hung in there for as long as they have? Unfortunately, a new string of transports come along, Alice comes to take my order, and I don't get to find out what happens at the top of the steps.

Hustling away from my table, she collides with a man who's appeared from nowhere, mutters something and carries on, leaving him bewildered. He's short, sixty-ish, and pleasantly stout—Santa without the beard. He's wearing a brown, leather captain's hat and rainbow-coloured suspenders. Another waitress comes by to ask if she can help him.

"I was hoping to find a table."

"Oh dear, I'm afraid we're full. Let me peek in the other room." Seconds later she's back. "Sorry, sir. Everything's taken. You can wait at the entrance if you'd like. Maybe twenty minutes."

"Oh fiddle-sticks, thought I'd beat the rush." His mouth forms a circle around his words, as if he were blowing smoke rings. There's a trace of Scottish accent.

I have no idea what comes over me. Maybe it's the couple who gulped their coffee to let me sit, maybe it's the woman who saved me from crashing at the dock. "You can join me if you like." As much as the words surprise me, his quick acceptance astounds me even more, as though he was headed my way all along.

"Thank you," he says as he grips the chair across from me. "This is most generous of you."

What am I doing? For all I know, he's a religious crusader on a mission to convert lost souls, or a peddler of snake oil. I nod to acknowledge his appreciation, but regard him carefully as he removes his cap and twists awkwardly to hang it on the chair. He has a ruddy face but a fish-belly scalp that hasn't seen much sun. After settling, he takes stock of me, his blue eyes twinkling through deep slits. Nicholas comes to mind as a better name than Santa.

"I see you've ordered the German beer." He extends a stubby finger, pointing. "It's on me, along with any refills."

"You don't need to—"

"My only wish is that I could join you. Lord knows, I miss a good bottle of beer." He raps a fist against his sternum. "Unfortunately, it doesn't agree with me any more."

Alice comes by to take his order of chopped steak and ginger ale.

"I'm famished," he says. "You're a life-saver to let me share your table."

"Busy day?"

"Oh, pumpernickel, you can say that again. This morning I was out doing some prospecting, must have walked ten miles. This afternoon I walked some more, witching a well for a German fella who bought some property down Centre Line Road."

"Did you find water?"

"For the first half hour, didn't get nothin, not even a tug, but then I saw this little gully and thought, ah ha. Well, once in the gully, the ground nearly pulled the willow branch right out of my hands."

I ask him about the prospecting, leading him on.

"Copper," he says. "You from anywhere around here?"

I mention the Soo, the sailing trip. He whistles softly, tells me I'm a brave soul, and returns to the topic of copper. "You probably know something about the history of Bruce Mines."

"First copper mine in North America."

"You bet. They closed her down a long time ago, wanting people to think they'd stripped her clean." He winks, "Take it from me, there's still a whole kit and caboodle of copper in these rocks."

"Why'd they stop mining?"

"The metal prices were low, but I've been keeping my eye on them over the years, watching them sky-rocket. They'll be starting to mine again any time now," he clicks his tongue, "you can be sure of it."

"And you're out to stake a claim."

"Yeah, but I'm David against Goliath. They've got most the land tied up, you know."

"The mining companies own it all?"

"Pretty much. The big-shot owners work in cahoots with the government so they both make a fortune." He rubs together his thumb and finger tips. "It's the government that controls what people can do with the land, right? They'll take the copper right out from under the feet of the farmers who can barely grow hay in this soil."

"Doesn't seem right."

"I could show you rocks with copper veins the width of axe handles sitting right out in the open."

"You should organize the farmers, come up with a plan."

"Too set in their ways." He sits back, snaps his suspenders in exclamation. "You know what their biggest problem is? They believe everything the government tells them. You'd think after—"

Alice arrives with our meals, tells us to give her a shout if there's anything else we need. He nearly yanks the plate from her hand, pouncing, attacking with both knife and fork, leaving it no chance to escape. He's still chewing when he points his fork at me, no doubt preparing to resume the conversation. In no mood to listen to conspiracy theories, I try to sidetrack him. "Tell me about witching wells. I hear it's a gift—you either have it or you don't."

He nods, tries to swallow and speak at the same time. "If you don't have iron in your blood the willow won't talk to you." And off he goes, relating one well-witching adventure after another, embellishing I'm sure. Nonetheless, he's an amusing story-teller and it's not a bad way to spend dinner.

Later, outside the restaurant, I begin to step away, telling him it was nice to meet him. He tells me "likewise" but keeps walking alongside. I see a pick-up with a missing front bumper and wonder if it's his, hoping he'll veer towards it. He doesn't. "I'd better get back to my boat. I've got charts to study," I tell him.

Glancing over his shoulder, he removes his cap, rubs his scalp, and moves even closer. "I can tell you something that'll blow the sails right off your boat. There's something about me you don't know."

I sure as hell hope so.

"How I'm going to make my fortune," he whispers through puckered lips.

I can only imagine.

"Fishing," he says.

"Fishing?"

"Oh yes. The wealth of this province is in the north, both in the mines and in the water."

"Commercial fishing?"

"Many years ago, these waters teemed with fish: whitefish, trout, pickerel, herring. That is, until the big companies came and cleaned them out. And once the fish were gone, the companies packed up and left, leaving nothing behind but ghost towns." I tell him I know a little about it from researching the North Channel. "The big shots aren't as smart as they think—they underestimate the resilience of the north." He snaps his suspenders and nods. "But the fish are back." I ask him how he knows. "Let me tell you. But first, let me show you my fishing boat."

He begins to board his boat but then stops and pulls back. "We haven't been properly introduced. I don't let strangers on my boat, you know." His eyes glimmer with delight, a jolly old elf for sure.

"One has to be careful these days."

"One can never be too certain, though you seem a nice enough fellow."

"I could be a wolf in sheep's clothing."

He likes that one but suppresses a chuckle. "The devil in disguise."

"Not at all who I seem to be." Gravely, I nod. "There's so much deception in the world."

He pauses, then proclaims, "They call me Ronnie McDougall—of that you can count on."

"Mark Weathers, from the time of my birth, I swear."

He slaps me on the back. "Well, follow me, Mark Weathers, and welcome aboard."

The boat is pretty much an empty shell, and aside from the fishing rod, tackle box, and fish finder, is no better equipped for fishing than a row boat. In the pilot house there's a table and chair, a two-burner stove, an empty can of coffee next to an old corning-ware coffee pot. Below, he points to a narrow door and tells me that the head needs some repairs. An open locker next to the berth is crammed with stuff—coat, boots, sleeping bag, tools, pots, pans, a small, inexplicable television. "Just got her in the spring and haven't had her out fishing yet, but I've been doing my research with the fish finder." On the basis of a Canadian Tire fish finder, he's asserting a commercial fishery for the North Channel? Back on deck he gestures to waters beyond the bay. "Out there about nine miles to the east, towards Gull Island are two razor-sharp shoals that run parallel. Sailors stay clear, but the water between them is deep and full of fish."

"They showed up on your fish finder?"

"Like a jar full of jelly beans. And you know what?" he scrunches his face like a pirate, "methinks it's salmon down there—orange gold." Salmon? "I could invest in commercial fishing, you know, get some nets and stuff, but there's no facilities here for processing fish. I'll stick to chartering and attract the big shots from down south—they'll pay a pretty penny for good fishing."

"You and the Bavarian can complement one another's business."

"Now you're thinking like me." A sobering thought. He points at Antonie. "That your vessel?"

I offer him the tour.

"You wouldn't by chance have coffee on board, would you?" I tell him I do and that he's in luck because I make good coffee. "You wouldn't happen to know the game of cribbage would you?"

"I would, though I haven't played in years."

"Splendid." He claps his hands and turns to descend the ladder. "Wait right here."

He's full of compliments for Antonie, but eager to start the game. "Low card deals?" He cuts a seven but I cut a two. On the first play of the game he lays down a six, I play a nine. "Fifteen for two." I move my peg two spaces on the board. "Hmph." He plays a seven and I'm guessing he has little choice to avoid a run. "Twenty-two." I play my eight to make a run of four—6,7,8,9. "Thirty for four." I move my peg another four spaces. "Go," he says. I move my peg another space, pegging seven points on the first three plays. And that's the way it goes throughout the game—I almost skunk him.

"Oh my," and he suddenly points to the design on the back of the cards. "Ah, I've brought the wrong cards, you see. This deck has always been unruly. I'll skip next door and bring back the other deck."

"Not a good idea. Go ahead and shuffle," I tell him. "New game, your crib."

He begins to shuffle but suggests I shouldn't be afraid of trying a new deck, "not if you're truly a good player."

I pause to see what he's dealt me. "Not a matter of being a good player. It's the sailor's curse I'm afraid of."

He throws a couple of cards to his crib. "Sailor's curse? Something I should know about?"

"You're not familiar with it?"

"Of course I am, though I might need a brief refresher."

"In the early sea-faring days, card games amongst the crew meant that the sea was calm, that the ship was tip-top." I pause to throw cards to his crib. "Considerable pressure, however, was exerted to keep the same deck in play for the course of the evening, probably to keep drunkenness and bad tempers in check as superstition had it that if the same cards survived the evening, three successive days of fair winds and general good fortune would follow."

"You don't say."

"Oh, but I do say." I set down my first card. "Three. A sailor could be having awful luck, the cards could get soaked from spilled ale, but the crew would be extremely reluctant to change the deck."

He sets down a king. "Thirteen. Oh yes, the sailor's curse. It's coming back to me."

"Good, then you'll remember that switching decks aboard a sailing vessel will bring five days of ill fortune. And you'll remember that doing so has been the cause of many shipwrecks." I rest my chin on my chest, play the final card in the series, "Thirty-one for two." Again I move my peg forward.

Ronnie shakes his head. He can't do anything right. I can't do anything wrong. "But you must know," he says, "that the superstition is out-dated, no longer seriously considered, not since they discovered the world was round."

"You better check your sources."

"Why's that?" He plays a nine.

I play another six. "Fifteen-two. Guess what the crew of the Bismarck was doing the evening before their great battleship was sunk?"

"No!"

"Ah yes. All because Captain Schmidt got off to a poor start in a game of cribbage and got out a new deck of cards."

"I hadn't heard that," he says, massaging his scalp. "Wasn't in the movie I saw." He plays his final face card. "Twenty-five for one."

"Now you know."

He picks up his cards, studies me with a furrowed brow. "The Titanic—please tell me that changing decks wasn't the cause."

I bow my head, slowly, and he does too, placing an open palm over his heart. I count my hand. "Twelve—lucky cut."

Antonie snoozes in the evening air. Trucks rumble on the highway, shifting down and then speeding up again as they leave the village, their noise subdued by the on-shore breeze. A mosquito, having buzzed us all evening, finally runs out of luck on the back of Ronnie's neck. Rubbing the blood from his hand, Ronnie asks for another cup of coffee, which means he wants another game. His luck has been awful, mine superb, even though I've had enough wine to make me stupid. I pour myself another glass and we begin our third match, Ronnie still mumbling about bringing the wrong deck.

"Sorry," he says, "but I'm going to have to give my luck the old flip-flop." He puts one hand on the table, palm down, and pounds it with his other fist, like a judge with his gavel. The stricken hand flip-flops, once and then a second time, before coming to rest again palm down. "There, that should do it." Immediately, he gets a good hand and takes a lead for the first time in the evening. "Ah, the old trusty flip-flop, never lets me down." I wonder why he's waited so long. "Tell you what—even though it's my invention, you have my blessing to use it whenever you feel the need."

"Why, thank you sir, I'm honoured."

He picks up his newly dealt hand. "One small detail," he says with a smirk and a shrug, "the blessing doesn't take effect till the end of the present game."

"A gentleman, but not a fool are you."

Over the course of the game I learn that Ronnie McDougall grew up near Thessalon, about twelve miles from here, and that he had a grandfather who mined copper. "My dad wanted to be a miner, too, but the mines closed so he decided to mine for fish instead."

"Commercially?"

"Whitefish, mainly, but he caught some pickerel and herring as well."

"Ever go out with him?"

He tells me he started as a young boy, joined the business full-time after finishing school, but then jumps over an unspecified number of years to tell me about his arthritis. "It's why I'm thinking about salmon and downriggers, so I won't have my hands in the water, pulling in nets." When I ask him how many years he fished with his dad he responds vaguely, but mentions he was expected to take over the business when his dad's health began to fail. "But the fish were almost gone by then and I felt no choice but to sell when a fair offer came along." He tells me that he had a falling out with his family over selling the business and that his brothers haven't spoken to him since, "but what did they know, they'd left Thessalon years before, buggered off to the big city." By the time he finishes his story I'm guessing that his father took him into the business when he dropped out of school and couldn't get a job, his brothers blamed his laziness for selling their father's business and for spending the proceeds on real estate that he claimed was rich in copper. He had wanted his wife, Dorothy, to get a job so he could pursue his get-rich schemes, but instead she left him to go live with her mother in the Soo. Recently, he used an inheritance from his mother to buy his fishing boat, in the belief it would make him his fortune.

Now he turns to his hunting exploits, telling me how he could live off the fat of the land, that his government cheques are mere supplements. It amazes me that he seems satisfied, and I wonder if he'll look back as an old man and feel the same. I hope so; though I think I'd prefer the misery of self-awareness.

Once again, Ronnie's behind late in the game. I was hoping he'd win this one. It's my deal, my crib, and almost certainly my third straight win. He notes the situation, "Oh my, I've been talking too much," and picks up the newly dealt hand. "Wait a minute, wait just a fish-frying minute." He looks from his hand to the board, moving his lips, counting the points he'd need, "Holy pumpernickel, would you take a look at this," and shows me his three fives and his jack of diamonds. Cutting the five of diamonds would give him the crown jewel of cribbage, a twenty-nine hand that would win him the game. People can play a lifetime of cribbage and never see this hand. He sits back, closes his eyes—"I have to visualize this, the five of diamonds, the five of diamonds"—opens his eyes and stretches his fingers like a pianist, inhales, and cuts . . . the three of clubs. So I win, and we agree to call it an evening.

"I usually win my share of games, you know."

I tell him I was just lucky, knowing he's not the type to dwell on his losses, anyway. A dreamer, he'll go away focusing on his close encounter with the ultimate hand, turn it around somehow to become a good omen.

He invites me to go out with him at dawn, to the fishing grounds, and I tell him I'll go, "if I can get up that early." And then, as he's about to leave, he says something that knocks me broadside. "You and I are alike, you know, true adventurers, entrepreneurs—people like us make dreams come true." He gives a thumbs-up and heads up the ladder.

After he's gone I have a couple more glasses of wine, maybe more. Now that I've met the scarecrow, I'll find the tin man and lion—we'll lock arms and head off to find the wizard. What a fool I've been, sailing farther and farther away from reality. I sit back, and laugh, and laugh, and it's the hateful laughter of humiliation. It's time to take a walk, time to take another look at the businesses here—Alice's Art Supplies, Norm's Upholstery & Live Baits, and the new sign I'll visualize: "Ronnie McDougall's Charters". I want to imagine this village rising from its coppery ashes, becoming a thriving community, drawing people from all over to work in its mining and fishing industries. And oh yes, most of all I want to visualize the sign that reads "Mark's Fair Weather Inn (Self-Improvement and Cruise Centre)."

And I thought Ronnie was a dreamer.

I walk past the park and out to the highway where traffic passes through town in the course of a minute, in one side, out the other, never leaving a trace. I hear the grumbling of a transport, shifting down, coasting into town, lit up like a circus, no doubt headed elsewhere, far from its origins. I want to interrupt its journey, open its doors, confirm now before any more miles are wasted that whatever's inside isn't worth the trip. I stare at it, willing it to stop, at the gas station beside the Bavarian will be fine. It keeps coming and I crouch, setting a hand to the pavement, palm down, giving it a rap like a judge with his gavel. A couple of things happen at once. A girl screams from a car sitting across the road, at the gas station where her mother's getting a fill-up, screaming something about a man on the road. A horn blares, and I think of Ronnie's fishing boat, lost in the fog. The scream from the girl gets louder—I back away. The truck passes, its horn blaring for another fifty yards, filling the night with bluster.

The ice-cream and pizza place is closed, unable to provide a double-dip pralines and cream. From across the street the woman filling her car is looking at me. I move out from under the streetlight and head back to the boat, disillusioned with dreaming, but needing some sleep so I can slip away before dawn.

14

THE NATURE OF REALITY

THE GIANT LAKE, ANISHNAABE Chi Gaming, is slipping by, its mythical powers along with it. Having abandoned entrepreneurial fantasies I've turned towards the spiritual, turned this way and that, but haven't found it. I've searched for grace with all the reverence I can muster, and nothing, not a whisper of epiphany, not a glimmer of magic, nothing close to the magic I felt when Zoe placed my hand on her heart to let me know what was happening to her, or what she thought was happening to her. But she was wrong and I've been wrong and how foolish it is to go on believing that life's meaning can be found in wonderful sensations. Having achieved nothing from listening to Beethoven, from smelling rosemary, from witnessing sunsets, from tasting wines, from feeling heartbeats, all that fills me is a terrible yearning for what I'm missing.

At Old Woman Bay, the cliffs that rise straight from the water, towering up to six-hundred-feet, make little impression. At Cascade Falls, where a river plunges over an escarpment and right into the lake, I shower under the icy downpour—but the experience is more fact than feeling. Fog grounds us for a time, but I don't remember it rolling in or drifting out—it comes and we stay, it goes and we leave. There are days with high seas when we take shelter in coves, and I think I pass the time sleeping, reading, and looking around, but the memories lie scattered. I think of my brain-injured patients who complained of losing their direct sense of things, feeling as if they were trapped in a bottle, and could only experience the world from inside. Have I fallen and hit my head somewhere along the way? I don't know if it matters.

I've worked hard, making it to the lands and waters of spirits and legends, and now they refuse to talk to me. I brain-stormed and planned and all I found was humiliation. I wonder about First Nations people living near the shore who might be watching and I wonder if they'd help if I asked them to. "Excuse me, I'm sorry for not speaking your language, but I've undertaken a quest and was wondering if you could tell me the right way to go about it." Maybe I haven't suffered enough. But I know, I just know, because otherwise I'd be willing to do it, that I could starve myself and stop drinking, but all that would happen is that I'd starve and die of thirst.

Ever so slowly, we close the distance to Thunder Bay, the finish line for which I strive, the point where I'll say I've done what I could. Now, sailing most days into the wind, nothing, not even this modest journey is progressing without a struggle. With the end approaching, "Please let me have my senses back," I pray, not having prayed before, but having nothing to lose, I promise to appreciate them more.

When I first noticed the cabin cruiser, I thought nothing of it, just another boat. But it's been tracking us for hours, on a parallel course and at a similar speed, slow for a motor boat. When I tack, it tacks for no reason. An hour ago when I hove-to and drifted while I ate some lunch, it drifted as well. Though pirates come to mind, the thought embarrasses me. I'm not sailing the Indian Ocean. After lunch, the tracking continues, except now the word *stalking* seems more appropriate.

The Slate Islands lie just ahead. I set a course to give the impression I'll be skirting them to the south, but as soon as I put land between us I haul in the sails, start the motor and double back to enter the maze of islands, hoping for a good place to hide. It isn't long before I find a bay at the end of a narrow strait. After going below to grab my rifle, ammunition, and a beer, I lie in the cockpit to listen, thinking how silly all this is, but still trying to come up with a reasonable explanation for the pursuit. The murmur of a motor gets closer and then farther, closer and then farther, following a grid pattern. Now it grows so close I can hear a voice. "Where can he be?" and then another, "Can't be far." Adrenalin flushes the blood from my veins—ice takes its place. What's going on here? I toss my rifle to shore, leap after it and head into the woods where I find a good lookout point maybe a hundred yards away. Already, the cruiser's anchored outside the bay, and four people, two men and two women, are in a Zodiac motoring down the strait, heading right for Antonie. After getting no answer when they call to my boat, they come ashore carrying what looks to be a huge camera, a case of beer, a picnic basket and a long, canvas bag. They're young and attractive, maybe in their early thirties, dressed casually in shorts, t-shirts, and halter tops. They set up the camera—maybe it's a beer commercial. No it doesn't make sense—wherever they're from, they wouldn't have to travel so far, and what reason would they have for stalking me? One of the men starts to gather firewood—damn, they're going to be here for a while. At least they're not organizing a search, not yet, and for now they're leaving Antonie alone. When the guy gathering firewood ducks into the woods I check that my rifle's loaded. I imagine headlines in the Thunder Bay *Chronicle Journal*: "Photographers Shot Making Beer Commercial, Sailor in Custody" or alternatively, "Sailor Found Burned In Pit, Cult Members Suspected."

They make a fire, have their picnic and do some filming. They stage a scene in which one of the women gets pushed playfully into the water, she scampers back to shore, soaking wet, shivering and shaking her fist—and that seems to wrap it up. They give her a big towel to wrap herself in and then they pack up and go, steering alongside Antonie to take a good look, but without laying a finger on her. After an hour, I go back, unroll my sleeping bag in the cockpit and stay outside for the night.

I leave at daybreak, stiff and tired, but anxious to get to open water where I hope to see no sign of the cruiser or its crew. Away from the islands, with nothing in sight except open water, I question whether the episode really happened. But of course it did. As puzzling as it was, hallucinations aren't nearly so coherent. Still, I need to get my bearings, to see people, to compare notes—how strange, me wanting to seek out people for a reality check. Ronnie McDougall, well in the past anyway, wasn't exactly the best reference point for testing reality. I need to get to Thunder Bay, walk around and talk a little.

The lake's getting choppy and I'm getting wet, so I head for some islands lying between us and the mainland. Large rocks scattered along the coast force me to anchor a little ways out, but taking a cue from last night's episode and thinking about how nice it would be to have a fire, I try the inflatable dinghy for the first time. Later, after it turns dark and I've gone blind from staring at the flames, I notice a movement between the beach and the woods. It's a breezy night and the trees are swaying, but a dark, fat, shape, low to the ground, appears to be lumbering towards me—a black bear, I figure, coming to sniff my supper pans. I grab the rifle and shoot over its head to scare it away. It doesn't flinch. I shoot again, before my eyes, adjusting to the darkness, see that the menacing shape is only a shrub. I need to get to Thunder Bay. I need to dock at the marina, talk to other sailors, other humans, make sure I'm intact. Because ending my life at the conclusion of this trip, if that's what I decide to do, must not be the result of depression, or paranoia, or any other mental disturbance. I'll need to be calm, determined, and rational when I decide the outcome.

15

Vladislav

THE WIND'S BEEN FIGHTING US for days, forcing us to zig-zag extra miles across the lake. The more I look forward to our destination, the harder the wind blows, at times almost pushing us backwards. Finally, we tack north towards Thunder Bay, the body of water that marks the gateway to its namesake city, now within sight only 25 km. across the bay.

Boats are converging from all directions. The cabin cruiser I've been keeping an eye on for the last twenty minutes is gaining on us; a cutter approaches from the west, its sails stiff as shark fins; a freighter materializes from the mirage that moments ago shimmered on the horizon. The cabin cruiser crosses our wake and then turns north, assuming a parallel course. An older couple wave from the bridge, toasting the air with their drinks, and I wave back as they pull away.

We've done it. Hurray for us. I congratulate Antonie, reach over to pat her on the stern. A damn good boat she's been, and after doing everything asked of her, she's still as fit as the day we left. I'm feeling good, at least for the moment, and lighter than I've felt for some time, ready to let go of the fights, flights, and fantasies. Still, the purpose of the quest was to find meaning, and unfortunately no epiphany has come, the obvious reason being that one doesn't exist for me. But this isn't the time for brooding, and after all, the conclusion I've reached does provide an answer of sorts. "Is it true, Antonie? Do I have my answer?" She remains silent.

Okay, but first we need to celebrate our small accomplishment. When we get to the city I'll freshen up, chat with some of the other sailors, ask about where they've been and where they're going, establish my sanity. Then, I'll find a nice restaurant, order a lobster, drink some wine, and take a bottle back to my boat. Finally, it'll be time for a last reflection, a step back to look at the gestalt of the journey, let it sink in. Maybe one more day and one more night will join the dots. Of course, that thought's born of desperation, like the guy who asks for an outcome to be determined by a coin toss, and then asks for the best two out of three, and then three out of five when he loses yet again.

I'll pick my time soon enough.

The wind dies and the sails sag, reminders that we haven't quite arrived, and just when we need it to make a triumphant entrance. Motoring the final distance is out of the question, like hitching a ride in the final mile of a marathon run. I wait, but soon the bay calms, leaving us stuck on a giant mirror. In the distant sky, a black, bulging mass, oozes over the city, veins of lightning criss-crossing within. Bastard, trying to deprive me, but no way, I'm in charge of this ending. Wolf Cove on the Sibley peninsula lies closer than the city. I start the motor, turn around, and head back.

A breakwater shelters the cove and the few berths tucked inside, one of which sits empty. The place is strangely quiet, no one around except a boy propped against his bike, watching our arrival. Leaning from the cockpit, I steer for the berth, wondering if he's going to tell me it's reserved, but he says nothing. I tie up, stretch my arms, and look towards the hazy sky. The boy hasn't moved. He wants something from me. A lane at the base of the dock tunnels into some woods and disappears around a bend, through a mix of pines and white birch.

The leaves of the birch are twitchy in the humid air. A rooftop on the far side of the bend is mostly hidden by the trees, but I feel as if it has eyes that are watching me.

The boy turns his bike as though preparing to leave, but doesn't. I should take a stroll to find where I pay, but fatigue is convincing me to take a nap first. Opening the hatch to head below, I glance towards the other boats, unnerved by the ghostly silence: no people, no voices, no traffic, and everything as silent as the boy with the bike. The boy, who can't be more than ten-years-old stands forlorn, as if he's just lost a friend or pet dog. I hope it's not part of himself he's lost. With both hands he clutches his bike as though it's his only possession, perhaps thinking I could take it from him. As if. All he has to do is leave. He's free to go. I have nothing to do with what he's afraid of. I take a couple of steps down the ladder. Why's he standing there? I feel like telling him that whatever he wants, I don't have it, but that not having something for him isn't the same as taking something from him. It's not.

"Hi there." I try to sound friendly.

He looks but doesn't speak. Well, there you have it, nothing I can do about *that*. I start down the ladder, until a voice, weak and high-pitched, asks, "Do you have any beer bottles?"

Ah, so that's it—a younger, less intrusive version of Ivan the bottle collector. "Do you want them full or empty?" Quickly, I tell him I'm only joking. I raise a finger. "Just a minute," and when I emerge with a six-pack of empties, the boy maneuvers his bike to meet me at the edge of the dock. His bike, which is too big for him, is an old-style single speed, with thick tires, padded seat, and a wire basket mounted on the handle bars.

"Sorry, these are all I have. I don't throw many parties."

"Thanks mister." Mister? Haven't heard that in a while. Without making eye contact, he takes the carton and puts it in the carrier, wrestling with the handle bars and the sliding six-pack while dipping the bike to get on.

"Is this how you make a living?" He looks to make sure I'm kidding. "Better than going to school, I'll bet."

He smiles and shakes his head, no doubt in agreement regarding the part about school.

"This a regular stop of yours, coming to meet the boats?"

He nods. "Lena pays me for the bottles."

"I see. Does Lena manage a beer store?"

"No." That's all. Asked and answered.

He's a handsome little fellow with features I'd describe as Slavic, not that I'm an expert regarding ethnic characteristics. What I note is his sandy hair swept to one side as if he's been traveling at an angle to the wind. His eyes are blue, squinty, and intelligent, and with his pale skin and thin lips, he's a pint-sized version of the famous Russian goaltender from the 1970s. The younger version of Vladislav swings his leg over the crossbar, groping for the pedal with his foot.

"Say hi to Lena for me."

He glances at me, his face reddening, as though I might say something about his awkward mount.

"Do you know who I'm supposed to see about docking here?"

He stops and stares.

"Do you know who owns the—"

"Lena. You're supposed to see Lena."

"Where—"

"She owns the restaurant, down behind the trees." He points in the direction of the rooftop.

"This Lena sounds like an important person." I look to where he's pointing, and I wonder again about the looming storm, still hidden from view. "Thanks. I'll check in with her a little later. By the way, I don't know if you're far from home but you should know there's a storm coming."

I expect a look of surprise, but "I know," he says. Maybe he's heard thunder. If so, his hearing's better than mine. "It'll be here," he looks the wrong way, out over the lake, "in about twenty minutes."

"What makes you think so?"

"The water."

The water on the bay is dead calm but it's been calm for a while. He looks the other way, "And the leaves are turning over."

"The leaves are doing what?"

"And the air's changing."

In the past few minutes it *has* cooled off a bit. And then—step, push, push, he's off, his little body lurching from side to side, pumping, creating the momentum he needs before he can sit to pedal, and then he's gone.

The day darkens, the temperature drops, a blast of wind comes ripping through the trees. I go below and lie in wait, ready to welcome what comes next because storms bring the best sleeping weather. When I wake, the cabin's darker, the rain's pelting the deck above my head, the wind is rocking us gently, and without switching on a light, I eat some cheese and drink some wine, and then settle back and sleep again.

16

THE CLASSICAL MUSIC HOUR

THE MORNING, THOUGH COOL and refreshed by a good soaking, smells fishy, perhaps from seaweed washing up on shore. I must have slept in, for several berths are already vacant. Not that it matters. I'm at the finish line, or awfully close to it, and I think about how I could have taken advantage of yesterday's storm to really finish things off. But I'm happy with my decisions, happy still to be in control of my own ending, determined to first set foot in the city known as the Lakehead.

I should have asked Vladislav about shower facilities. The marina is tiny and might not have any, but I'd like a change from the in-and-out baths in Superior that shrivel my manhood. Choosing to be optimistic, I grab my grooming kit and set off down the lane whose potholes are already drying in the sun, their outer crust curled like corn-flakes. Twigs and branches lie strewn like bones on a battlefield. A blue-jay darts across the lane and lands in a tree, fluffing its feathers, displaying its colours, white like the clouds, blue like the sky. The jay's a beauty, but I wonder if two companions loom close by. Leaving isolation behind when I sailed into Thunder Bay, mingling with the other boats, docking at this marina, and talking with a young boy, has stirred my senses, aided now by the freshly cleansed and fragrant pines that intoxicate the air. Either that or my senses are mustering a final rally, like things do near the end, cramming for a final burst— I can't be sure. Living and dying are so closely related, separated by moments, often determined by a fluke no more predictable than the number of blue-jays encountered, sometimes by a simple choice.

But right now, there's just the solitary jay chirping at me, reminding me that I'm the only thing around that hasn't had a shower.

A short path veers from the lane to a small building with a sign saying, Washrooms & Showers. A building I presume to be the restaurant, with a parking area containing half a dozen vehicles, stands a little farther down the lane. I'll have to go for breakfast after I get cleaned up. Hallelujah, the showers work, the water's hot and high-pressured, and I enjoy the longest shower I've had for weeks. Finally freshened and with the kinks steamed away, I return my grooming supplies and head for breakfast, both famished and curious about this out-of-the-way settlement.

Closer, I see that the restaurant is part of a small resort, one side a clearing containing a large fire pit surrounded by playground equipment, and beyond, cabins nestled in the woods. The restaurant, white with green trim, is wood-framed with an outdoor veranda protected by overhanging roof and perimeter railing, and over the front steps, a sign saying: "Grandma's House." On the veranda, a colourful wooden woodcutter and grandma stand on one side, Red Riding Hood on the other, beside a wolf that looks more like the family pet than the drooling, teeth-bearing menace that appears in story books. The place is either quaint or kitsch, depending on one's taste, but how does it stay in business in the middle of nowhere?

Inside, I hear the twang of country music, like finger-nails scraping a blackboard. Through an archway on the left, is a formal dining area with checkered table cloths, and to the right, a café where I join the dozen or so other patrons. The décor is small-town functional, scuffed pine tables and booths with green, plastic upholstery. The pine-paneled walls display a smorgasbord of historical moments: yellowed newspaper articles about silver mines, pictures of old boats and freighters, photos of grainy, grim-faced men with drooping moustaches, and stiff, dazed-looking women balancing hair buns on their heads. A swinging door at the back leads to the kitchen. Everyone stops to look as I enter, but just as quickly turn back to their food and conversations. I seat myself at a booth.

A woman with Mediterranean skin and long, bouncing, black hair swishes between the tables in white blouse and flowered skirt, making the rounds, offering coffee, her appearance at odds with the music. I can easily imagine her with a tambourine instead of a coffee pot, stepping barefoot, the sandals tossed aside, the blouse fluttering, skirt flowing, her body swirling around a campfire, letting her hair fly free after a day with the children pick-pocketing the tourists. From around the circle in which she dances, arms reach out, glowing in the firelight, wanting a piece of her, clapping, cheering, urging her on. Is this Lena, I wonder?

"Morning, some coffee to start with?" Her voice is deep and lustrous, her smile secretive.

"Yes, please." I use my calm, self-assured tone.

She goes to pour, but suddenly stops herself. "I'll bring some fresh, and be right back with a menu." A customer from a nearby table calls out, teasingly, "Oh yeah, preferential treatment for the tourists— a second ago, the coffee was good enough for me."

"Hell, you're a caffeine addict, *any* coffee is good enough for you." This brings a round of chuckling as she heads for the kitchen, music in her movements, not from Nashville, but from where I wonder. What's she doing in Wolf Cove? I'd bet her story's a good one. Whoever she is, her persona is just short of flamboyant, a definite style, a nice thing to have, maybe second to talent, though I'm guessing she has *that* as well.

In minutes, she's back at my table, pouring my coffee. "You must be Number Nine."

Number Nine? The table number? Wouldn't she know? The only other associations that come to mind are the sweater numbers of famous hockey players—Rocket Richard, Gordie Howe, Bobby Hull, and I don't resemble any of them.

She chuckles, not unkindly, at my bewilderment. "Did you arrive on a sailboat, about a twenty-five footer, late yesterday afternoon?"

"Uh-huh."

"You're in the last berth, closest to the breakwater?"

"That would be me."

"The berth's are numbered. You're in nine."

"Oh. Is that okay?"

"Perfectly fine."

I realize she was teasing. Alright, I can do this. "Number Nine's a nice name, I've been called worse. But give me a second to come up with *your* name—I've got a knack for guessing names solely on the basis of a person's appearance."

She chuckles with that throaty sound of hers. "Oh yeah?"

"Let's see, the dark hair with the colourful clothing, the eyes of a gypsy, hmm, the name Lena comes to mind."

She feigns surprise. "Very impressive, able to deduce my name from that small hint Peter gave you."

"Peter?"

"The boy who—"

"Oh, Vladislav." The name wins me a quizzical look—at least that's something. "What do I owe you for the berth?"

"Depends on your stay."

"One night only—last night."

154

She nods, almost imperceptibly. "You can settle up with your breakfast bill." She sets a menu in front of me, a single laminated page, and tells me she'll give me a few minutes to look it over. Half-way through turning away she turns back. "The eyes of a gypsy?" I shrug. "Can't say I've heard that one before." Again she hesitates as she begins to turn away. "Vladislav?" I raise my hands as if to say, *Come on now.* She half grimaces, half grins, and then she's off, shaking her head at the silliness.

The various combinations of egg, bacon, sausage, hash browns, toast, pancakes, and muffins are numbered one through nine. I'll have to ask if she has a thing for single digits. At the bottom of the menu, however, are unnumbered entries that catch my attention: herbed omelettes, orange-cinnamon French toast, eggs benedict, and an entry called chedda-feta-quiche.

"I'll try the quiche," I tell her when she comes back. Someone laughs from the booth in front of me and Lena smirks as if in response, but I tell myself the timing's a coincidence that has nothing to do with me.

"That's a fine choice, you won't regret it."

She's right. The quiche is delicious and everything else about the breakfast is good as well, the orange juice tastes freshly squeezed, the coffee exactly the way I like it.

A short time after taking my plate away, she returns with separate bills, one for breakfast, one for dockage. I'm finishing my coffee as two people from the booth in front of me prepare to leave. A man of height with crinkled eyes and frisky beard, unfolds himself, untangles his arms and legs. He turns to get my attention, his body stuttering like an old tractor engine trying to get started. If I *could* guess names, his would be Ichabod. A long, bony finger points to my bills. "Tell Lena you should only have to pay one of those."

"Why's that?"

"She owes you. Because of you, she won a bet at my expense." His movements are revving up, his smile is mischievous.

"How so?"

"At the start of the week she came out with this new breakfast menu featuring her fedora-cheese quiche, or whatever she calls it. I tell her that no one this far north eats quiche, she won't get more than a half-dozen takers for the week, and none will be male." He leans in and lowers his voice. "Most of us men don't have that good of taste— we're kind of boring that way." He breaks into one of the warmest and friendliest grins I've seen. I'm thinking I like this guy. A woman, casual in jeans and a quilted vest, slides out from the other side of the table, smiles sympathetically, acknowledging me as just another victim of her gregarious partner, a partner she obviously loves judging from how she sidles alongside of him.

"I wouldn't listen to him," she says, "he likes to stir things up."

"You never know," I reply, "a free breakfast is worth a try."

As they head for the counter, he gives me the thumbs-up with a thumb the length of a shoehorn. As they leave, the country music stops, the speakers crackle and, surprisingly, a cello suite by Bach begins. In mock alarm, Ichabod stops, covers his ears and calls out, "It's 11 o'clock, get out as fast as you can, it's Lena's classical music hour." Shaking her head, his partner pulls him towards the door and out.

As two women get up from the booth behind me one of them calls out, "If you want to get rid of us Lena, for heavens sake, all you have to do is close up for an hour." At the till, Lena's waving her arms like the music conductor, a contented smile on her face. "We read about your strategy in the newspaper," the other woman chirps in, "the same thing they do in the big cities, in the malls and subway stations, playing this type of music to keep teenagers from loitering."

Lena calls back, "Just think of it, Dolores, as country music from Vienna."

"Sorry, my imagination isn't that good."

The banter's good-natured, everyone enjoying each other.

At the till, Lena asks me if I'm heading out. I tell her I am.

"You're getting a late start."

"Only going to Thunder Bay."

"Oh, you live there?"

"No." I have a hard time thinking of what else to say. "I'm on a trip. For now, Thunder Bay's my destination." She looks up, expecting me to continue, and I don't want to be the only one in the place who can't contribute to the atmosphere. "By the way, I happen to think that breakfast with Bach works a lot better than breakfast with Garth or whoever it was." There, I've made an effort.

"You know Bach?"

I cock an ear towards the speaker. "Well enough to know this is one of his cello suites—Suite #1, but don't be too impressed, it's the only one I can identify by number."

"Bach a favourite?"

"Wouldn't say that. I like some of his stuff, like his cello suites and violin concertos, but a lot of his music sounds pious, makes me think I should be in church flogging myself or something."

She chuckles. "I think I know what you mean."

She's giving me my change when a small, hawkish-looking woman wearing an apron and hair net comes up behind her. The net is loose, almost sloppy, as if she started to pull it off and got interrupted. Grey hairs stick out from the bottom. Her nose protrudes like a weapon. She hands Lena something that looks like a bill. "Thanks," Lena says, "I was looking for that." She checks it over briefly. "Auntie, have you ever thought of Bach's music as pious?"

"Pious?" She sucks in her cheeks, stabs me with her eyes. I prepare to be pecked to death. She glances upwards, lifts the bottom of her apron and wipes her hands with it. "Yes," she says, studying me, "makes me feel like I'm in church. Not this, though, not his cello suites."

Lena looks startled, but only for a second. "You been eavesdropping?"

"Whatever are you talking about? And don't be questioning your auntie."

I laugh. "Have a good day," I tell them. My announcement has come a little abruptly, perhaps, and somewhat awkwardly, I backtrack. "How about you? Who's your favourite composer?" The question's for both of them but it's Lena who answers. "I can't say that I have *one* favourite composer. Depends on my mood, on the particular piece of music. And you?"

"I know what you mean about moods, but I do have a favourite." Auntie cocks her head, leans forward as though daring me to give the wrong answer. "His name is Ludwig Van Beethoven, maybe you've heard of him," I smile.

Lena looks at her aunt but the older woman doesn't take her eyes off me. For seconds, no one says anything. "He's not the one in number nine, is he?"

"Yes, Auntie, he is."

Auntie's stare bores deeper. "And you're sailing a vessel by the name of Antonie."

"Yes, that's my boat."

"Well then."

17

Brave Explorers

RRRM. RRRM. RRRM. RRRM. Rrrm, rrm, rrm.

Now what? The gear's in neutral. The throttle's in the start position. The choke's out.

Rrrm, rrm. This, I don't need. We're so close to the end and I'm anxious to get the journey done with. With both hands, I tighten my grip on the starter rope, widen my stance, hunch my shoulders, coil my hips, and yank like a madman. Rrrm, rrrm. I muster my strength like an Olympic weight lifter preparing for the *clean-and-jerk*. Rrrm, rrrm, rrrm, rrrm.

With a gentle sway, Antonie suggests I calm myself, suggests in the same gentle manner that I'm acting like a ninny, that something's wrong with the motor and that how I pull the rope won't make a difference. Okay, thank you Antonie. I'll use my head. Let's see, the motor can't be out of gas as it hasn't run for more than an hour since I last filled the tank, and I'd be able to smell a leak. I check the gas tank anyway, and just as I thought, it's three-quarters full. The hose going from tank to motor looks secure at both ends. I sit in the cockpit and stare at the motor, thinking back. Yesterday, in the mouth of the bay, the motor started immediately, just like always, I used it to approach the berth, right up till I pressed the stop button to turn it off. I check

159

the button to make sure it isn't stuck shut and it isn't. I close the choke and try again. Rrrm, rrrm, rrrm. I open the choke. Rrrm, rrrm. Not even a stutter. I take the cover off, knowing nothing about motors but hoping to see something obvious, like a cable popped from a connection. Everything looks intact but what do I know?

I expect to hear bellowing laughter coming from the same fate that yesterday prevented us from reaching our destination. What the hell, forget the motor. I'll shove us clear of the berth, get some canvas up and let the wind take us out—except there is no wind. But what's the hurry, a wind will come soon enough. Maybe after I digest my chedda-feta-quiche, my brain will turn its attention to figuring out why the motor won't start. If that doesn't work, I could simply forget about going to the city, wait for some wind and head southwest towards the centre of the lake. Thunder Bay the body of water, Thunder Bay the city, who the hell cares?

I stretch out on the bed, prop the pillows under my head and pick up the book I've been reading, resuming where I left off, in Antarctica, with the story about two explorers racing each other to the South Pole—Scott vs. Amundsen. I read for hours, captivated by the contrast in approach. Amundsen's the methodical planner, the thorough researcher, the one who learns from those who've encountered the climate before him, the one who went to the Inuit to ask for advice. He's purposeful and patient, unpretentious and humble. And then there's Scott, a vain Englishman who believes that grit and a jolly good effort will win the day, who believes in his nation's superiority and who looks only to the customs and traditions of his country, who sets off for the South Pole in the same way his countrymen had set off to conquer other lands—with horses. Bloody hell, so what if hooves sink right through the snow and fix the horses in place like butterflies stuck with pins: *Push ahead lads. We shall not give up. Keep a stiff upper lip and all that.* Amundsen wins the race, yet Scott wins the publicity and becomes the more famous. Amundsen becomes depressed, lives out his life in misery, denying himself credit for planning such a remarkable feat, the fortitude for enduring the pain and hardship. What was wrong with this guy? I'd be ecstatic to experience such success. Hell, I'm having trouble making it from Windsor to Thunder Bay, two cities in the same province, and in the warm summer months.

I'm embarrassed. Considering the courage of both explorers, fighting through circumstances where the possibility of freezing, starving, getting lost, or falling into a bottomless crevasse was more likely than not, I realize how pathetic I am, feeling sorry for myself after waking up on a warm August morning and having a good breakfast of chedda-feta-quiche in the company of cheerful characters.

"Okay, Antonie, you're right about me needing to adopt a calm manner. I promise we'll get to Thunder Bay. By the way, Lena's auntie seems intrigued by your name. I'll have to ask why."

My eyes are feeling heavy, surprisingly so, after the marathon sleep I had last night. Maybe it was the big breakfast, or reading about magnificent deeds. I'll get more rest before deciding how to proceed.

18

The Slippery Slope

I LISTEN BUT HEAR NOTHING—no wind, no traffic, no waves slapping against the hull. I strain to hear more distant sounds, a chainsaw or lawn mower, or a jet flying overhead. Nothing. The world is soundless. To rule out deafness, I click my tongue against the roof of my mouth and hit upon a deep, hollow, *klock*. Experimenting with the different tones that come from placement of the tongue, I produce, perfectly, the sound of water dripping inside a cavern. I wonder if in deafness, one can hear his own internal world, if one may hear it even more acutely *because* of deafness to the outside world. I knock against the wall, "Hello, is anybody home?" and am relieved to hear both my voice and the knocking. Still, except for my own sounds, the world is quiet.

It's motionless as well. After so much time sailing, it's eerie to be so still, and suddenly I get the feeling of being left behind by a tide, like a clam caught in seaweed. All I feel is the weight of my body, the depression it's making in the bed, the clamminess that fastens me to the mattress. I inhale deeply, sniffing for the scent of fish or seaweed, but unlike this morning I can't sense anything. The world seems to be pulling away from me.

The cabin, however, stays put like an outer shell of myself, and provides evidence that I have eyesight. I see the fake wood paneling, the book about Amundsen and Scott, the hatch over the bed looking out into oblivion. The enclosure reminds me of a recurring dream in which I'm fleeing from something, a bear, soldiers, or an angry man, relentless in pursuit. Eventually, I lose them for long enough to find a hiding place, yet regardless of how perfect it is, they proceed directly to it, and I'm trapped inside. At that point the dream ends.

Only now do I imagine an ending; the pursuers seal me inside and I'm left to die with no chance of rescue.

Maybe I've already died. Maybe I sailed out into yesterday's storm, capsized, and drowned. Perhaps the trauma of death causes the brain to erase the event, replacing it with the illusion of life continuing as normal. While the rest of the world goes on living, the deceased end up in a parallel *la-la* land, none the wiser. God, what a disturbing thought—to exist only as a deception. Please, I'd rather be dust. What if I'm dead but want to get back? What if I try to move, and can't?

I bolt from bed, scramble through the cabin and emerge from the companionway like a diver from the depths, gulping for air. I need to keep moving.

Peter's on the lane, checking the progress of an incoming sailboat, though looking no less like a Vladislav than he did yesterday. I turn to my motor, perplexed about its sudden illness. Perhaps I only dreamt it wouldn't start, or maybe I was more tired than I thought and simply forgot a step in the process. Choke out, gear in neutral, throttle in position, a good, solid pull. Rrrm, rrrm. Rrrm, rrrm, rrrm. There's something wrong, it's not going to start.

"Peter, you wouldn't happen to know anything about motors, would you?" I'm joking, but he shakes his head *no*.

After grabbing a beer I return to the cockpit, slip on my sunglasses, and watch Peter watching the boat, curious to see if he greets it with the same reticence he did me and mine. This one's a beauty, about thirty-five feet long, spiffy and sleek, as are the two men and two women on board, dressed for the royal regatta, complete with white belts and sneakers. The helmsman knows what he's doing, making adjustments, calling out instructions, the wheel in one hand, a beer in the other, a good sign for Peter, who leaves his bike and positions himself to catch the rope should they decide to throw it to him, offering a little something in exchange for their bottles. Maybe they look friendlier to him than I did.

One of the women calls out, "Looks like we have a welcoming party," and the others are quick to chime in.

"Maybe he's the mayor."

"Maybe the o.p.p. looking for *dwunken* sailors."

"We'd better make a run for it. Reverse engines, full throttle!"

"Hell with that. Offer him a bribe or something. Hey there, would you like to join us for a beer?" They're giddy, tittering like they've had a few too many.

"Why don't you embarrass the hell out of the little guy?"

"He's not embarrassed. Look at him, he's soooo cute."

"Try throwing him the rope."

Peter's retreating, about to step from the dock when a rope lands at his feet. He freezes.

"Okay fella, pull us in." Peter looks at the rope but doesn't move. I think he'd just like to get out of there. "The rope kid, the rope—you know, the long thing lying there in front of your feet."

The helmsman calls out, "Leave him be, I think he might be slow or something."

"He collects beer bottles for the owner of the marina." My voice surprises me as it does everyone else. They all look, pausing to appraise me and my boat before their expressions turn haughty, passing judgment on our relative social standing.

Showing he has no desire to engage me, the helmsman glances back at Peter and tells his crew, "Looks a little young to be dealing in beer products anyway. Ken, could you pull us in at the stern?"

Not ready to be dismissed, I call back: "He doesn't *drink* the *product*, he collects the empties." The tipsier of the women guffaws, probably a little more loudly than intended. The helmsman glares but doesn't say anything. Not wanting to ruin Peter's chances, I adopt a friendlier tone. "Empties get in the way, take up space—beautiful boat by the way—many sailors don't want to waste time hunting for places to take them. He'll be happy to take care of them for you if you don't want the bother."

The red-haired, scruffy-bearded Ken looks up from where he's tying off the stern. "Maybe if the kid spoke for himself and asked politely, he'd get somewhere."

The helmsman is even less conciliatory. "If you ask me, it's the same as begging. Might as well sit on the ground, hold his cap out."

Still hoping that one of them, maybe one of the women will come through, I try again. "The owner of the marina has problems with sailors throwing bottles overboard before they leave. Young Vladislav has no need to beg. He's paid to help keep the place looking clean." Peter does a double-take, nearly falls over his bike. "It's an environmental service more than anything. The owner appreciates it."

Clearly, the helmsman has a burr up his ass. "Environmentalists out to save the world usually learn to speak."

Peter won't be getting any bottles from this group. He's straddling his bike, preparing for take-off, but looks back to see if I have anything left.

"Ah, the young lad would like nothing more than to be able to speak." They're all ears. "Unfortunately, he was born mute. He's very intelligent, has an i.q. in the superior range, but he also has detached vocal chords and the doctors say there's nothing that can be done about it. He knows sign language like you wouldn't believe, but he isn't going to sign to *you* because he's guessing you wouldn't understand." For a moment, no one says a word.

"Sorry. We don't have any bottles," proclaims the helmsman, finally. His crew members twitch, holding evidence to the contrary.

"Yeah, I can see that." The final words are mine.

The crew busies itself, tying the boat, wrapping the sails. When I turn to Peter, a sly smile crosses his lips and in a flurry of finger flicks and wrist twists, he pretends to sign something to me. I come close to bursting out laughing but manage only to nod and wave as though I've understood. With a big grin, he nods and takes off down the lane.

After going below to get my backpack I set out in the same direction, in search of a mechanic. While I'm at it, I'll pick up some groceries. I'll explore, see what there is to this community and if I don't find a mechanic, myself, I'll ask Lena if she knows of anyone who could help me. Surely a marina serious enough to have showers has access to minor repair services.

A wooden post, covered top to bottom with signs, stands at the parking lot entrance. Several signs point to the left, to Scenic Trails, to the Sea Lion, and to No Exit, and several to the right, to the Village, to the Provincial Park, to Highway 17, and one suggesting, Probably The Way You Came. The sign at the top of the post points up, the one at the bottom points down. The first says, in old English script, Pearly Gates, the other, pointing down and printed in red, says, Hell, Come As You Are. Funny people.

The village has exactly what's needed for a place situated at the end of a peninsula, where tourists go mainly to camp, hike, and fish. They can clean their clothes at the laundromat, buy groceries at the Red & White, get a snack at the coffee shop, and buy just about anything at either the general store or souvenir trading post that has a LCBO attached. On a treed lot at the village edge, sits an old wooden house in ornate trim, with a sign over the door identifying it as an antique shop. A few yards over, on the same lot, sits a pink and purple shack with a sign saying, And Here Sits An Ice Cream Parlour—Go Figure.

Apparently, the people of Wolf Cove like to amuse themselves. It must come from living in the middle of nowhere, enduring the long, frigid winters. Now, however, in the middle of August, the village is teeming with tourists walking about with wide-eyed optimism. My own hopefulness takes a leap when I spot a yard full of boats, and a sign announcing, Clarke's Boat & Lawn Mower Place. The building, which looks like a former gas station, is surrounded by boats, most of them aluminum and chained together to discourage theft. A half-dozen riding lawn mowers sit chained to a light pole mounted on a concrete pad where the gas pumps once sat.

Full of cheer, I proceed to the door of the building. The Closed—Please Call Again, sticker in the window tells me the shop closes at 4:30 on Friday afternoons. I peer through the window to a clock inside that says 4:10. The sticker also says that he's closed on Saturdays and Sundays and will be open again at 8:30, Monday morning. Great. How nice for Clarke to own his own business in a small community where he can do whatever the hell he wants. I tell myself to take a breath, stay calm. Serenity and wisdom are two virtues I've always wanted but never managed to achieve—I'll have to work on them during the time I have left. What should another few days matter? In the meantime, I'll take advantage of the hiking trails, get some exercise, try to absorb a smidgeon of nature's wisdom.

On the way back, I stuff my backpack with groceries, wine, and a six-pack of beer, the latter mainly for Peter's benefit. At the trading post I buy some worms and fishing lures so that if I have another sleepless night, I'll forego the twisting and turning, the words playing pinball in my head, and go fishing instead.

The night is cool. I read from Beethoven's biography, but put it away after a chapter and return to the more relaxing lull of fiction. I try hot chocolate instead of alcohol wondering if it might be more soothing, and I pull some blankets around me. Hours go by waiting for a sleep that doesn't come.

With longjohns under my jeans and sweatshirt under my jacket, I grab my fishing gear and a life jacket to sit on, and head for the breakwater. I start with worms but when I don't get a bite in the first hour, I switch to lures. Another hour or so and still nothing. I go back to worms and move up and down the breakwater, from shallow to deeper water, from weedy sections to rocky ones. Bass are supposed to feed after dark, but where are they? It gets darker and colder. I switch back to lures and keep moving, walking and casting to stay warm. I cast into the black and shiny water, where falling stars have settled deep below to form underwater cities. Again and again, my lures come up empty, and still I keep casting, watching the lures glimmer with starlight before they go plunk, and disappear into the blackness.

19

AUNTIE &
DAVID DIEFENBAKER

TWENTY-FOUR HOURS AFTER MY FIRST visit to Grandma's House, I'm back, hoping to escape my own company. The place is packed and full of life, voices yacking, dishes clattering, chairs scraping, the noises all twined together by country music. That last part I could do without, but the top of the hour is nigh, and I'm hoping it will bring a change of music just as it did yesterday. A teenaged girl with spiked hair bursts from the kitchen, bum first, hoisting a tray above her head and waltzing through the tables, shifting her hips this way and that to balance the family of breakfasts she holds aloft. Three people at a corner table are leaving so I mosey in that direction. The older man recommends I try the blueberry pancakes, the younger man agrees, tells me they use home-made maple syrup, and the woman who has plump, rosy cheeks, pokes me in the ribs and tells me she's left me a warm seat next to the window.

"Thanks," I say, "nothing better than finding a warm seat on a cool morning."

"You have yourself a nice day, dear." Good therapy they serve here.

My seat provides a good view of the clearing and the cabins beyond. To the left, a giant map showing multicoloured routes provides information about nature trails, and at the edge of the driveway several people are pulling tables and chairs from the back of a truck. I spot Ichabod running a string of pennants from tree to tree along the perimeter.

"Good morning." Hands have come from nowhere to clear my table. "You're still here," Lena says.

"Yeah, but not by design, I'm afraid."

"So which was the clincher—quiche, music, or scenery?"

"My motor's refusing to start."

"Hmph," she says.

"Motor aside, any one of the quiche, music, or scenery would have kept me an extra day."

"Now there's an endorsement. We'll cite your testimonial on our tourist brochures: "Come To Wolf Cove. You'll Be Tempted To Stay A Day." She pauses, smiles, waits for a comeback.

"I've tried your breakfast, toured your village, spent my money, behaved like a perfect tourist—what more could you ask for?"

She proceeds with clearing my table. "You'll have to see Clarke."

"Oh yes, I found Clarke's shop minus the shopkeeper on my tour, and it was well before his closing time when I got there, I might add."

"Tell me you've never left work a little early on a Friday afternoon, and anyway, maybe Antonie's decided she's not ready to leave."

Interesting. "I wonder," I say.

"Maybe you should ask her." She sighs. "That's the trouble with men, they don't bother to ask."

"Oh, here we go."

"Would you like a menu?"

"If you don't mind. I remember entries one, two, and three, but I'm having trouble with numbers four and—"

"Okay, funny man, we'll get you a menu. You should count your blessings, getting stranded in a place like Wolf Cove." She pokes me in the shoulder, the second time in ten minutes I've been poked by these people, and on neither occasion do I brush away the touch. I must be mellowing—either that or I'm dead tired from lack of sleep.

My eyes follow her, noting how differently she's dressed this morning, looking nautical in a blue and white top with navy slacks, apron-free and bearing not a trace of ketchup, egg, or coffee. Her hair's different as well, tied back out of the way. On her way to the kitchen she stops to say something to the young helper who's making the rounds with a pot of coffee. The teen nods in my direction, disappears into the kitchen and then reappears, the coffee in one hand and a mug in the other.

"Coffee, sir?" Her voice is strong, her gaze direct, poised for one so young. So young she regards me as *sir*. Or is it that I'm really that old? When did that happen?

"Thank you." I'll need the whole pot to stay awake as any sleep today will beckon more sleeplessness tonight.

My mug's different from the rest, and different from the one I had yesterday. The others are white with a picture of a quaint little building and the words, Grandma's House. This one's brown, with a treble clef and musical notes on one side, and a picture of Beethoven on the other.

"Nice mug."

"It's the owner's. She collects mugs with musical themes. Rarely uses them though. "

"I'm honoured. If you see her, tell her she can forget the menu. I've decided on French toast."

"French toast, coming up."

"And tell her I like the mug."

"She said you're a fan of Beethoven." She smiles and goes back to her rounds just as Vivaldi's Four Seasons takes over from a song about a broken-stringed guitar. I watch the girl as she serves the coffee, the curves of her body as she slips between people and reaches across tables, the wide smile that comes so easily, the tilt of her head as she listens to a request. I hope that her teenage years are good, that she can experiment, that she gets more than one chance at things, that people are good to her, that opportunities blossom, that after the spring-time of her youth, she gets to experience the best of each season, that she never becomes a broken-stringed guitar.

I turn back to the window. Two men and a woman are unfolding the chairs and placing them around tables. Another man and a teenaged boy are at the fire pit unloading firewood from a pickup. A young couple is sitting at a picnic table outside a cabin, enjoying their toddler, the mother blowing bubbles through a plastic ring while the toddler tries to catch them. Every time the child reaches above his head he plops back on his bum and the well padded diaper that cushions his fall. Time after time, as his father rocks with laughter, the child rolls to his side, rises on his stubby legs, and tries again. I'm cheering for the toddler, wishing he could catch a bubble, possess it, cherish it, have his persistence rewarded just once before his optimism pops and dissolves. Finally, after a couple more tries, the child loses interest and heads for the woods with his mother in hot pursuit.

"It's the day of our annual cornfest, in case you're wondering."

Lena's back with my French toast, motioning with her chin towards the window.

"The Day Of Our Annual Cornfest—what a silly name for a piece of music." I turn an ear towards the speaker. "I could have sworn it was called, The Four Seasons."

"Oh brother," she says, rolling her eyes. "*Something* in here is silly, but it's not the music."

"I was merely trying to contribute. Isn't that the idea behind a cornfest, to be a little corny?" Extreme fatigue, like drunkenness, makes me goofy.

She shakes her head. "How long you been sailing by yourself?"

"Sorry."

'I don't know—your motor we should be able to fix, but your sense of humour—well, you might be out of luck. I'll talk to Les, see what he thinks." She gazes past me and out the window, as though looking for him.

"Okay, I give up. What's with the corn festival? I didn't think sweet corn grew this far north."

"It doesn't, but that's why we take one day a year to celebrate it." I'm tempted to ask if they have a pineapple festival, or maybe an olive festival. "Every year at this time, Greg and Audrey Murray go to visit relatives in southern Ontario and bring back a truckload. It started about eight years ago when they brought some back for themselves, then some neighbours asked if they would bring some back for them, and next thing you know, they're bringing it back for everybody with thoughts of making it into a festival for the entire community. It's been going strong ever since." As she looks away from the window a patron catches her attention. "Oops, gotta go, but we'll be expecting to see you this evening. Everybody comes. There are games for the kids, and the feast complete with drinks, salads, and desserts, and then my favourite part, a storytelling contest around the campfire. Wolf Cove has some great storytellers. You could enter the contest if you wanted. A sailor like you must have good stories. "

I chuckle, not taking the invitation seriously, and call out as she moves away. "I like the Beethoven mug, by the way."

"I'm serious. Residents, visitors, cottagers—everyone comes to the cornfest." She's gone before I can tell her about my lack of sleep, that I'll be turning in early.

Later, when I'm at the counter paying the bill, I mention the hiking trails and she asks how ambitious I'm feeling.

"A good workout with something scenic along the way." Something that will tire me out, help me sleep, get me back on schedule.

She suggests that I turn left at the road, follow it to the end, and take the trail that leads to the Sea Lion—a large rock formation that stands out from the cliffs and overlooks the bay. She explains that there's a longer hike, one that starts at the edge of the parking lot that would take me as far as Thunder Cape at the end of the peninsula, but the round trip would take five or six hours and I might want to save that for an earlier start.

As I'm thanking Lena for the travel tips, Auntie, the hawk lady, emerges from the kitchen wiping both hands on an apron that wraps her from neck to knees, a hair net sitting lopsided, as before, on her head. She looks at her hands, grunts, and wipes them again, adding to the palette of food stains already there. "What's his name?" she asks, just like that. Her voice is deep like Lena's, but older, a bit craggy around the edges. She stares, waiting for an answer, looking again as if she might peck me with her beak.

"We've been rude," Lena says, "and haven't asked him his name. He'll think we only think of him as Number Nine, and that's awful." Lena closes her eyes and shakes her head. "No way to treat a guest. I'm afraid we've forgotten our manners."

"What's this *we* business?" hawk lady asks sharply. *You're* the PR person, I'm the cook. *You* didn't ask him his name." It's all huff. The ease and affection between them is palpable. I felt it immediately when I saw them together yesterday.

"And I do apologize," Lena says. "This is my auntie. Her name's Carmella." Carmella squints at me, sizing me up. I don't offer my hand for fear of losing it, but nod and tell her I've enjoyed her cooking. They stand, staring, waiting to hear my name.

"I'm David."

A scowl crosses Carmella's face. "You don't look like no David to me."

"Auntie! Speaking of rudeness—"

"Name doesn't suit him. Not my fault."

"David's a nice name." It's Lena to my defense. "What's wrong with David?"

"David Diefenbaker," I tell them.

Auntie scrunches her nose and a furrow digs deep between her eyes. Her expression reminds me of a picture in a social psychology book of a native from the jungles of New Guinea demonstrating the universal facial expression for disgust—like David Diarrhea would be no worse a name. "No relation to a previous prime minister." I smile, pretending I've gone over this a thousand times before. "Everybody always asks me that."

Auntie's gaze is piercing. I swear she hasn't blinked. "So, Mr. Diefenbaker," she begins.

"David."

"So, Mr. Diefenbaker, your favourite composer is Beethoven."

"No other comes close."

"And what would your favourite piece of music be?"

"Easy. His Ninth Symphony."

"Of course, The Ninth, and what would your second favourite piece of music be."

Lena looks at her auntie as though she's gone loonie. But she's also intrigued. She calls out to her helper, "Gwen, would you mind checking on table ten for me and make sure my tables have coffee?"

"My second favourite piece of music—that's a tough one." I pause to consider. "Quite a few are tied for second, I'm afraid."

"For instance."

"For instance, Beethoven's Fifth, Seventh, Sixth, and Third Symphonies, his Violin Concerto in D Major, his Romances for Violin and Orchestra, his Piano Concerto No. Five, the Appassionata, his Moonlight Sonata, his Choral Fantasy, the Kreutzer." I'm surprised at how fast the titles come to mind, and surprised even more at my playfulness in pronouncing *Kreutzer* with a German accent.

Auntie purses her lips, continues to study me.

"The Kreutzer," she echoes, gargling the accent the same way I did. "Tell me, Mr. Diefenbaker—"

"Please, call me David."

"Please, tell me Mr. Diefenbaker, from what ethnic background does the name Diefenbaker come from?"

Damn. How the hell did I come up with Diefenbaker, anyway? Jones or Smith would have sufficed. "Good question, I have no idea. My parents were funny about it, would never say, regardless who asked. They'd always say everyone in the family was Canadian and that's all anybody needed to know."

"I see. Would you consider yourself an authority on our favourite composer, Ludwig Van Beethoven?"

"Not really."

"Would you happen to know his mother's name?" I feel as if I'm being grilled, on the verge of being arrested.

"Auntie," Lena interjects. "I don't think that Mr. Diefenbaker—"

"David. Call me David."

"All right, I don't think that David came to the restaurant this morning hoping to get tested in classical music." She puts her hand on Auntie's shoulder. "If you're not careful, Auntie, you're going to scare off one of the few customers who actually enjoys classical music hour."

"No, it's fine. That you ask me this question is extremely odd," I say, looking at Auntie. "Unnerving, too. A short while ago, I couldn't have told you her name, but I've done a lot of reading this summer, and coincidentally, one of the books I'm currently working on is a biography on Beethoven."

"Uh huh."

"His mother's name was Maria Magdalena."

"What a nice name," says Lena.

"And listen to you, claiming you're not an authority."

"Auntie, reading one biography doesn't necessarily make you an expert on the subject."

"Let me get this straight. He knows the mother's name, he rattles off his music, he sails a boat by the name of Antonie, and he tells us he's not an expert. Does he think I just fell off the beet wagon?"

I have no idea what she's getting at.

Abruptly, Auntie changes the subject. "Well, Mr. Diefenbaker, we'll be expecting to see you at the cornfest this evening."

"Oh, I don't think so. I'll be needing to—"

"Yes, we insist," says Lena. "Peter will be there. He asked me this morning if I thought you'd come. He's been talking about you, and Peter doesn't talk much about anyone." Gwen passes by on her way to the kitchen, smiling but looking harried. Lena notices and heads back to her customers. "See you later," she says.

I look at Auntie and shrug. "Sorry, sounds like a great event, but I'm really in need of a good sleep." Auntie puckers as if she has a mouth full of lemon, and for the moment, says nothing. "Sorry," I repeat.

I'm almost at the door when I hear the squawk. "Don't be a party crapper." She says it loudly enough that a few patrons look up. I twirl around in time to see her snapping her fingers, looking around, "Hell, what's the expression?" A patron calls it out and Auntie shouts, "Thanks, that's it—don't be a party pooper. You're in Wolf Cove now and you're expected to be there."

Am I now? Now that I'm being ordered, I'm even less inclined. God, I can only imagine mingling among the Clarkes, the Ichabods, the Aunties, the Dorises, the country music clan, every single one of them reminding me how much I don't belong. With my luck, I'd find myself trapped at a long table beside the village blabbermouth, having to listen to every detail about every cornfest that ever was. Later, the village drunk would find me, fix me in his sights, stumble over chairs and discarded corn cobs to get to me, ask me for money, throw up at my feet. There'd be nice people there, interesting people, but they'd be with each other. In passing they might inquire where I was headed, and I wouldn't be able tell them. They'd want to know what I do for a living and I wouldn't be able to tell them. They'd ask my name. David Diefenbaker. "Hey, that sounds like a good Irish name," and I'd chuckle but wouldn't know what to reply. If I mentioned I was from Windsor, the Murrays might probe to find if I knew some people they knew, and then I'd have to explain that I wasn't really from Windsor but from a rural area on the outskirts, and then they might ask if I knew people with a certain name who grow sweet corn close to the Harrow area and I'd tell them I didn't, and then they'd be at the end of the road with me and move on to their neighbours.

Sorry Auntie, you can threaten me with that beak of yours, glare at me with those piercing eyes, rake me over with that saw-toothed voice, but I ain't going. I won't go, even though I imagine a kindness under your harshness. But imagination is probably all it is. So, no, I won't be going even though there's something I admire about you, you old buzzard.

20

THE SEA LION

BACK ON ANTONIE, I PREPARE my backpack before setting it aside to read another chapter on my guy, Ludwig. Not that it makes a lot of sense, but Auntie's interrogation has enhanced my interest in him. Of course I'm unafraid of the small, elderly woman, and the questions she asks, but still, I read carefully, looking for details I could impress her with.

Finished with the chapter, I set out with my backpack, noticing as I pass the restaurant, that it has a sign out front: GRANDMA'S HOUSE CLOSED AT 1:00—SEE YOU AT THE CORNFEST, and in small print at the bottom; Don't Forget To Bring Your Own Toothpicks. Nice image. I'd love to know if the sign's supposed to be taken seriously. Elsewhere, I'd assume it was tongue-in-cheek, or in this case, tongue-in-teeth, but the folks who live here are several eccentricities removed from elsewhere, and difficult to read. What am I to make of a restaurant called Grandma's House with wood carvings on the patio to reinforce the theme, or of the signposts pointing to heaven and hell, the classical music hour, the inquisitorial hawk lady, and the celebration not of local fish or moose-meat or blueberries, but of sweet corn from southern Ontario.

At this point there are enough tables and chairs for a couple hundred people, set up in neat rows, encircled by orange, blue, and green pennants, perhaps recovered from earlier service at a used-car lot. About a half mile down the road I come to a western style ranch complete with sprawling log house, split rail fence, and grazing Appalachian horses, a scene more appropriate to Montana than the north shore of Lake Superior. An archway constructed of twigs and branches supports a sign welcoming visitors to The Brouhaha Ranch—what is it with these people and their signs? It's as if the entire community is misplaced, yet inhabited by people who are more amused than distressed by their plight.

Beyond Brouhaha, wilderness closes in on the road, and after a mile or so chokes it to an end, leaving only a parking nook and a sign pointing the way to the Sea Lion. I follow the path to a cliff overlooking an inlet with the most luminous body of water I've ever seen, sparkling and clear, casting its turquoise glow upon the rocks, trees, and sky. The lion sits sixty yards away, looking cool under the sun, its front paws in the water, its head tucked between its shoulders as though preparing to yawn in the moment of being turned to stone.

I sit propped against a pine, close my eyes, inhale deeply, and listen for whatever there is to hear. Should sleep come knocking, I'll get up and get moving, request that it return this evening. At first, the whispering of the pines makes the only sound, but a little later, a pummeling noise begins to intrude, first from a distance, then growing closer and closer until I recognize the sound of hooves approaching from behind a ridge. Suddenly, the sound stops, and when I peek out from my hiding place I see Indians on horseback strung along the ridge, like a war party in old westerns, Apaches, or Comanches, or Sioux, whichever is scariest. The warrior with the headdress raises a spear, signaling the others. I consider revealing myself, walking towards them, holding out my arms in an overture of peace, showing my respect, explaining how I've always wanted to learn more about their history, their culture. Too risky, don't be a fool. Trusting could be a big mistake. So I sit quietly and watch these First Nations People, hoping for cues about what they're up to. The warrior I presume to be the chief conveys little belligerence behind his beard and jiggly eyebrows, unusual features for a First Nations Person. He scans the area, looking more amused than tense, friendly even, if not a little ridiculous, his feet dangling near the ground on a horse that's too small for him, a pony, really. A hawk circles directly overhead. Oh God, what if it squawks and blows my cover. A white couple wearing funny hats, clunky shoes, and heavy clothing with over-sized buttons appear between the horses—Pilgrims, no doubt, captured and taken prisoner. Their wagon sits farther down the ridge, not of the canvas-covered variety I remember from westerns, but a square, wooden one with writing on it, covered with bells and trinkets, more like a gypsy wagon. Several other paleface are scattered about, a few of them with their own horses. An oriental looking man is wearing a Dr. Zeus hat. I'm starting to wonder if any of them are Apaches. Renegades perhaps? I see a swarthy, olive-skinned man, carrying a suspicious looking package. A suicide bomber? If the bomb detonates, horse-shit will cover the earth. Geezus, he's opening it. I crouch lower, barely able to peek through the brush. He pulls a book from the package, shows it to the person next to him. I can see the title on the cover: *Company's Coming For Dinner—Easy To Prepare Recipes From The Middle East*. The rat-a-tat-tat of snare drums and the drone of bagpipes start the procession moving, now joined by a xylophone, tinkling like wind chimes. Well, what do you know about that, a harmless parade is all this is. I'm safe! But now when I try to wave, I find myself paralyzed, under six feet of water, looking up through a world of turquoise. I gasp for air, water fills my lungs. Please. They're marching by without seeing me. I want them to see me. I need help. With all my energy I try to get up.

My head jerks awake, I look around. There's no ridge, no peoples of any nation, no funny hats, no parade. I hope I didn't nod off for long, it doesn't seem like I did, though that was an awful lot of dream to be crammed into a few minutes. I take a moment to reflect on the details, hoping for the *Aha,* promising I'd be thankful forever. But, of course, there is no eureka, just a dream, day residue bouncing about in a tired mind.

When I get back to the driveway at Grandma's House I see Peter coming from the dock with three or four empties in his carrier. Dismounting his bike, he grabs the bottles and heads for a storage shed behind the restaurant. I wave, knowing his hands are full and that he can't wave back. He offers a big smile. Seeing him reminds me of something I was planning to do. I return to Antonie and notice the new boat, a cabin cruiser a few berths away, no doubt the source of Peter's latest treasure. Two people are seated on deck, but they're looking the other way, so I retrieve the six-pack I bought yesterday, uncap the bottles, and one by one pour the contents over the side, saving only two for myself, preparing to give Peter the four empties.

After making myself a sandwich and getting my fishing gear together, I see Peter riding around in circles, entertaining himself at the end of the lane. I take him the bottles and tell him I found them while cleaning up. "Soon, you'll be able to buy a boat of your own," I tell him. I smile and start to walk away—the last thing a shy young boy wants is to be coerced into conversation with an adult he doesn't know.

But, "Going fishing?" he asks.

"Yep. I think I'll catch my supper for tonight."

"Where you going to fish from?"

"From the breakwater," I tell him, gesturing ahead.

Several seconds go by, then, "You're not going to catch any fish."

His comments surprise me. "Why not?"

"The fish don't live there." He stands, motionless, shielding his eyes from the sun.

"Oh yeah? Then where do they live?"

He shrugs, apparently all talked out for the moment.

"Maybe I'll get lucky, find a fish that's lost his way. You think it's possible?" I smile to assure him I'm only kidding. He grins, ever so slightly. Again, I start to walk away. Tentatively, he follows, keeping a distance—until I've made about five or six casts into the water. Gradually, he moves closer.

"If you catch one are you really going to eat him?" His voice is clear and innocent but seems fragile, a tiny speck of sound against the din of a mighty lake brushing against the dock. How easy it would be for his voice to drown, or be blown away, unheard.

"I don't know. I might feel sorry for a fish that's had so much bad luck. Think about it. First it gets lost, and then it gets caught by a fisherman who's fishing in a place where fish never visit."

"Yeah, he sure would be unlucky." He stoops to pick up some stones and chips of cement. The flat pieces of cement he tries to skip along the water. With the rounder stones, he aims for a piece of driftwood. It's an instinct that boys are born with. He moves closer. After a few throws he speaks again, as though he's been giving the topic some thought. "It would be a really unlucky fish."

"I know."

"A really, really, unlucky fish." He has something else to tell me.

"I know. A fish who gets lost and then caught by a pretty bad fisherman."

"And a fish who gets caught by a lure that looks like an orange torpedo." He tries to keep from giggling but can't.

"What? You don't like my lure?" I look at it dangling at the end of the rod. He giggles harder. I don't know much about lures, simply attached the brightest one I had. Feigning determination, I cast again. "You just watch, I'm going to catch him. And then you'll be really, really, sorry that you laughed at my lure."

"No fish is dumb enough to bite an orange torpedo," he erupts into outright laughter, "but maybe the lure will hit him and blow him up." Now he has me laughing right along with him. "I can think of a way for the fish to be even more unlucky," he says. He's gathering steam. I stop reeling, dying to hear. He stoops again and picks up the largest stone he can find. "Watch this," he says. Facing the water, he leans forward, his throwing hand tucked behind him like a pitcher on the mound, squinting at the batter awaiting the pitch. Then he aims and throws, watches intently as the stone hits the water, hoping it might hit something—something that might happen to be swimming by. Slyly, he turns to look at me, again starts to giggle.

"Oh yeah?" I set down my rod, grab a handful of stones and mimic the same motions of a pitcher, throwing the stones, one after another. Quickly, he joins in, and there we are, the two of us, throwing in quick succession, faster and faster, but always pausing to look to see if we hit anything, pausing then for longer and longer as we try to catch our breath, recover from our laughter. Anyone watching us would think we were daft, and it wouldn't matter.

Later, when we walk back to his bike he thanks me for the bottles. In return I thank him for the fishing tips. Then, as he pulls away, he calls back to me: "See you at the cornfest." He's gone before I can tell him I won't be there.

21

WOLF'S COVE CORNFEST

CARS ARE PARKED ALL THE WAY to the breakwater—it seems the entire population of Wolf Cove and surrounding area has come for the cornfest. Early arrivers stroll along the dock where they stop to gaze at the lake. A young couple disembarks from a newly arrived sail-boat, discussing salads, hoping their favourites are back from the previous year, while three middle-aged folks from the boat next door stand on the dock, all holding sweaters or jackets, waiting for the guy who's locking up the cabin. When one of the women catches me looking, she points to her watch and calls out that I should get going, "the food will be flying off the tables." I give a friendly wave and call back that I'm not crazy about corn, that my mother still can't get me to eat my vegetables. As untrue as this is, it makes for good banter.

"Oh, you should come anyway," she says. "It's great fun. This is our fourth year. We come across from Thunder Bay." She gets distracted when the man locking up calls out, asking if she has the camera. A moment later, off they go.

Strollers pass by looking at the boats, see me sitting in the cockpit enjoying the fresh air. "Not going to the cornfest?" Some holler, "It's almost six." Others do everything but break into song: "You're going to miss the won-der-ful foo-ood, all that sweet, butt-er-y, coe-orn." I feel as if I'm on display, but the weather's pleasant and it's too early to go below. Besides, I *am* curious. I decide to take a stroll.

There's a carnival atmosphere at the cornfest grounds where two white-haired women at a cash box collect admission fees and stamp the hands that pass the money. The women are laughing. A man, mostly hidden from view, squatting on the far side of the women, appears to be the source of their amusement. One of the women, in particular, is beside herself, holding her side with one hand, waving him off with the other, signaling she's had enough—but he's on a roll and she can't resist. She leans towards him to hear what comes next and whatever it is cracks her up even more, and now she has both hands aflutter, again pleading with him to stop. The man takes hold of the table to pull himself up. Too late I recognize him: it's Ichabod, glowing with delight. He spots me before I can duck away.

"Hey there!" He waves with one of those giant hands of his. His crinkly-eyed grin could charm a grizzly. "I see you survived the cowabunga quiche." Quickly, his expression changes as his waving hand drops to scratch his neck. "Was it cowabunga? No, that's not right, what the hell did she call it?"

"Chedda-fedda, I believe."

Instantly, his face brightens. "Yes, yes, that's it, and good to see you again. Welcome to the cornfest."

Damn, I should have known better than to take this walk. He's coming over to corral me and before I can come up with an excuse I'm lassoed by the longest arm I've ever seen, guiding me towards the cash table.

"This here's a fella who's adventurous enough to try Lena's chatanooga quiche," he says to the women by way of introduction.

I tell them I'm just out for a walk, and follow this up with my little white lie about not liking corn-on-the-cob.

"Seven dollars" says the woman closest. Not the one who nearly laughed to death; this one's scowling and impatient.

"For all you can eat," chirps the pleasant one, "while the food lasts, so you better get in there."

"Sounds like a great deal, but—"

"Salads like you wouldn't believe, baked beans from a secret recipe, dinner rolls, lots to eat besides the corn."

Before I know it, the stern-looking one has snatched the ten dollar bill I wasn't fully aware of removing from my wallet. Apparently, my right arm's on automatic pilot. She smooths and flattens the bill, lays it neatly in the cash box on top of the other tens, carefully pinches out my change. With rubber stamper in hand, the jovial one reaches out. "It doesn't take people long before they're going back for seconds and thirds, so don't be shy. Get right in there."

Ichabod jumps in. "Now Audrey, he's going to think we're gluttons." He feigns concern, and then, looking back to me, breaks into that boyish grin of his. "Unfortunately, it's true," he says. "We all get eating corn-on-the-cob at the same time, butter dripping everywhere, and you know, it's probably not the prettiest sight."

Not to mention the collective picking of teeth that comes after, the toothpicks brought from home.

Ichabod introduces me to Audrey Murray, "Wolf Cove's corn buyer and fund raiser extraordinaire," and to Evelyn Frith, "teacher and principal of Wolf Cove Elementary," advising that if anyone gets out of line this evening, they'll be sent down to Evelyn's office first thing Monday morning. "Child, adult—doesn't matter." I believe it. Her stern expression holds as she stares at me over the top of her glasses, making me feel that I'm already in the principal's doorway. Ichabod pauses, giving me the chance to introduce myself, but my mind is lagging, still trying to remember how I reached into my back pocket for my wallet and the ten bucks.

"Leindert Roosevelt," he says, and sticks out his hand. It might be smaller than a banjo but not by much. "But everyone calls me Les."

I think the name Ichabod suits him better. "In case you're wondering, *no,* I'm not related to Theodore," he says with a jiggle from his eyebrows.

"David Diefenbaker," I tell them. "Not related to John."

At once, they look at one another, pursing their lips and shaking their jowls. Evidently, they all remember John Diefenbaker. The sight of them would be comical if not so weird—a trio breaking in unison into an impersonation of John Diefenbaker at the mere mention of his name. Peculiar place, peculiar people.

Les's partner emerges from out of nowhere to announce that the games and races are nearly over, that the food's coming out, that the corn's nearly ready. Les introduces his wife, Wilma, to David Diefenbaker—unrelated to John. Instantly, she shakes her jowls and jabs her finger at me, as if she were the Right Honourable John Diefenbaker and I were Lester Pearson. Her impersonation is the goofiest but also the funniest. "Come, join us for supper," she says.

Hell, now that I've paid, I might as well eat.

Inside, we stop at the games area, where the final event of the day is about to start. A woman holding a megaphone announces that the three-legged race is open for same-sex and mixed pairs, for ages nine through twelve. I look but see no sign of Peter either among the participants or the spectators. The teams line up, the gun goes off, the race begins, and through the cheering, squealing, and toppling over, twin girls with perfect rhythm are first to cross the finish line.

The next race involves people rushing for a row of tables near the trail map, where women armed with utensils stand ready to serve their community. Everything's in order: the plates, cutlery, and napkins, followed by breads and dinner rolls, followed by lettuce, fruit, vegetable, jello, and pasta salads—and then, Baked Beans by Betty, simmering in their secret sauce. The fragrance suggests mustard, bacon, and something else I'll need to taste to figure out. As we move along, I give vague answers to questions about my trip and make subtle attempts to change the subject, until finally we come to the corn, simmering in vats of water on a giant barbecue. Two women tend to it, one overseeing the cooking and moving the corn from pots to platters, the other moving it from platters to plates held by outstretched hands. Just as I think I'm done with the questioning, the server looks up—it's the hawk lady. "Wilma, Les! How ya doin? Mr. Diefenbaker, it's good to see you." With her long-handled tongs she reaches for one of the platters. "Piping hot for special friends," she says.

"It never hurts to have connections," says Wilma. "Looks like another good turnout."

Auntie looks up at her friend, redirects the tongs, waves them first towards the sky and then towards the woods. "Ah, the day is gorgeous. We need to squeeze out every bit of summer we can. The corn looks better than ever, and yes, it's a great turnout."

Les is looking back and forth between two punch bowls. The contents of one are a deeper pink than the other. Apparently, he doesn't see the sign beside the darker version that advises, Not For Children. "Which one is the world famous kick-a-poo punch?" Using both hands to grapple with the tongs, hawk lady gestures with her nose, "The dark one." And then, "I see you've met Mr. Diefenbaker." She grimaces and gives her head a shake.

"Carmella's kick-a-poo punch is a must," Les tells me, "but you need to go easy with it—it packs a hell of a punch, so to speak." Les chuckles at his joke. Wilma groans but agrees with his assessment. "You want to be careful around that stuff, drink very slowly, one sip at a time."

"Hell," Carmella says, setting Les's corn on his plate, wriggling it into his salads to make room, "look at what he eats. A big man like your husband would have to drink half the bowl to feel anything at all." Both Wilma and Les roll their eyes. Obviously, they know better. Les sets a finger on my chest. "Two little dixie cups of this stuff will make you tipsy, a third will finish you off. I'd suggest trying one for the experience, and then, well, drinker beware."

"Nonsense," Carmella squawks. "And what are you doing, trying to scare Mr. Diefenbaker like that? He's not driving, he's not boating. His motor's broke—hell, he's not going anywhere."

"Sorry, Carmella, you know we love your kick-a-poo, it's just that—"

"He wasn't even going to come. I told him he had to." Carmella looks from Les to me. "You were wise to listen," she says. Then she looks back to Wilma and Les. "He's an expert in classical music, you know that?"

Les and Wilma respond in unison: "You don't say."

I tell them it's not true, not even close. Carmella gives Wilma her corn and then reaches to the platter for mine. Biting her lip, squeezing the tongs with both hands, she seizes a cob and twists around quickly to get it to my plate, holding the thing well out from her body as if wrestling a live lobster tempted by the size of her nose. "Don't let him fool you," she says. "He knows his classical music, has two very good ears for it. So here," she says, dropping the corn on my plate, "have another ear and make it three good ears." She snorts out a laugh, elbows her partner in the ribs. The corn cooker laughs as well. Les and Wilma groan but then start to laugh at the laughter of the two women. Good grief. Attempting to be a good sport, I ask Carmella if she's been sipping the punch. "You no-like-a my pun? What's za matter for you? Take your friends and get away from my table, go and finda your own." She raises the tongs in warning. A satisfied grin crosses her face as we turn to go. "And Mr. Diefenbaker, owner of Antonie, don't be in a hurry to rush off afterwards. I'd like to have a chat with you. Do you hear me, Mr. Diefenbaker?"

Neither Les nor Wilma appears to have heard her. They're looking for a place to sit, making their way through the banter that reaches
out and snags them like underbrush. "Hey Les! How's that hound of
yours?" "Bessy's fine, thanks. It was a thorn in her front paw—Wilma
found it and took the tweezers to it." Wilma chimes in: "Yeah, and I
paid for it, got a little nip on the hand for making her yelp." The neigh-
bour quips back, "You know what they say about the hand that feeds
you." "And you know what?" Les asks. "The two of them sound exactly
the same. I couldn't tell whose yelp belonged to whom." No sooner
are they past that exchange than they're into another, and then another. Either Les and Wilma are in the thick of everything, or everyone's
in the thick of everything in this community.

Eventually, we find a seat. The food tastes as good as it looks.
The punch goes down easy—in the same way that Margaritas do,
cool and refreshing even while making a person thirsty for more. Sitting across from me, Les and Wilma make easy conversation. When
I ask about their backgrounds, about what kind of a life they live
in Wolf Cove, they tell me they're the owners of the antique shop
and the ice cream parlour beside it, explaining that they live on the
second and third floors over the business. After providing the fascinating history of their old house they tell me I should drop by. "Not
to buy anything," they add, "just to take a look, join us for tea." They
regard their ventures as more hobbies than businesses. Every year in
the off season they travel the province looking for antiques and unusual gifts, "and new friends amongst the buyers and sellers," Wilma
adds.

Leindert is full of stories. If he were to leave to go to the washroom, I bet he'd return with an intriguing tale to tell, and I'm surprised
to find he's not among the evening's storytellers. "Some friends talked
him into it one year," Wilma explains, "and he bombed. Said he didn't
know how to turn normal conversation into storytelling."

Les shrugs. "For me, it was like entering a breathing contest, didn't know what I was supposed to do that was special."

Wilma comments on the quirks of the people around her, while acknowledging her own. When I ask what prompted them to combine an antique business with an ice cream outlet she tilts her head and draws up her shoulders, "It was a whim," she says, "just like we've decided to start buying rocks—especially amethyst. People love amethyst, especially when you tell them that it's native to the area. So we're now in the business of antiques, ice cream, and rocks." She pauses for effect, then adds, "Go figure," stifles a laugh. Something tells me she sets up this line every chance she gets. Surprisingly, I don't find it annoying.

I catch glimpses of Lena running errands. No doubt she's one of the organizers, along with her aunt and the other women serving food, Audrey and Evelyn. Gwen, the young waitress, seems to be helping out as well, along with two other teenagers, including a teenaged boy who keeps looking at Gwen. He's smitten with her, I can tell. I still see no sign of Peter.

"That was very good," I say when I'm down to cleaning my plate.

"Yum." Wilma tells me she enjoys the cornfest more than she does Christmas dinner. "Especially since I don't have to cook," she adds.

Les points to the wild rice and mushrooms, giving his wife credit. "Oh, big deal," she says. "One simple salad."

"Simple, maybe, but year after year, it's the prize winner." He takes a forkful, chows it down. "Delicious." His mouth half-full, he asks me what I think of the punch.

I tell him I like it, perhaps a little too much. "Carmella brews it from scratch?"

"Oh yes. One of her secret recipes." Then he does what I do— swirls it, takes a sip. "She brews it in a shed behind her house, never lets anyone watch. I tease her about being a witch, stirring it with a broom handle, cackling about casting her spells."

"Yes, it fits."

"She's a great old gal, though, nothing like a witch." He pauses. "A soothsayer of sorts, but definitely not a witch."

Wilma tries to steer him off. "Les, I don't know if Carmella would appreciate you—"

"No, no, it's not an insult, there's nothing wrong with being a soothsayer." Les offers an innocent shrug. "She just has this way of foretelling things. Just an eccentric older lady with special talents and who happens to have a prominent nose—and who never seems to be far from a broomstick," he adds with a wink.

A man of great circumference two chairs down from me rises to his feet. Holding his empty plate, he glances towards the food tables and then looks back at us, pointing his fork at Les. "Legend has it that she'll put a curse on anyone who tries to steal one of her secret recipes."

"So you've heard it too," Les says.

Wilma shakes her head as if to ask what she's supposed to do with this husband of hers. The comment about Carmella being a soothsayer stokes my interest. I ask Les if he can give me an example.

"Are you a believer?" he asks.

"Nah, no more than I'm a believer in horoscopes, or weather forecasts that predict the sun might peek out during an otherwise partly cloudy day that has a thirty percent chance of rain. Still, I'm interested in hearing about her."

"And well you should be, David," Wilma says. She leans towards her husband. "Tell him about the July 1st weekend."

Les proceeds to describe how Wolf Cove celebrates Canada Day, "another major event for the community." I'm starting to think that the citizens of Wolf Cove are big party people; or maybe it's just what people do when they don't have ready access to movies, theatre, and professional sports. At any rate, he explains that the celebration includes an all-you-can-eat fish fry, the consumption of a giant birthday cake, games, and then the fireworks display. He's in the middle of telling me how they launch the fireworks from the end of the pier and how impressive the display is for such a little village when he's cut off by Wilma, who's been smiling patiently, rolling her eyes. She reminds Les that he was telling me a story about Carmella, that he can get back to the fireworks later.

He tugs at his beard as if to change the channel. "Oh yes," he says. "Well, here's the thing—Lena always orders lots of fresh fish for the event. As usual, she's well stocked, but a couple of days before the event Carmella tells her she'd better get more. When Lena asks why, Carmella tells her that it's a holiday and that tourist traffic might be particularly heavy that day. Now this doesn't make sense to Lena because she's been doing it for years and knows exactly how much to order. Carmella insists that they'd better be ready, that she has this hunch about an influx of visitors, a lot more than usual. So what do you think happens late afternoon on Canada Day?"

"The Royal Yacht Britannica steams into port?"

He points at me like *I'm the man*. "You're awful close," he says. Then, leaning towards me, his voice lowered to a whisper, he tells me, "a charter bus full of Japanese tourists pulls into town."

"They've heard about the fish fry and fireworks?"

"No. They haven't a clue. They've come to travel the Sleeping Giant, visit the Sea Lion. They have no intention of visiting Wolf Cove. But then, on the way back from the Sea Lion—" Les's eyes go wide, he slaps the table, "boom, the bus breaks down, and then as evening's coming on, they need something to eat, right? So they all come to the fish fry. Carmella's done it again." At once, Les and Wilma glance around as though expecting Carmella to burst on stage to take a bow.

Of course I'm skeptical, not because I think Les and Wilma are lying, but because people are drawn to the inexplicable and are prone, subconsciously, to distorting perceptions and memories in the interest of fostering legends. How people long to hear evidence supporting the existence of Big Foot and the Loch Nest Monster, and how the citizens of Wolf Cove would like to believe that the old gal among them has magical powers. Whereas the truth probably involves little more than an innocent question from Carmella regarding whether Lena had ordered the fish, and Lena responding that she ordered more than enough. And then bit by bit, detail by detail, the story expands. I keep that thought to myself, though, and make a quip about Carmella being a good person to take along to the horse track.

Les stares straight into my eyes, as if he's reading my mind, detecting the doubts. "You'd be especially interested to hear about her latest prediction," he says soberly.

Again, Wilma tries to head him off. "Les," she says. "I don't think that David would particularly care to hear—"

"Why not? After all, he's the main feature in the prediction."

"Yes, but he's just a nice man on a sailing trip. You don't want to spook him."

"It's not bad or anything. Do you get spooked easily?" he asks me.

"Not at all. Go ahead. Tell me."

Again, Les goes through the routine of looking around, feigning concern about being overheard.

"About three weeks ago Carmella and Lena were gabbing with a few of us in the restaurant. It was late in the morning, things were fairly quiet and I was teasing Lena about her classical music hour, reminding her that there isn't anyone in Wolf Cove besides her and Carmella who can name a single piece of classical music. And she said, yeah, she was thinking of dropping the Classical Music Hour. I almost fell on the floor. And I could tell it bothered Carmella too, the way Lena said it, like she was resigning or something."

"I told her I hoped it didn't have anything to do with Les's teasing," Wilma interjects, "but she assured us it didn't. Afterwards we got to thinking that it had something to do with the anniversary of her mother's death." Wilma lowers her head, continues solemnly. "We think she started the Classical Music Hour a long, long time ago as a way to keep her mother's memory alive, but Carmella has arthritis and the kitchen work is making it worse. Lena knows it and is trying to talk her into retiring."

"The thought of their partnership coming to an end has her feeling down, especially at this particular time," Les adds. "She told us it won't be the same without Auntie, that she doesn't want to pretend otherwise, and so wants to start making changes."

"What's Carmella saying?"

"No friggin way, there's to be no more talk about ending the classical music hour," Wilma squawks, pounds her fist, impersonating Carmella at her ornery best, "at least not before Thanksgiving, and the same goes for any talk of retirement." She describes how Lena was gentle but insistent in telling Carmella to start taking better care of herself, that it was time to accept a little pampering, just as she had always pampered Lena. "And that's when Carmella said something very strange." Wilma pauses, glances back to Les.

"It was very touching," he says. "Carmella's eyes got glassy. She took Lena's face between her hands and told her the Classical Music Hour was needed as a beacon for a lost soul, perhaps a sailor, who at that very moment, could be headed in their general direction." Les raises a brow as if to ask what I thought about *that*. "Lena didn't know what to say, maybe wondered if her aunt was losing it, but also saw the desperation in her expression."

"At first," says Wilma, "no one takes this business about the sailor literally. We're trying to figure out if it's some sort of symbolism."

"That's right," Les agrees, "until Lena questions, softly, how the sailor is expected to hear the music when it can barely be heard inside the restaurant. Carmella doesn't know how to answer, just sits there looking confused, then asks Lena to *please be patient and trust me on this*. Lena asks if we'll know when the sailor gets unlost. Carmella assures her we will, when he arrives in Wolf Cove. When Lena reminds her that lots of sailors come to Wolf Cove, Carmella closes her eyes and smiles: *We'll know it's him because he'll be unique, or his boat will be unique—there will be some kind of sign."* Abruptly, Les ends the story. "And there you have it. According to Carmella, here you are."

What? I wait for the punch line, for Les to jab me with a finger, shouting "Gotcha!" but the punch line doesn't come. This is the most preposterous tale I've ever heard, and yet, there across the table the two villagers sit staring as though I'm the one with some explaining to do.

"Carmella thinks I'm the lost sailor?" I wait for sheepish grins that don't come, "the sailor guided to Wolf Cove by a beacon of music emanating from a place called Grandma's House?" They exchange glances with one another, turn back to me with shrugs. "Don't you see, Carmella's prediction has come true like the catch-all weather prediction comes true." Nothing. I take a deep breath. "The theory has some weaknesses, don't you think?" I begin my rebuttal. "First of all, except for a little fog here and there, I've always known exactly where I am—in fact, I've almost always been within sight of shore." I give them a little nod. "Secondly, the only classical music I've been aware of has come from my own CDs." Patronizing expressions appear on both their faces, as if my testimony supports rather than refutes their theory. "The very first time I heard classical music coming from Wolf Cove is when I stepped into Grandma's House, yesterday, *after* I arrived on shore. I neither saw nor heard anything that drew me here."

"What we know is that you do like classical music and that you're the only sailor this summer to express such an interest."

I remain patient. "I'm not the only sailor around who likes classical music. It was quite by accident that I happened to be eating break-

197

fast at eleven o'clock." I study their faces—I'm getting nowhere. "And thirdly, my boat is a twenty-five foot sloop, a very average day-sailer, cream and black, white sails, hardly one-of-a-kind."

"Antonie," Wilma says. "The name of your boat is Antonie. Carmella says that's why it's unique. It's the name."

"She told us about it this afternoon," Les adds.

"So?" I do remember Carmella's interest in the name and wanting to know if it was my boat. "Boats are known for having unique names—think about it."

"Everyone was in a rush this afternoon so she said she'd explain it to us later." On Wilma's face is the faith of a disciple.

"She assured us we could trust her on this," says Les. He's every bit as spellbound. "And when Carmella says we can trust her on something—"

"Despite what I've told you about my trip?" I give them a more plausible theory—that Carmella wants a partner for Lena, that Lena's more likely to meet someone with an interest in classical music if she keeps the classical music hour, that— It's no use. I'm winning nothing from them. "Okay, so what does it matter? Now that the sailor's arrived safely, is Lena going to put an end to the Classical Music Hour?"

"I think we're about to find out," says Wilma. "And I think we're going to find out why it matters."

Les is looking down, scratching the back of his head. "According to Carmella's prediction, this lost-and-found soul would be staying for awhile."

Awhile is another one of those perfect words for catch-all predictions—applicable to minutes or decades. "I don't know how Carmella defines *awhile*, but I've already been here longer than I meant to be and I'll be leaving as soon as I get my motor fixed—planning to see Clarke about it on Monday. With any luck I'll be out of here by Tuesday and off to Thunder Bay to complete my trip," I add quickly, "but thankful I got to visit this wonderful community of yours." I sit back to offer my summation. "So not staying for awhile will be the fourth criterion that eliminates my candidacy as the lost sailor."

Wilma looks at Les. "Did you get that last part about criterion and candidacy?"

"I think so."

"Good. You can fill me in later," she says.

The needling is tongue-in-cheek, at least I think it is, but it pricks my skin, nonetheless.

"By the way, is Clarke around? Maybe I could get a word in about Monday morning."

"No. Haven't seen him," Les says.

Wilma shakes her head. She hasn't either. "He's not really one of Wolf Cove's socialites," she adds. "But rest assured, you don't require an appointment to drop in."

I scan the area hoping to spot Lena, who up until now has impressed me as the voice of reason. "And how about Lena, what does she say about this lost sailor business?"

Just then, Wilma is distracted by something on my left. "Speak of the devil—Hi there Lena! Hi Peter! Great cornfest."

Les asks if they got lots to eat.

"We sure did, didn't we Peter?"

"Where you been hiding?"

"Over there with Doug and Carrie." Lena stands on her tiptoes, pointing a few tables over. Wilma cranes her neck and then tries to point them out to me—like I'd recognize them if I saw them.

"Hi there Peter."

"Heh-heh-hello Mi-mi-mi-Mister Baker," he says, obviously ill at ease.

"I was looking for you at the races, Peter."

Lena sees his discomfort and jumps in. "Peter was volunteering in the kitchen," she says, "he's a great worker, this one." Then quickly, she turns to me. "Here, I brought you a special treat." She hands me a dixie cup of the darker-coloured punch, notes the reactions from Les and Wilma. "Oh, you've been into it already—oh well, you're going to have to drink it anyway, after the effort I made to get it here without spilling it." I take it and thank her.

"Peter told me about your house-cleaning, how you found some more bottles."

"Yes, and he was nice enough to take them off my hands." I give him a pat on the shoulder.

"That's the thing about sailboats," Lena says, cocking her head and smiling, looking back and forth between Peter and me. "With all that closet space, you never know what you're going to find during a clean-up."

"Things you never knew you had."

"And he told me about your fishing exploits, all the latest techniques."

"I hope you didn't tell her about our secret bait." I make a side-arm throwing motion which prompts a giggle, and an exchange of glances between him and Lena, an obvious giveaway that he's told her every detail.

"And I hope you didn't tell her about catching more than our legal limit." I'm shaking my head *no*. Peter follows suit. "Good man." I give him the thumbs-up.

"He's got something he wants to ask you, don't you Peter?"

"I wa-wa-was—" He sees something that makes him stop—the approach of an older woman who's wearing big sunglasses and a hair-do that's clamped to her skull like a swan-feathered bathing cap. Her smile looks forced, like she found it on a table and stuck it on. Wilma is the first to greet her. "Hello Nelley, it's good to see you." Lena whispers that Nelley is Peter's grandmother, that Peter stays with his grandparents for the summer.

Not addressing anyone in particular, Nelley replies with a "Hello" of her own. "Would have helped out with the cornfest had God given his blessing," she says, "but with Bridge's bad back, I have my hands full at the cottage," she pauses to draw a breath, "with our young summer guest and all." There's a hint of resentment in her voice, something that's turned a ten-year-old grandson into a summer guest. "Only came this evening for Peter's sake," she says. I doubt it. "He loves his corn-on-the-cob, don't you Peter?" She's moves alongside him, takes hold of his shoulders. "But, unfortunately, we gotta get going—Bridge needs his after-supper medication and he needs help with his exercises. I swear the man would just sit all day if I wasn't there to get him off his butt. Well, good to see everybody." And then she steers Peter away, both hands still on his shoulders as if she were pushing a wheelchair.

"Say hello to Bridge for us," Lena calls after them. Once they're out of hearing range, she adds, "Great outing for Peter, I'm sure it'll be the highlight of his summer."

"Oh, give her a break," says Wilma. "Just think of all the sacrifices the poor woman's made to give her grandson a summer he'll never forget. And you know how bad she feels about not helping out with the cornfest this year—or last year, or the year before that."

"Yes, that's exactly what I'm thinking."

Les pipes up, "At least Peter got something to eat. How about poor Bridge? He's probably starving to death."

"Poor, poor, Bridge, he'd choose starvation over having to get up off his arse."

Lena interjects. "Aren't we awful? We're not like this all the time you know."

Wilma agrees. "Bridge and Nelley seem to bring it out in us."

When the person in the seat next to me leaves, Lena's quick to take it. "As you may have noticed, Peter isn't fitting in well with other kids, and that's why you didn't see him in the races." Just then, an oval-faced man with cherry lips walks up behind Lena, pokes her shoulder and congratulates her for the "better-than-ever" cornfest. Lena cringes a bit as she acknowledges the compliment but informs him that she was only one of many who contributed. "Yes, but let's not be overly modest, I know you played a leading role." His tone is excessively reverential and I wouldn't have been surprised had he added *my child* to the end of his sentence. I hear the slight dismissal in her voice when she responds. "Well, I'm glad you're enjoying yourself, Richard, always nice to run into you." He takes her cue, gives her a pat and moves on.

"That was Lena's boyfriend," Wilma says, mischievously.

Lena sighs. "The man's persistent, I'll give him that." Though she doesn't say it disparagingly, it's easy to see that the aspirations are one-sided.

I ask her what the problem is with Peter making friends.

On the other side of the table, Les and Wilma have turned the other way, busy with the never-ending parade of people who appear to be seeking them out.

"At the start of the summer, a boy thought it would be funny to mimic Peter's stuttering. Unfortunately, others thought it was funny and joined in. Kids can be so cruel at that age."

"I was surprised to hear him stutter just now. I hadn't heard it before."

Lena looks away, to clear the glassiness from her eyes. "He's very sensitive, so it's the worst thing that could have happened to him. Afterwards, except for the ringleader, I think the boys felt bad about it, but Peter's avoided them ever since."

"Until this evening, I wouldn't have guessed he had a problem."

"That's remarkable, especially since you're new to him." She studies me as she might a son who's just done the family proud. "He's taken to you, you know. Sometimes when I'm with him, one-on-one, the stuttering almost disappears, but never completely. Of course, the more anxious he is, the more he stutters."

"Yesterday, he was waiting for a boat to come in." I'm reflecting back, wondering if I saw any signs of his problem. "The people on-board tried to engage him but they were drunk, behaving like louts. Peter just stood there without saying a word."

"That is, before the boy with the superior IQ began signing to you."

"Aren't you the confidante?"

"Yes, and I like what I hear."

Suddenly, everyone goes quiet as if they've all been eavesdrop-ping, eager to hear what comes next. But the lull creates a vacuum that needs to be filled. The atmosphere shifts, marking a transition in the proceedings. The reception line across the table disperses, some people start picking up, others begin moving chairs around the fire-pit. Wilma and Les look over to check on us. "So, you two got it all figured out?"

Lena's scanning the area. "We're getting there," she says. "I see that Gwen and Auntie are gathering up the food, so I'd better give them a hand." Les and Wilma volunteer to chip in, as do I.

As I drop off the last of the leftovers and spot Lena loading a dish-washer, I go over to thank her for the hiking advice, tell her how im-pressed I was with the Sea Lion.

"You're enjoying your stay, then?"

I tell her I am, that Wolf Cove's an intriguing place.

"I love it here," she says. "It's where I belong." Etched by the bright kitchen lights, her smile reveals fine lines around her eyes and mouth. She may be closer to my age than I thought, though no less appealing. Her gaze slips away and I wonder if it's sadness I saw or just something imagined, stoked by the concern expressed by Les and Wilma.

"What is it that you do when you're not sailing the oceans blue?"

"I sail the *Gweat Lakes.*" Oh dear, the kick-a-poo's kicking in. I'm hoping she'll think I pronounced it like that on purpose.

"And when you're not sailing?" Good, she didn't notice.

"I've been a psychologist."

"Really? You've *been* a psychologist." Apparently she's not one for missing nuances. "Have you *been* enjoying this profession of yours?"

"It's made me a living."

She asks if I'd mind passing her some bowls from the end of the counter.

"Now there's some enthusiasm for one's profession if I've ever heard it. Not surprising though, you strike me as the outdoors type, and I doubt if psychologists get to practice much outdoors." Her appraisal surprises me, but sounds like a compliment.

"How about you? Do you enjoy being a restaurant, bar, marina, resort operator?"

"Yes indeed. I'm very lucky." She flashes a smile, but she's pre-occupied with what she's doing. "See any small dishes that could be crammed in?" she asks. I look around, pick up a garlic press, and spot Auntie on the other side of the kitchen, spooning leftover food into plastic containers. Seeming to sniff the air, she spins around. "Ah, Mr. Diefenbaker, I knew you'd be dropping in." Oh, yes, Carmella the soothsayer. She drops what she's doing, comes directly to me, takes the garlic press, hands it to Lena, and tells me we're going for a walk. "Let's take a look at that boat of yours."

"Auntie," Lena begins to protest, "I don't think that David—"

"You don't think that David what?" Auntie gives her no time to answer. "He's the captain of this vessel named Antonie, is he not?"

"He'd probably like to hear our wonderful storytellers." Lena checks her watch. "They'll be starting soon."

"Hell, they won't be starting for twenty minutes or so. Captain

Diefenbaker, how long will it take to do a tour of your ship? You have how many rooms on that vessel?"

"Approximately two."

"See there Lena, my lusty-voiced little angel. We'll be back in a jiff."

Lena abandons her role of saviour. "Alright. Maybe the walk will do him good, help him work off the effects of the kick-a-poo. And you listen to me Auntie, don't be giving him any more of that stuff, he's getting too much of a *gweat* thing." She turns away with a grin.

22

HAWK LADY

SO DOWN THE LANE WE GO and I'm pretty sure that my walking is normal and steady. Or maybe it only seems normal relative to the spasmodic activity occurring next to me. With beak held high and elbows flapping, she's like a vulture with road-kill dodging traffic. I take evasive measures, drift to my left, away from the elbow that keeps poking me. It's no use, she keeps drifting right along with me.

"Tell me what you think of our village, Mr. Diefenbaker?"

I tell her it's a very nice community.

"Nice?" She scrunches her nose. "Most who were born here, were born with Wolf Cove in their blood and have never left—or, at least, have properties that they never sell, so they can come back. Others, who have come by accident, take root before they know it, like jack pines in the earth between rocks."

I ask if she was born here.

She tells me she was. "And by that I don't mean I was born in Thunder Bay and raised here. I was delivered here in a cabin on the shore of the mighty lake. They tell me the lake was in a fury that day, roaring along with my mother as she pushed with all her strength— had to, cause, as legend has it, the wild critter wasn't about to join the world peacefully."

I try to imagine what she must have looked like as an infant. The image that comes to me has a yellow beak, bulging eyes, fluff sticking straight up from its head.

"Something strike your funny bone, Mr. Diefenbaker?"

"I can imagine your feistiness, right from the get-go."

"You'd be wise to keep it in mind, young man."

When we get to the boats I offer my hand to help her navigate the embankment. She slaps it away with her right and follows through with a left that misses. "Didn't we just establish that I'm not some helpless old woman."

"I was only displaying chivalry, my response to all classy women."

She looks at me, tells me I'm full of shit and then sidesteps down the embankment, proceeds to Antonie's stern, reads the handsome black print.

"How'd you come up with the name?"

"She had the name when I bought her."

"Have you ever known anyone with that name?"

"Nope, never seen nor heard that name before."

"Tsk, tsk. People always believe they're sure of things they can't possibly be sure of. Did you look at many boats before you bought this one?"

"No, I knew she was the one as soon as I saw her."

Carmella looks from the name to me, as though I have more to reveal. When she sees I don't, she looks back at the name. "Yes, yes, no doubt."

I climb aboard. It's a tricky step from dock to cockpit and despite her feistiness she'll need a hand. What do I do? I fear she'll pounce on me if I offer help, flap me to death.

"I've seen all I need to see," she says. "We better get back for the storytelling."

I tell her I'll walk her back but that I'll take a pass on the stories, explaining that I didn't sleep well the night before and plan to turn in early.

"Not this evening you won't—we haven't had our chat."

I tell her we can chat as we walk, that we can take our time.

"Our chat will take longer than a few minutes, Mr. Diefenbaker."

When I ask her what she wants to discuss, she swings around, pokes me in the ribs, tells me to shoosh, and then hoofs it up the embankment. Seconds later, when I catch up to her she stops, surprises me. "So, what do you think of my Lena?" Just like that, without warning.

Not trusting what she's up to, I play it safe by telling her that she seems to be a very nice woman and that Carmella must be proud of her. Again, she scrunches her face. "Nice? Nice community, nice woman, you sound like death warmed over." She gives her head a shake, rakes her fingers through her hair and resumes walking. "Lena was born and raised in Thunder Bay. As a young child, she spent summers here with her mother and older sister. Her mother's name was Anna. Anna was my younger sister." I'm assuming our chat's underway and I'm guessing it will involve Carmella talking and me listening. "Lena's father would come to visit, but he was a busy man who'd never stay for long. Still, to accommodate him, Anna and the girls would move into the guest house for the summer. The property had been left to both Anna and me by our father who bought the property and built a tiny log cabin on it. Over the years, he worked hard, made some money when silver was discovered, got married to mama, built the main house, and a few years later, the guest house."

I have no idea why she's telling me these things but, nevertheless, find myself intrigued.

"We're talking about Lena's grandparents, then."

"Yes, my mama and papa—so who else? Try to pay attention, would ya."

"Sorry, I'll do my—"

"Mama, you'd be interested to know, was a composer, although of course as a woman in that day and age, she was never recognized for her talent. Still, she composed some of the most beautiful music I ever heard—was a pianist as well. Whenever we asked her to play something new, she'd tell us we had to be very quiet so she could listen for music from the wind. After a few moments of silence, she'd scratch down some notes and next thing you know she'd be playing something—a gift carried from heaven, she'd tell us."

"Classical music?"

"Every kind of music, she had no bounds."

As we approach the break in the fence, Carmella slows. "Mama died very young, and we've never known from what—probably some sort of cancer. In those days, people died, we grieved, we buried them—didn't matter much why they died." She pauses. "Too young," she says, "much too young. The same with Lena's mother, Anna, she died much too young." Slowly, she shakes her head.

"Come on," she says. "We need to find a seat for the storytelling."

Looks like I'm staying after all.

Carmella directs us to a picnic table framed between two pines but well back from the fire that snaps and crackles as it beckons everyone to gather round. I spot Les and Wilma but they're busy mingling in the large circle that surrounds the campfire. Lena must still be inside. The air cools with the setting sun, a sun that's retiring earlier these days, as if weary from the long summer. Carmella says she's going to get a sweater and that I'm to stay put. She's back in moments, wearing an oversized cardigan and carrying a couple of cups of punch. "Coffee comes later, after the storytelling," she says as she hands me a cup and takes a seat.

A tall man, bald except for a feathery fringe of hair, pulls a chair towards the fire, stepping carefully, looking for a flat piece of ground.

He sits, wriggles, and then seemingly satisfied, looks up, clasps his hands on his lap. Everyone notices, and the ensuing hush leaves only the sounds of a campfire, settling in for the evening.

"Here's to storytelling." Carmella raises her cup and I join her in a toast, reminding myself to sip slowly.

Carmella tells me the guy in the chair is Gerald, that he's the best story teller in the village. "He usually scares us with a ghost story." And so it starts.

"Most of you know I live close to here, only the length of a freighter away, on the shores of our magnificent Lake Shuperior." He has the deep, resonating voice of a Shakespearian actor and a small impediment that causes him to shssh his Ss. "Ash well, most of you know I live on a bluff with a good view of the comings and goings on the lake. And let me give thanks for the eye-shight the good Lord hash allowed me to retain over my aging yearsh. Yet, when the thick fog comes to shit upon Shuperior, it's hard to tell the difference between sheeing and imagining." I whisper to Carmella, asking if it's true the fog can be so rude. She gives me an elbow but seconds later she has a hand to her mouth and I feel the quiver of suppressed laughter. "The fog, like the lake, is always changing. At times, it stands like a wall, at times it tumbles and rolls, and on the night I wish to speak about, it was a shwirling mass of ghosts. So let me shtart by shaying that fog plays tricks on your mind. However, you need to know there was nothing wrong with my mind that night, that my imagination was shafely on its leash, that I never drink after shupper," he lowers his voice, "and that I shaw what I shaw. So please hear my shtory, and afterwards you can believe one of two things—that either I've lost my marbles, or, indeed, I shaw what I shaw." He pauses again, takes time to study his audience, lets us know he can look anyone in the eye as he tells his tale. It's an effective ploy. After all, if he can gaze this deeply into people's eyes, then why not into the shwirling fog that's come to shit upon Shuperior?

Damn, I've been guzzling this refreshingly flavoured brew and I remind myself to slow down. "Drinker beware." Les had warned me.

"Go ahead and enjoy it," Carmella says, "it'll help you relax. You've been a bit of a tight-ass, if you don't mind me saying."

"Thanks for that."

"Someone has to tell you." She speaks as if it's been the talk of the town. "Now, I was telling you about Lena's mother—" Just like that, she starts up again, her voice low and guttural, for just the two of us. God only knows why she's telling me this. "She was vulnerable, developed mental health problems before she was twenty, maybe earlier. Occasionally, the demons would leave her alone, but then would always come back. They went away for a while when she was dating Douglas, and I was hoping their relationship would protect her. He was smitten. He saw her as a sensitive young woman who was seductive without trying to be, and he couldn't resist her despite her fragility. They were happy for a time, but the depression crept back. She had another good stretch when she got pregnant with Mary, Lena's older sister, and she held it together through Lena's first years. Life's milestones, it seemed, could distract her but could never set her free, for sooner or later, she'd slip back. And then she was devastated for not being the mother she wanted to be." I note the strain on Auntie's face, the set jaw, the moist eyes bulging above her nose—looking like a baby bird whose appearance has never changed except for the aging. I'd like nothing more right now than to put my arm around her. "Poor Anna," she says. "Like Mama, she was very musical, two of the most beautiful voices I've ever heard—don't know what happened to me. I guess Anna inherited the music and I got the recipes. Anyway, Lena has her mother's voice—and I'm telling you, it's something to hear." Carmella closes her eyes and listens. Almost immediately she begins to sway, she smiles, her face softens. Breaking from her reverie, she gets to her feet, tells me she'll be right back. I could take advantage of the moment to pull one of my disappearing acts, but now the mere thought of it reminds me of what a louse I can be.

Gerald's casting his spell, has everyone imagining a shchooner that appears in the fog, greyish, shlightly darker than the shurrounding mist, drifting aimlessly. Intrigued, he decides to check it out, goes to his shed to grab a lantern, heads for his rowboat. I'm there with him as he enters the shed, hearing the shqeak of rusty hinges, lifting the lantern from a nail in the wall, rowing, dipping the paddles in and out of the water as shilently as possible.

Gerald's about to board the boat when Carmella returns, handing me another cup of punch, reminding me to sip it. Real helpful she is. Maybe if she'd stop bringing me the damn refills. When she's not paying attention, and after I take one more sip, I'll reach around and set it on the table.

From this point, things get blurry and I don't know if I get everything straight. Carmella tells me about Anna being admitted to the psychiatric hospital in Thunder Bay, at first for brief visits, followed by increasingly longer stays—that eventually she couldn't look after the girls, that she had a major breakdown when Lena was only four. She explains how Douglas had to take full responsibility for the girls, how difficult this was for him as his job often took him out of town, and how Carmella took the girls for the summers, when Anna was at her best and able to take leaves from the hospital to help care for the girls. Lena would catch frogs and turtles as gifts for her mother, hoping they'd cheer her up. Even without the gifts, Lena was the one who could make her mother laugh—and oh how they'd sing together with their beautiful voices while Mary retreated, became her father's girl, embarrassed by her mother.

My ability to focus falters. Gerald's below deck, calling out, wondering if anyone's on board, and hoping not to trip over any bodies on a boat that sheems to have been abandoned. He feels wary about trespassing, but also justified, concerned about the vessel, and a crew that's left shigns of very recently being on board. Where is everyone, and what made them leave?

Lena got her mother to walk with her every day. Most often, they'd walk to the marina and sit a spell before proceeding to the Wolf Cove Inn for a snack, although from the start Lena, with her vivid imagination, had referred to the inn as Grandma's House. In those days, the village was even more wooded than it is now, and the highway was narrower. So there they'd be, walking down little more than a path in the woods, the little tyke asking questions about why the hamlet was called Wolf's Cove, thinking there must be lots of wolves around. "Am I right about that, Mommy?" And then, when they'd come to the large house in the clearing, Lena would laugh and proclaim their safety, that they had nothing to worry about as long as they stayed in Grandma's house and waited for the woodcutter—a ploy used to get her mother to stay as long as possible so they could prolong their talking and eat their ice cream. Anna said it was the best therapy she'd ever received, much better than that provided by the shrinks who were determined to uncover mythical trauma. Oh yes, the psychoanalysts always looking for boogeymen from the past.

Gerald hears a creaking coming from the deck. Breathlessly, he listens, wondering if it's only the waves, shtirring things up. But no, it's footsteps he hears, and they're doing their own listening. After a moment, he hears the shteps descending the ladder and on impulse he does shomething he immediately regrets—he extinguishes his lantern.

Anna gets worse. Her visits from the hospital grow shorter and then come to an end. After years of deterioration, after she begins asking her husband who the hell he is and why he's trying to swindle her. Douglas, a successful ergonomics engineer who'd been making a name for himself, opts to accept a job with General Motors. Auntie tells me that he moved with his girls to Dearborn. Dearborn—the suburb of Detroit? My mind's awash with kick-a-poo, wandering from Carmella to Gerald, and back to the corn, wondering if it came from Essex County, perhaps from the field next to where I grew up. I probably fabricated Dear-*born* from corn. I must try harder to focus. The letters from Lena's mother stopped as Anna lost the ability to write. Devastated, Lena turned her attention to singing and joined her high school choir.

Upon Anna's death, the girls became the beneficiaries of an inheritance left by their grandfather, in trust to Anna until their respective twenty-first birthdays. At some point later in Carmella's story—and I wonder how much I've missed of it—the Wolf Cove Inn came up for sale and Lena was there to pounce on it.

I have no memory of how things ended on Gerald's schooner or, afterwards, of stumbling back to the marina, insisting I could make it, contrary to the learned opinions of others. Nor do I remember veering off the lane and into the woods where I tripped and fell and barfed my guts out, overseen by Carmella who stood at the base of the lane to follow my progress, and who sent the rescue squad to save me.

23

AFTER THE CORNFEST

I DON'T MOVE A MUSCLE FOR FEAR of vomiting in whoever's bed I'm in. Thumbtacks jab my brain, not at all blunted by the pillow under my head. Light pries open my eyelids, forcing them to take note of the old-style dresser, chair, and desk. Thankfully, curtains filter the sunlight. I have no idea where I am. Windsor, Killarney, the Soo, Dearborn? Why in the world would Dearborn cross my mind? As my ears begin to work I hear a clattering from close by. I scan the room, hoping to see a bathroom, though I'm not sure how I'd get to it.

For several minutes I keep still, taking long, deep breaths until I feel settled enough to sit up. Moving as gingerly as possible, I get out of bed, take a step, and then another. There on the dresser, propped against an old photo of a wedding party, is a note addressed to me. Lifting it, I smell the ink left by a felt marker and the taint of alcohol nearly triggers my stomach. I cease all movement until this latest wave passes.

> *David:*
> *Good morning. Right now you're probably thinking it's not so good. But take heart, while Auntie's punch packs a wallop, its hangovers tend to be short-lived—let's hope. Anyway, you're*

215

in the guest room at Grandma's House. If you look out the back door you'll see a walk-out patio with lawn chairs and a picnic table. Behind the clump of woods is the marina. The front door of your room leads to a hallway with a storage area to the left and a washroom (with shower) to the right. There's a towel and wash cloth for you on the end table beside the bed. Through the hallway is the door to the restaurant's kitchen. Let Henry (the cook) know when you're ready for breakfast and he'll prepare it for you, compliments of the house. Feel free to eat on the patio. It's very peaceful.

Lena.

P.S. Obviously, you still have your clothes on. There was quite a debate about this. Auntie thought you should have them off, that you'd be more comfortable. I insisted that we leave you be. You don't seem the type who would appreciate having strangers pull your pants off. Wilma agreed with Auntie. Les sided with me. I hope we made the right choice.

I try to picture the scene, myself flopped on the bed, the good citizens of Wolf Cove standing over me debating the dilemma, Auntie adamant, convinced she knows best, chastising Les and her niece for their prudishness, while questioning aloud what kind of a man I am, not able to hold my kick-a-poo.

I consider slipping out the back door and returning to Antonie where I can be sick in the privacy of my own quarters. However, getting something into my stomach, something neutral like toast and a few sips of coffee might help make me feel better, especially if I can avoid the activity required to prepare these things myself. After taking a near-motionless shower, I enter the kitchen and spot a young wisp of a man chopping vegetables. "Are you Henry?" He turns. "Morning champ, you must be David, survivor of the kick-a-poo?" His rooster-like gusto hurts my head. "Define survivor," I mutter. He laughs, "We need to get some breakfast in you. You name it, whatever will help."

I tell him toast with a cup of coffee with double milk might settle things down.

"If that's what you want, but it can be anything, you know. Lena's given the word, and it's on the house." He points his knife at me. "My eggs benedict get rave reviews, if I do say so myself."

I tell him eggs benedict might be a little rich, that they might come up faster than they went down.

He gives me the once-over. "Yeah, you're probably right, but how about some homemade blueberry jam with the toast? Blueberries are said to thin the alcohol so it runs right out of your system."

I try hard not to imagine this. "Thanks, but plain will be fine."

He tells me he'll put a little on the side in case I change my mind. "And where would you like to eat it—the restaurant, your room, the patio?"

"Patio, thanks."

He tells me he'll bring it to me and that I'm to leave the bedroom door open when it's okay for him to come through.

The air's damp from morning dew and almost too fresh for me to handle. Leaning against the railing, I inhale a little bit at a time as I look over the backyard. The yard is all garden, mostly vegetables and herbs arranged like neighbourhoods, with a business section at the centre marked by tall structures that house the green beans, and—in a feat for this part of the country—the ripening tomatoes, accomplished no doubt with an early start in the garden's small greenhouse. I'm heading down the steps for a closer inspection when I feel the swell of revolt. For a moment I'm afraid to move either up or down, but then, slowly, make it back to the picnic table. Needing urgently to sit, I plop down on the dew-covered bench. An itchy bum from wet blue jeans will be the least of my problems.

Moments later, slumped forward, my head heavy as a bowling ball set upon my arms, I hear the back door and look up, surprised to see Lena standing there with my toast, and a thermos with two cups.

"Mind if I join you for coffee?"

She's all bright-eyed, clearly hangover-free, dressed in a white t-shirt, and calf-length jeans that accentuate her sandals and painted toe-nails. She pours the coffee, asks how I'm doing, and I give her the summary, warning that I'd better stay very still for the moment. I nibble the toast and sip the coffee from the special Beethoven mug, telling her it makes the coffee taste extra good. When she asks how I slept I answer truthfully that I have no idea, but I thank her for the accommodations and the rescue effort that brought me here.

"I don't know how thankful you should be, considering that Auntie kept pushing that stuff on you."

"She didn't force me to drink it."

"Don't know what the hell she thought she was up to."

"Her way of being a good host?"

"No way, it's out of character. By the way, I made her confess what her little talk to you was all about." She shakes her head. "I could strangle her." I can tell from the blush she's embarrassed. "She's been acting funny—up to something but I don't know what it is." She looks at me as if hoping I might guess.

I shrug, telling her I don't know, have no idea. "She's one-of-a-kind, I do know that."

"Anyway, she's going to apologize, at least for making you sick, if not for the inappropriate history lesson about our family. I've made that clear to her."

Tongue-in-cheek, I suggest Carmella relates the history to every stranger that comes along, but maybe hasn't got caught before.

"Ha. She's extreme in the other direction, very reticent, very protective of me, especially around men."

218

"Really?"

"Are you kidding? She tells me I should get myself a man, but whenever one comes along and even looks at me, she can't discourage him fast enough." She chuckles. "A few weeks ago a couple of guys come over by boat from Thunder Bay, stay a couple of days. Because they're outgoing, Auntie suspects their intentions." Lena waves, dismisses the possibility. "Anyway, Auntie and I are relaxing on the veranda when they happen to walk by. They make the mistake of inquiring about the restaurant, asking how long we've been running it, where we get our supplies, if we have them brought in or if we go for them ourselves. Well, doesn't Auntie jump all over them, demanding their reason for asking, wanting to know if they're the KGB, lecturing them that the KGB has no jurisdiction over Wolf Cove, that Wolf Cove doesn't need any Mr. Nosies hanging around, that if anyone should be supplying answers it should be them, like how long they're planning to stay. All this because Auntie suspected they were interested in me, though she wouldn't admit it—never does. Not surprisingly, they left later that evening." Again, Lena shakes her head. "Great for business I tell you. Come meet the friendly people of Wolf Cove, where hospitality comes first."

"She has spunk, that woman. I wouldn't want to tangle with her."

"Tell me about it. But then, she goes from that, her typical reaction, to telling you my life history. I don't get it." She pauses, scratches her head. "Alzheimer's doesn't cause people to act like that, does it?"

"If you're asking me, sounds more like menopause," I say with a straight face.

Lena throws her head back and laughs. "Menopause, that's great. I'd love to tell her that—that in the eyes of our visiting psychologist, Dr. Diefenbaker, she's acting menopausal." Saying it aloud makes her laugh even more. She leans forward across the table, her face lit with mischief. "Can I tell her that?" she asks. "Please, I really need to tell her that."

TOM MANAGHAN

Matching Lena's frivolity is out of the question. Under the circumstances the best I can muster is a smile. "No way, a hangover would be the least of my worries."

"Well, raging hormones or not she has an apology to make."

"Ah, that won't be necessary. Like I said, she didn't exactly pour it down my throat."

"I'd better finish my coffee and get back," she says checking her watch. "And, oh yeah, besides my dear Auntie, there was something else I wanted to talk to you about."

"Alright."

"Peter. He wanted to ask you something but didn't get the chance."

"Oh right, he was interrupted by his grandmother."

"The grandmother who sacrifices so much for her grandson." She grimaces, obviously not proud of her sarcasm. "Anyway, he and I are going for a hike today on a trail that follows Superior's shoreline. We go every year, on the day after cornfest, and every year as he gets older, we go a little farther. One of these years, we'll make it all the way to Thunder Cape, hopefully before my age slows us down."

"How many years you been doing it?"

"We started five years ago when we hiked to the end of the pier for a picnic with some of the leftovers. It keeps evolving. Yesterday, he asked if you could come."

I'm touched. "But it's always been just the two of you?"

"Like I said, things evolve—and it would really mean a lot to him. He has no males in his life—Bridge doesn't count."

I feel honoured, but unworthy of whatever impression he has. If they knew how self-absorbed I've been, they wouldn't be bothering. Except for the cost of a six-pack, I've invested nothing more than a simple decency that requires no more effort than rudeness. The poor little guy's desperate for a friend.

"Would you like a refill?" Lena motions with the thermos. She notes my hesitation. "Has the coffee and toast helped at all?"

"A little, I think." I reach across with my cup. "Thanks."

"Of course, yesterday we couldn't predict that Auntie was going to poison you. Peter would understand if I told him you got sick from something you ate."

"I'd appreciate that, especially leaving out the part about me getting drunk and passing out."

She sips her coffee and stares into her cup. "He'll be disappointed—understanding, but still disappointed."

What does she expect me to do? "Sorry, but I wouldn't get far feeling like this, and I don't think you'd appreciate having to stop every hundred feet to watch me throw up."

"What if you're feeling better a couple of hours from now?"

Fat chance of feeling that good. Still, I don't want to leave the impression I'm happy for the excuse. "When will you be setting out?"

She checks her watch, makes a tick-tocking motion with her head to help with the calculations. "Tell you what, Peter and I will wait at the big map at eleven o'clock. That gives you over two-and-a-half hours. If you're feeling up to it and if you'd like to join us, meet us there at eleven. We'll head out at 11:05 if you're not there."

As she gets up to leave, I thank her for the breakfast, and again for the rescue effort and accommodations.

"You're very welcome."

I have to reach for what comes next. "And for your company this morning." She smiles in a way that makes me glad I reached. "And for your auntie—I like her, you know."

"Yes, I've seen that, and she quite likes you, as you must know."

She's at the door of the guest room when I think of one last thing. "And thanks for your excellent judgment."

"Sorry?"

"My clothing. Last night. Thanks for letting me keep my clothing."

Obviously caught off guard, she studies me for a moment before a sly smile crosses her lips. "Not the comment I'd expect from a man the morning after a social affair, and I don't know if I want to say you're welcome—I'll have to think about it. In the meantime, lie down, take it easy, and try to get ready for a hike."

24

PETER THE GUIDE

AS MORNING PROGRESSES, my condition improves from critical to crappy. My stomach's cramping, my head's hurting, and when I see them across the clearing I'm thinking it's not too late to turn back. They're fidgeting with their backpacks when Peter looks up and spots me. His reaction, the big grin, the eager way he tugs her sleeve, the hand raised to engage her in a high-five, takes me from crappy to just a little under the weather. I'll try my best.

Although the first section of the trail is well-marked, it's strewn with rocks and roots that lie waiting for daydreamers to stub a toe or twist an ankle. In places, the path leaves the woods to follow the shoreline, relying on arrows painted on rocks to mark the way. Inland, the terrain varies from marsh, to forest, to rocky highlands.

I assign Peter the task of guide, telling him his job is to advise us of danger, and to point out wildlife such as foxes, beavers, and bears. He giggles when I ask him about the chances of encountering the seven dwarves and he responds with a joke of his own, saying they'd probably be afraid of us but that we might see Dopey, because he wouldn't know how to hide. He relishes his assignment as guide, frequently running ahead and returning a short time later with a report: "The guide reports there's a steep hill ahead," and, "The guide reports a sighting of poop, probably bear poop because it's purple, lumpy, and full of blueberries." I ask him if he thinks the bear poop is the product of a one cup, one quart, or one bushel meal. "A bushel for sure," he says, "maybe two, you should see it."

"Oh yuck, stop it, both of you." Lena pulls a face as though she's stepped in it.

"And trusty guide, how fresh would you say it is—a couple days, a day, a half-hour ago?"

"Judging from the smell, I'd say—"

"Never mind! Peter, did you really have to invite this guy? In all the years we've gone hiking, we've never had a conversation about bear poop."

I act dumbfounded. "You go hiking in bear country and never talk about bear poop? What does she talk about, Peter—about going back to school, who your teacher's going to be, things like that?"

Peter's giggling, "Yeah, pretty much. Sometimes she talks about how my mother's doing." He puts his arm around her, gives her a squeeze, showing he still loves her.

"You guys." Lena mutters something about men getting together, what they do to intelligent conversation.

"You must understand, Lena, that in the wilderness, intelligent conversation is about survival. Not school, not the clothes you're going to wear, but survival." I look back to Peter. "So, what do you think—those blueberries still usable?"

"Stop! Enough!"

Peter and I exchange glances, grinning, shrugging: What's up with her?

Later, along the shore, in a pile of driftwood bleached white by the sun, I find a walking stick for Peter, perfect with its long knobby shaft, and handle in the likeness of a fox head—a crack for the mouth, indentations for eyes, and nubs for the ears. "Guides often have code names," I tell him. "Yours should be Fox."

"Fox," he says, clearly enthralled, "I like that name."

We stop for lunch on a peninsula where we look back along the shoreline to appreciate the distance travelled from Wolf Cove. The water beside us is deep, but clear enough to reveal a bed of smooth, oval rocks, almost perfect in shape, lying on the bottom. They have faint but coloured markings, some with stripes and some with zig-zags. I point them out to Peter, kidding about them being Easter eggs left by a mama and papa dinosaur.

"Noooo!" he says.

"Why not?"

"Because Jesus didn't make Easter until a long time after the di-nosaurs were gone."

Lena, who's been spreading out a blanket, looks up. "Has you there, doesn't he?"

"He's a pretty smart guy."

Just then, Peter spots a bottle lying amongst the coloured rocks.

"Hey, there's a bottle down there. You think there's a message in it?"

I tell him it's probably just an old beer bottle, that if the water wasn't so deep I'd be happy to jump in to get it for him.

"It looks green, though."

I remind him that some beer bottles are green. "And besides, the bottle's lying on the bottom which means it's full of water, so even if there was a message in it, it would be all wet and ruined by now." I feel like a killjoy. Fortunately, Peter's quick to move on.

I help set out the paper plates, the cutlery, the containers of food. Lena was right about the kick-a-poo not leaving a lengthy hangover— either that or the exercise has done me wonders. Whichever it is, my appetite's back and I enjoy the picnic.

Later, when everything's packed away except for the blanket, Lena announces she's going to take a twenty minute break to bask in the sun. Peter tells us he'll be back shortly, that there's a cove on the other side of the point he wants to explore, that he'll bring us a scouting report. "You never know where you might find buried treasure," he adds, and off he goes.

We're lying on the blanket, looking up at some clouds when Lena confides she hasn't seen Peter this happy all summer. I ask how they became such good friends.

"I'm his godmother—his mother and I have been friends since elementary school. Things haven't gone so well for them, so I try to help out."

"What's the problem?"

"His father left them five years ago, returned to the east coast where he grew up, and except for the odd birthday card he doesn't keep in contact. Both Patty and Peter were devastated, though I've noticed in the past year that Peter has stopped asking about him."

"Ah geez, poor little guy."

"I know. I give him what I can, but in the big scheme of things it doesn't make up for his loss. He's very shy, doesn't make friends easily, and so it's been tough. And though Patty loves him, she can barely look after herself."

I tell her he's lucky to have her as a godmother, that I wouldn't underestimate the good she's doing.

"Anyway, thanks for being so good to him. It means a lot."

"I haven't done much—"

She sighs and rolls away, cutting me off as she closes her eyes to signal the official start of basking. I was only going to tell her how I'd love to make a difference, how I'd like to leave him with something he could use in life, like hardiness, or a fable he'd always remember, something more than a few hours of hiking that will have no more lasting value than a good Walt Disney movie. I'm glad he has Lena, the woman lying next to me with the good heart, the generous spirit, and the nice curves that rise and fall along her body. She lies peacefully, but not asleep—I can tell by her breathing. I wonder what she's thinking.

Peter returns and sits quietly at the foot of the blanket, but not for long. He's antsy to give us his report. When Lena senses this as well and begins to sit up, I see my opening. "So our fearless guide is back."

"Your fearless guide, Fox," he says as he sticks out his chest.

"I have a code name, too, you know."

"Really?"

"Kind of, though it's not a cool code name like yours."

"What is it?"

"Sometimes when sailors sail on their own for too long, they daydream too much, start to imagine that they're other people, you know, just to pass the time. Trouble is, when they finally get to shore they forget and start telling people they're somebody else."

Lena clears her throat and looks away.

Peter's getting it in his own way. "They forget and tell people their code name."

"Exactly. They're not really trying to lie, it's just that—"

"What was your code name?"

Lena turns back to watch his reaction.

"David Diefenbaker."

"Cool! So that's just your code name?"

His godmother does a double-take, but her relief at Peter's reaction is obvious.

"My real name is Mark. Mark Weathers."

"Does anybody else know?"

"No, just you and Lena, but when we go back, I'll be letting other people know."

"I liked Mr. Diefenbaker, it sounded important." He catches me raising my eyebrows. "But Mr. Weathers is pretty cool, too."

Lena looks at me tight-lipped and squinty-eyed. "You didn't fool Auntie, she said she'd wager the restaurant that David Diefenbaker was bogus. I don't know how she knows these things, but she does." She's doing her best not to sound angry in front of Peter who chirps in wanting to know what bogus means. She tells him, while never taking her eyes off me, that it's like a code or special language that people invent when they want to be secretive. Peter looks back and forth between us, wondering what's up. For a moment no one speaks but I think we all realize that it's Lena who needs to say something to determine where we go from here. Slowly, she turns towards Peter, releasing me from her gaze. "Mr. Weathers seems to like stories, so Peter, why don't you tell him the story about how Wolf Cove got its name?"

"But I don't know it good enough."

"Sure you do. You listen carefully every time I tell it—I'm sure you can do it."

"I need to practice on somebody but I want Mr. Weathers to hear it the way you tell it—please."

"Okay," she agrees, "but we'd better ask him if he's interested in hearing about it."

Peter scrambles over to sit next to me. "Oh, you'll like it Mr. Weathers, it's a great story."

"I'd love to hear it."

Lena suggests we have a fruit punch while we listen, and pours a cup for everyone.

"You ready, Peter?"

"Oh boy!"

"You ready, *Mark*?" Her smile melts my heart. They've let me off the hook, both of them. I don't deserve their kindness. For the time

I have left, I vow to be a better person. She explains that the village became a settlement soon after a silver vein was discovered running towards the mainland from a tiny island, charted only as Island No. 4. While the silver was impressive, the prospective mining site on the island was not, and it soon became apparent that the mighty Lake Superior was angered by the intrusion. Labourers toiled long days to protect the site from the lake, building breakwaters, foundations, and coffer dams around the vein. The appropriate buildings were constructed and mining got underway—but never for long as the lake would not allow it. Time and time again she gathered her forces and attacked, flooding the shafts, smashing it all to smithereens. Due to it being one of the richest mines in the world, the mining company would make repairs, extend the break-walls, and try again. It was dangerous work at the best of times. On one occasion, a fiery debate occurred over whether a shift should proceed on the eve of Thanksgiving. The local supervisor, Ted Simpson, had argued to give everyone the night off because of the holiday, and because of how tired and stressed everyone had become working long hours for little pay. The manager, a man by the name of McGuigan, ordered the shift to go ahead, threatening action against anyone who refused to comply. During the evening in question, however, when Simpson was home eating supper, he heard timber wolves howling in the woods behind his house. He'd heard wolves before, but never so many of them, never so close, and never with such persistence. They kept it up for over an hour, desperate it seemed, to get his attention, as if trying to warn him of something. Despite the forecast of clear weather, he began to suspect a storm was brewing. Unable to dismiss the howling, he went to the wharf, untied his boat, and made the crossing. He insisted on telling everyone, himself, that the shift was over, that he'd assume full responsibility with McGuigan, and that they really needed to be home giving thanks and preparing for turkey.

No sooner had the men cleared the island than the winds began to build. The storm was one of the most violent on record and before the night was over, Superior had obliterated the break-walls and reclaimed the island. Every worker, whether above or below ground, would have perished. The locals wanted to name their settlement, Simpson, to honour the supervisor, but the man would have no part of it, though finally he did give in to their insistence that he name it. It's been Wolf Cove ever since.

Another legend full of embellishments? It doesn't matter. If it's good enough for Peter and Lena, then it's good enough for me. If they're going to accept, without question, the transformation of David Diefenbaker to Mark Weathers, then I'm going to accept without question the naming of Wolf Cove. I thank them for the wonderful story. As we ponder it, I tell Peter my hunch that he, too, will do something special someday, as special as saving lives. My hunch is really a hope that this comes true, that he will get the opportunity to accomplish something special in his life.

Regarding a more urgent concern for the hours ahead, I hope to be far from Carmella when she hears about my name.

25

THE NATURE OF
MYSTERIES

FRESH SCENTS PACK THE CABIN, compliments of trimmed
beans, minced shallots, and chopped parsley. Olive oil waits alongside the broth and Madeira, ready for reduction in the skillet, while
a blend of butter and flour prepare to thicken the sauce. The steaks,
sprinkled with ground pepper have returned to the fridge. I've cleaned
the mess, showered, changed my clothes, and set a candle on the table
beside the wine—a vintage no less. Prepared, I sit in the cockpit with
Ludwig's biography, and try not to lift my eyes after every sentence
to watch for Lena, reminding myself that well into mid-life and in the
aftermath of Zoe, respect and fondness are all I hope for. The candle's
for ambiance, to enhance the dining.

A short while ago, we were sitting on the steps of Grandma's
House sipping lemon-aid and congratulating ourselves on a fine hike.
Evening was approaching, and it wasn't long before Peter had to go,
leaving Lena and me to wrap things up for the day—or not. I was
enjoying her company and was in no hurry to leave.

"I think he had fun."

"I know he did."

"He's quite the guy."

"Sure is."

"Lots of energy."

"Yep."

"I told you he didn't stutter."

Lena shifts until she's almost facing me. Briefly, her knees touch mine.

"You did, didn't you? I've known him to make it through a few sentences but never through a whole day."

In silence, we watch as he rides away and disappears around a bend.

"Well," she says, slapping her thighs, "I say we help ourselves to some leftovers. I can get some plates, find some wine—"

"Absolutely not. Except for organizing community events, caring for godchildren, and rescuing drunken sailors, you've done nothing but feed me since I arrived. This evening, dinner's on me."

"Oh no, I couldn't ask—"

"Listen up. I'm stocked with groceries, I know how to cook, and you wouldn't believe the wine I was able to get at your liquor store. You're coming to my place for dinner."

"Sounds inviting, but, um, I don't know what to say."

"Then don't say anything. Just show up as you are, in how about an hour from now?"

I got quickly to my feet. Lena, on the other hand stayed put, leaned back against the steps giving me an appraising look, perhaps needing to contemplate the David Diefenbaker deception. Then, as if making up her mind, she stood, stepped forward, and looked me straight in the eye. "Thank you. I'll be there in an hour with a salad."

An hour later I'm telling her she can pour the wine and prepare the salad, adding that the steak and beans won't take long. She's brought ambiance enhancers of her own—the lustrous hair loose on her shoulders, tan-coloured jeans, silk top that matches the wine. During dinner, she responds patiently to the questions I have about her and her business, glowing by candlelight as she tends to her steak, ensuring every bite gets swirled in sauce, savouring as always everything she comes in contact with. She describes what Carmella has meant to her as an aunt, a mother, a sister, a friend, a business partner, whoever she's needed her to be, whenever she's needed it. "Occasionally, we'll have our spats, usually when she forgets I'm an adult and lectures me about what I should or shouldn't do, but I'm great at making faces and there's this one outrageously hideous face I make where I stick my tongue out and—" She sits back in her seat. "I'm telling you far more than you need to know."

"Please, don't stop."

"We're a little weird at times, that's all." Her voice is velvety, like the wine.

I ask her if Carmella's ever been married.

"Not quite, but for most of her life she's been in love—still is, I think."

"Tell me."

"She and her high school sweetheart, Vince, got engaged on his birthday, the day he became old enough to join the war. She didn't want him to go, but it was 1945 and things were looking good for the allies. He said it was the least he could do to help finish off the Nazis after so many countrymen had sacrificed their lives. He promised he'd return soon to marry her, assuring her that a world war wasn't big enough to keep them apart, and that regardless of what she might hear about battles and casualties, she wasn't to fret—he'd come back to her. But after they said goodbye, she never saw him again. The army figured he was ambushed on a scouting mission in France. For a long time he was listed as, missing in action, and though his body was never found the time came when the army officially declared him dead. At first, Auntie believed he'd suffered a concussion and was probably wandering around Europe, lost. She even went to look for him, made inquiries in the towns and villages he should have passed through on his mission. Although she doesn't talk about it any more she continues to wait."

"I can't imagine how sad that would be, waiting and hoping for so long, from before we were even born."

A strange expression crosses Lena's face.

"What is it?"

"Nothing," she says, looking away.

"Hope it wasn't something I said—please tell me."

"I'm not sure. Last night when we were helping you into bed, Auntie began muttering something about love knowing no bounds, about it conquering time and distance. She seemed to be talking to you even though you were out of it, and it spooked me to think that somehow she was seeing something of Vince in you."

"A bit unnerving."

"Tell me about it. At her age, you start thinking dementia, right?"

"The thought might cross my mind, but I really don't think—"

"Anyway, she must have caught the look I gave her, and didn't like it. *This has nothing to do with me*, she says in a huff. Then she calls me a damn fool and marches out of the room."

As she considers this, I pour some wine, giving myself just a tad, still wary from last night. "And how about you, have you ever been married?"

"What? Auntie didn't get to that part of my history?"

I shake my head.

"I'm surprised."

"Maybe she told me and I don't remember like I don't remember what happened on Gerald's shchooner."

"I'll tell you what happened on the schooner, it's the more interesting story."

"Later. First we need to finish with you."

"Whatever." Cupping her glass in both hands, she sits back, takes a sip. "I was married once to a guy named Ian." She stops and for a moment I wonder if that's as far as she's going to go—asked and answered.

"And?"

"And? And?" She leans forward, caricatures my wide-eyed curiosity.

"Make fun of me all you want, but I still want to hear."

Again she sits back, takes a breath. "I was twenty-two, had just started a job with the school board as a music teacher. We met because of Handel's Messiah. The Finlandia choir and the Lakehead Symphony Orchestra still get together every Christmas to perform it. He played the French horn. I sang in the choir. He was seven years older, sophisticated, and came from a family with connections in the music world. In the vows we made for ourselves, we promised that nothing was going to be more musical than our love, that we'd make one long symphony from our life together no matter how much practice it took to get things perfect. He was a perfectionist, so that part was his idea. Well, our lifetime together lasted for two-and-a-half years, until he was offered a spot with the Toronto Symphony Orchestra. Suddenly nothing else mattered to him, and that was about it."

"The offer went to his head? You didn't want to go? What was it?"

"All of the above, but the main problem was that he accepted without even consulting me. I asked if he'd taken even a moment to consider my plans and preferences. He said I was inflexible and afraid of change. I reminded him of our vow to always plan things together. He told me that people need to be open to once-in-a-life-time opportunities and that partners should support one another in such times. And you want to know something? I was considering the move to Toronto, just to please him, when he announced he wouldn't be turning down the offer, not for anything or anybody. It was the unilateral decision and the clarity of his priorities that convinced me to let him go."

"So he left and you stayed?"

"That's my story."

As we finish the clean-up, Lena pulls a bottle of wine from her tote bag. "A Chateaux Neuf du Pape," she boasts, "been saving it for something special."

"Oh yeah?"

"Yeah, but I should probably open it now before it gets too old." She's laughing half way through the punch line.

"I should have invited Auntie for dinner—she might have considered the occasion more special."

"Oh no, I appreciate steak far more than she does."

"You're a regular comedian but you're forgetting who helped you set a new long distance record for your annual hike."

"You're right, Peter was truly inspirational."

"Get off my boat."

"You order me off your boat, I'll order you out of my marina." She raises a finger to her chin, pretending to ponder. "Oops, there's that little problem with your motor isn't there, wouldn't be able to get rid of you if I wanted to. So why don't you grab our glasses so we can head outside and drink this wine before it grows any older."

I bow graciously, and with a flourish point to the ladder. "Game, set, match, to the gypsy woman."

"Gypsy woman?"

Outside, despite the chill she declines my offer of a jacket, proclaiming herself a hardy northern soul, before adding, "maybe later I'll need it." She hands me the bottle and I pour a glass for her, and discreetly, a half glass for me, and then I hesitate as she settles and makes herself comfortable, wondering if I should sit next to, or across from her. Not wanting to give the wrong impression, I choose across from her. She tells me again how much she liked the meal, noting how little things like shallots and parsley can make all the difference.

"I'm delighted you enjoyed it." After tasting the wine and proclaiming its excellence, we take a moment to sip, breathe in the cool air.

"Do you ever see your ex?"

"Oh come now, we're back to me?" She sighs, making me think I should back off a bit. "We've remained friends, believe it or not. He's an entertaining guy, has lots of stories, knows how to embellish his experiences, I'll give him that. With his mom still living in Thunder Bay, he comes up about twice a year to visit, usually calls me when he's in town so we can go out for lunch or coffee, compare notes for an hour. He enjoys his little rituals, maintained the visits with me even through his second marriage."

"How is his wife with that?"

"Ellen didn't mind. Apparently, she let him do whatever he wanted, that is until—" a Mona Lisa smile crosses her lips, "she discovered that he and a flautist were fornicating rather flagrantly after rehearsals." She shivers and rubs her arms, "If you don't mind, maybe I *will* take that jacket."

When I return, she stands, allows me the gentlemanly gesture of holding the jacket as she backs into it. "He's on his way here as we speak, with a kayak and friend, a male friend he tells me. They're staying in one of the cottages for the night before they head off to Red Rock Bay."

I find myself distracted, trying to place the scent of her shampoo. "Who's on his way?"

"My ex."

"Yes, your ex."

"Maybe you'll see him. He'll be the better dressed of the two." She chuckles as she sits, buttoning the snaps of the jacket. "Hell, he's the type who'll fret about what to wear on his kayak. Anyway, if you see them, he'll be the one with long wavy hair combed straight back like a maestro getting ready to take the stage."

She looks up. "Now, how about you? Cooking doesn't give you the right to avoid talking about yourself, you know. "

"One more question?"

"Fine," she points her finger, issuing a warning, "but make it quick."

"No problem. I'll even reveal something about myself in the asking."

"I'm listening."

"I'm not sure of everything that Carmella told me last night, since she told me lots of stuff, and then I dreamt lots of stuff, and I'm not sure which was which. But here's the question: Did you live in Michigan for a while as a teenager?"

"Yes, why?"

"You didn't sing in a choir for a Dearborn High School, did you?"

"That's question number two, but the answer to it is also yes."

"Did you sing for any other high school choir when you were there?"

"That's question number three and you're on thin ice." Again, she takes aim with her finger. "No—I mean yes. It wasn't a high school choir, it was an American-Canadian international choir. I was a member for a short time before we moved back to Thunder Bay."

"An international choir."

"Yes, but international on a small scale, essentially a Detroit-Windsor choir."

"Unbelievable. How old are you?"

"My, haven't we grown bold? Someone's been hanging out with Auntie." She swirls the wine, sniffs it, and takes another sip. "Or is this just another question to distract me?"

"No, I promise. Please tell me. I may have a surprise in store."

"Now there's a new line. Alright, Dr. Snoopy, I'm forty-seven."

"I'm forty-eight."

"Congratulations, but hate to tell you I'm not really surprised. Don't get me wrong, you're a fit looking forty-eight, but I know lots of people around our age, and—"

"Ah, maybe so, but how many of them," I slow down, lean towards her, "watched you with the Border Cities Teenage Choir, in the Cadillac Auditorium, on a rainy May evening, at the age of seventeen, belting out Beethoven's Ode To Joy?"

I'm half-expecting to hear evidence to the contrary, that she was never with the choir when it sang in the Cadillac Auditorium, or at least never in May, or never on an occasion when they performed The Ninth. But the rebuttal doesn't come. She draws back, her jaw drops, her eyes widen, so big and round, and then good God, I recognize that same expression from thirty years ago—the mouth held open in an O, her eyes fixed as though she's focusing on a point in the audience, at a spot right where I happened to be. I don't know who's more shocked.

"Auntie told you."

"She told me about you singing in a high school choir in Dearborn. She didn't say anything about an international choir, or about a Cadillac Auditorium, or about an Ode To Joy in the month of May. "

"You're guessing, making it up." I note the fear and accusation. She believes she's being tricked but doesn't know how and doesn't think it's the least bit funny.

"No, it's the truth, and I remember so well because—"

"How can you claim you saw me when you didn't even know me?" She stands, doesn't know what to do, sits down again. "What's this all about? Who are you? What are you doing here, anyway?"

I apologize for frightening her but ask that she listen to me. I explain about Malcolm and Cathy, about how the evening was memorable because it was the first time I'd been to a symphony, unforgettable because I'd never before fallen in love with music. I tell her about Malcolm not letting me concentrate on the music until I located Cathy in the choir. "A dark, wide-eyed girl was standing next to her, singing like there was no tomorrow. You were attractive, I was eighteen, I noticed. And at the time I could have sworn—" I check myself. "Do you remember a Cathy?"

She thinks maybe, but isn't sure. Her tone softens. "And now, here you are." Her comment is half statement, half question. "A long way from Detroit, in a place called Wolf Cove."

"Yes, and I can assure you that coming here was a fluke. You'll remember I'd already sailed past when I turned back because of the storm. And I wouldn't be here right now, telling you about this incredible coincidence, if my motor hadn't quit." I rest my case, knowing she'll find me innocent.

Another emotion, perhaps a let-down of sorts, flickers across her face and I hope she hasn't misinterpreted what I said as lack of interest in Wolf Cove, or in her.

"A fluke," she says, addressing her wine as if expecting an answer. She turns sideways, leans back against the cabin, gazes towards the lake, obviously reflecting on what she's heard.

I position myself the same way, but look down the shoreline to where we hiked, noting the blazing sky upon the horizon. A woman in a Tilley hat appears on a cabin cruiser four berths over, joined a few seconds later by a man wearing the same type of hat. As the woman turns to him, pointing out the sunset, he presses close, places both hands on her shoulders. Their movements are jerky, their bodies stoop from age, but merged together they grow straighter, less brittle, gain strength from one another. I think of Carmella and her beloved Vince, and what they missed. How sad to keep yearning against hope. I'd cry for their loss, if only it would help. Lena reaches across the divide, her glass in need of a refill. "A fluke," she says again. "Too incredible, don't you think?"

I shrug, wondering if the coincidence is that improbable. "Maybe not, it's a small world where millions of things occur simultaneously. So it's inevitable that unrelated events cross paths, share the same time period, share the same space. Coincidences seem exceptional because we only pay attention to the small range of events relevant to us while we're oblivious to the millions of other coincidences that aren't coincidences at all because they're inevitable. Know what I mean?"

She's frowning, trying to sort it out. "I'm not sure, are you?"

"Not really. But think about the Murrays. They have family from southern Ontario in the vicinity of sweet corn, so their relatives can't be far from Windsor. Windsor has places where lots of people congregate—a large shopping mall, a sports arena, a university campus, a riverside park that hosts an annual freedom festival that attracts tens of thousands of people. Isn't it possible or even likely that I've come across the Murrays before without knowing it, or if not them, then maybe their friends or relatives? I could have talked to the Murrays last night and easily identified people or events or places that connect us in some way. Do you see? Not so much a matter of coincidence as noticing or not noticing."

"No," she says, shaking her head. "I understand what you're saying but, no, I don't agree. Did you see me in the Cadillac auditorium? Sounds like you did. Is it probable that we happened to cross paths back then, but didn't meet each other for another thirty years, hundreds of miles away in a place called Wolf Cove, and that we discovered this coincidence just now while drinking wine together on a boat in Wolf Cove? Nope. I accept that all this has happened, but the why of it, that's a mystery—an intriguing one if I may say so. She swivels around to face me again. "So what does that rational mind of yours say about Auntie's fascination with you and with the name of your boat?"

"I was hoping you'd tell me."

"Haven't a clue."

"Another mystery, then."

She raises her glass. "To mysteries."

As we toast, she sees my glass, realizes I've been nursing my drink. "Hey," she says, "that's hardly fair. I've been doing all the disclosing, and apparently all the drinking as well."

"I know, but you really can't blame me for taking it easy after last night."

"Okay, maybe for the drinking but you still haven't said bugger-all about yourself, except that once you went to a symphony about thirty years ago, had a friend by the name of Malcolm. So let's have it, you promised."

"There isn't much to tell."

"Oh puh-lease. You've been a psychologist, you lived in Sault Ste. Marie, you're alone on a sailing trip—you trying to get away from something, trying to find yourself, what's the story?"

"Sounds like you've figured it out."

"You grew up near Windsor, you like classical music, you like food, that's what I know. You have a few gaps to fill in. I told you all about Ian and I notice you're not wearing a ring, so maybe that's a topic you'd like to start with."

"You're too much."

"You're not enough."

"You're right about that, and that's the problem." Not wanting to go down that road, it's a slip I immediately regret. "I was married a long time ago, for not a whole lot longer than you."

"And?"

"I shouldn't have got married but I'd given up living my own life, was becoming exactly what my parents would have wanted, married a girl they would have picked. Not surprisingly, it didn't work out."

"And what did you want?"

"Something that would make me feel good about myself, maybe a special talent I'd have passion for. Seems I've been looking forever."

"And you're still looking."

"That night, when I went to the symphony, the Ninth did something to me. My appreciation for it was so overwhelming, I felt—I don't know—like I must have some type of creative potential that needed to be discovered. You were in the choir and played a part, but it's hard to... Anyway, I left the auditorium that night vowing to take a year off, feeling I needed to do some exploring because of dreams I had about sailing north through the Great Lakes. For whatever reason, I felt a calling. Sorry, this is sounding pretty silly."

"Not at all. Where in the north did you go?"

"Didn't go anywhere. My dad had a heart attack that summer and couldn't go back to work as a customs officer. He had to rely on a cabinet-making business that until then was mainly a hobby. He didn't say anything, but I knew he was afraid of an early death and concerned about my mother having enough money. Thing is, he couldn't run his business without help, and my older brother was already part way through college, so guess who? My parents had been dead set against me taking time away to travel, so they were quite pleased to have me stay home, help out my dad, attend the local university."

"What happened?"

"I kept going to school, kept getting degrees, kept helping out, until my brother decided he wanted in on the business, all eager with plans to expand it. That was okay with me, I had no passion for cabinet-making and it was also quite alright with my dad. He and Dennis always got along whereas he was forever picking fights with me, trying to bully me into believing what he believed. If anything, that just increased my rebelliousness, which made him resentful. He never liked me much, but I like to rationalize that it wasn't as much about me as a person as it was his interpretation that *I* re-jected *him*."

"But your release from the business would have freed you to trav-el, right?"

"Too late. I had too much invested in school and was planning to become an environmental psychologist. Unfortunately, those plans didn't work out so well, either."

"So you gave up on yourself?"

"It seemed that fate was running the show."

"And how about a love life? You never found someone you want-ed?"

"I'd say we're even-steven in the self-disclosure department, wouldn't you?"

"Auntie's right, you can be a bit of a tight-ass, which is surprising considering your love of the outrageously free and uninhibited Sym-phony #9." Teasing or not, she's forgetting the section of the Ninth that contains uninhibited fury.

"Then let me tell you, freely, about Zoe. I'll keep to the highlights and make it brief." She assures me she has all the time in the world. "Af-ter questioning for so long whether there was any meaning to life, I met Zoe and fell in love with her. It didn't happen instantly. It couldn't—for you see, Zoe was married. And so we were friends at first, but really clicked. We made each other laugh like no one else could, we antici-pated each other's reactions and read each other's moods like magic. We could talk for hours and it would seem like minutes. At first, we were responsible, agreed on the limitations of our relationship, but as time went on we lost that restraint. At last I found meaning, and it was my love for Zoe. It would bring upheaval but it would be worth it, we belonged together. I said all that to her, she said the same to me, and I believed her. Nothing, we agreed, could be more real. Of course, we discussed her husband, how he was a good man who didn't deserve what was happening. They'd fought about children—he didn't want any, at least not for the foreseeable future, and she did—but then the day came when he changed his mind, when he told Zoe he felt he was losing her and would do anything to keep that from happening. He said he'd reconsidered and really did want to have kids with her, as soon as possible. Within months she was pregnant and everything about the world I'd believed to be true showed itself to be farce, and I wondered if I could even be sure that my name was Mark." Recognizing the bitter tone creeping into my voice, I try ending on a lighter note. "So perhaps Gerald can look at something and conclude that he shaw what he shaw, but I have trouble doing that."

Poor Lena. Her face is red. What can she possible say? So much for capping off a wonderful day with a pleasant evening. I offer a warm smile and sympathetic voice. "Aren't you glad you asked about my life?"

"Come over here," she orders, patting the space beside her. "Say no more, I'll read your palm, review your life, and explain things so they make sense to you."

"Yeah, right."

"Come, come," she says. "You've wasted enough time." She takes my hand and cups it in hers, brushes it off as if it were a mirror covered in dust, traces the lines, does some muttering.

"Ah," she says, "it's all so clear."

"Please, I'm dying to hear."

She proceeds in a low, sensuous voice. "It's well past the time to let your feelings go regarding this so-called love affair. In a state of desperation, needing an anchor to grab on to, you made a juvenile mistake, but that's all it was. When did the affair end?"

"A couple of years ago."

"Well, if a sixteen-year-old can get over things like that, you should be able to." Her audacity stuns me.

"Easy for you to make light of it," I try to pull my hand away, "but I'll forgive your glibness and blame the wine."

She keeps hold of my fingers, grabs my wrist with her other hand, won't let go. "It has nothing to do with the wine. The whole episode was pretty predictable."

"Glad you think so."

"Obviously you'd been looking for something to believe in for a very long time and when Zoe came along, you were vulnerable. Love—what a worthy virtue to hang your hopes on, certainly one worth living for. Except, you must realize that reality was always there, right in front of you, and that it was you who distorted it. Considering her wish to have a baby and her husband's response about not wanting to have one in the foreseeable future, I'm guessing she must be a lot younger than you."

"Early thirties. Very much an adult wouldn't you say?" I sound feeble.

"An adult from a younger generation, who had a husband, a family she was raised in, her own circle of friends, an entire life that carried on outside of the small amount of time she spent sneaking around with you. You knew better. You knew you were fooling yourself into thinking that a special friendship would be okay, but it was you who rejected reality."

"You weren't there, you can't—it doesn't matter, I don't know why we're even talking about it." I turn away to watch the colours that fade upon the horizon. The sun's been gone for quite some time. Minutes later, I feel her tugging the hand she hasn't let go of, trying to pull away my bitterness.

"So much for mysteries," I say.

"What do you mean?"

"I mean you've just given me a very rational explanation for how an experience like love can be totally false. Back then, I considered love a mystery."

"Back then. You've known better for quite some time."

I feel the urge to throw my wine glass against the rocks. "So I've done well to adopt a much more realistic outlook, wouldn't you say? Like the rational explanation I just gave you about the coincidence of us crossing paths, you know, without the silly interpretation that an adolescent might give it." She nibbles her lip, lets my hand fall away. I've hurt her feelings. I'm the king of jerks. "I'm sorry."

"For what?"

"For being such a sourpuss. I'm a forty-eight-year old boy who has a hard time getting an ice-cream cone and then when I do, it's a lop-sided one that falls to the ground. So I sulk a lot."

"And you vow to never buy another one, and choose instead to go away on your sailboat for a good long sulk."

"You're thinking I should be able to let go of the disappointments. And I admit that compared to other people's, including some I've met on this trip, mine are not all that exceptional."

"Life requires effort. I'm betting you've come across lots of people in the midst of struggles."

"Early in my trip, I met a man with developmental disabilities who was born without my advantages, yet he seemed content, much happier than me. There was a woman who dreamt as a young girl of being a lifeguard, who now has a demeaning job as the sexy host of a car dealership; another woman who loves her bookstore but barely earns enough to live from month to month; a man who's spent a lifetime chasing rainbows, prospecting for copper; a woman who lost a beautiful and talented mother when she was very young; another woman who lost her fiancé before they could gaze together at sunsets."

"So why can't you let go?"

"Cause there'd be nothing left. I'd still be left with nowhere to go and with nothing to contribute. God, I hate the sound of me. Okay, I'm letting go of it all, right now. Ah, I feel it going. What do you think of that?"

"I'm cheering for you."

"Poof. All gone."

"Now what do you do?"

"I get my motor fixed and head for Thunder Bay, finish my trip."

"And after that?"

I don't answer. Instead, "There's a mystery I'd like to solve before I go."

"What's that?" She's eager, a little hopeful I think, leaves herself open.

"The fascination Carmella has with Antonie. To find what it's about?"

She turns away. I remain the king of jerks.

"How about I ask her?"

"Would you?"

"Sure." She swings around and stands up. "I'd better get going," she says. She takes my face in her hands and kisses my forehead. "Thanks for the great day. It was fun and full of mystery, and I'm sure it was that way for Peter, too."

"It's still early, not even dark yet."

"I know, and it's been a wonderful day, the type of day that makes life worth living, don't you think?" She pulls away before I can answer.

26

MIDDLE AGED MEN

IT'S SIX-THIRTY IN THE MORNING and cold as the dickens, with no campfire, no coffee brewing, no sizzle of bacon and eggs to soothe the chill. Crystal Lake lies just ahead, haunted by fog and the call of loons echoing across its surface. An hour ago I was enjoying my best sleep in a long time, compliments of steak and wine and most of all the time I spent yesterday with Lena. The day was the best I've had in a long time and I plan to look her up later today to tell her that, as well as how much I've appreciated Wolf Cove and the people who live here. I woke from my lovely sleep, however, wishing that I had only dreamt the part about sitting on the steps of the restaurant yesterday afternoon, sipping lemon-aid, noticing the glum look on Peter's face as he got up to return to his grandparents, asking him where his grandparents lived and how long it took him to get there on his bike. That's when he told me about Crystal Lake, a short distance down the road that branches to the left just before Clarke's garage. I was trying to make him feel better about going back to his grandparents, asking if it was a nice lake, if it was good for fishing, and his face brightened as he told me that Crystal Lake was great for fishing, "ten times better than Lake Superior." I should try it, he'd said.

"Maybe I will sometime."

"How about tomorrow morning? There's perch and bass and everything. If you come early, we'll catch something for sure. Grandpa and I always did, but he doesn't fish any more because of his bad back. I could get up early and catch some worms." He looked so hopeful. "I use worms but you can cast if you want." I didn't have the heart to turn him down.

He meets me in the driveway, looking as if he could hug me, and takes us to a spot two-thirds of the way down his grandparents' dock where he says there's a grassy bottom that attracts perch. I'm glad he knows where we are because the fog's so thick we can't see anything except the damp, wooden boards that creak under our weight and get our bums wet. Neither the cold nor wetness wipes the smile from Peter's face. After a few minutes I stand to cast, trying to keep warm more than anything. With each cast, the lure disappears into the murk, calling kerplunk to announce its arrival. Finally, when the fog lifts enough, Peter points to a row boat tied to the dock. "We should fish from that," he says. "A little way out, there's a clump of rocks and then a deep drop-off where we'd catch something for sure. You should use worms, though, because the fish are directly below in a deep hole."

He's right. After dropping anchor it's only a matter of minutes before I catch a perch. "I told you," he says proudly. Then, minutes later he snags a bass that jumps and dances on the water, Peter twisting and dancing right along with it, letting the fish expend some energy before reeling him in. It's obvious my young friend has done this before. He anticipates Mr. Bass's final move, where he comes to the side of the boat and pretends to give up before taking a plunge, pulling the line under the boat. A moment later, when the battle's over, Peter directs me to scoop the bass with the net. He slips him onto a stringer and holds him up for display. I reach over to raise his arm in victory when our attention gets diverted by a commotion on shore.

His grandparents are running down the dock, yelling and waving frantically in our direction. I look to their cottage, thinking fire, but see nothing unusual except for the old folks dressed in pajamas, on the verge of hysteria. Proudly, Peter points the fish in their direction. "Gra-gra-grandma, Gra-gra-gra-grandpa, loo-loo-look what I caught!"

Arms motion us to shore, screams echo over the water. "Peter, Peter! You get in here. Bring the boat back to the dock, Peter. He's got no business being in that boat. Tell him if he doesn't bring you back right now, we're calling the police!"

What the hell's going on? My mind races, searching for an explanation. Maybe something's come over the news about an escaped convict using a sailboat to evade capture.

"We-we-we just go-go-got out here," Peter answers. "We-we-we're catching fish."

The woman's voice grows shriller. "Peter, do what you're told, right now!" The man's voice gets louder as well, more authoritative. "Bring the boat in, Peter."

Grandma grasps him by the arm as he steps from the boat. "Come on," she says, "we're going back to the house."

Peter raises the stringer, trying to present evidence that will exonerate him of whatever it is he's accused of. In a huff, Grandma snags it and throws it into the water. Peter's face whitens.

"Wha-what are you doing? Tha-that's my fish!" Bewildered and on the verge of tears, he yanks his arm from her grip and runs to the boat to retrieve his fishing pole. As he steps back to the dock she grabs him again. "You watch yourself, young man." Again, Peter yanks his arm away. Now grandpa steps towards them. "Do what your grandmother says." Peter scoots out from under his reach but heads towards their cottage, doing as told. Grandma's in pursuit, calling out that she'll take care of him and that grandpa's to take care of me.

He steps towards me, wagging a crooked finger. "You," he spits, and keeps coming. If he so much as touches me, old man or not, he's going for a swim.

I shout back, hoping to stop him in his tracks. "What the hell's going on here?" He squints, still pointing, but stops a few feet away, telling me I know damn well what's going on. There's a fury rising inside me that recognizes the accusation before I do. "You going to tell me, or are we going to stand here all day?"

"I can assure you that you won't be standing here much longer. You're trespassing on private property right now and need to leave. Nelley will be giving Jim a call as soon as she gets inside. Jim's the OPP around here, so I'd suggest you get moving—on the double."

'On the double.' I want to tell him how frightened I am, so frightened that maybe I'll wait right here for Jim to arrive. Suddenly, a few feet from shore, Peter turns and runs back to the edge of the water, throws his pole like a javelin, as far as he can into the lake. Whatever this is about, I'm afraid it's going to stay with him for a long time. I try to control my outrage.

"I met your grandson when he came to the marina looking for empty beer bottles. I'm guessing you know that he gives them to Lena, who pays him. I gave him the few bottles I had. Yesterday, I joined him and Lena for their annual hike—at their invitation. He invited me to come fishing. He's a great kid. Here I am. You're going to call the cops on me for what?"

His mouth curls and he makes a whistling noise as he inhales through his nose. "You think you can get away with luring little boys to diddle with, or do whatever it is you think you can get away with?"

"What the fuck?"

And then I get it. I look at an innocent boy's grandfather, this judgemental old bastard, this cottage-owning, tax-paying, hypochondriac; this uptight and likely sexually repressed paragon of society, and I get it. I get it from this jaw-thrusting jerk who thinks he can threaten me as he stands there with jowls quivering with two-day-old, reddish-grey stubble, who stands withered and stooping inside his baggy pants and shapeless wool sweater that must be picking at him as much as his beard—this asshole who thinks I have no choice but to stand here and take it because he has everything on his side—society, seniority, and probably the Lord. I stand in judgement—a middle-aged man who's befriended a boy, and fortunately for grandpa, a man who's too civilized to let his rage run amok.

There's nothing for me to do, no way to react, but to leave. I put one foot in front of the other and take a step, and then another, and pray he doesn't bump me. My retreat emboldens him. "I better not see you around here again." I take a couple more steps. "And I'd better not hear about you spending any more time with him—down at the marina, or anywhere."

I stop and turn around. If my eyes could burn a hole in him, they would. He thinks that he's won. Maybe he has.

After easing my blood pressure over stale coffee at a gas station diner, I head over to see Clarke. The bells over the door jingle to announce my arrival. At the back, behind a counter that looks diseased with peeling yellow paint, I see a man a little older and a little shorter than myself puttering about, opening tool boxes and turning on a coffee maker. He looks up, sees me and without saying a word carries on, walking out from behind the counter to open the hood of a lawn tractor. With his grey and closely cropped hair, his wire-rimmed glasses, and intense expression, he looks like a spy.

I ask him if he's Clarke. He doesn't answer. Nice manners. Not my fault he missed the cornfest. I look around at the used lawn mowers, at the boat motors clamped to a wooden rack. Boat motors, yes! I must be patient. On the wall are blown-up photos of speedboats—the big ones that look like spacecraft with little cockpits at their centres. In a picture over the counter, Clarke and some other men dressed in over-alls are standing with a driver in front of a boat called Miss Valvoline. I'm definitely in the right place.

I try again, louder this time. "I have a sailboat at the marina. I was headed for Thunder Bay when my outboard quit on me. It's a nine-and-a-half horsepower. I need it for getting in and out of dockage."

Nothing. A few seconds later, in response to some pawing and whimpering, he opens a back door. He goes out, brings in a bowl, fills it with water from a laundry tub at the back of the shop and takes it back out. I see a black tail wagging through the gap in the doorway before Clarke re-enters the shop, closing the door behind him.

"I was wondering if you'd be able to take a look at it."

He leans over the tractor with the opened hood. "Open your eyes, there's a few other things I'm working on right now," he says, drawing out the words.

I take a breath and bite my tongue. "Yeah, I can see you're a busy guy." I do my best to sound respectful, but it's not easy, especially not the way the morning's going.

He takes another look at me, smirks, and with a grunt walks over to his coffee maker.

I ask, politely, if he has any idea when he might be able to take a look at it.

"God-damned tourists," he mutters, shaking his head. He pours himself a coffee, reaches into a miniature fridge to get some milk. He sips his coffee, testing it. Satisfied, he sips again. "That's the thing with you tourists," he says. "You think you're entitled—that for some god-damned reason you should get priority. You see that John Deere over there? That belongs to Steve. You don't know Steve and you're not go-ing to be here long enough to meet Steve. I've known Steve for years, will continue to know him for years, because we both live here in Wolf Cove. He's the one who gets priority around here—not you. Got it?"

I remind him that I never suggested otherwise.

"Not with words you didn't." With his coffee, he heads back to the lawn mower, picks up some tools and starts working on it.

I'm going to have to get out of this place before I knock his counter over, take Miss Valvoline off the wall and throw it at him, before I go over and smash his coffee maker.

"Well, it's been a fucking pleasure doing business with you," I tell him. "I never asked to be a priority, with words or otherwise." I turn to open the door. "I'll drop by the Wolf Cove Better Business Bureau and mention to them that it's been a total delight doing business with you. I'll tell them people like you make me want to come back, pay another visit, tell my friends about the place." I give him the same smirk and grunt he gave me. My dam's ready to burst. "At least you could give me directions to the fucking Better Business Bureau. I'll bet there's two or three in this fucking place. Any one of them will do."

Without looking up he asks me what it is that my motor isn't doing. I answer him, suspecting his question's setting me up for another rant about god-damned tourists.

"It's probably nothing more than a spark plug," he says.

I tell him I had a new spark plug put in with a general tune-up to start my trip.

"God-damned tourists," he mutters. "Why the hell do you ask when you already got all the god-damned answers?" He rises and turns to face me. "Sometimes people sell cheap spark plugs to god-damned tourists and the god-damned tourists find that the plugs are no fucking good, that they misfire and go black, and then these god-damned tourists come round debating things they don't know shit about."

"Well, you don't know how sorry this god-damned tourist is for fucking asking." I open the door.

"What kind of motor is it?"

I tell him.

"And what year is it?"

"This god-damned tourist doesn't know what year it is."

"What's your best guess…three, five, ten years…older?"

My guess is five. I remember buying it.

He turns away. "I'll be out late this afternoon. I'll bring some plugs with me." His voice is as ornery as ever. I wonder if I've heard him correctly.

"Thank you."

"Be sure to drop by the Better Business Bureau to tell them about the great fucking service you're getting." He gets the last words before the door closes behind me.

On the walk back to the marina, a police cruiser pulls alongside, slows to my speed and starts to escort me. Cop or not, I've just about had it. "You looking for someone?" I yell it so he can hear me through the closed window, so grandpa can hear me from the cottage. This must be Jim. Good grief, he has the same scowl and the same squint as the grandpa—they obviously belong to the same family. He points a finger at me, cocks his thumb, holds it long enough to get his message across before pulling away. Fuck this place.

Back on Antonie, I can't help obsessing about the morning, worried about what Peter's hearing from his grandparents, trying to convince myself he'll know better. After a while I head for Grandma's House, hungry because I haven't yet eaten. Last night, Lena dulled my urgency to get away as fast as I can, so maybe she can do it again. Maybe I'll see Les and Wilma and they'll confirm that no one pays much attention to Nelley and Bridge, and that their relative, Constable Jim, is a bit of a dork who isn't respected either. And Clarke? Maybe I'll learn he's the community trouble-maker, the tourist-hater at odds with the rest of the villagers who actually like the tourists and the business they bring. Maybe the lunch hour won't be too busy and I'll get a chance to banter with Carmella, ask her myself about her interest in my boat. Why wait for Lena to solve the mystery? The thought of Lena makes me want to reach down deep, search for the positive in all this. Have wisdom, be serene.

Unfortunately I don't see Les and Wilma, and though the lunch hour isn't busy, not once does Auntie emerge from the kitchen, not during the whole time I linger over a veggie burger and the extra cup of coffee I don't want. Nor do I see Lena—not till I leave the restaurant and hear her laughter.

Lena and two guys are sitting at a picnic table next to a cabin, a few feet from a Mercedes. They're animated, clearly enjoying one another's company. The maestro, just as she described him, seems to be in the middle of telling a joke, puffing up his cheeks and thrusting a fist back and forth from his mouth, mimicking someone playing the trombone. Whatever it is, the guy sitting across from him thinks it's the funniest thing ever. He keeps slapping the table and throwing his head back in laughter. Lena's trying hard to control her own laughter, covering her mouth with both hands. No doubt about it, they're making great music together. I watch from the veranda as Lena gets up and disappears into the cabin, joined a moment later by the maestro himself. I'm on the verge of turning away when they reappear, Lena with two bottles of beer, the maestro with one, his free hand on her lower back guiding her forward. When she gives the other guy his beer, he takes her hand with it, pulls it to his lips and kisses it—Lena, the queen of the gypsies. Playfully, she swats him away. When the maestro sits he tries to pull her onto his lap, obviously looking for a kiss as well, his mouth searching for hers. Laughing, she manages to thwart him, and like the heart-broken lover he is, he clutches his heart with both hands. So what does she do? She leans forward and gives him a quick peck on the forehead. I guess kissing guys on the forehead is something she does—Lena, queen of the gypsies and forehead kisser.

I forget that I'm standing like a statue watching them. She looks up, sees me and waves, gesturing for me to join them, not waving quite as wildly as grandma was a little earlier—but grandma's wave, I have to say, seemed more natural. There's something a little contrived about the one I'm seeing now. Quickly, I scan the driveway, like that's what I was doing all along, not really noticing anything in particular, just breathing in the fresh air. I'd yawn if I could. But I can't, so I simply look away as if I didn't see them and head off down the driveway and then down the road, to somewhere I won't be found. Maybe I'll go for another hike to the Sea Lion and close my eyes and take what's coming to me, the sound of fate laughing its ass off at its favourite target—the one who's so easily fooled, a regular Charlie Brown who gets convinced each and every time that Lucy won't pull the football away at the last moment.

27

The Decision

WITH NOBLE POSE THE SEA LION keeps watch, never flinching as he absorbs, day after day, both the battering and soothing of the lake. Now, this is a guy who appears serene, perhaps awed by the water's ever-changing moods, the way it flexes its muscles with might and fury, the way it shimmers silent and blue in its quest for eternity.

There will be no eternity for me. I won't be building any pyramids or composing any symphonies. Less ambitiously, I won't be able to better the world as an environmental psychologist, nor will I be able to make a decent living from something that interests me, whether it's running a bookstore, restaurant, outfitter shop, tour business, or seminars at a small resort. After forty-eight years I'm nothing more than a nomad without talent. No, worse than that, I'm now a pedophile, a god-damned tourist, a jilted adolescent watching from the sidelines as Lena gets back with her ex, feeling naïve for not being able to see the inevitability of it all. The traces of kinship I've felt for this place are as false as everything else in my life. I don't belong here. My quest is over—I've tried and failed.

I make my decision. I'll end my life by heading out to where the water meets the sky and there I'll drown. Immediately my rage cools, like boiling water poured upon the ocean. Is it numbness I feel, or peace?

I reflect upon my voyage, wondering if it was all a waste of time. It wasn't. Although it didn't conjure meaning, it gave the satisfaction that comes with giving a good effort. I opened my mind and tried my best. I confronted a challenge, took some risks, talked to nature, talked to people, adopted hope, explored options—and here I am, not with serenity, exactly, but perhaps with a measure of resolve. Still, the final step may not come easily for fate will not be pleased to relinquish control, and may yet try to thwart my plans—plans that still need to be worked out.

Exactly how and when?

To start with, I need to anticipate Clarke failing to show up today as promised, and maybe not even tomorrow or the day after that. I won't fret, won't give fate the satisfaction. If he doesn't show up after a reasonable amount of time, I'll wait for an offshore wind and try to sail out. Still feeling a need to reach Thunder Bay, I'll worry about docking when I get there, prepared to throw the anchors out to moor offshore if I have to. And if I end up in Wolf Cove for a few more days, I won't avoid talking with Lena. She's a pleasure and I have no more reason to avoid her than I do a beautiful sunset or favourite violin concerto, though I'll be wary of fate using her to distract me from doing what's necessary. From what I saw this morning, however, that seems unlikely—I wouldn't be surprised if she and Ian were engaged in some type of duet at this very moment. Nevertheless, I shall remain wary.

How else shall I behave? If I see Carmella, and I probably will, and Les and Wilma, I shall joke and banter. I won't be surprised if I don't see Peter, as I suspect his grandparents will restrict his movements until his mother arrives to pick him up on the Labour Day weekend. I'll be sad not to see him. My feelings towards Bridge and Nelley have become irrelevant, as I now view their behaviour as having been established long before I came along. Especially in this tiny village, but in other places as well, my passing through is inconsequential—nothing to do with their past, and with no bearing on their future. I regret this. As corny as it sounds, I would like to have done something, somewhere, to make a difference. Unfortunately, there was that old problem of inadequacy, the absolute lack of genius, the paucity of skill.

On the walk back to the marina, I promise to deny myself pity. In fact, I'll go with spirit and vigour, exercising perseverance right to the end. I'll listen to weather forecasts and wait for a storm, knowing sooner or later one will come, and then I'll shove off and head for the centre of the lake where I'll thumb my nose at the crushing waves. If the storm eases too soon, I can jump overboard from the centre of the lake and swim for shore, knowing I can't swim a half mile—not even that in frigid water. But I'll swim as far as I can.

I wait, reading in the cabin, prepared for either a visit or no visit from Clarke. Lo and behold, he arrives at 4:15, replaces the spark plug, pulls on the cord and starts the motor. Thank you Clarke, I'll never argue with you again. I barbecue a burger and return to the cabin, not in the mood for seeing anyone else.

Of course, it's not long before I hear footsteps, and then her voice. "Mark, are you in there?" Seconds later, Antonie dips to one side as Lena boards and knocks on the hatch. "Mark, you there?"

We talk in the cockpit. She asks why I didn't answer right away, wants to know if I was trying to ignore her. I tell her I was merely having a nap. It mustn't sound convincing. Instead of apologizing for wakening me, she questions why I ignored her earlier when she gestured from the picnic table. "I was hoping you'd join us for a beer. When Ian asked me what new and exciting things were happening in Wolf Cove, as if that was too unlikely, I told him about a Beethoven-lover who had sailed into port, saved Peter's summer, cast a spell on Auntie, and who—" she slows down and lowers her voice—"had me alone on his boat last night, wining and dining me." She's back to being playful. "I was hoping to introduce him to this sailor."

I plead obliviousness, telling her I must have been day-dreaming as I left the restaurant, looking around, perhaps, but not paying attention. "How's the old ex doing?"

"Fine, for Ian, I guess."

Yeah, yeah, I'm done with being naïve. The pause is filled by squawking seagulls, circling low over the water, clearly in a flap about something.

"Probably a dead fish or something," she says.

"The water's so cold that dead things are supposed to sink and never resurface, right?"

"Depends."

Depends? On what?

"Clarke dropped into the restaurant a little while ago, had some pie and coffee."

"He got my motor running. As he predicted, it was just a spark plug."

"He told me he got a kick out of meeting you."

"I'll bet."

"Said you dished out as good as you got, that you were pretty witty for a tourist."

Lena sees me shaking my head and laughs at an encounter she can only imagine.

I ask if she'd like a drink. "Wine, beer, coke?"

"No thanks."

"Strange guy."

"He can come across as a jerk, but he's just a harmless grump. He complains and he huffs and he puffs, but he'd get up at three in the morning if there was an emergency you needed him for."

I ask if she'd mind me having a beer without her and she says no, but once I'm below, she calls down to say she's changed her mind and asks if I'll bring her one. "By the way," she calls, "I want to hear how the fishing went. Haven't seen Peter around to ask him."

Back on deck I describe my encounter with Bridge and Nelley, and how it accounts for Peter's absence. She takes a deep breath, follows it up with a good slug of beer. "I'll be paying those two a visit," she says through her teeth.

"Nah, just let it go."

"I'll do nothing of the sort. I'm his godmother and they're going to get a good piece of his godmother's mind. I'll tell them their daughter's going to hear about it as well."

"You sure it's worth it? Labour Day's only two weeks away, Peter will be going back to his mom's, I'll be leaving."

"When?"

"Soon, now that my motor's fixed."

"Where to?"

"Thunder Bay, remember?"

She ponders as though recalling something from long ago, and when she asks if I'm in a rush, I tell her I'm playing it by ear. "You'd better not be planning to leave tomorrow."

"Why's that?"

"I'm driving to Thunder Bay to buy some paint for the cabins and wanted to invite you to keep me company. The cabins need a fresh coat before fall arrives. After getting the paint, if you were interested I was going to take you out to Old Fort William. Ever been there?"

"No. I lived in Thunder Bay, briefly and long ago, but the fort hadn't been opened yet."

"I'm thinking that an explorer such as you would enjoy it."

Explorer? I like the description. It comforts me, even as I consider that all places on earth have already been discovered. Maybe that's my problem—I should have been born a few hundred years ago.

"It's been a while since I've been there. If we left early, we'd have a fair amount of time."

Why not? While I was reading, I had the weather radio on and heard the forecast of clear skies for the next few days. Not only will I go with her to visit the fort and get the paint, I'll help her with the painting—do something nice for someone before I go, make myself useful until the forecast changes. If, after the painting's done, there's still no storm, I'll head out anyway, and go for that swim.

When she spurns my offer of painting, I tell her that she'll have to make the trip to the city without me. I say it firmly but with a smile. She concedes, but then says she'll pay me. Of course I scoff at this but suggest we could do some bartering—painting for dockage fees.

"I charge a pittance for dockage."

"Maybe you should charge more."

"Don't be ridiculous. You just treated me to a wonderful meal."

"That was for you. The painting would be more a general contribution to Wolf Cove—you know, helping to give it a face lift, not that it needs one. So come on, let me do something that will make me feel altruistic."

"Think of what you've done for—"

"Shoosh. You going to let me help with the painting or not?"

She pauses, scratches her head, and then her face lights up.

"Tell you what. I'll let you help but only if I can make a special dinner for you."

I pause, stroke my chin. "Depends on what you're offering to cook."

She swats my arm. "You'll eat what I give you, and you'll like it."

"Alright, but on one more condition."

"Now what?"

"We leave quite early, and we go by boat so I can test the motor."

She's surprised but recovers quickly. "How good a sailor are you?"

"I've made it this far, haven't I?"

The motor works, Thunder Bay is a fine place, the historic towns of Port Arthur and Fort William joined at the hip to make a city. I answer Lena's questions, explaining why I left my profession and confessing that I sold my home in the Soo, so no, won't be returning there. "Antonie's my only home these days." Having made the big decision, the facts feel lighter and easier to talk about. We have breakfast, which I tell her is not nearly as much fun as it is at Grandma's House, and then we walk to a car rental where we rent a sub-compact to take us to the fort. On the way, we stop at a hardware store and buy the paint— lots of it, forest green and eggplant purple. Back in the car, she turns solemn, but I catch her stealing glances at me, and I wonder what she's thinking. Finally, she works up the nerve to ask if I have cancer or something. "Forgive me for asking, but I'm getting these vibes from you—this talk of you wanting to do good deeds before you go. Not that I can't imagine you being helpful."

"No, I'm quite healthy as far as I know. I'm one of those middle-aged men who suddenly quit what they're doing to start over, one of those converts who move from the city to the farm, from stock brokering to growing sunflowers. You read about them in the weekend editions of newspapers. They end up wondering what took them so long to make the move."

"What's your plan? You've bought a sunflower farm?"

"Not sure what I'm going to do—that's what this trip's about." I feel bad about deceiving her.

She gives me a funny look. "Your journey's almost over."

"I'm thinking it might not come to me until the journey's completely over and I take some time to figure out what I've learned from it." I make a point of looking in the rear-view and side-view mirrors, to keep from making eye contact. "I hope you're paying attention to your navigation duties." She tells me we keep going straight for a while. "So you were telling me that Ian was doing fine for being Ian."

"Yeah, he's his usual self except for going a little overboard with his buddy-buddy routine, but that's to impress Jeff about his prowess as a lady's man. He'd like him to think that not even his ex-wife can resist his charms." She pauses as I pull out to pass. "When we were talking and joking at the picnic table, he tried to get me to kiss him. I wriggled away, told him if he wanted to put his lips on something he could get out his French horn—the instrument with the curvy figure he left me for. Of course, I said it lightly, but it was funny how he guzzled down his beer and left soon afterwards."

I feel sheepish for jumping to conclusions. Still, it makes no difference. It's too late for me—I'm water under the bridge, or is it over the dam? Whatever it is, I've passed the point of no return, have exhausted all the cliches. Besides, in the next breath, she could start telling me about some new guy she's interested in.

I ask about her plans, the future of the resort, about Carmella being forced from her role by the mean-spirited arthritis. She tells me how difficult the transition's going to be for her aunt, that it'll break her heart, though she'll try hard not to show it. She tells me of her own plans to carry on with the business, that she'll always look after Auntie, make sure she gets the care she needs—without ever leaving Wolf Cove.

"Do you guys ever get away?"

"What?"

"Do you ever get away, other than to Thunder Bay? Like travel to other parts of the country, go to Europe, anything like that?"

She answers sharply. "Why would we do that? We have everything we need right here."

"I wasn't suggesting you move. Was just curious about whether you get out for visits, to see what else there might be to see."

"I left Wolf Cove once and it was a big mistake. I should have never agreed to go." At first, I have no idea what she's talking about. I glance over and see her eyes welling up. She turns and stares out the passenger window but I hear the quiver in her voice. "We abandoned mom when she needed us most. She'd given me so much, tried so hard for me, and then just like that I disappear from her life."

"You were just a girl and it wasn't up to you. Maybe your dad realized your mom would be devastated for you to see the way she'd become. Besides, it sounds to me as though you were able to give her more than anyone else could."

"The least I can do is take care of what she passed on to me."

"No doubt you've done that, and maybe neither you nor Carmella has any desire to travel—who am I to say? All I'm suggesting is that you guys could reward yourselves in a way that could help your aunt picture a new stage in life, as opposed to seeing her retirement only as an end."

"Thanks for the tip." Little more is said until we get to the fort.

Lena was right in thinking I'd enjoy the fort, an impressive reconstruction built upstream from Superior on the Neebing River, brought to life by buildings and barricades cut from local timber, and by inhabitants in period costumes engaged in everyday activities that would have been typical for the times. Blacksmiths are working their bellows, bakers are baking in stone ovens, and canoe makers are preparing birch bark. We're there at mid-day when natives arrive by canoe, carrying furs, hoping for trade. Tanners are tanning, and cheese makers, themselves smelling a little curdled from their work, are busy churning. They answer questions, but most of the time talk among themselves as they would have way back when, spreading gossip based on news brought by voyageurs. The trapper, Pierre Boucher, is drunk inside his cabin, as always, according to the weaver who weaves next door. We go in to check on him. It's hot inside because he likes to keep a fire going even in the summer, even now when he's perspiring and his clothes are soaked through. He staggers about with his whiskey bottle, disheveled and spouting gibberish, muttering something about Bonnie, that whore of a woman who abandoned him. He eyes Lena, turns to me, pointing a finger at me in warning. "You gotta keep from getting mixed up with women if you ask me, they just ruin a man is all they do." I tell him I appreciate the advice, especially its timeliness. Lena gives me an elbow, tells me I can forget about that supper.

"Run for the hills, my friend, run for the hills." He staggers away, falls face down on his bed. If he's a drama student, and I'm betting he is, he has a great summer job.

A perfect westerly breeze is much appreciated for our trip back. Lena remarks that this sailing business seems a lot easier than she thought it would be and asks if I'll give her a lesson. I give her the tiller and tell her she first needs to learn the parts of the boat. She informs me she already knows most of them. "The sheets are ropes you don't have to wash. Those halyards are looking a little loose, don't you think? This is so easy."

"It involves a little more than sitting with your hand on the tiller."

"If you ask me, it doesn't seem like there's much more to it."

"Okay, then, Captain, I'll ask that you head us into the wind, port side that is, and take us through a tack."

"Well, you haven't told me about that yet. Just tell me what to do and I'll do it."

After explaining the steps involved in tacking, I tell her that the very first thing she needs to do is issue the proper command. "You're the captain, I'm the crew, you need to prepare me for the impending maneuver. *Coming about!* You need to shout it out."

"That's silly. Why would I do that? You already know what we're doing."

"It's absolutely critical. One of the captain's most important roles is to issue clear commands. If the boom swings around unexpectedly it could take someone's head off."

"Okay, but isn't there something else I could say? I'd feel a little weird calling out to everybody that I'm coming about." She pauses to consider. "No way, it's embarrassing."

"The command is *coming about*—not, oh baby, I'm coming."

"Sounds pretty much like the same thing to me," she says.

"Then you're going to have to let me be the captain." I make a move for the tiller.

"Oh, for crying out loud: Coming about. There, I've said it."

"What the hell kind of a command was that? You can't mutter it. The wind roars, the water splashes, the crew won't hear you. You have to shout it."

"No way."

"Come on. You can do it. Coming about!" I yell it out for her.

"Coming about." She manages to raise her voice but starts to giggle.

"We still can't hear. Somone's going to enter the cockpit, cross the path of the boom, come on, get your lungs into it."

"Oh hell. COMING ABOUT!" She screams. And then she keels over laughing and so do I, and we never do carry out the tack.

As we approach the marina and I take the sails down, strap them, and start the motor, I feel her staring at me. "What?" I ask.

She smiles and tosses the hair back from her face. "Nothing."

28

CHOIR PRACTICE

WE BEGIN PAINTING THE NEXT DAY, Wednesday, with Lena taking purple for the trim, me taking green for the walls. Her concern about maintenance notwithstanding, the existing paint has worn well and is easily covered. Scaffolding borrowed from a local contractor enhances our progress while Carmella manages the restaurant, assigning extra responsibilities to Henry, the cook, and hiring a teenager back from planting trees for the government to help Gwen wait on tables. Wednesday's the only day Lena and I don't eat lunch together, because of an errand she has to run. It turns out the errand is a visit to see Bridge and Nelley, "to set things straight."

"I hope you didn't make a fuss."

"I made a damn big fuss. Apparently, so did Patty. After I called her last night to give her the low-down, she called them, so they got an earful from both of us."

"What did they say?"

"Doesn't matter what they said, but I can promise you, if they don't want to see their daughter showing up like the Tasmanian devil before the weekend, we'll be seeing Peter around fairly soon."

Within the hour a relieved-looking Peter arrives on his bike, asking if he can help. Lena hands him a broom and tells him he's in charge of cobweb removal. Later, he helps us move the scaffolding, and he loves it when I hand him my brush to finish off a wall. When Lena tells him about her sailing lesson and I see his enthusiasm, I ask if he'd be interested in a lesson or two. He looks to Lena, his excitement rising by the second until his body starts to vibrate and I fear he might pee his pants. I tell Lena that we're a crew and she'd have to come too.

This evening on Antonie, a new passion is born. During the initial tour of the boat he absorbs everything I tell him and asks for more. Later as he steers the tiller, looking the epitome of contentment, he watches intently at what I do, and to how the boat responds to the wind. He recounts aloud with remarkable understanding what he thinks is going on. After watching me crank the winch to tighten the sails, he asks to do it—and does it well. After hearing my references to port and starboard, he uses the terms a dozen times, never referring again to left and right. During the return trip, and with the wind directly at our back, I ask to take the tiller, explaining the danger of an accidental gybe. Peter keeps his eyes on the sails, watching for slight shifts in the wind, seeming to understand exactly what I mean. Back at the dock he asks if he can tour the boat one more time. I tell him to feel free and then watch as he runs his hands along everything, patting and stroking as he goes.

It's the same every evening after that. He takes to sailing like a monkey to trees. I'm amazed, not only at how fast he learns the technical aspects, but at his sense of the wind. He anticipates its gathering, its weakening, predicting shifts by watching its play on the water. I think back to my first lessons, the way I had to reinforce my on-board training with extra study, the consistent practice I required before mastering the basics. I wasn't a natural—Peter is.

On Thursday, Lena announces that she won't be able to join us on our outing, that Thursday evenings she goes to Thunder Bay for choir practice.

"Choir practice?"

"The Finlandia Choir, I told you that."

"From a time decades ago. You're still singing?"

"Something strange about that?"

"Not at all, and good for you."

When I ask if they're practicing for an upcoming performance, she tells me they are, that the choir greets the start of each new season with a special performance. "This time, for the end of September, we're going to welcome the fall equinox and combine it with a Thanksgiving celebration." I ask what they'll be performing. "I'll tell you more about it over dinner on Sunday." I feel a little guilty, knowing that my dinner commitment depends on the weather. "Anyway, I phoned Patty last night and she's perfectly fine with Peter going with you without me around." She sees the look on my face. "Sorry it's like that, but she's his mother, and she has to make the call."

"Us middle-aged men can be pretty creepy."

"Mark."

"Sorry. I appreciate you calling, getting permission for him."

The days go by, getting warmer, not cooler. I keep listening to the forecasts. On Sunday afternoon, the restaurant closes at three as usual, but tonight it's opening again to accommodate the special dinner first proposed by Lena but since hijacked by Carmella, our host, cook, and server for the evening. On the way, I duck into the woods to pick an assortment of variously coloured flowers. Carmella shocks me when she greets me at the door wearing a dress. In jeans and sports shirt, I wonder if I'm underdressed. "Those for me?" she asks. "How thoughtful, I'll get a vase." If she's teasing, I can't tell from her straight face. I guess I'll know by whether they end up on the table between Lena and me or not. I tell Carmella how lovely she looks, and she tells me I'm a man of impeccable taste and to give her a shout if her niece

turns out to be a prude. She winks at me. "Lena's been out of circula-
tion for a while, so you may have to be patient." She enjoys a hardy
laugh at this. "Come on in." She steps back, beckons me inside and
then leads me to a corner table, the only one dressed in white lace and
holding a wine cooler, complete with bottle of wine. "I'll go and tell
the little princess to get her butt out here."

After ten minutes or so, Lena arrives, indeed looking like a princess. She's also in a dress—it's light and summery and something
about it, maybe the tiny yellow tulips, makes me think of Holland. Her
dress goes nicely with my flowers, now arranged in a vase, brought to
the table by Lena who has placed a yellow flower in her hair. "Auntie
says I have to give the flowers back after dinner."

Carmella, the chef, outdoes herself, her piece de resistance a lobster fettuccine with sun dried tomatoes and black olives in a feta sauce.
She, herself is a highlight, albeit of a sideshow sort, regularly emerging from the kitchen looking impeccable, except for the one time she
almost forgets and I see her dashing back to remove an apron covered
in tomato and olive stains. Occasionally and on the sly, she winks at
me. The food's delicious, surpassed only by Lena's company. Twice,
however, Lena deflects specific topics. When I ask about the choir
rehearsals, she tells me, "Later." She does the same in response to a
question about Carmella's interest in my boat. I don't ask what *later*
means, but when I suggest, teasingly, that maybe I should ask Carmella myself, she gives me a stern "No," adding that it's better if she
explains. A smile flashes across her face, as fast as the winks I've been
getting from her aunt. During dessert she tells me about one of her
best friends, one who happens to be in the choir and happens to work
as a secretary in the psychology department at Lakehead University.
"Apparently there's a job posting for a faculty position—they're looking for someone to teach and do research in the area of developmental
disabilities." I tell her I've been too long removed from research, but

I try to sound light-hearted about it, reminding her that it's the sunflower business I'm after. She's not deterred. "Considering what you said about psychology not yet having the knowledge to affect the lives of many people, I thought you might be interested in trying to discover some of that knowledge." She lets the subject go after I reiterate that no one would be interested in someone who's been away from research so long.

As we're sipping our after-dinner cognacs, Auntie comes out of the kitchen to announce her departure. Her duties fulfilled, she'll leave Lena and me to finish our drinks. I tell her how much I enjoyed her food and that I've never been served by a tidier chef or wonderful host. "And you never will be," she says, pleasure clearly etched on her face. Lena stands to tell her how much she appreciated it. "Auntie, I love you for everything—today and every other day." They exchange kisses and hugs and just when it looks like tears might flow, Auntie swats Lena away, tells her to drink her cognac, and heads off, taking the flowers with her.

After she's gone, Lena asks if I'd like a tour of the living quarters upstairs. Perhaps noticing an expression I didn't intend, she tells me not to get any wrong ideas. "The thing is, I'm getting a sore bum from sitting here. These chairs were never intended for long sittings. We could finish our drinks in comfort if you'd like to come up." I tell her I'd love to see her place.

The main quarters on the second floor are an open concept arrangement defined by rugs and furniture, except for the bedroom which is sectioned off by a half wall, beyond which the foot of the bed is clearly visible. A main seating area separates the bedroom from the kitchen which overlooks the lake. The stools around the kitchen island are varied in colour, as are the rugs, the cushions, and book shelves, but it all comes together, everything seeming to belong except for the clock hanging in the kitchen. Trying hard, with green rim and pink petals, to look like a daisy, it looks tacky where everything else looks funky. I can't help noticing it because it's exactly like the one my parents had hanging in the kitchen throughout my childhood. Because it never stopped ticking and always gave the correct time, my dad refused to get rid of it. "That clock has perseverance," he'd say, "and there's nothing I admire more than perseverance." I ask Lena where she got hers. She tells me Auntie gave it to her as a keepsake from the homestead, that it was likely purchased in the fifties, and if not for its sentimental value, would have found its way to the dump by now. She asks me what I think, about the whole place, that is. I tell her it's great that it has everything she needs and that I envy her view from the kitchen. "Follow me," she says, "there's more."

She leads me up another set of stairs to the attic, where about a third of the space has been converted to a music room, "where I practice my singing", furnished with a leather couch and matching chairs and an impressive stereo system. The entire wall facing the lake is window, providing a panoramic view even more magnificent than the kitchen's. The two side walls as well as the peaked ceiling are plastered with stucco. The back wall is a showcase of musical memorabilia, pictures of choirs, orchestras, and opera scenes, pressed and laminated right into the wall. Some are new, some are old, and some are in between, and there appears to be a chronological sequence to them. They're all unframed so it's necessary to look carefully to see where one starts and another ends. A large picture of the Mozart monument that stands in Burggarten, Vienna, is placed in the centre, its naked cherubs, some with musical instruments, some without, clambering up the sides. Beethoven is represented in a sketch by J.D. Bohm, a famous portrayal that has him out on a walk, wearing a top hat and wrapped in a long coat. As well, there are segments from Beethoven's Frieze, the visual representations of the Ninth Symphony painted by Gustav Klimt. Much of the artwork is sensuous, even erotic, like

Klimt's image of the female, Music, painted with mysterious and symbolic attributes, and like Raphael's painting, Apollo among the Muses, in which a half-naked Apollo is playing a fiddle surrounded by women wearing loose, flowing garb. What else could be expected from the combination of art and music, if not something sensuous? In places, musical scores appear between the artwork, early drafts scribbled on parchment by their composers, the incomplete works of creativity striving for fulfillment.

"What do you think?" Lena asks.

"It's amazing."

She holds up her glass of cognac. "To music," she says, and to music, we toast.

She directs me to the couch, tells me to get comfortable because she has an interesting tale to tell. She sits kitty-corner on a chair, reaches over with the cognac, tells me not to think about turning it down, assures me I'll need it. Giving herself a little more as well, she sits back and begins.

"A long time ago, not long after Ian left me, I was practicing in this very room, getting ready for a performance of the Ninth, a joint effort between the Finlandia Choir and the Thunder Bay Symphony Orchestra. Although we've performed it a few times since, the time I'm talking about was our very first attempt at it. Typically, I practice with the windows closed—why disturb the neighbours—but this day was very hot and I didn't have air conditioning back then, so I opened them. Because it was a late Sunday afternoon, I figured no one would be around. I hadn't considered Auntie, who heard me singing from her cabin, and tip-toed over, and made herself at home on the patio to listen. Afterwards, she told me she'd never heard me sing so beautifully, that I sounded like an angel singing to heaven, trying to get Beethoven's attention, so I could thank him for the music. I told her there was little chance of that because heaven was so far away and because, after all, Beethoven was deaf. Up till then, Auntie had never been especially interested in Beethoven, but afterwards, she went to the library, got some books and started reading about him. She became especially fascinated with the story about his Immortal Beloved and began teasing me that perhaps I was the reincarnation of this mysterious loved one, the love of his life whom he had never identified. She said it would account for the magic in my voice as I sang for him. The teasing comes and goes but is always prevalent around performances of the Ninth. She's developed a real fantasy about it, telling me every time I should practice with the windows open in case Ludwig, too, has been reincarnated and is trying to find me."

"Ah, the reason she had for wanting to continue with the Classical Music Hour."

"Exactly."

"And she believes that true lovers get reunited no matter how long it takes."

"You've got it. Now, for the skill-testing question: When the choir-orchestra schedule was developed for this year, guess what was chosen for the Thanksgiving-equinox celebration?"

"You've got to be kidding."

"I swear."

"So along I come, proclaiming Beethoven to be my favourite composer, with The Ninth as my favourite piece of music."

"Brilliant deduction, Sherlock!"

"Sherlock? Don't you mean, Ludwig? What a preposterous story. Un-friggin believable."

"I swear I've had nothing to do with any of it."

"I believe you. You're far more rational than Carmella."

"Given the circumstances, however, can you imagine Auntie's perspective about you—and me?"

"I have to admit to being a little spooked."

"Think of what it's like for me. I see her every day, she's my closest relative."

"I mean, everything about it is utterly absurd, but the way it's come together in her mind—do you think she actually believes it?"

Lena grimaces, cocks her head and shrugs. "A little more cognac?"

"Please. Do you have another bottle?"

"I think so. If not, I've got wine, beer, or whiskey."

"Good." I take a gulp. "Truly amazing how someone can concoct such a fantasy and then have circumstances unfold that support it. But surely she'd have to accept that millions of people like Beethoven and if it wasn't for the timing—"

"There's one other thing."

"I can't imagine."

"Something you're forgetting to ask me."

"Like what?"

"Like the story behind Auntie's fascination with Antonie."

"Do I still want to know?"

"Auntie's researched all the theories regarding Beethoven and his Immortal Beloved and favours a recent one, put forward on the basis of previously undisclosed evidence."

"And that would be?"

"Early biographers had various theories based on subjective impressions of women he was known to favour. However, based on the newer evidence, a more recent biographer has deduced, rather convincingly, that only one woman satisfies all criteria necessary for qualifying as his Immortal Beloved—based on timing, geography, travel locations, and the correspondence between them."

"Don't tell me her name was Lena."

"No, not Lena. Her name was Antonie—Antonie Brentano. Auntie says it wasn't a coincidence that your boat led you here.

"Antonie." I hardly hear my own voice. "Wow. I suppose this does qualify as an incredible coincidence."

"Either that, or it's just another one of those mysteries." She shrugs, expressionless, sipping on her cognac.

We sit without speaking for several minutes, taking turns looking at one another when we think the other isn't looking. She's first to break the silence. "Would you like me to put some music on? The acoustics in this room are really terrific."

"No thanks."

"I could play the Ninth, see if it does anything for us." She's teasing, doing her best to make light of it all. "I have a version performed by the English Chamber Orchestra accompanied by the Tallis Chamber Choir—my favourite."

"No thanks. It must be getting late, and the food and cognac have made me dopey. I should probably be turning in."

"It's not that late."

"We've got some painting to do tomorrow, some cabins to finish."

"Depends on your priorities," she tells me.

29

LENA

THE WEATHER'S BEEN HOT and increasingly humid. Yesterday, Thursday, the forecast called for relief, predicting thunder storms by late afternoon or evening today. This morning the forecast was updated to include a thunder storm watch with the possibility of hail and gale force winds. Boats are being advised to stay off the water.

We've been painting all week, proceeding from the cabins to the shed, and then to Lena's garage. Yesterday we finished at noon, thankfully, as it was the hottest day yet. By mid-morning, clothes were damp, limbs were listless, and moods were somber, mainly due to anticipating Peter's departure. His mother's arriving this afternoon to take her son back to Thunder Bay tomorrow morning. It's the beginning of the Labour Day weekend, the unofficial end of summer, when kids return to school and many adults return to work. A new cycle begins, except this time I won't be going along for the ride. The timing of the storm is as good as I could hope for. I'm overcome with sadness, but determined not to show it. I like Wolf Cove and I care a great deal about Peter, Auntie, and the beautiful woman named Lena who I believe is showing an interest. Though I've been friendly to a fault, I continue to act oblivious to the feelers she's putting out. I remember Zoe and how I couldn't have been more certain—if I couldn't read that reality, I can't read any.

This morning, Peter's been particularly quiet. He's had fun with us all week, especially with the sailing lessons, and though he doesn't want to end on a glum note, he's having a difficult time. Lena's feeling bad for Peter, and I think she's feeling bad for the two of us also, suspecting that something's askew. The saddest moment comes when it's time to bid farewell to Peter. The three of us rise from the steps of Grandma's house. Lena hugs him and kisses him on the forehead, promising to call him sometime next week. I shake his hand, telling him with a quivering voice how much I've enjoyed getting to know him, and that he's the finest guide and sailor I've ever met. I want to give him a hug and tell him to be happy but I don't. Neither one of us needs that much emotion. He's a trooper, this little one. The tears well in his eyes, but he refuses to let them fall. Off he goes, pedaling like a demon. I don't know what goes wrong—maybe he's going too fast, or loses his concentration, but he hasn't gone far when his bike slides, and he falls. Quickly he gets up and scrambles to get back on his bike, with one arm and then the other wiping at his eyes.

Lena gives a tug on my shirt. "Please, wait here." After a few minutes she comes back with a tote bag. "Come with me." She leads me to the garage and opens the door. "I'd like you to go for a ride with me."

She drives us through the village, past Peter's road, past Clarke's garage, for two or three miles before she pulls off the road onto a slab of rock. The rock forms a narrow lane that dips into the woods. Slowly, she draws ahead until we're hidden by trees.

"I want to show you a place my mother discovered." Without waiting for a reaction she gets out of the truck. I follow. "Watch your step," she says. And then we're side-stepping down an embankment to the edge of dense forest. She takes me along the perimeter to where the woods seem impenetrable, to a spot where she points out a tiny opening between a pine and a boulder. We slip through, climb a rock, and then descend a long slope on the other side. We follow a grassy ridge through some lowlands and soon I hear the gurgle of water. A couple of minutes later, we come to a small pond surrounded by green, spongy, moss, surrounded in turn by a thicket of soft-needled evergreens, the colour of dill. I think they might smell like dill as well, but that's probably just my imagination. It's the pond that's doing the gurgling, though I see no brook that leads from it. The pond, the size of a merry-go-round, is filled with emerald green water, foamy, like a bubble bath, around the edges. Lena stops at its shore, sets down her bag and takes my hand.

"It's fed by an underground spring—a hot spring. My mother brought me here for picnics when I was young. She said it was a magic pond and that no one else knew about it. To this day, I haven't heard of anyone else who's come across it. She called it the fountain of youth and claimed that immersing yourself in it prevented you from getting old. Maybe she was right. She may have lost touch with reality, but she never got old." Lena grows quiet, staring at the pond.

I squat and reach forward to feel the temperature of the water. It's warm. Here in the northern woods, with an icy Lake Superior not a mile away, lies a hot spring. It's hard to believe.

Lena crouches to join me. "Feels good, doesn't it?"

While we're both crouched she reaches and gently caresses the side of my face, one brief stroke, and then turns away as she stands.

"During our picnics, we'd always take a dip," she says. She pauses, glances at the sky, and then looks all around the tree line, checking to make sure we're alone. We might as well be on the moon when it comes to the likelihood of having company. "I've never brought anyone here before." She reaches for the buttons on her shirt and starts to undress. "You should join me. You won't believe the amazing sensation—hard to describe, but it's different from a hot tub, the bottom's spongy but nice spongy." She takes off her shirt and then puts her hands to her shorts and shimmies them off. She reaches for her bag and takes out two towels which she sets on the bag, close to the water's edge. She notes that I haven't budged. I'm too stunned.

"You're an explorer, after all," she says. "Really, this is something you should try. You've traveled so far, looking for something, and now you've found this, like finding buried treasure, don't you think?" Quickly, she slips off her underwear, takes two short steps and jumps in. The water's deep, up to her neck. What the hell—I follow her lead, remove my shirt and pants, slip my underwear down, doing my best to emulate the same deft movements, in part to hide my self-con-sciousness. But I'm in too much of a hurry and begin to dash for the pond before my shorts have cleared my ankles. Down I go, my head and shoulders smacking into the water as the rest of me sprawls along the spongy edge. As graceful as a walrus I roll myself over, and in. Lena laughs, but not so much as to shelve my manhood—tells me my entry needs a little practice. Generously, she moves on. "So what do you think?" It feels great, pulsating like some kind of living thing. She lets me get accustomed to it and then wades over to me, puts her arms around my neck, and kisses me.

As promised, the cold front's on its way. The clouds stretch black across the horizon, like mountains rising from the sea. Though still miles away, it'll be coming fast. Already the temperature's dropping, pockets of cold air bouncing across the water like tumbleweed. The waves are starting to roll. I'll have to get away soon. I think about Lena, about today, about what a fool I am for thinking about love, though that's what today has done to me. But love is partly about offering things to share. Lena has so much to share while I have so little—nothing more than what I started with this summer. Still, I need to say good-bye, and I owe her something of an explanation:

Dear Lena,

Please forgive me for not saying a proper goodbye. Our departure certainly warrants one. As well, you deserve a heartfelt thank-you for everything you've given me. Please believe that I mean this. Because of you, Wolf Cove has been the highlight of my trip. In my heart, I thank Peter and Auntie as well. And to think that stopping here was just a fluke.

Leaving would be so difficult, perhaps impossible, if I were to say goodbye in person, and have to hear your voice. I'd wish to hear it again, and then again after that. I'd end up wanting to stay long enough to hear it singing from the choir. But then what? I'd so wish to give you something back, if only I had something of value to give. My savings won't sustain me over the long run. As you know, I'm done being a psychologist, although I believe that everyone in Wolf Cove could probably use one (just kidding). I do believe there's some truth in your claim about me being an explorer. But though I've followed the careers section of newspapers for over thirty years, I've never seen an ad that reads: Wanted: Explorer. Nothing from the Hudson's Bay Company, nothing from Jacques Cartier And Associates, nothing from The Christopher Columbus Adventure Cruises. Perhaps I don't belong in these times. Still, I want you to know that this identity as an explorer has given me some comfort.

Unfortunately, all I have to give you is this journal. It's a record of my thoughts during the trip. The writing isn't good, there are no revelations, there's lots of ranting, and it's pessimistic if not downright depressing. Great gift, eh? Yet, this is all there is of me to give. Please don't feel obligated to read it. I trust that placing it on the driver's seat of your truck should keep it safe until you find it. I've left some money in an envelope. As Peter's godmother, I'd like you to set up a trust fund for him, for when he's older, preferably for his education, or to help him buy a boat—whatever you determine to be most suitable. I'm also leaving it to your discretion to reveal (or not) where the money came from. It may seem weird coming from an acquaintance he knew for two weeks. Please feel free to say it came from you.

Finally, I'd like you to keep some of the money to take Auntie on a trip while she's still healthy and full of spunk. I suspect that your first reaction to this (and maybe Auntie's too) will be that you have no desire to travel. If you promise to give it serious consideration and still end up hating the idea, then so be it, but do think about it. The good citizens of Wolf Cove won't let anything happen to the resort while you're away. The precious gift your mother left is not at risk of abandonment. Wouldn't Auntie love to see a place such as Vienna? I was there once and even stood in Beethoven's apartment, overlooking the university. What a thrill that was. Just an idea.

It's time for me to go.

With Love In My Heart,

Mark

P.S. This morning when you went into the restaurant to get us drinks, I used the outside staircase to sneak into your apartment. I stole your tacky clock to take along on my trip. I'm very sorry.

30

FATE

AFTER PLACING THE LETTER AND JOURNAL on the seat of
Lena's truck, I return to Antonie, start the motor, and shove off, not
bothering to retrieve my weather gear from below, the prospect of
catching a cold no longer relevant. Beyond the breakwater I kill the
motor and raise the jib. It doesn't take long to put a mile between us
and shore, and then two miles, and then three. As the thunder and
lightning fast approach led by the first sting of hailstones, I feel chastened already for having dismissed my weather gear. Thankfully, after
a minute or two, the hail turns to rain, the downpour as cold as my
surging adrenalin, making me wonder if without the distraction of a
storm, I'd be able to withstand the terror of what I'm doing.

With wind and waves making it difficult to stay the course, I re-
duce sail, at the same time apologizing to Antonie for taking her with
me. Antonie—quite the story she's turned out to be, leaving me intrigued about how her name was chosen in the first place. I'll never
know. I'm still gazing over my fine vessel when, suddenly, the head of a
young boy pops through the companionway. WHAT THE HELL? SHIT!
SHIT! No, it can't be! My stomach leaps into my throat as the frightened looking boy appears from below. "Peter! Good God, what are
you doing?" I scream because of the wind, and because of the shock,

not intending to frighten him even more. "Peter, for God's sake, how did you—"

He says something that I can't hear, but I can see he's close to tears.

"Doesn't matter. It doesn't matter, Peter." I can't let him think I'm panicking. "Don't worry about it, we're heading back to shore." But blinded by rain and facing an increasingly angered lake, I have no idea how we're going to do this. I reach inside the seat beside me, grab the life jackets and throw one to Peter. From our previous outings he knows what to do. Otherwise, I don't know what to tell him. If I tell him to go below and we capsize he might be trapped. If I tell him to stay on deck, he could get swept off. Already, the waves are splashing over the deck. He's looking at me trying to figure out how much trouble we're in. In seconds he'll see, and he'll see I'm not in control, and he'll be scared like he's never been scared, and—"Go below, Peter. Things are getting a little rough—but stay close to the ladder in case I need your help." He hesitates, trying to read me. The waves are building and we get hit by the biggest one yet. I've got to turn around, get pointed towards shore, but having consistently backed down from bad weather over the course of my trip I'm ill prepared. I tighten the jib and steer the tiller to swing us around. The wind takes us with it, directly east, a direction that will never get us to shore. Watching intently, Peter has yet to move. I pull again on the tiller, trying to angle us in. "There we go. We're heading back." Almost instantly a wave hits the corner of the stern and swings us broadside. Afraid the next one will roll us over, I lessen the angle. "There, that should do it." I doubt it, but announce it anyway, feigning confidence for Peter's sake. "Okay, Peter, go below, but stay close, I'll need you to help us land." He's obviously frightened but trusts what I say. I'm thankful he doesn't know better. "And remember, Peter, you're a sailor now, and true sailors never panic."

"Okay, Mr. Weathers," he shouts as he heads below.

What have I done?

We're carried along, escorted by the thunder and lightning that has caught up and is now lambasting us from directly overhead. If the waves don't get us then a shoal surely will, emerging from the depths to rip us apart. I'm at the mercy of forces I can't control. Hell, what else is new? Only I could lose control over my own suicide, fate intervening once again to show me who's boss. But none of that matters now. All that matters is Peter. Screw fate and its cruelty for involving an innocent young boy. I must focus, persist, and take any opportunity I can to save him, gladly willing to sacrifice my own life (or death) to do so. All I need is a break, so please, just give me a break, just this one time, and please give Peter strength—these are the only things I ask, so please—Who do I think I'm talking to?

I have no bearings, no idea where we're headed, can't even tell if the wind has shifted. For all I know, it could be taking us out and away from land so it can capsize us with assurance we'll never be found. Wasn't that my initial plan? Then during a lull in the rain, land appears on our port side, running right alongside us. As anticipated, however, the shoreline is pure rock and getting to it without crashing and getting splattered over the rocks will be close to impossible. That's if we even make it to shore. The probability of hitting a shoal this close to land increases by the second. There's little time. Scouring the shoreline, I spot a small cove, nothing more than an indentation, but I angle towards it. If I can clear the jut of rocks and get inside to calmer water—it's our only chance. Again, with the angle I need, a wave almost flips us. Damn, if I don't get closer we'll get swept right on by. The next attempt is better and we do get closer and yes, the water's calmer but it's not calm enough. Still, the wind drives us forward, right for the rocks, each wave carrying the weight of the lake. Peter won't have a chance.

I call for him to come up from below.

At the top of the ladder, he takes a quick look around, yells out, wanting to know if I plan to anchor in the bay.

Anchors! Yes! Geezus! I don't dare leave the tiller.

"Get the anchors from under the seat." He does as he's asked. "Tie off their lines and throw them in as fast as you can."

"Okay" His voice is shaky but his movements are clean and bold as any sailor.

"The water's shallow so don't let out too much line."

Seconds after the second anchor disappears below the surface I feel a jolt. They're dragging, slowing us down, and then there's a second jolt but this time it comes from the keel scraping bottom. I wait, but the ripping and tearing doesn't come. Incredibly, we're brushing over sand, not rock, but the contact is brief and doesn't stop our course towards shore.

"Come on, Peter, take my hand, we're jumping overboard. Keep your mouth shut, don't gulp the water. We'll swim for shore. Try to keep hold of me." On the count of three we jump, right into a wave that knocks us flat and takes us under, life jackets and all. Somehow, I manage to keep hold of him. But for how long? We break through the surface but only momentarily, and again we're sucked down and thrashed about like rags in a washing machine. Again and again, we fight to break the surface, gulping for air, and again I shout at him to hold tight, to keep his mouth closed. With one arm looped through his life jacket, I use my free arm to side-stroke, making little or no progress. I fear an undertow is pulling us out. No, no, no, Peter is not going to drown, I won't allow it. I kick, and pull, and thrust forward with all my might, but again we're sucked under as a ton of water rolls over us, pushing us down. Down, deep, the water's calmer. Strangely, the panic subsides and even more strangely I think about Lena's clock heading for oblivion, imagining my father's rage that I let this happen. Then, the image dissolves, replaced by another that surprises me—

my father telling me not to worry, that the clock doesn't have half the persistence that I do, that I'm too stubborn to give up. He chuckles about this, the chuckle turns to laughter, and then, incredibly, we're laughing together, and it feels good, it feels—

Suddenly, miraculously, the lake spits us out, thrusting us upon a small patch of sand—an unlikely oasis enclosed on all sides by rocks. I check Peter to see if he's alright, letting him know that he's the bravest sailor ever.

"I kept my mouth shut the whole time, just like you told me," he says, shivering.

"That a boy."

"I held on really tight, didn't I?"

"You certainly did."

"I knew you wouldn't let me go."

"Thank you, Peter. Now, lets' climb out of here, shall we?"

The rocks are slimy and we proceed carefully. I go first, pulling Peter along whenever I find solid footing. When we make it to the top, I look down to see Antonie moving slowly towards the rocks, the anchors failing to hold. I need to go back to see if I can save her, pull her towards the sandy part of the shore. I tell Peter to stay where he is, that I'll be right back. Climbing down the rocks is even more treacherous, and I cling with my fingers to whatever I can, as my feet stretch, probing for the next foothold.

Then, on a small ledge, the moss gives way and my feet shoot out from under me.

31

ECHOES OF THE NINTH

A PARADE IS PASSING BY, SPRINKLED with floats, some horses from the Brouhaha, and the entire population of Wolf Cove—but again, I find myself separated, looking through turquoise, watching helplessly as they start to fade away. If only I could move, reach through and wave for help. The whole world's pulling away, getting darker. I've got to raise my arm. I try and I try, and God do I try. Thunder shatters the blackness, ushers in light. I'm sitting, but not in water. I'm in bed in a foreign room, and someone is holding my outstretched hand.

"Mark? Mark?"

Oh God, it's Lena. "I fell—"

"I know."

"I slipped on the rocks—where's Peter, is he—"

"Peter's fine, he's in the waiting room. How are you feeling?"

"Sore, my head hurts, my—"

She reaches over me. "I'm just going to let the nurse know you're awake. You've been out for a while." She grabs a button from over my head, squeezes it, then sits back, my hand still in hers. I see rain driving against the window, hear rumbles of thunder. "Mark, what the hell were you doing out in that weather?" The look on her face tells me she

291

has a guess which she hopes is wrong. How could she have not found my letter? I'm staring at her, searching for words when a nurse walks in, pulls my eyelids, tells me to wiggle my toes, first one foot and then the other. "Not now, you need some rest, but I want an explanation, Mark. Peter posed the same question. I told him you picked up a distress signal from a boat coming in from Thunder Bay and went out to offer assistance. I had to lie to him."

"Thanks, and I'm sorry." My eyes are getting heavy again. "He's really alright?"

"Oh yes. You guys were lucky. You landed on shoreline that belongs to the Shuttleworths. Peter found an ATV trail that leads right to their house. He's telling everyone that he's a true sailor for not panicking. Of course, after today, he's going to be a sailor who's grounded for a good long while."

The nurse tells Lena that my vitals seem fine, that she'll have the doctor take a look when he comes back, that Lena should step out and take a break, let me get my rest, assures her she'll keep watch. As I drift off I hear Lena telling the nurse about how I scared the hell out of her when I regained consciousness, bolting to a sitting position right on a crack of thunder.

The next time I wake, Lena's back in my room. She leans over to feel my forehead, shakes her head and asks softly, "What's going on in that mind of yours? You're going to have to talk to me, you know."

"I've never been much of a talker. As a psychologist, I learned to let others do the talking."

"Well, here's your choice. You can either open up to me or you can tell Auntie your story and answer *her* questions. Take your pick."

"Oh God."

A moment goes by in silence as we both check the rain still slapping at the window, neither of us able to find words to suit the occasion. Finally, it's Lena who breaks the spell.

"Were you just being pessimistic or do you really have no chance to land that university position?"

I remind her of my age, the length of time that's passed since I've done any research. "It's not going to happen, Lena."

"Yeah, I guess I know that and that it's probably not something you'd want anyway. I was just thinking—forget it, it doesn't matter, we'll just have to hire you as chef and handyman for the resort. Henry wants to retire and...well maybe you could breathe some new life into the marina or something."

"Too bad you'd never be able to afford my hourly rate." I chuckle but pay for it with a flash of pain that shoots through my head and down my neck. "You and your aunt would end up in the poor house."

"Maybe you should lower your expectations—perhaps start by moving into one of the cabins for awhile, see how things go."

"Hmm. Could I expect regular visitations from you—you know, in the manner of Constance Chatterley?"

"Your daily chores might tire you out—it would be a real pity if you couldn't keep up, wouldn't it?"

The reference to tiredness hits me like an anesthetic.

"Speaking of tired..." As I start to fade I wonder about our jesting, her invitation to stick around the resort for awhile. Was it jesting? It all seems a bit far fetched, just like everything else in Wolf Cove, yet, surprisingly, I do feel a strange kinship with this place—the people and their signs, the cornfest and its storytellers, Peter, Auntie, and something a lot more with Lena. Can I trust it?

But, ah yes, the storytellers.

"Lena?"

"It's okay. You need the rest."

"No, no. I've been meaning to ask you something, about Gerald and his schooner."

"Yeah?"

"How did it end?"

"You want to know now?"

"The last thing I remember is Gerald extinguishing his lantern when he heard someone on the ladder. The suspense was building, so now that I'm not hopelessly drunk, I should be able to stay awake long enough to hear the ending—if you don't mind."

"Strange guy, wakes up from a concussion, asks about a campfire story... but, whatever, if it'll make you feel better."

"If I don't hear it now, I'm afraid I never will."

"Alright. You'll recall Gerald's instant regret over turning off his lantern. Just a sec, I'm trying to remember exactly how it went so I can tell it the way Gerald did. Okay, here goes. *Whoever or whatever it was on the ladder froze the instant the light went out, but then, in a hoarse whisper, called out: Is there shomeone down here?... Please, I need your help... the other shurvivors are trapped.*

Her impersonation's hilarious, better than her fellow villagers doing Diefenbaker.

I must shay, the plea shounded convincing but only a moment ago I'd been on deck and hadn't sheen a thing. Was it a trap of shome kind? I'm sure you'll understand that I had to consider this. I shtood frozen, the sheconds passing like hours, my life shuspended within a vacuum without shight, shound, or motion. Then, shuddenly, shurprisingly, the presence on the ladder began to ascend. Shomething told me I needed to act fast—but just what was I shupposed to do?...

When, once again, I wake up, Auntie's in my room, slumped in a chair, snoozing, a book spread open on her lap. I call her name in little more than a whisper.

Her eyes open, her chin lifts from her chest. "So you've decided to wake up and join us?"

"You too."

"Nonsense, I was just resting my eyes." She drags her chair closer to the bed. "I'm not going to waste any time here, life's short, so I have a couple of things to say to you, and then you're on your own. By the way," she reaches into a large straw bag and pulls out my journal, along with the letter, "I found some items of yours in Lena's truck—I'll keep them safe till you come around to pick them up." She tucks them back in her bag. "My Vince is alive, you know, I keep him alive in my heart. That's what it's about, getting to know each other, bringing each other to life, keeping the spirit of loved ones alive." Auntie looks over me towards the window. "Vince, he had a tender spirit, you know—he rescued a rabbit once after it got struck by a car. The vet told him to forget it, but he didn't, he nursed it back to health. I don't know if he had to shoot anybody in the war, but if he did he would have broken down and cried." She pulls even closer, looks at me with eyes old and moist. "You listen up. People are more alive because of you. Before you, Peter's spirit didn't have anyone to shine through. Lena's a wonderful, beautiful person, but she's more wonderful and more beautiful because you're here to notice—even more than most people would. And nature—well, the sounds of the wind, the sounds of the lake, would not be so magnificent if you weren't here to receive them, now would they? You have a gift for seeing, feeling, and hearing these things, and it's a great gift, because your senses are so ready to bring things to life, if only you'd let them. Got it? Okay, enough of the sappy stuff. There's just one more thing—I want to read you a passage from this biography of Beethoven." She raises the book from her lap, reaches into her bag and takes out her glasses. "Last night when we heard about the accident and came to the hospital, I brought the book along, not knowing how long you might have to stay here and thinking you might appreciate the reading material. But I'd like to read you a passage, now. She opens the book.

In the middle of a snowstorm on March 26, 1827, thunder shook the streets of Vienna, rattling the window beside Beethoven's bed where he'd been lying in a coma for two days. In a flash of lightning he opened his eyes, and reached his fist into the air. Then, his arm fell back, his eyes closed, and he began to mutter something. Anselm Huttenbrenner, a friend who was at his bedside, leaned forward to listen. Ludwig described how a voice had come to him in his coma, to confirm that the end was nigh and to ask if he had used his gifts wisely, if he had taken advantage of the wonderful opportunities life had offered him. Ludwig then squeezed the hand of his friend and told him, "Anselm, it was only then that I realized how much of life I've wasted on misery. Oh, how ungrateful I've been, and what desperation is overtaking me at this very moment when it's too late. And so my last moment is a moment of hell and I have only myself to blame. If only I could return and live another life. I swear I'd be willing to forego my musical genius, if only I could have my ears, my eyes, my nose, my skin to appreciate the beauty which I have so dishonoured in this life." An enormous sigh escaped his lips and the maestro was gone.

Auntie closes the book and gets up. "I'll go and see if Lena and Peter are still hanging around." She's halfway to the door when I call out, asking if she could leave the book behind, because I'd like to take a look at it. I don't tell her I suspect there's no such quotation, that she made the whole thing up on my behalf. "The nurse says you'll be leaving here soon, so you can wait and read your own damn book." She grins and heads off. "Auntie," I call. She turns. "I guess it's a good thing you have me around to appreciate that awful, grating, voice of yours." She sticks her tongue out at me and continues on her way.

TOM MANAGHAN has practiced as a clinical psychologist for over thirty years, and has served in various jurisdictions as Chief Psychologist and Clinical Director for the past twenty years. His appreciation for personalities prompted him to invent the board game *Psychologizer*, the rights to which he eventually sold to a major Canadian game and toy company. Tom and his wife Carol have made their permanent home near Sudbury, Ontario, where he divides his time between private practice, writing, and nature. *The Bottle Collector* is his first novel.